Groombridge Log

THE UR-QUAN MASTERS SERIES

Groombridge Log
Eternal Doctrine

GROOMBRIDGE LOG

Tommi Salminen

Based on the universe of

STAR CONTROL

By Fred Ford and Paul Reiche III

Third edition

This book contains quotes from the computer game Star Control 2 which was made by Fred Ford and Paul Reiche in 1992. The book is printed with their permission.

Publisher:
BoD – Books on Demand, Helsinki, Finland
Printed by:
BoD – Books on Demand, Norderstedt, Germany
ISBN 978-951-568-418-9

CHAPTERS

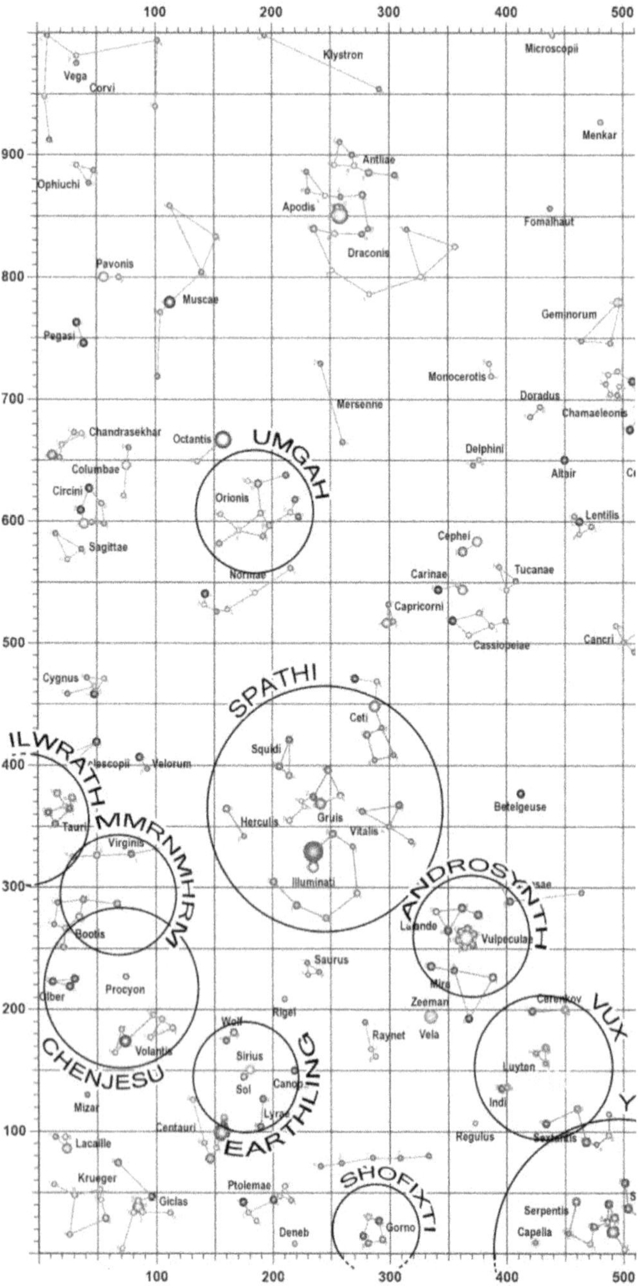

100
200
300
400
500
900
800
700
600
500
400
300
200
100
Klystron
Microscopii
Vega
Corvi
Menkar
Antliae
Ophiuchi
Apodis
Fomalhaut
Draconis
Pavonis
Muscae
Geminorum
Pegasi
Monocerotis
Mersenne
Doradus
Chamaeleonis
Chandrasekhar
Octantis
UMGAH
Delphini
Columbae
Altair
Circini
Orionis
Lentilis
Sagittae
Cephei
Normae
Carinae
Tucanae
Capricorni
Cassiopeiae
Cancri
Cygnus
SPATHI
Ceti
ILWRATH
Squidi
Velorum
Betelgeuse
Tauri
MMRNMHRM
Herculis
Gruis
Vitalis
Virginis
Illuminati
ANDROSYNTH
Lalande
Vulpeculae
Bootis
Saurus
Mira
Procyon
Zeeman
Cerenkov
VUX
Rigel
Wolf
Raynet
Vela
Sirius
Luyten
Volantis
CHENJESU
Sol
EARTHLING
Mizar
Indi
Centauri
Lyrae
Regulus
Lacaille
SHOFIXTI
Krueger
Ptolemae
Giclas
Serpentis
Gorno
Deneb
Capella

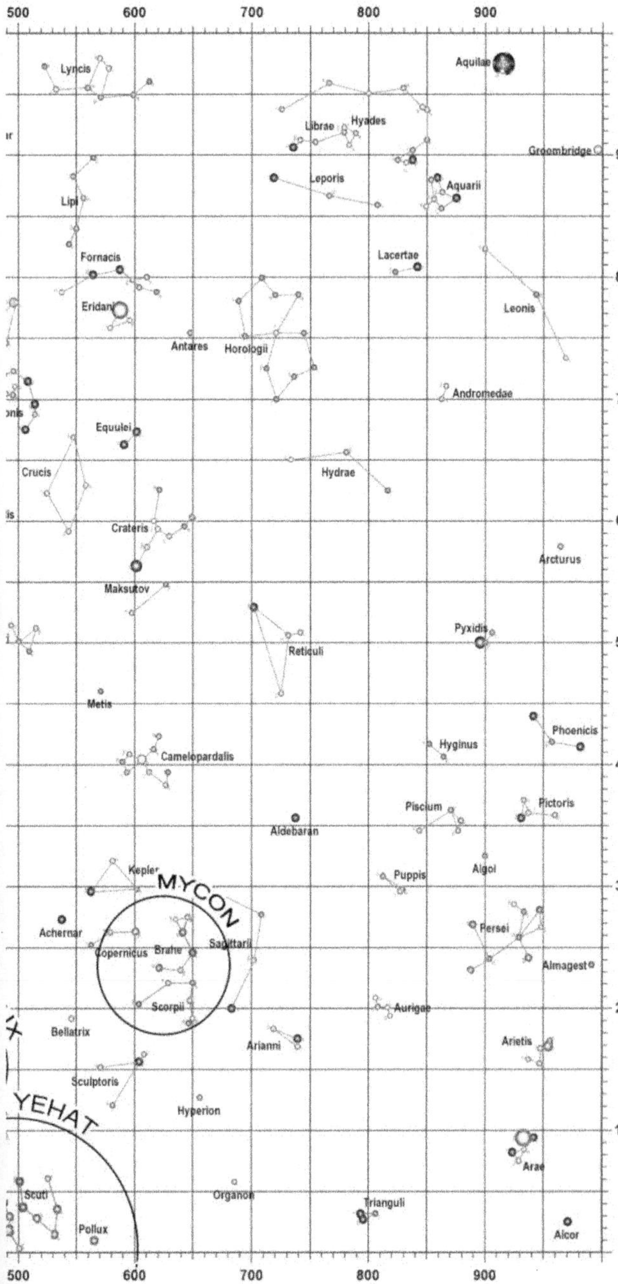
500
600
700
800
900
Lyncis
Aquilae
Librae
Hyades
Groombridge
Leporis
Aquarii
Lipi
Fornacis
Lacertae
Eridani
Leonis
Antares
Horologii
Andromedae
Equulei
Crucis
Hydrae
Crateris
Arcturus
Maksutov
Pyxidis
Reticuli
Metis
Phoenicis
Hyginus
Camelopardalis
Piscium
Pictoris
Aldebaran
Kepler
MYCON
Puppis
Algol
Achernar
Sagittarii
Persei
Copernicus
Brahe
Almagest
Scorpii
Aurigae
Bellatrix
Arietis
Arianni
Sculptoris
YEHAT
Hyperion
Arae
Scuti
Organon
Trianguli
Pollux
Alcor
100
200
300
400
500
600
700
800
900

The map on the previous pages details the spatial relationship between the stars in our known region of the galaxy, as well as the spheres of influence for each alien race as of AD 2133. The positions are based on hyperspace coordinates, which may be unsettling to some students of true space astronomy. Defined long ago by Chenjesu stargazers, the constellations are now accepted by all Alliance races as the standard.

Due to the great difficulty in pronouncing the Chenjesu language, each race has translated the names into their own tongue. When it came time for Earth to adopt this system, the United Nations decided to use traditional astrological designations, assigned at random. This has caused some confusion, but it is considered preferable to the suggested alternative: using the names of past politicians.

PROLOGUE

Neutron chain reaction, the basic principle of atomic bombs, was discovered in the 1930s. In 1939, the United States, the United Kingdom and Canada started the Manhattan Project with the sole purpose of creating the first nuclear weapon. It was dropped onto the city of Hiroshima in Japan on August 6th 1945. Three days later a second bomb was used against Nagasaki. Over a hundred thousand were killed.

In the following decades humanity was on the edge of destroying itself in an all-out nuclear war. Lack of mutual trust prevented the United States and the Soviet Union from coming to an agreement on limiting nuclear weapons. The whole world was waiting for either side to make the first strike, but in the end, neither of them did. Eventually the cold war ended and the immediate threat for planet-wide destruction started to fade away, but the vast number of nuclear weapons remained.

In 2015 nuclear combat broke out between several Middle Eastern countries. Fortunately, only a dozen warheads were launched and global disaster was narrowly avoided. Still, almost a million died.

The incident forced governments around the world to sober up. The United Nations General Assembly decided unanimously to strengthen the authority of the U.N. immediately. Within six months, the U.N. had assumed control over all weapons of mass destruction. They were dismantled and their components stored in huge subterranean bunkers, later known as “Peace Vaults”, where they remained for a hundred years.

The era of large-scale wars had come to an end and humanity continued to make breakthroughs in science. In 2019 a Swiss scientist, Hsien Ho, perfected the artificial parthenogenesis – cloning – of humans. Although the clones were, to all external appearances, human, Hsien Ho modified their genes so that they were incapable of producing offspring.

The clones faced a tough world. Major religions were against cloning and fought to have the clones declared sub-human, in which they eventually succeeded. The clones, now called the Androsynth, were stripped of their human rights. As the years passed, they became little better than well-treated slaves.

By the middle of the 21st century, colonization of the solar system had begun. First there were orbital factories and lunar bases, then a colony on Mars and, not long after, outposts in the asteroid belt. But still, because of the great distances and relatively slow speed at which spacecraft could travel, humanity was imprisoned in its own solar system. A great effort was made on technology for warping to distant stars faster than the speed of light.

Because the Androsynth were stronger, smarter and more adaptable than normal humans, many of them were doing sophisticated research, but with little autonomy. The inevitable happened in the spring of 2085. The tens of thousands of Androsynth across the planet staged a world-wide rebellion with help from a sympathetic human underground.

The uprising had been carefully planned. Within 24 hours the clones had seized control of nearly every space-flight facility on the planet. The Androsynth working at the facilities had secretly prepared over a thousand spacecraft and only two days after the rebellion had begun, the clones had taken over almost all of the orbital and lunar bases. Soon there wasn't a single Androsynth left on the face of the Earth.

Star Control, the recently established wing of the United Nations' military forces, tried to suppress the revolt. But every time their ships approached, the Androsynth burned them to ashes with colossal maser-weapons which they had fashioned out of formerly harmless energy broadcast units.

After two months the U.N. decided to open the Peace Vaults. But before the weapons of mass destruction were reassembled, Star Control patrol ships reported an amazing sight: Eight of the largest space stations were accelerating out of Earth's orbit. The Androsynth had somehow managed to modify the stations* for flight.

Star Control chase ships couldn't keep up with the space stations, but an ore freighter on its way home from the titanium mines on the asteroid belt was able to catch a glimpse of the escaping fleet during an important moment. According to the pilot's testimony, a "great red hole" appeared in front of the space stations. They flew into it one by one and vanished. Only seconds after the last one had entered, the hole disappeared. It took over 30 years for humans to meet the Androsynth again.

In 2112 the most distant human space installation was built on the dwarf planet Ceres. Three years later the base received unexpected publicity when it became the setting for humanity's first contact with extra-terrestrial intelligence: An alien ship had suddenly appeared out of nowhere, positioned itself three kilometers above the base and begun broadcasting the following message:

People from Earth: We are the Chenjesu. We mean you no harm. We come in peace with an urgent message. Heed

---

* including the recently finished Starlight Hilton

these words: There is a horde of conquering warriors advancing toward your solar system from deep space. They are called the Ur-Quan. They know you are here. They will make slaves of you as they have made slaves of a thousand races across the galaxy. They will enslave both our species, Chenjesu and Human, unless we stop them now. We are not alone in our struggle. There are others who will fight with us against the Ur-Quan. Together – in an alliance with the remaining free stars – we may yet turn back the enemy, defeating the Ur-Quan and its Hierarchy of battle thralls. We beseech you to join us, for we desperately need your help. But we do not have much time. What is your answer?

For over a week the only answer from Earth was stunned silence, but the Chenjesu representatives were patient. They understood the great psychological shock their sudden appearance had on the humans – a race that amazingly had never been in contact with another intelligent species.

The crystalline silicon-based Chenjesu soon became familiar to all humans. For several months they conferred with political, military and scientific leaders of Earth. Meanwhile, the Chenjesu starship transported U.N. observers to visit several worlds that had been attacked by the Ur-Quan.

One of the most amazing things about the Chenjesu's unprecedented biology was their natural means of communication. Their bodies were able to send extremely powerful hyper-wave signals that could reach across solar systems. As a gesture of good will, and to ease inter-species communication, they gave humans technological means to artificially produce hyper-wave signals, although no artificial transmitter could match the Chenjesu's natural abilities.

Amidst all the confusion, life continued on Earth. The Ice Cream King, Britain's largest ice cream manufacturer, was about to introduce a new product. It was “The Chenjesu Icicle”, which resembled their ice-like form and had their semi-transparent, reflective texture. The authorities were horrified, fearing that the Chenjesu would feel offended, and banned the product before it reached the stores. The news of the censorship soon traveled to far ends of the world and it launched a heated debate. Some said that the icicle was a symbol of racism and would lead to hatred against humanity’s new friends. Others argued that the anti-racism campaigning had gone too far and that the icicle symbolized our friendship with the Chenjesu.

The Chenjesu themselves heard about the debate and had a hard time understanding the importance humans sought in such trivial matters. Even though the Chenjesu insisted that they didn’t have a problem with it, the ban remained.

On August 1st 2116, Earth officially joined the Chenjesu and their other allies – the Mmrnmhrm, the Yehat and the Shofixti – to form the Alliance of Free Stars. The Chenjesu were the leaders of the Alliance, although they refused to formally accept the title.

The Mmrnmhrm were purely mechanical beings that had a close relationship with the Chenjesu. All that humans knew of their history was that they were a product of a distant unknown culture, which sent a giant factory-ark into our region of space many centuries ago. The ark, which the media called Mother-Ark, churned out millions of robots before it finally broke down. If the Mmrnmhrm had a specific purpose, they never told anyone what it was.

There was a lot of discussion* on whether the Mmrnmhrm should even be called a race. It was pretty much

---

* Only on Earth. Other races in the Alliance didn’t see any point to the topic, least of all the Mmrnmhrm.

undeniable that the robots were sentient, but many argued that they were just well-designed tools and not living beings.

The Yehat were an avian race of ancient warrior clans that had been traveling the stars for many centuries. The clans were highly competitive and sometimes waged war on each other, but they were all loyal to the Queen, who managed to unite the clans against common enemies.

The Shofixti were a race of intelligent marsupials that had been "civilized" for only a few decades. They were discovered by the Yehat, who adopted and "uplifted" them, giving them advanced technology and cultural definition.

Star Control was placed under direct authority of the Alliance Command Council. The Chenjesu expected humans to play a major role in the Alliance both as combatants and suppliers of war material. Although human technology was primitive, Earth had thousands of modern factories and millions of skilled workers able to manufacture both munitions and spacecraft. The tens of thousands of thermonuclear weapons stashed away in the Peace Vaults were an additional bonus which surprised even the Chenjesu.

On the day following Earth's induction into the Alliance an unknown alien ship landed on the Moon. The ship transmitted a request to meet with Alliance representatives and soon afterwards a delegation of human and Chenjesu diplomats went to the lunar surface. The newcomers, who disturbingly were little green men in flying saucers, introduced themselves as the Ariloulaleelay. They explained that they too were threatened by the Ur-Quan and that they had come to join the Alliance of Free Stars. The Arilou, as the media called them for simplicity, were extremely secretive and unwilling to discuss even the location of their home world. But they provided additional strength to the Alliance and everyone welcomed them with open arms.

The Ur-Quan resembled larvae, like green caterpillars found on Earth, except that they were several meters long and carnivorous. They had arrived in this region of space from the direction of the galactic spin over ten years before humans joined the Alliance. Upon arriving here they had first enslaved the Umgah, a solitary blobbish species in the Orionis constellation. Shortly afterwards they conquered the Ilwrath, a race of overly religious and hostile spider creatures in the Tauri constellation. The Chenjesu and the Mmrnmhrm were next, but together they were able to fend off the invading armada. The Ur-Quan fleet then changed direction and subjugated the Spathi instead, a race of cowardly but highly mobile clam-like creatures, facing little resistance. Earth joined the Alliance shortly after this.

In 2119 humanity's first new-age battleships, the Earthling Cruisers, were ready. They were on their way to support the Yehat and the Shofixti when the fleet encountered a battle group of Vux, a species of green one-eyed semi-humanoids only the Yehat had known to exist. It was then that the biggest mistake of the war was made. The details are unclear, but it is said that Captain Jeffry L. Rand somehow inadvertently insulted the Vux in a way that made all Vux deeply despise humans. The Vux soon joined the Ur-Quan Hierarchy as battle thralls and became a feared enemy for the Alliance.

With their new Vux allies, the Ur-Quan immediately tried to break through Alliance defenses, but were stopped by the combined might of the Yehat and the Shofixti, supported by the first wave of Cruisers. The Ur-Quan fleet didn't waste any time and instead turned away to attack a new race, the Mycon.

Not much was known about the Mycon back then. They were more like fungi than animals and they thrived in temperatures close to the melting point of lead. In any case, they voluntarily became fighting slaves and soon the Ur-

Quan fleet returned, accompanied by hundreds of devastating Mycon Podships. The Alliance was only barely able to hold the line.

When several Earthling Cruisers were patrolling the coreward front near the Vulpeculae star cluster, the Alliance received more bad news. With a blaze of red light, unknown alien ships appeared in front of the fleet. Not giving their opponents time to do anything, they ruthlessly chopped down every Cruiser into tiny bits. It took a while for the Alliance to figure out that the attackers had been the Androsynth.

Later on the Alliance learned that shortly after the Ur-Quan had subjugated the Spathi, they moved to Eta Vulpeculae where the Androsynth had set up a colony after fleeing from Earth. After a short but intense battle the Androsynth had surrendered and become Hierarchy battle thralls.

Ever since the first encounter with the Androsynth humans were a lot more afraid during missions on the coreward front. There was nothing more dreaded than an Androsynth hit-and-run squadron. And to make it worse, everyone knew very well that the Androsynth had a good reason for despising humans.

In 2120 one more race joined the conflict. The Syreen had lost their home world in a mysterious and horrible cataclysm in 2035 and had been wandering the stars ever since. When their slow-moving habitats were attacked by the Ur-Quan, they escaped into human space and became unofficial members of the Alliance.

The media was all over the Syreen as they resembled humans in almost every way. The only external difference was that their skin had a blue tone. In addition, all Syreen starship officers were female, which made the media even more enthusiastic. It was soon revealed that humans and Syreen could even have children across species.

The opposing sides in the war were as follows: In the Alliance were the Earthlings, the Chenjesu, the Yehat, the Mmrnmhrm, the Ariloulaleelay, the Syreen and the Shofixti. Fighting alongside the Ur-Quan were the Mycon, the Spathi, the Androsynth, the Vux, the Ilwrath and the Umgah.

In 2124 the Ur-Quan concentrated their forces, trying to break through the Indi and Mira star systems. The Alliance ferociously stood their ground and managed to hold the line, but the Ur-Quan didn't give up. Over the following ten years there were many great battles between The Alliance of Free Stars and The Ur-Quan Hierarchy. Then, in 2134, the course of the war suddenly changed dramatically.

The fleets of the Alliance were pushed back to beyond the Raynet star system and the Chenjesu forces were suffering great losses while holding the strategically important Rigel star system. Recognizing this, the Ur-Quan focused their forces on Procyon, the Chenjesu's home star. After that, the Chenjesu and the Mmrnmhrm were never heard from again.

A few weeks later Sol was attacked from all directions. When the Ceres base fell, humans knew that they had been defeated, but they kept on fighting anyway. Three days later the Ur-Quan destroyed the last laser-forts on the Moon and then there was nothing left to fight back with.

Ur-Quan Dreadnoughts took positions above Rome, Moscow, Beijing, Tokyo, London, Buenos Aires and Washington. Humans had lost the war and they knew it, but the Ur-Quan decided to make the fact really clear. That's why Buenos Aires can't be found on any of the post-war maps.

After the U.N. had submitted their formal surrender, Earth had one week to decide the nature of the servitude.

The Ur-Quan demanded that the decision would be made through a popular vote. Either humans would join the Hierarchy as battle thralls and preserve some autonomy, such as traveling through space, or be forever imprisoned on Earth under an impenetrable slave shield.

Humans chose not to fight for the Ur-Quan. One month was given to withdraw all people and equipment to Earth. Anyone or anything left outside would be destroyed when the shield went up. Then the Ur-Quan sent an odd message: All human constructions older than 500 years were to be abandoned.

The meaning became evident when the Ur-Quan Dreadnoughts opened fire on Earth's surface with their fusion weapons. The flaming rain lasted for 40 hellish hours and afterwards it took days to realize that most of the history of mankind had been lost.

Large sections of European cities were incinerated. The Ur-Quan had also erased the Parthenon, Stonehenge, the Giza Pyramids and similar targets. Curiously, the United States was almost untouched. The Ur-Quan also destroyed some places that weren't thought to be significant. From their positions in orbit the Dreadnoughts blew away a kilometer of land in central Iraq, vaporized several targets in the Amazon rain forest, punched a big hole through the Antarctic icecap to destroy something deep under the surface and melted a broad swath of ocean floor in the South-Eastern Atlantic.

Just a couple of days later the slave shield went up, cutting all communications with the outside universe and giving the sky a red glow. What happened to the other alliance races – the Syreen, the Arilou, the Shofixti and the Yehat – remained unknown.

The Ur-Quan set up a starbase in Earth's orbit to service Hierarchy ships. Nearly 2000 humans, all skilled professionals, were selected to work there. The starbase was to be resupplied every five years by the Ur-Quan. During the resupply, the personnel would also be substituted with new members from Earth. A group of Ilwrath and Spathi ships were stationed on the Moon to keep an eye on the starbase.

The first two resupplies went as scheduled, but the third one never came. It has now been eight years and the starbase is running dangerously low on supplies. The starbase hasn't been able to make contact with the base on the Moon either. Without replacement radioactive elements for the starbase's power cores, the station will run out of heat and air in a matter of weeks…

CHAPTER 1

THE FIRST CONTACT

February 18th 2155, Earth's orbit

Two men were sitting at the starbase's cafeteria. The older of the two squeezed his hand tightly around his mug, which contained a small amount of brown liquid. It wasn't coffee, though, since coffee beans hadn't existed in decades. Instead it was the crown jewel of humanity's scientific prowess. Some guy from the Scandinavian Union got the Nobel Prize in Chemistry for it in the late 21st century. The drink had the same refreshing effect as coffee and it even tasted just as bad, but it wasn't unhealthy.

The older man raised the mug with the intention of drinking from it. He stopped in the middle of the process, holding the mug half way between the table and his mouth, and then put it back on the table, not letting go of it. The younger man didn't pay any attention to his company. His eyes were focused on the table to the spot where the mug was, was not, and was again. His mind was obviously somewhere else.

The cafeteria was quiet. The two men were the only people there. The only sound was the silent hum from the air vents.

"Two weeks" the younger man suddenly said. "In two weeks we have to decide which goes first – heat or air. Then we have our comfortable last few hours either choking or freezing to death. Do you think we should have a poll?"

The older man didn't say anything. He knew the question was rhetorical.

There wasn't actually that much of an age difference between the two. The older one merely looked old. He had grey hair and a beard and moustache that circled around his mouth and then went up to his hair line in front of his ears. His forehead was wrinkled and he always looked serious.

The younger one had neatly cut brown hair and no facial hair. The sum of their ages was an even 100. The younger one was the station's commander, Andrew Hayes. The older one was second in command, Adam Gruber.

"I can imagine the looks on the Ur-Quans' faces," Hayes said, "when they finally come here and find 1900 frozen corpses. They will probably say 'oops', get the reactors running again and order a replacement crew to come play a second round in this fun little game of death."

Gruber switched his position and leaned forward a bit. He held his head down, looking at the table. He opened his mouth, but took a few seconds before he started talking.

"I don't think that the Ur-Quan would willingly neglect us like this," he said after careful consideration. "They went through a lot of trouble setting this place up. It would have been a lot easier to just kill us all."

They both fell silent for a moment again. Then Gruber raised his head and looked at Hayes.

"I'm more concerned about the base on the Moon," Gruber pointed out. "The Ilwrath don't necessarily care, but the Spathi must realize how foolish it would be of them to let us die here. The Ur-Quan would most likely punish them severely."

He waited a few seconds and then continued: "When did we last check the surface for activity?"

"A few months ago that I'm aware of," Hayes replied. "I told Leonov not to waste any power on the telescope. After all we're still picking up the same old transmissions."

Ever since they started working on the station eight years ago, they've been receiving a constant encrypted signal from the Moon base.

Gruber looked at the ceiling. He was thinking about recent disturbances where some of the starbase crewmen had been at each other's throats. First five years at the starbase had gone practically without incidents. Then, as the resupply vessel's scheduled arrival date passed and no information was given, things had slowly started to escalate.

"Morale is getting low," Gruber said. "We might kill each other before the power runs out completely."

Hayes lowered his eyes and said nothing. Gruber looked around for a while and then raised his mug to his lips. With one sip the mug was empty, but he didn't place it on the table. He just silently looked at it.

The silence was broken by distant rapid footsteps that were getting louder. Someone was running their way. Soon the cafeteria door opened and a short, oriental man stormed in.

"Commander!" he yelled, looking anxious, still running towards the two men. "We've detected a ship! I think it's the resupply vessel!"

Hayes and Gruber both immediately stood up.

"Gruber, come with me to the control room," Hayes said with a decisive and commanding voice.

"Aye," Gruber replied and they both made their way towards the door.

"Walk with us and fill me in," Hayes said to the messenger.

"Yes sir," he replied.

The three of them were walking in the corridor towards the main elevator. Lights were dimmer than usual because power was being saved for life-support. All men had the same kind of uniforms – light grey shirts and darker grey pants with even darker grey knee pads and belts. The man who had just brought the news was Lei Wu, a structural engineer. He was shorter and skinnier than the two and he had short black hair. He started explaining the situation.

"Since our deep radar is offline we couldn't see it until we detected its gravity waves – which are exceptionally strong."

"We didn't try to contact the ship," Wu continued. "I came to get you right away. I'm not even sure if we still have enough power for the hyper-wave broadcast."

"If it comes to that," Gruber said, "we can always squeeze some extra juice by shutting down non-vital sectors."

Gruber had thought of it before. Shutting down non-vital sectors while transmitting wouldn't be a problem. They had already considered doing this to get a few extra days of heat and air.

"Have you told anyone else?" Hayes asked Wu.

"Leonov detected the ship so he knows, but that's all," Wu explained. "He should be in the control room right now."

"Good," Hayes replied, "I want to make sure it really is the resupply vessel before the whole station is informed."

They reached the central elevator. They were on level five and the control room was on level 16, to which Wu set the dial.

The elevator moved swiftly and silently. Nobody said anything while they were inside. Soon the doors opened and they entered the control room. It was a spacious room with lots of computer consoles on the left and a big window to the right. Above the consoles in the middle was a big screen, which was currently displaying nothing.

In contrast to the greyness inside, the view from the window was spectacular. Almost half of the view was occupied by Earth, which glowed red because of the slave shield. Slowly the planet slid out of sight as the station rotated, bringing the Moon into view.

"Leonov, tell me what you know," Hayes said as they stepped out of the elevator.

Leonov was sitting in front of a computer console below the big screen. He was a middle-aged Russian man with dark grey hair tied with a blue bandana. He hadn't shaved his beard in a while and he had dark circles below his eyes. He was looking at a monitor which showed the gravity waves of an unidentified object.

"Ah, Commander," Leonov said. "I've been analyzing the gravity waves and I'm pretty sure this ship type is not in our data banks. Whatever it is, it's bigger than an Ur-Quan Dreadnought."

"I'll try to contact it," Hayes immediately decided. "Put them on the main screen."

Leonov tried to set the system to transmit mode on a common open hyper-wave frequency, but it didn't work.

"Looks like we don't have enough power for a normal broadcast," he said. "I can decrease the bandwidth to a level where we can send and receive text only. That might still work."

"Alright," Hayes said and took a sturdy position looking at the blank screen. Leonov signaled him that he could start talking at any time. The computer would convert his speech into a text message.

"Attention unidentified space vessel!" he said in an official tone. "I am starbase Commander Hayes of the slave planet Earth. Our hyper-wave broadcast is extremely weak. Our situation is critical. Energy cores are exhausted. Scanners and deep radar are non-functional. We cannot identify your vessel. Are you the Hierarchy resupply ship?"

They waited for a response. After about a minute, a message was displayed on the screen:

"Slave planet! Hierarchy resupply vessel! What is going on here?"

"So they're not the resupply vessel," Gruber immediately concluded in an 'I knew it' kind of voice.

Hayes was already composing the next message:

"I don't know who you are or why you're here, but right now **you** are our only hope in saving the lives of the 1900 men and women aboard this starbase. I can't keep the transmitter on too much longer since we need the power for heat and air. If you don't have any radioactives on board your vessel, please get some and bring them back here before it's too late."

"If they don't know what is going on here," Gruber reasoned, "they obviously aren't with the Hierarchy."

Leonov was looking at a monitor which showed the constant encrypted signal from the Moon.

"In that case," he said, "the Ilwrath and Spathi squadrons – or at least the Ilwrath – would surely have intercepted them. But I'm not picking up anything out of the ordinary."

Hayes looked at the signal, leaning over Leonov's shoulder. He nodded and straightened himself up.

"We can leave speculations for later," he said. "Let's just wait for their response and hope they have at least some radioactive elements with them."

As soon as Hayes was done talking, a new message was displayed on the screen:

"We have something you can use. We will start transferring them to you right away."

"Splendid," Hayes stated while making a positive gesture with his fist.

Gruber wasn't as happy. He felt like an unknown ship suddenly appearing with radioactive elements to spare was too convenient. It would be foolish not to be prepared for a trap or a trick of some kind. But then again, what difference would it make?

Hayes took a personal communicator device from his pocket and touched the screen several times. After a few seconds he turned to Gruber and Wu:

"Dave's communicator seems to be offline, so you two go to the hangar and explain the situation to the loaders. I'll make an announcement and keep you informed."

"Understood," Gruber and Wu said at the same time.

As the two were going back to the elevator, Gruber thought that the most rational thing for them would be to trust the sudden arrivals completely. But he could not shake one disturbing thought from his mind. Wu interrupted his thought process as he set the dial to level 10.

"Who do you think they are?" Wu asked.

"I'd put my money on the Umgah," Gruber replied. "This could be one of their pranks again."

"Would they really go this far?" Wu asked in a slightly skeptical tone.

"You've never engaged them so you wouldn't know," Gruber said. "We know more about the Umgah than most races, because they had a tendency to converse with us – before, after and during battle. To them it was all just a big joke."

The elevator soon reached the destination. A big yellow number 10 was painted on the hangar door, which soon opened to both sides, sliding silently inside the wall. The hangar was a huge hall with an opening to the vacuum outside. The only thing between the warm inside and the cold, dark outside was an invisible force field.

As Gruber and Wu walked through the hangar they passed several crates that were lying in the middle with no apparent purpose. Some of the crates were stacked in what one could call an artistic formation. Behind this piece of modern art was a man in a pneumatic loader suit. He looked provokingly pleased with himself as he saw Gruber.

"Hey, chief! Isn't it beautiful?" he asked Gruber, clearly knowing that he should be doing something else at the moment.

The man was Jonathan O'Donnell, a common joker and trouble-maker. Gruber had always considered him a sub-par worker and an arrogant asshole they were stuck with. If he could have been sent back to Earth, they would've done it a thousand times already. Every time something went wrong, O'Donnell had something to do with it. Someone found in the women's locker room? It's O'Donnell. Green water in the shower? It's O'Donnell. An illicit still found in the air ducts? O'Donnell again.

"Get out of that suit," Gruber coldly ordered. He was used to giving such commands to him and he hadn't shown any emotion towards O'Donnell in years.

"I suppose you've already fixed the door on docking bay three?" Gruber asked, although he knew that O'Donnell probably had neither seen the door nor the order. He probably hadn't looked at his job list in weeks.

"No problem, chief," he replied, sounding sincere. "I got Johnson working on it. We had a bet which I, obviously, won."

He showed no intention of stepping out of the suit. Gruber didn't have time to get on O'Donnell's case so he continued walking.

"I heard his family was in Buenos Aires," Wu said to Gruber, keeping his voice down.

"Everyone lost something in the war," Gruber replied, implying that O'Donnell deserved no sympathy. They didn't talk after that.

Soon they reached the hangar control center. It was a small booth with big windows and a good view of the hangar. Gruber opened the door. He saw David O'Hara, the man in charge, sitting in his chair, his legs up on the computer consoles. Dave was a chubby Irish guy with a touch of orange in his otherwise brown hair. There was a half-eaten snack-bar on the table. Questionable pornographic content was playing on one of the screens.

"Dave," Gruber said with the intention of getting his attention.

Dave said nothing and didn't move. Instead he soon let out a very loud snore. He had his headphones on and seemed to be sleeping quite comfortably. Gruber took quick steps to reach Dave's side.

"Wake up! We have a situation here!" he yelled.

Dave screamed in terror and nearly fell from his chair. His feet hit the floor hard. He grasped his chest and gave Gruber a look which is usually only given to Death or the tax collector.

"Holy crap, man," he said as he was gasping for air. "Are you trying to kill me?"

The pornography was still playing. Realizing this, Dave quickly took off his headphones and turned off the screen. He took a deep breath and leaned backwards.

"So what's this 'situation' you mentioned?" he asked.

"An unidentified vessel is sending us something for our power cores," Wu explained.

"We don't know who they are and they don't seem to know anything about us," Gruber continued. "In any case, they said they would help, so get the loaders ready immediately."

Dave took a few seconds to process the information.

"Right…" he finally said. "Right…" he said again, turning to face the computer panel. "I'm on it."

When Dave was doing his thing with the controls, Gruber's communicator beeped to notify him of an incoming call. Gruber took his communicator from his pocket and answered the call. Hayes' face appeared on the communicator's screen and his voice came out of the speakers as clear as if he was standing there:

"They said they would send one unit of astatine. Are you at the hangar control already?"

"Yes, we just arrived here," Gruber answered. "Loaders have been informed and Dave will have his communicator turned on from now on." He looked rather angrily at Dave while saying the last part.

Dave showed a sign of remorse and turned on his communicator.

"So one unit of astatine it is," he said. "That should keep us going for a few more months."

"I'll make the announcement to the base now. Out," Hayes said and didn't wait for a response before closing the link.

Gruber tucked the communicator back into his pocket. Soon a cheerful ding-dong sound effect played from the station wide speaker system indicating an upcoming announcement:

"Your attention please, this announcement concerns everyone. This is Commander Hayes. We have been approached by an unidentified ship. It is not the resupply vessel, but they will give us radioactive elements for our power cores. We will now initiate the transfer. Stick to your routines."

"What else do we know?" Dave asked Wu.

"Since there's no power for the deep-radar," Wu replied, "we've only been able to determine that the ship is bigger than a Dreadnought, based on its gravity waves."

"Can't we look out the window and see for ourselves?" Dave asked innocently.

Gruber thought about it for a second and then felt stupid for not seeing such an obvious solution himself.

"I'm pretty sure it's too far for the naked eye to see," Gruber said. "But if we know its position, we can use the telescope on the observation deck."

All three of them kept nodding their heads for a while.

"I'll go there and ask Leonov to determine its position," Gruber decided.

He called Leonov as he left the room and soon Leonov's face appeared on the communicator's screen.

"Can you figure out exactly where the ship is?" Gruber asked. "I'll go to the observation deck and take a look at it with the telescope."

"There's no power in the telescope so it's no use," Leonov said. *"I did already calculate the position, though. It is 10 -50 200."*

"I should have known… Out," Gruber said feeling stupid again and closed the link.

He had only walked about 10 meters from the hangar control door so he turned around and went back. Wu and Dave were staring at the pornographic material from a while ago on one of the big screens. Dave quickly turned the screen off as Gruber entered. Gruber didn't bother to say anything about it.

"Of course there's no power in the telescope," Gruber stated in a disappointed voice.

Dave spun around in his chair to face Gruber.

"Do we have an old fashioned mechanical telescope lying around somewhere?" Dave asked.

After a few seconds of silence, Wu opened his mouth:

"I have one," he said plainly.

Dave and Gruber both looked at Wu, waiting for him to understand the situation. It took him a while.

"Oh..." Wu finally mumbled, indicating that he realized that he had to go get the telescope and try to locate the ship with it.

"I have it in my quarters," he said as he left the room.

Dave took a sandwich from one of the drawers and stuffed half of it in his mouth. He had obviously put a lot of effort into making it from the ingredients available at the starbase. Dave and Gruber were both looking at the screens showing the progress of the loaders. An unmanned transport vehicle was approaching the station from the direction of the ship. It was so close that they could see it from the cameras mounted on the loaders. It was clearly not of human design. The form was very smooth and round. It looked like an advanced piece of equipment.

"Do you know that design?" Dave asked.

"No," Gruber replied with a puzzled look on his face. "I can say for sure that its origins aren't in the old alliance."

Gruber sat down.

"Suddenly my old fears are returning," he said.

Dave looked at him with a big question mark almost visible over his head.

"Ever since the war was lost," Gruber continued, "I have been waiting for the Androsynth to return and have their revenge on us, ignoring the Ur-Quan's commands. Actually, that was what I feared the most during the war. Unlike the Ur-Quan, they had a reason to get rid of humanity for good. I was even slightly relieved when the slave shield went up. Now the Androsynth could only kill us aboard this starbase."

"Would their grudge really be that deep?" Dave asked rather skeptically as he took another bite from his sandwich. He continued talking with his mouth full: "I believe they have a lot of their own problems so they wouldn't waste their resources on revenge." He swallowed and pointed the sandwich at Gruber. "– at least not any more. Hell, the youngest ones should be around 70 by now."

"I'm not counting on them not reproducing," Gruber said. "I'd be surprised if they haven't overcome that by now."

Dave raised his eyebrows.

"So are you saying that this supposed astatine delivery is actually some Trojan scheme to blow up this starbase?" he inquired.

"It's a possibility," Gruber stated.

The elements arrived at the loading area and Dave sent a message to Hayes about it. The transport vehicle left as soon as it was empty. Just then, Wu entered the room holding an old telescope.

"Good," Gruber said. "We might locate the ship more easily if we follow the transport vehicle. Let's go to the Edge quickly so we don't lose it."

The part where the hangar ended and space began was called the Edge. From there one could look into the black infinity, standing one meter away from the end of the platform. The force field was like an invisible solid wall so it was impossible to fall off.

Gruber and Wu hastily walked across the hangar. Gruber told Wu about the transport vehicle and Wu adjusted the telescope on the move. They soon reached the Edge and tried to locate the vehicle. It had been so close just moments ago, but it could already be so far that it would be indistinguishable from all the stars. The station slowly rotated and the sector where the vehicle went was about to slide out of view.

"There!" Gruber nearly shouted as he pointed at a little dot moving away from them.

Wu rushed next to Gruber, aiming the telescope by Gruber's arm which was still pointed at the vehicle.

"I see the transport vehicle," he said, "but I don't see the mother ship yet. It has to be… over… there… CRAP!" The hangar wall blocked the view. Now they would have to wait almost 20 minutes for the station to rotate another round if they were to see the ship from the hangar.

"Let's go to the observation deck," Gruber said quickly.

They jogged across the hangar towards the same elevator that had brought them there. Along the way they passed O'Donnell who was still in the loader suit.

"Hey chief!" he shouted at Gruber. "What's going on here?"

Gruber ignored him. There was no time for chit-chat. O'Donnell tried to catch their pace, but he couldn't move fast in the suit so he was soon left behind.

"Chief! Come on, man!" O'Donnell shouted at their backs.

They reached the elevator. It had gone to another floor and they had to wait for it. Gruber thought that he had never had to wait for the elevator so long.

After an eternity of 15 seconds they managed to enter the elevator and set the dial to level 30 where the observation deck was. The elevator once again moved swiftly as it always did.

"How are we going to find the ship?" Wu asked. "The transport vehicle has to be too far to notice by now."

"Right, I forgot to tell you..." Gruber responded. "Leonov calculated the ship's approximate position so we can narrow down the search enough."

The door to the observation deck opened. It was a big round hall with a massive telescope in the middle. The roof was shaped as a dome and it was completely transparent, like it was made of a single piece of glass. There was a small platform which could be freely moved anywhere inside the room. Gruber knew without looking that the station was aligned in a way which made it impossible for them to see the ship from the floor. They climbed on the platform and Gruber started to maneuver it with a small joystick.

"Leonov said that the ship is at 10 -50 200." Gruber explained as he steered the platform into a proper location.

Wu had never used the platform controls and he looked quite surprised that Gruber operated them with such confidence. Wu set the lenses of his telescope to match the distance. Gruber pointed at a direction which was about directly opposite of Earth.

"It should be over there." he said.

Wu looked through the telescope and started scanning the direction Gruber was pointing. Suddenly Gruber's communicator beeped.

"It's Hayes." Gruber said and opened the link.

"We'll have power in a matter of minutes." Hayes said. *"Get over here, you might be needed."*

"On my way," Gruber responded, "out."

"It's all up to you now." Gruber said to Wu as he steered the platform down as quickly as possible.

"I don't know how to operate this." Wu said in a complaining tone, pointing his hand at the control panel.

They reached the floor.

"I'll set this to move automatically to the last position" Gruber grumbled. He pushed a button and jumped off the platform. The platform quickly accelerated to the opposite direction which nearly made Wu fall down. He barely managed to grasp the railing and pulled himself up.

"How do I get down from here?" Wu shouted at Gruber who was already running towards the elevator.

"Call me when you find the ship!" Gruber shouted, not looking back.

Soon Gruber reached the control room. Leonov and Hayes were both exactly where they had been when Gruber left the room. There was a message on the big screen:

"We will wait for your signal."

Hayes was looking at a display which showed the energy output of the reactor and the distribution of power to different parts of the station.

"Ah," he said in a very relieved tone, "power readings are climbing and life-support is coming back into the green."

Then he turned to look at Gruber with a smile on his face.

"We should have a visual link in a few seconds." he said.

"Deep radar is online." Leonov said. "I'll get a view of their ship in no time."

Just then Gruber's communicator started beeping again. He took it out of his pocket and looked at the screen which showed Wu's image. He answered the call.

"I found it, but I have a hard time believing it," he said, sounding as if he'd seen a ghost. *"I've never seen anything like it. One thing I can say for sure though... It really is huge."*

"The scan is complete." Leonov reported.

He looked at the silhouette of the ship from a small monitor in front of him. It took him a while to get any words out of his mouth.

"What the hell kind of a ship is that?" he finally said in disbelief.

"What do you mean?" Hayes asked.

"See for yourselves." he continued and put the image on a secondary screen next to the big screen.

"It looks like a skeleton..." Wu simultaneously managed to describe it. *"A skeleton of a starship much more advanced than we've ever seen!"*

Wu's description was not far off from what Gruber thought.

The ship seemed to consist of three long, thin beams. Two of them were symmetrically arranged under the third one at an angle of roughly 45 degrees. The two were connected to the third one from both ends and several Earthling Cruisers would easily fit between them. In front of the middle beam was what looked like an enormous cockpit. The middle beam had about a dozen large holes, as if the ship was missing some vital parts.

"We have a visual link!" Leonov announced.

A picture appeared on the big screen and they saw who they had been dealing with. Gruber didn't know which was more unbelievable: The ship they had just seen or the fact that they were now conversing with a young human male in a Star Control officer's uniform.

CHAPTER 2

LUNAR EXPEDITION

February 18th 2155, Earth's orbit

"Uh... hello." the man on the screen said.

Hayes' eyes were wide open. He looked at the screen as if all rationality had just vanished from the universe.

"Who are you?" he asked after a few seconds.

"I am Robert," the man said, *"Captain Robert Zelnick of the starship Vindicator."*

"The starship what?" Hayes asked, but shrugged the question off immediately. "Never mind... Where did you come from?"

Captain Zelnick took a more formal position standing straight, holding his hands behind his back.

"We are survivors from a Star Control science mission to Vela."

Gruber found that hard to believe and assumed that so did Hayes. But then again, everything about the current situation was rather uncommon.

"A Star Control science mission, eh?" Hayes said with disbelief in his voice. "Captain, I served as a Star Control officer during the war aboard several cruisers in the coreward front. If there had been any 'scientific mission' to Vela, I would have heard about it."

Zelnick seemed offended.

"The mission was highly secret," he explained. *"About 20 years ago we were sent to the second planet of Vela to investigate an ancient Precursor installation. While we were there, the Ur-Quan broke through the Indi-Mira line and our*

ship returned home to assist in defending Sol. Some stayed behind to continue the research, but our ship never came back."

The story sounded believable in Gruber's opinion, but it still didn't explain that huge starship they were flying.

"So how do you explain that huge starship you're flying?" Hayes hive-mindedly asked.

Zelnick looked irritated.

"It turned out to be a spaceship factory we were investigating," Zelnick replied. *"We were eventually able to get it up and running, but the raw materials ran out before this ship was finished. However it was already capable of flight, so... But now you tell me – What did you mean by Earth being a slave planet?"*

Hayes didn't answer immediately and instead sought advice from Gruber who was just outside the view of the communication link. He wondered how much Captain Zelnick and his crew actually knew.

"So we can assume that they know the history to the point when the line fell in 2134," Gruber said. He could speak freely since the communications program filtered out external noise. "But they don't know that the war was lost only a few weeks later."

Hayes waited for Gruber to finish and then answered Zelnick's question:

"The Alliance lost the war right after the line fell," he explained. "An impenetrable slave shield was cast upon Earth. This starbase is the only thing humanity has outside the shield – with the exception of you apparently."

"Commander!" Leonov suddenly cried out. "There's an Earthling Cruiser behind the ship!"

Hayes looked at one of the secondary screens which showed a detailed picture of an Earthling Cruiser. He raised his eyebrows higher than Gruber thought possible.

"Now that's something I haven't seen in a long time," he said.

"I couldn't see it from the gravity waves earlier," Leonov explained, "because the other ship is so much more massive."

Hayes' eyebrows returned to their normal level. He turned to face the screen again.

"So what is this starbase?" Zelnick asked. His irritation had changed to curiosity.

"Ur-Quan slave law requires that we maintain an orbital space platform to assist Hierarchy vessels which are in need of repairs or fuel," Hayes briefly replied. "But now you explain how you can have a Cruiser with you. Didn't you just mention that you were stranded on Vela?"

"That's a very long story," Zelnick said, suddenly looking sad. *"For now let's just say that we* ***found*** *the Cruiser on our way here."*

Hayes' face was more worried now.

"Before the slave shield went up," he explained, "the Ur-Quan said that everything man-made outside the shield would be destroyed. I have a hard time believing that an intact Cruiser would be just 'lying' around somewhere. Anyway, if the Ur-Quan find out that we have a functional Cruiser here, they will kill us all."

"So let's not let them find out," Zelnick suggested.

"There's a big problem right there," Hayes said, pointing at the Moon which had slid into view in the big window behind him. "There's a hierarchy base on the Moon. I don't know why they haven't come after you yet, but I suppose there are at least a dozen Ilwrath Avengers and Spathi Eluders down there."

"Should we destroy the base?" Zelnick asked in an innocent voice.

Hayes took a while to analyze Zelnick's face to see if he was serious.

"Captain… What do you want from us?" he asked.

"We came here to give you the technological secrets of the Precursors," Zelnick proclaimed, *"and to help fight the Hierarchy. Although now it seems that we are too late."*

"That you are," Hayes stated. "We can't oppose the Hierarchy now, no matter how much we want to. We have no ships, no weapons and no allies."

"We have two ships now," Zelnick said either proudly or as a joke. *"Although the Cruiser doesn't have a captain so we can't use it in combat."*

"**That** is not the problem," Hayes commented. "We have plenty of qualified captains here."

Hayes turned to Gruber.

"Bring Trent here," he requested.

Gruber nodded and took out his communicator.

Matthew Trent was commonly regarded as a tactical genius. He was the captain of one of the first Cruisers alongside Captain Rand during the first encounter with the Vux. Later in the war Trent became famous for coming out on top even in the most desperate situations. The Indi-Mira line probably would have fallen years earlier without him coming up with new brilliant tactics again and again for countless battles. When the line finally did fall, Trent was on Earth recovering from a wound he had received in the great battle of Zeta Illuminati, where only a handful of Earthling Cruisers and Chenjesu Broodhomes repelled a nearly endless fleet of Spathi Eluders and Umgah Drones.

Gruber called Trent on his communicator. Soon his face appeared on the screen.

"Yes?" Trent answered in a polite, yet efficient manner.

Trent was only a bit older than Gruber, but he looked like an elderly man. He was mostly bald, his face was wrinkled and there was a scar on his forehead. It wasn't a battle-scar though. He got it on the starbase when he fell down some stairs – or that's what he says. His story doesn't check out, but nobody seems to know the truth.

"Come to the control room immediately," Gruber ordered.

"Roger that - out," Trent responded. He never asked any unnecessary questions.

"If we could supply the factory on Vela with sufficient materials," Zelnick speculated, *"we could probably upgrade this ship to its full potential, which is still mostly unknown to us. We might even be able to build a whole fleet of these. Are you saying that we wouldn't have a use for that fleet anymore?"*

Hayes sighed.

"The problem is," he explained, "that it would have to be kept a secret from the Ur-Quan until we were ready. We simply can't do anything in secret with the Hierarchy outpost watching over us. But regarding your ship – I'm sure that our facilities here could be adapted to work on it as well if we had the plans."

"We have all the plans," Zelnick replied. *"How about we destroy the base on the Moon and then you take us more seriously? After that we'll get the factory on Vela running again, build a strong fleet and liberate Earth."*

Hayes seemed amused.

"Ahh... fight the Ur-Quan!" he gloriously declared. "Win back our freedom!"

Then he continued more seriously.

"I remember having such thoughts myself...once, a long time ago. But that was in the first years after the defeat, when it was still terrifying to look up and see the bloody glow of the pulsating slave shield overhead. Through day and night we gazed up at the impenetrable wall as though the sheer power of our hatred would pull it down. But over the years I spent so much of my time struggling down on the surface under the shield and then later up here trying to keep this station alive that I'd forgotten what it means to be free... to hate our Ur-Quan Masters! And now, here you are, in an alien ship of unknown power, offering me your assistance to fight against the Hierarchy again, after all these years."

Hayes stopped talking even though he seemed like there was more to come. Zelnick waited for Hayes to continue, but just then Trent entered the room. He looked at Zelnick's face on the screen. Then he looked at the ship screens showing the Vindicator and the Cruiser. Finally he looked at Hayes who looked back at him.

Hayes returned his focus on Zelnick.

"Captain, your offer is intriguing," he continued. "It's tempting to think that with your advanced Precursor technology we can somehow crack Earth's slave shield and reassemble the Alliance to attack the Hierarchy. And this time, win the damn war! But consider the consequences if we should fail… The Ur-Quan won't just punish us here on this station. They will exact a gruesome retribution on the surface below as well."

"Won't they do that anyway unless we smash both of these ships into some remote asteroid?" Zelnick pointed out.

"You're right," Hayes had to agree. "We are almost forced to take our chances here. So here's what we'll do…"

Hayes looked at Gruber. His eyes weren't asking for approval. Rather, they seemed to tell him that it was about time they did something. Then he continued:

"If you can eliminate the base on the Moon and get rid of that threat at least… Then I will commit this station to help you with this rebellion you are about to start."

Trent was listening closely.

"Are we attacking the moonbase?" he silently asked Gruber.

Gruber made a very small gesture with his hand. It clearly indicated that all Trent's questions would be answered shortly.

"You mentioned that you have capable Cruiser captains," Zelnick remembered. *"Could you send one over?"*

"Yes," Hayes responded. "You will get Matthew Trent."

Trent's face showed a slight surprise, but not for long. Zelnick also seemed surprised. He clearly knew Trent's name.

"Alright," he said, obviously pleased, *"shall we send a shuttle to pick him up?"*

"That would be best," Hayes replied. "Trent, come over here and say hi," he then suggested.

Trent walked next to Hayes and took a formal standing position. He was probably three times older than Zelnick.

"Matthew Trent," he introduced himself.

"Robert Zelnick," the young captain said. *"It's a pleasure to meet you. You will command the Cruiser Tobermoon."*

"Tobermoon, you say?" Trent replied, looking surprised. "I remember Tobermoon from the time when Isadora Burton was its captain. I knew her father rather well back on Earth. I suppose Burton is not with you?"

Zelnick's good mood seemed to vanish instantly.

"No," he said plainly. *"She's dead."*

Suddenly Zelnick looked devastated, like he was about to burst in tears.

"We'll send the shuttle," he barely managed to mumble and then terminated the communication link.

"Looks like there's some kind of a story there," Gruber commented on the sudden stop in negotiations.

"Let's not dwell on that," Hayes decided and turned around.

"Go to the hangar and wait for the shuttle," he said to Trent. "Gruber can tell you everything while you wait."

Then Hayes addressed both of them: "You should also tell Dave to expect the shuttle. I'll try to get the connection back."

"This is a tough game we're about to start playing," Gruber pointed out. He then turned to Trent. "If you are destroyed, the Spathi will probably notify the Ur-Quan immediately. Then we will have to hope that the Ur-Quan get here fast enough, before the Ilwrath sacrifice us all to Dogar and Kazon*."

"That would be unpleasant," Leonov said, joining in on the conversation. "There is absolutely no chance of the moonbase failing to notice two ships approaching this station. We must consider the possibility of a trap."

"Of course," Trent agreed. "Even if it isn't a trap, they will have to know that we're coming. We'll just have to hope that they're unprepared for battle and that Captain Zelnick's ship is as powerful as it looks."

"Do any of you oppose this course of action?" Hayes asked.

There was a short pause. When it was evident that nobody had any objections, Gruber ended the silence:

"I agree with this. If this Precursor ship is powerful enough to give us any chance of opposing the Hierarchy, getting rid of the moonbase will have to be possible, if not trivial."

"And if it isn't," Leonov continued the thought, "then it wouldn't have been any use anyway."

"Wait a second," Trent interrupted. "Did you just call it a 'Precursor' ship?"

---

* The Ilwrath gods of darkness, pain, death, cruelty… basically everything that is evil.

"Oh, right, there wasn't a chance to tell you," Gruber answered. "They said the ship is from some ancient Precursor factory on Vela II."

"What were they–" Trent tried to ask, but he was interrupted by Hayes:

"Get going you two. Gruber can tell you everything on the way."

By the time the elevator reached the hangar floor, Gruber had succeeded in his task.

"A Star Control science mission, huh?" Trent commented. "You know, I remember some rumors that Corridor Nine, the special operations division of Star Control, was directing some hush-hush operation near Androsynth space. The Vela star system actually is in that direction.

They started walking through the hangar towards the control booth. There was nobody around. All idle crewmen had probably gone to the observation deck.

"How much do you know about the Precursors?" Trent asked.

"Not much." Gruber answered. "I know that they were an ancient highly advanced race that suddenly appeared about 200 000 years ago and just a few thousand years later they just as suddenly vanished. All that is known of them has been learned from countless relics found throughout the quadrant – from an orbital platform in Alpha Centauri, to a stack of data plates in a cave on Pluto, to some nameless widget found in a voodoo shop in New Orleans."

"You seem to know the same facts as I do," Trent said. "I often wondered what a Precursor ship would look like. I can't wait to see how it performs."

"Captain Zelnick said that the ship was not finished since the factory ran out of materials," Gruber pointed out. "So don't get your hopes up too high."

The artistic crate formation had been scattered across the landing area. The crates would have to be picked up before the shuttle arrived. For the first time Gruber felt angry for not seeing O'Donnell anywhere. Gruber could do almost any work on the station, but he was not qualified to operate the loader suit and neither were Trent nor Dave. He would quickly have to find someone else to do it.

As they approached the hangar control booth, they saw Dave through the front-side window. He seemed to be talking while looking at the console and typing something. Dave's eyes met Gruber's.

They opened the door and saw who Dave was talking to – O'Donnell was in the booth, looking through Dave's porn collection, which seemed to have achieved quite a high status. Dave turned to face Gruber, but O'Donnell didn't move. He had headphones on and was sitting with his back towards them.

"Any news?" Dave asked.

"They're sending a shuttle," Gruber told him. "The landing area needs to be cleared right away."

O'Donnell didn't move a muscle. He either didn't hear them or acted like he hadn't. He was sitting at the very edge of the chair, focused on what was happening on the screen.

Gruber grabbed O'Donnell's chair and pulled it backwards with full force. O'Donnell fell to the floor, hitting his head on the chair's edge, which made his headphones fall off.

"There's a shuttle coming -" Gruber said in an extremely polite and quiet tone,

"- SO CLEAR THE LANDING AREA!" he shouted in a less polite manner.

O'Donnell took his time getting up. When he finally got to a standing position, he looked Gruber in the eyes with a blank expression for a while. Gruber looked back at him. Their faces were awfully close to each other.

"Okay," O'Donnell finally said and made his way to the door, saluting half-assedly on the way.

"So what's in this shuttle?" Dave asked when O'Donnell had left the room.

"Nothing," Gruber replied, "it's here to pick up Trent."

Dave looked at Trent, then at Gruber again.

"It turns out they have an Earthling Cruiser with them," Gruber continued, "but no captain for it. So with help from Trent, they are going to attack the moonbase."

Dave scratched his head.

"That's pretty heavy."

"Yes it is," Gruber agreed.

They all looked at the landing area through the control booth window. O'Donnell actually was in the loader suit, picking up the crates. He moved very quickly. If he didn't have such an attitude problem, he would be an excellent worker. Soon the area was cleared and O'Donnell saluted towards the control booth with the suit's arm.

"Just in time," Dave said, "the shuttle is coming."

True enough; the shuttle soon came into view. It approached the hangar opening and then slowly glided through the force field. The shuttle was of familiar design. It was the standard shuttle on every Earthling Cruiser.

Dave stayed inside the booth as Gruber and Trent approached the shuttle. O'Donnell was already near the rear end, waiting for the entry ramp to be lowered. Gruber and Trent took positions in front of O'Donnell. Several other people were now entering the hangar.

After a while the entry ramp started to move. Slowly they could see more and more of the inside of the ship. Standing at the top of the ramp was a middle-aged woman with blonde hair, wearing a Star Control uniform. As soon as the ramp was all the way down, she started walking towards

Gruber and Trent. They waited for her to come down before saying anything.

The woman looked around curiously. She smiled at everyone and then stopped in front of Trent.

"Hello, Jane Jenkins," she introduced herself and shook hands with Trent. "I'm supposed to take you to the Tobermoon. You are Matthew Trent, aren't you?"

"Yes I am," Trent replied.

Jenkins' face seemed to be filled with joy. Her dark brown eyes were beaming with enthusiasm. She looked around once more and then turned to Gruber.

"Are you in charge here?" she asked and shook his hand too.

"No," Gruber answered, "I am Adam Gruber, chief of staff and second in command. Commander Hayes is in the control room."

"Should we leave right away?" she asked, meaning her and Trent.

"Yes you should, you can have a guided tour of the starbase later," Gruber replied with a grin.

Jenkins returned the grin and beckoned Trent to enter the ship. With no other words exchanged, they walked up the ramp. Soon the ramp closed and the shuttle's engines started to roar again. The shuttle left as quickly as it had arrived.

People in the hangar began to scatter. O'Donnell was pestering Gruber about why Trent alone had been taken. Gruber explained everything O'Donnell needed to know in a few sentences.

"Commander Hayes will probably inform everyone soon enough," Gruber concluded the topic.

"I want to go too," O'Donnell said to Gruber as if it was in his power to decide. He got no response.

Since Gruber had nothing else to do at the moment, he decided to return to the control room. He called Hayes and told him that Trent had left with the shuttle.

"Good," Hayes replied, *"now all we can do is watch and wait."*

Gruber called the elevator. When it arrived, it wasn't empty. There was Doctor Vincent Chu, head of the research section. He had the stereotypical look of a scientist – old, small frame, white coat, round glasses, progressing baldness, bushy white hair and a neat moustache. Even though Chu was also among the highest ranked people on the starbase, Gruber didn't know him very well. He rarely had any business with the science division.

"Are you going to the control room?" he asked Gruber.

Gruber noticed that the dial had already been set to level 16.

"Yes," he answered, "I suppose you are as well?"

"Commander Hayes asked me to look at something," Chu explained.

When they entered the control room, the main screen was displaying a tactical view of the surroundings. There was Earth, the Moon, the starbase, the Vindicator and the Tobermoon. All were portrayed by distinguishable symbols. Two secondary screens were showing the ships' bridges. Zelnick was standing on the Vindicator's bridge, but Tobermoon's bridge was still empty.

"Doctor Chu," Hayes greeted, "I'm sure you know that we have quite a situation on our hands here."

"Actually," Chu replied, "I know nothing more than what you said in the announcement some time ago. I had been in the clean room alone for over an hour when I got your message."

Gruber took a seat by the consoles next to Leonov while Hayes explained everything to Chu. Gruber and Leonov were looking at the Tobermoon from one of the secondary screens. Seeing a Cruiser after 20 years was a real moment.

Gruber thought back to the time when he was the first officer on Artemis, one of the second generation Cruisers. He remembered the battle in Draco, where humans clashed with the Ilwrath for the first time. It was still early in the war and the Alliance had the upper hand that time. The Ilwrath were arrogant and rushed forward without any tactics, making themselves easy targets for the Cruisers' homing nuclear missiles. The Ilwrath were blown away like fireworks.

During the first years on the starbase, Gruber often looked back on that battle with Hayes, who was also an officer on one of the Cruisers. However, they had run out of old battle stories long ago so they hadn't talked much about the war in years.

After finishing his explanation to Chu, Hayes lowered his voice a little, indicating the start of a private conversation. It could have easily been overheard, but Gruber thought that it was none of his business, so he tried not to pay any attention. It turned out to be too difficult with nothing else to do so he started up a conversation with Leonov.

"Can you show me where the shuttle is going?" he asked Leonov.

Leonov touched the controls a few times which made the screen show an image of the shuttle docked with the Tobermoon.

"So we should soon see Trent on the bridge," Gruber stated.

As if on cue, Trent appeared on the communication screen.

"Commander," he said to get Hayes' attention.

Hayes turned to face the communication screens and Chu took a seat near Gruber and Leonov.

"How does it feel?" Hayes asked Trent.

"It's like getting on a bike after 20 years," he replied. *"It all feels very familiar."*

Trent sat down on the captain's chair. The Cruiser's bridge was round with the captain sitting at the center. The communication screen didn't show much apart from the captain. The Vindicator's bridge remained a mystery. What they'd see on the screen was just a very large empty room.

"Can you hear me, Trent?" Zelnick asked. The link was open for all three of them.

"Loud and clear," he replied. *"What's the plan?"*

"We might have to change that now that you're in control of the Tobermoon," Zelnick considered.

"Alright," Trent said, *"so tell me what your ship can do in battle."*

Zelnick paused for a while.

"I don't know," he finally said.

"WHAT?" Trent and Hayes shouted in unison.

"Hey, it's not like this thing came with an operations manual," Zelnick defended himself. *"We flew here straight from Vela and haven't tested the main gun yet. As far as I can tell, it is the only weapon we have."*

"What about maneuverability?" Trent asked with a deep sigh.

"Very poor," Zelnick said. *"I understand that this ship could be incredibly fast, but the engines are not even nearly finished."*

"I see," Trent said. *"Under these circumstances, our best bet would be for you to bombard the base directly and for us to nuke the enemy ships while they are still on the ground. If they take off before we are in position, it will get a lot more difficult. While we would get a gravity whip from the Moon, you would have to draw their fire and endure much more than any known ship could handle."*

"In that case," Zelnick decided, *"let's get going so they have less time to take off."*

"Alright, set course for the Moon," Trent agreed.

"Everything is in your hands," Hayes said. "Good luck!"

Everyone in the control room watched on the tactical display as the symbols of the Vindicator and the Tobermoon slowly approached the Moon. When the enemy ships would take off, their symbols would also appear on the display. It would take approximately 30 minutes before the Vindicator and Tobermoon could get within firing range of the moonbase. There was an estimated time of arrival counter at the lower left corner of the screen.

The atmosphere was tense. Any second now the enemy could launch their counter attack. Nobody dared to say anything as they just gazed at the display. Gruber was fiddling with his beard and swallowing every 10 seconds. Leonov had taken off his headband and was tapping his fingers on the console and his right leg on the floor. Gruber had always hated the leg tapping. Doctor Chu was sweating like a fat pig even though the room was quite chilly. Hayes was standing stiff as an iron pole. Trent looked like an ordinary Cruiser captain doing ordinary things. Zelnick on the other hand looked almost too relaxed - like he didn't understand the seriousness of the situation.

After what felt like hours, the ETA counter had dropped to 10 minutes. With shaking hands, Leonov managed to put the telescope view of the moonbase on one of the tertiary screens. It was business as usual at the moonbase. They seemed to completely ignore the incoming ships. There was the same movement on the surface as ever and the same incoherent broadcast they had been listening to for years. Gruber didn't know whether to consider it a good thing. Were they just laughing and waiting to set off their trap?

Had they been idle for so long that they didn't care to monitor the starbase anymore?

Finally the counter reached zero and the enemy still hadn't shown any sign of movement.

"I can't find any targets down there," Trent said, *"at least neither ships nor any other weapons. There are just a bunch of construction vehicles moving on the surface."*

"Should we fire at the base?" Zelnick asked.

"They seem unarmed," Trent pointed out.

"If you conclude that they have no weapons, take control of the base," Hayes ordered. "It might contain valuable information and materials."

"Let's wait and observe for a while," Trent decided.

"Okay," Zelnick agreed, *"we'll prepare a landing team. We have a few handguns."*

They watched the base silently for a few minutes, but nothing happened.

"I just noticed something," Trent suddenly said and broke the silence. *"The construction vehicles' movement is random. Take a look. They are just moving moon dust from one pile to another."*

Everyone focused on the vehicles. The randomness of their movement was quite obvious now that they knew to expect it. It was hard to imagine a reason for them to move like that.

After a while the landing team was ready.

"Should we send the landing team to the surface?" Zelnick asked.

"I think now would be a good time," Trent said. *"We've seen enough."*

"Yes," Hayes agreed, "I don't think we'll learn anything important from watching anymore."

Leonov relayed a view from the shuttle to one of the screens. On another screen he put up a split view showing everyone in the landing team. There were 12 crew members in total. Jenkins was piloting the shuttle, which was the same one that had picked up Trent from the hangar. Gruber noticed a peculiar detail in the crew – three of the men looked identical. For a second he thought they were Androsynth, but soon he scrapped the idea, since there was no production line those three would even slightly resemble. However, he would have to ask about it later to confirm it.

The shuttle took off, leaving the Vindicator and the Tobermoon in orbit. Again everyone was doing their own thing to cope with the excitement. Jenkins was giving readings as they got closer to the surface.

Suddenly the communication link with the shuttle got very unstable and noisy. Just a few minutes later, the connection was lost completely. They could still see the shuttle approaching the moonbase, so nothing had apparently happened to it.

"Interference," Trent recognized. *"Judging by how it started, it was probably on before we got here."*

"Can't we do anything?" Zelnick asked.

"Not without firing at the communications tower on the surface," Trent replied.

"Don't fire," Hayes commanded. "The landing team might be able to disable the transmitter."

Once again all they could do was wait. They watched as the shuttle landed inside the base's territory. Both Trent and Zelnick had their fingers on their triggers ready to bombard the base if there were any hostile actions. They could see nine team members enter the base interior while two were left waiting outside. Presumably Jenkins was still inside the ship.

They waited. Gruber grasped the opportunity to ask what was on his mind.

"Did you notice that three men in the landing team were identical?"

The others shook their heads in silence.

"Well take a look and see if the communication link is restored," Gruber advised them.

Soon after he had said that, the link was completely restored in the blink of an eye. One of the landing team members immediately transmitted a report:

"This is Joseph Fritz reporting from the moonbase. We have explored most of the interior and just now disabled the hyper-wave transmitter that was interfering with our communications. This place is like a ghost town. It must have been abandoned years ago, but great care has been taken to make the place appear active. Life-support systems are functioning and fusion generators are at full output. The transmitter was broadcasting the same message over and over again. We weren't able to translate the message, but Thomas Rigby, the xenotech, believes the message was some kind of an alert or mayday."

"What about the equipment?" Hayes asked.

"This place is filled with all kinds of useful stuff," Fritz continued. *"We shall bring the most valuable materials and equipment aboard immediately."*

"Commander," Gruber began, "what if the purpose of that broadcast was to see how long the base stays untouched? Now that we turned off the broadcast, the Ilwrath and the Spathi might know that something has happened to the base."

"Ah, crap, I didn't think of that," Hayes said.

"What?" Zelnick and Trent inquired as they couldn't hear what Gruber had said.

"I think we should turn the broadcast back on," Hayes explained to them, "so that the Ilwrath and Spathi might think that the base is still untouched."

"There's a point," Trent agreed.

"Can you turn the broadcast back on?" Zelnick asked Fritz.

"We'll try," he replied.

Fritz was doing something for a while before coming to a conclusion:

"No can do, I'm sorry. The transmitter seems to be rigged in a way that the broadcast can't be reactivated."

"So it was a trap after all," Gruber said.

"We don't know that," Chu pointed out. "There are thousands of reasons for the transmitter to suddenly stop working with nobody around to fix it. I doubt they relied on that alone."

Suddenly Hayes looked repentant.

"All these years of watching and listening and we never even guessed that the base could be empty."

"What would it have changed if we knew?" Gruber asked.

The look Hayes gave to Gruber clearly indicated that there was nothing they could have done and that Hayes was a fool to fret over it.

"Let's continue with the original plan," Hayes decided after pulling himself together.

He then addressed Zelnick.

"Salvage what you can from the base. We can return there later if needed. Then come back here and we'll take a closer look at your ship."

"Alright," Zelnick complied and relayed the orders to the landing team.

"What's with the three identical men on the landing team?" Hayes asked Zelnick.

"What about them?"

"They're not Androsynth, are they?"

"What? No. They are the Liebermann triplets – Fred, Paul and Alex."

After about an hour, the shuttle was ready to return to the Vindicator. Then suddenly Leonov almost fell from his chair as he glanced at the radar screen. His sudden movement caught the attention of everyone in the room.

"Commander!" he shouted. He quickly straightened himself and switched the radar display to a bigger screen for everybody to see. "There's an Ilwrath Avenger approaching the moonbase at full speed from 160 10!"

Hayes immediately relayed the information to Zelnick and Trent.

"Listen closely!" he said with a serious voice. "Our long range sensors show a ship closing in on your position, fast! The computer identifies it as Ilwrath, Avenger-class. It probably hasn't seen you yet, but it very soon will."

"Should we hide?" Zelnick asked, sounding completely neutral.

"No," Trent said. *"You stay here and keep them occupied for just a little while. We will circle around the Moon and surprise them from behind. If they think that you are alone, we will nail them."*

"That's a good plan," Hayes agreed, "get going."

Both ships prepared for battle. The Tobermoon thrusted with maximum force away from the Vindicator. Soon it would be behind the Moon, out of sight and out of reach for the hyper-wave transmission.

"We will lose the link in a few seconds," Trent said, *"Converse with them for a while if you can to distract them. We will come back from the other side in about ten minutes."*

Right after Trent had said that, the Tobermoon disappeared behind the Moon and the link was lost.

"Captain, try to stall them for as long as possible," Hayes advised. "But also be ready to engage them yourselves."

"No problem," Zelnick assured him in an over-confident manner.

Very soon afterwards, the Ilwrath ship was hailing the Vindicator on a common frequency.

"Relay the link here as well," Hayes said to Zelnick.

Zelnick answered the call and a view from the Ilwrath ship appeared on the screen. It was just as those who had seen the Ilwrath before remembered. Zelnick's conversation partner was a large, red, spider-like creature with many green eyes and sharp teeth.

"By The Fetid Breath Of The Dark Twin, Kazon!" The Ilwrath said with both joy and surprise. The translation computer did a good job making the voice sound evil. *"A Hu-Man In An Alien Starship... How Fascinating! I Never Expected To Find Such A Remarkable Vehicle In The Hands Of A Hu-Man. Hu-Mans Are Prey Animals - Weak And Helpless. But Here Is A Hu-Man In An Armed Starship! And Therefore In Direct Violation Of The Oath Of Fealty. I Am Sure Our Masters, The Ur-Quan, Will Punish Earth Most Severely For This Treachery When I Present Them With The Twisted Wreckage Of Your Ship And Your Many Charred Corpses."*

Zelnick seemed to be caught by surprise by this overly aggressive message.

"Where the hell did you come from?" he asked.

"Since You Will Soon Be Dead, I Will Gladly Explain," the Ilwrath said cheerfully. *"We Have Spent Many Years Gleefully Preying On The Pkunk. They Are A Pitiful, Easily-killed Species And We Would Have Continued In This Divine Worship Of Dogar And Kazon But We Required Additional Crew Members And Repairs. So We Set Course For Home. But Before We Had Reached Our Region Of Space, We Detected The Passage Of A Nearby Vessel - An Ur-Quan Drone. It Informed Us That An Unidentified Starship Had Approached Earth, So Here We Are!"*

"The drone!" Hayes cried in agony and slapped himself in the forehead. "Of course the drone would have seen the ships approaching this station."

“This is a good thing,” Gruber pointed out to Hayes. “The drone didn’t reach the Ur-Quan. Instead, it relayed the information to this Ilwrath ship. If it is destroyed here, the Ur-Quan won’t even know.”

“It will be a pleasure blasting your ugly face out of the stars,” Zelnick replied to the Ilwrath in a polite manner.

Now it was the Ilwrath’s turn to be surprised.

“Fool!” it shouted. *“As Alien As Your Ship May Be, Our Sensors Reveal How Few Weapons You Have On Board. Your Threats Mean Nothing To--“*

The Ilwrath was interrupted by Zelnick:

“Let’s see what you think of those few weapons when they are shoved down your throat and up your ass – or equivalents. Surrender now, foul creature, and we might spare your life!”

The Ilwrath seemed angered. It let out an indescribable sound, which was probably used to scare prey animals in the wild.

“I Have No Fear Of You, Feeble Mammal!” it declared while showing its teeth. *“My Gods, Dogar The Black And Kazon The Unseen, Have Personally Confided To Me That They Despise You Hu-Mans, And That They Will Help Us To Kill You All!”*

“Oh yeah?” Zelnick said aggressively. *“Well your mother—“*

He stopped talking since the Ilwrath had cut the transmission and was now flying straight towards the Vindicator. In a few minutes they would be in range of the Ilwrath’s Hellfire Spout.

Zelnick ordered the ship to face the Ilwrath head on. They would be in range at about the same time as the Tobermoon was supposed to appear from behind the Moon. It was going to be a rather heavy situation for the main cannon’s first test.

"How did you like his diplomacy?" Gruber asked Hayes, lightening up the mood a bit.

"It was very appropriate," Hayes replied.

They watched the tactical display as the Ilwrath's symbol got closer and closer to the Vindicator's. Suddenly, before anyone could say Jack Robinson, Tobermoon's symbol appeared next to the Moon. Tobermoon was in sight for the starbase, but not for the Vindicator and the Ilwrath ship yet. Tobermoon could fire in less than a minute. Trent appeared on the screen again.

"Everything is going as planned," Hayes reported to Trent.

An Earthling Cruiser had a much longer range than an Ilwrath Avenger. Normally the Avenger would use its cloaking device, making the Cruisers' homing missiles work as unguided rockets, but for some reason it wasn't using its cloak now. Maybe they thought it wasn't necessary since they didn't know about the Tobermoon. Very soon they would, though, and then it would be too late for them.

Something was happening on the Vindicator's bridge. Zelnick didn't seem to know what it was.

"I think the ship is telling me that we can fire at an approaching enemy," he guessed.

At the same time Tobermoon had circled the Moon and could now fire at the Avenger.

"Fire!" Trent and Zelnick commanded in unison.

Two nuclear missiles blasted off from the Tobermoon and a bolt of energy was shot from the Vindicator towards the Avenger, which was now starting to activate its cloaking device.

The bolt hit the Avenger in about two seconds. The damage seemed rather severe, but not enough to destroy the ship. The missiles would hit in less than 10 seconds.

"Fire again!" Zelnick ordered and another bolt was shot off.

The Avenger started to fade out of sight as the cloak got more power, but the missiles were already so close that their shockwave would do severe damage in any case. The second bolt from the Vindicator hit and the heat from the impact guided the missiles towards their otherwise invisible target.

The missiles hit the Avenger, drowning it in the bright light of a nuclear explosion. After a short light show, there was nothing but debris left.

Hayes was triumphant.

“What a beautiful sight!” he commended the two cheerfully; “I haven't seen an Avenger blown away like that since the Battle in Draco. Good work you two!”

Zelnick ordered the landing team to return to the Vindicator.

“Should we return to the starbase?” he then asked.

“Yes,” Hayes replied, “we need to get the Precursor equipment and software over here so that we can make it work with our ship repair fabricators.”

They all looked at each other with smiles on their faces. The mood was light and cheerful. Hayes continued:

“So we do what we can to your ship and you go back to Vela… But then what, Captain?”

“Then, Commander,” Zelnick declared, *“we will proceed to kick some major alien butt!”*

“Yes, Captain,” Hayes laughed, “we'll do just that!”

CHAPTER 3

THE NEW ALLIANCE OF FREE STARS

March 5th 2155, Earth's orbit

A dozen people were sitting in the starbase briefing room. There were Hayes, Gruber, Chu, Zelnick, Trent, two women and one man from the Vindicator and three men from the science division. In addition, Doctor Eva Fredrikson, leading scientist in the technology division, was standing before the others. She was a picturesque blonde woman in her mid-thirties from Northern Europe. She was one of the very few crew members who were under 30 when they were selected for duty on the starbase eight years earlier. She asked the others to quiet down as she was about to start her presentation.

"During these past two weeks we have successfully integrated the Precursor technology from the Vindicator with our own facilities," she explained. "We have performed minor repairs on both the Vindicator and the Tobermoon. We have also rigged up an emergency warp escape unit for the Vindicator. Do note, though, that because the ship is so massive, the emergency warp will consume vast quantities of fuel. And speaking of fuel, the Vindicator's hyperdrive uses the same stabilized antimatter technology as Hierarchy vessels, on a much larger scale of course, so we can synthesize the fuel here."

Everyone was listening carefully even though the beginning was just a recap on what they already knew. The last two weeks had been the busiest in the history of the starbase. Nobody had had any idle time and everyone had signed up as a volunteer crew member for either the Vindicator or the Tobermoon.

"As you all know," Fredrikson continued, "we have obtained the blueprints for the Earthling Cruiser and can now build them in our shipyard – provided we have the required materials."

The blueprints she was referring to were no longer supposed to exist. The only designs that were in the starbase's data banks were incomplete Hierarchy ship designs which were of no use. But, when the Vindicator's technologies were being integrated to the database, one of the maintenance engineers had let everyone in on a big secret: She had been a starship production assistant at the Detroit shipyards during the war. When Earth was conquered, she was ordered to destroy all ship construction databases, but she secretly made copies of the blueprints and had kept them with her ever since.

"Theoretically we could even build alien ships here if we had the plans," Fredrikson speculated.

They wouldn't be of much use though. It was a well-known fact that alien ships just couldn't be flown in combat without native starship captains at the helm. Zelnick was the only known exception here as he somehow understood the alien interface of the Vindicator. After the starbase scientists' hopeless attempts to get to grips with the Vindicator's computer, Zelnick had been forced to tell his part of the story.

On their expedition to Vela, their most respected and also least liked Precursor expert was Professor Jules Farnsworth. He was well known for his formidable intellect and his extensive knowledge of the Precursor civilization. He was also widely disliked for his flamboyant egotism and rude impatience with those who did not hang on his every word.

The man was simply impossible to work with for anyone with even a hint of self-respect.

When the team had arrived at the site, Farnsworth located the central computer quickly. He hadn't had time to more than scratch the surface before the Alliance's Indi-Mira defensive line fell and their ship had been called back to defend Sol. They got orders to destroy the factory so it wouldn't fall into the hands of the enemy. However, the majority of the team had wanted to stay on Vela and they promised to detonate a nuclear bomb in the factory if the Ur-Quan would ever find them.

Days turned into months as they waited for a rescue vessel from Earth. Eventually their rations ran out and they had to establish a self-sufficient colony to stay alive. Then months began to turn into years. They named the planet Unzervalt, which simply meant "our world".

Over 10 years after they had been left by themselves, Farnsworth declared that he had unraveled the secret of the computer and, without permission, had given it the order to continue its primary function, which was still unclear. Suddenly all the machinery inside the factory had come to life and started to build something. In a few days it became clear that it was a starship. It also became clear that the construction would take a very, very long time. For years they couldn't do anything but watch the robots build a huge vessel. Then finally, after nearly a decade, the robots suddenly stopped, returned to their original positions and shut down. The computer explained that the factory had run out of materials and that there weren't any substitutes on the entire planet.

The ship was incomplete, but it was tested to be capable of flight. There was a problem, though. The controls of the ship were not designed for humans. It became obvious from the interior layout of the starship that the Precursors were giants, and seemingly not bipedal. Levers were almost impossible to move, three people were required to actuate a single switch, and the chairs, beds and other furnishings were better suited for a woolly mammoth than a human. Some kind of an automated control system was needed.

Farnsworth was ordered to remove the central computer from the factory and configure it to run the ship. When he was pressed to begin programming the computer for its new task, he broke down and admitted that he didn't have the slightest idea how to do that. It turned out that he had never understood the computer at all. Instead, for years he had secretly employed the natural computer talents of a young genius. This gifted child, Robert Zelnick, now a young adult, had been born on Unzervalt – the son of a starship officer and a research team engineer. Farnsworth was thrown into the stockade and Zelnick was made the pilot of the Precursor ship, which had been named Vindicator.

"Pay attention!" Fredrikson shouted at Zelnick who was counting the ceiling tiles. He quickly straightened up.

"Now then, about the Vindicator…" she continued. "Our engineers and Precursor specialists agree with the scientists from Unzervalt that the Vindicator is designed to be a 'workhorse' vehicle. It can be easily reconfigured for different missions by adding or swapping self-contained equipment packs which we call 'modules'. From the Vindicator's data banks we found blueprints for some basic modules: crew pods, which after modifying them to fit human needs, provide life-support for about 50 people; storage bays, which are basically just huge empty containers; fuel tanks, which hold around 50 units of fuel each—"

Junior scientist Edward Hawkins whistled. He was one of the men from the starbase's science team and Dr. Chu's subordinate. 50 units was a huge amount and the ship could be theoretically fitted with 16 of these tanks.

"—additional power generators, or 'dynamos' as we call them, which increase the energy fed to the combat batteries, thus improving the rate of fire; and finally weapon modules – Ion-Bolt Guns. These are not especially destructive, but very usable. The 'barrel' can be mounted in any direction, so the ship can be made into one tough hedgehog."

"Why is it called the 'ion-bolt gun'?" a middle-aged woman from the Vindicator's science team asked.

"Because it fires ion bolts," Fredrikson answered, trying to be polite. The woman slightly blushed and nodded. The following silence was a signal for Fredrikson to continue.

"Anyway, theoretically there are no limitations on the modules, other than their external measurements and connectivity. If we could get our hands on some other module designs, we could easily build them here."

"Where could such designs be found?" Trent asked after raising his hand.

"I have no idea," Fredrikson answered, "possibly from some museum labeled as 'modern art'."

Some of the attendants laughed a little. It was rare for Fredrikson to crack a joke.

"So here is the good news," Fredrikson got back to the point. "We managed to finish the incomplete thrusters of the Vindicator. We haven't done a test drive in hyperspace, but if our calculations are correct, you are in for one hell of a ride. The maximum cruising speed should be close to 1000 hyperspace milliunits per hour. The Vindicator should now be faster than any ship we have data on, which includes all Alliance and Hierarchy ships. The hyperdrive is also so massive that the Vindicator can 'drag along' at least 10 Cruisers without losing speed in hyperspace."

Everyone seemed impressed. Speed surely was of the essence here. The Vindicator could maybe even push straight through Ur-Quan space without worrying about unwanted encounters.

"And then some bad news," Fredrikson said lowering the pitch of her voice a little. "First of all, the massive hyperdrive gulps fuel like an old American car. Our calculations predict a consumption of…"

She paused for a while to take a breath. She gave an apologetic look which made everyone prepare for the worst.

"…10 fuel units per 100 hyperspace units."

There was a mixture of loud gasping, laughter and head scratching.

"Also," Fredrikson continued, "using the emergency warp I mentioned earlier will gulp approximately 5 units of fuel."

Nobody dared to laugh anymore.

"So using the emergency warp is like taking a trip to Alpha Centauri?" Gruber asked, but it was really more like a statement. "Where are we going to get such quantities of fuel?"

"It will be a huge strain, sure," Fredrikson explained, "but we can make enough if we have the resources. We used up almost all on the thrusters, so we don't have any fuel reserve at the moment. We also couldn't do anything for the maneuverability. The 'turning jets', as we call them, are still very simple and overstrained. Currently the ship is extremely vulnerable to flanking."

"Be sure to keep your face towards the enemy," Hayes said directly to Zelnick.

"So we won't be building more Cruisers any time soon?" Trent asked.

"Sadly, no," Fredrikson answered, "and that brings us to the next question – materials. We don't have to worry about the Moon Mining Act now, so we can get a steady supply of base metals from there. However, building the required mining equipment takes time and I assume we will be 'out of stock' for at least a month. As for more exotic resources, we will at first be completely dependent on what you can scavenge, for example from the debris of enemy ships. We have already used up everything that was salvaged from the wreck of the Ilwrath Avenger."

"So that's why you insisted on building that storage module," Zelnick realized.

"Yes," Fredrikson replied.

She touched a console and a view of the Vindicator appeared on the screen behind her. On the display there were no modules attached.

"So when you arrived here, the Vindicator had one Ion-Bolt Gun in the first slot, mounted forward, and one fuel tank in the second to last slot."

As she explained, the mentioned modules appeared on the display into their respective slots.

"We added a storage module into the ninth slot and a crew module into the fourth. We concluded that the first three slots and the last slot are ideal for weapon modules, so we currently have left those alone."

"So how much firing can the combat batteries handle," Zelnick asked, "since there are no additional… dynamos?"

Fredrikson pushed some buttons and a visualization of the Vindicator's combat batteries appeared on the screen.

"If the batteries are full, you can fire rapidly up to 15 shots," she said. "But note that if you do so, the batteries will be completely empty, leaving you unarmed for a long time."

"That doesn't sound so bad," Zelnick casually said.

"That's right, it's not bad," Fredrikson agreed, "but if we later on build more weapon modules, more energy will also be needed."

She looked around the room, waiting for questions. None were asked.

"One more thing…" she said, "We managed to build a second shuttle so now both the Vindicator and the Tobermoon have one."

She took a seat at the table where everyone else was sitting.

"That is all," she concluded her presentation.

"I'll continue," Hayes said without standing up. "You have all seen the proposed roster for the Vindicator and the Tobermoon. Are there any objections?"

Vindicator was going to have a crew of 50 and Tobermoon a crew of 18. Gruber was assigned as the first officer of the Vindicator and Zelnick's advisor on alien affairs. After all, Gruber's wide knowledge on all known alien races was what initially got him the job on the starbase.

Nobody seemed to have any objections. Then suddenly, to Hayes' surprise, Gruber asked a question:

"Why was O'Donnell selected for the Vindicator's crew?"

It wasn't that Gruber disliked the idea of having to deal with O'Donnell on the Vindicator, even though he did dislike it. But more than that, he was genuinely upset about rewarding O'Donnell's bad behavior by giving him one of the few positions that everyone was eager to have.

"We wanted the best possible crew," Hayes explained, "and he is the best loading worker even though he is sometimes tough to handle."

Gruber had to agree.

"Let's go over the plan once more," Hayes said, meaning that he would be the one doing all the talking. "The first step is for you to reach Vela and figure out what materials the Precursor factory needs in order to build more ships. You can also evacuate those colonists who would rather be here than on Unzervalt."

Hayes leaned forward and put both his elbows on the table. His hands touched his chin.

"Then, it's time to get down to business," he continued. "Simply put, the ultimate goal is to destroy the Ur-Quan and their armada of battle thralls completely. At first the

Vindicator will be too vulnerable to permit frontal assaults, but even if it were at its full potential, it would still be just one ship. The Hierarchy has thousands of ships so we can't win the fight alone. We need allies."

Hayes stood up.

"I hereby declare the re-foundation of the Alliance of Free Stars," he said in an impressive voice.

After a short silence someone clapped their hands. Whoever it was, their hands were under the table so the original clapper could not be determined. Very soon the clapping infected everyone else and the room was filled with cheerful applause and smiling faces. When the ovation was over, Hayes continued.

"We should first find out what has happened to the other races of the old alliance and recruit them if they are in any position to help us. I think it would be reasonable to start with the Chenjesu."

"Commander," Trent said, asking for a place to put in a word. Hayes made a slight gesture with his hand giving him permission to speak.

"I wasn't going to mention this at first," Trent began, "but then I thought that it is something that everyone should be aware of."

Trent looked at everyone in the room. His face left no doubt that he was serious.

"When the Ur-Quan broke through the coreward front, there was a rumor which the highest authorities of the Alliance forcefully silenced. It was said that the Ur-Quan had unleashed some kind of a super-weapon which was unstoppable by normal means. Maybe it was just because the line fell so suddenly, but in any case, we need to find out whether that rumor is true or not."

"The means at our disposal are not 'normal' either," Zelnick pointed out.

If it wasn't for Zelnick's quick remark, the mood might have dropped.

"Both of you are right," Hayes agreed. "If there is some unknown super-weapon, we need to find a way to deal with it. Also, we have a 'super-weapon' of our own this time. Still, I don't think we should focus too much on that rumor right now, simply because it won't do us any good. For now, let's keep the rumor between us so it won't affect morale."

Everyone agreed.

"That is all from me as well," Hayes said. "Does anyone else have something to say?"

He waited for a while, but nobody showed any signs of opening their mouths.

"In that case," Hayes concluded, "this meeting is over."

Hayes checked the time and then continued.

"You have six hours before the shuttle takes off, so do what you must. Don't make the shuttle wait for you."

Gruber went to his quarters after the briefing. He had already gathered all the stuff he would take with him aboard the Vindicator. During these past two weeks he had never had the chance to get familiar with the ship. Amongst all the other excitement, he was really eager to see the ship from the inside.

As he was packing his bag, he paused to look at a very old photo. It was a picture of a man, a woman and a young boy. The boy was Gruber's father, Karl. The man was Gruber's grandfather, but the woman wasn't his grandmother. Gruber never met his grandmother, who had died a long time before he was born. Instead, the woman was his grandfather's girlfriend as they called her, but Gruber never met her either. He had only heard stories from his father: After his grandmother had died, when Karl was very young, this woman had come into the Karl's life. At first Karl had rejected her completely, but as months went by, he had to acknowledge that she was a good woman. She was very kind, loving, beautiful and a good woman for Karl's father. Eventually, she became like a mother to Karl and they all had a good life in a small town in southern Germany.

There was one big problem, though. The woman, Karl's new mother, was an Androsynth, although Karl didn't know that until the day of the rebellion. He was only 11 years old and his life had turned upside down in an instant. His new mother had been gone for a few days when suddenly his father had told him a very long story about how the Androsynth were oppressed and how he had helped them escape from their slavery. After telling Karl everything, he broke down and just sat at the kitchen table, not saying anything, looking at the same spot in the wall. After a few hours, the military police came and took him away, saying something about treason. Karl was taken into custody and he never saw his father again.

Later on Karl realized the harsh reality most of the Androsynth had had to live in. At first Karl blamed his father for destroying their family, but as he grew older, he understood why his father had done what he did. The very strong anti-Androsynth propaganda, which continued for years after the Androsynth had disappeared, only made Karl angrier at society. He joined an underground group of Androsynth sympathizers, which had pretty much lost its purpose after the rebellion. It was then more like a club where people gathered to vent their frustration about any current events. As years passed, sensible people continued their lives, but the extremists remained in the group, turning it into an anarchist far-left terrorist faction. And, of course, they considered themselves to be the good guys.

After the bombing of the Mediterranean skyway in 2090, Karl snapped out of his hatred and realized that their actions had had no clear purpose in a long time. He anonymously tipped the police regarding some recent activities, which led to significant arrests. Karl himself went back to his home town and started a new life – which eventually led to the birth of a son, Adam.

"Shuttle leaves in one hour," a vivid female voice echoed over the starbase from the speaker system. The announcement made Gruber wake up and realize that he had accidentally slept for almost five hours. He sat up and groaned for no reason. He knew that sleeping was actually a very rational way to spend the last hours before takeoff, but he didn't like the fact that he hadn't done it on purpose.

The female announcer voice was a common mystery, since nobody knew to whom the voice actually belonged. Someone was once quite certain that the voice actor was a certain movie star from the early 22nd century. It was checked and re-checked a dozen times, but finally they had to conclude that it wasn't her. The voice was just changed to sound like her. Eventually someone started calling the voice Heidi, which caught on. "Did you hear what Heidi said?" was a popular saying.

Gruber stood up, took his bag with him and started to make his way towards the hangar. He wasn't carrying that much – mostly clothes.

The corridors in the living quarters were empty. The hangar, on the other hand, would most likely be crowded. The silence made Gruber very conscious of his own footsteps as he was approaching the elevator, which was conveniently only one level away. It arrived in a few seconds.

As he guessed, the hangar really was full of people. There were some emotional scenes, which was understandable. They had been on the starbase for eight years, so naturally some close relationships had been established. And now, some of the crew were going to leave on a mission with no guarantees of ever coming back.

Gruber wasn't that close with anybody, although one particular woman from the supply division seemed to be rather fond of him. Gruber half expected to see her there. He wasn't sure whether he wanted to or not.

Walking through the crowd he suddenly bumped into Zelnick.

"Captain," Gruber greeted him in a serious and formal way.

"First officer," Zelnick replied. "I'm sorry, but I forgot your name."

"Adam Gruber, sir," he answered.

"Ah, yes, of course," Zelnick said, "I remember reading through the roster a hundred times and your name was always on the top of the list. I'm just terrible with names, you see. We didn't have that many people on Unzervalt so it was easy to remember everybody's name there. I guess I'm still not used to all this."

"No offense taken, sir," Gruber replied.

Gruber became aware that amongst the crowd, there was a vacant ring around him and Zelnick. He also realized that Zelnick really stood out with his red uniform in the grey mass.

"So, what happened to the previous first officer?" Gruber asked.

"There was none," Zelnick answered. "I suppose you should know what really happened…"

Zelnick looked like he was about to say something painful. Gruber assumed that the captain meant there was more to the story than what he had told everyone earlier.

"As we took off from Unzervalt," Zelnick began, "Isadora Burton was the captain of the Vindicator and I was just a pilot, since nobody else understood the ship's computer. A few days later we—"

"Zelnick!" they heard a voice call out from behind them. They turned around to see Hayes making his way through the crowd. "Ah, Gruber, it's good that you're here too," Hayes said. "I suppose you didn't notice my attempts to contact you with all this commotion."

Gruber looked at his communicator and, surely enough, it showed that Hayes had tried to contact him a few minutes ago. Zelnick had also been given a communicator and he checked it to notice the same thing.

"Let's step out of this crowd so we can talk," Hayes continued, "I have important news."

"The story will have to wait," Zelnick said to Gruber as they followed Hayes through the crowd.

Once outside the crowd, they found themselves right in front of the hangar control booth.

"Let's go inside," Hayes suggested.

Against all instructions, the booth was empty. This time, however, it was better that way. Hayes sat down and so did Zelnick and Gruber. Hayes leaned forward and made a serious face.

"We have detected faint alien signals coming from the edge of our solar system," he said, "at least as far as Uranus, but definitely from within the solar system."

"It could be a Hierarchy spy," Gruber suggested. "We should check it out."

"I think so too," Hayes agreed. "Conveniently for us, Uranus, Neptune and Pluto are currently aligned in the same direction. You can check out all of them at the same time."

"Right," Gruber said, "and we'll probably be able to pinpoint the source when we get closer."

"Excuse me, but," Zelnick asked, "what are these 'Uranus', 'Neptune' and, uh…? I forgot the third one."

Hayes and Gruber looked at Zelnick to check whether this was a setup for a joke.

"Ah, yes, you aren't a local," Hayes then remembered. "Uranus and Neptune are the outermost planets in this system. Pluto is a small rock a little further out from Neptune."

Zelnick nodded. Nobody had anything more to say about that subject so they waited a while in silence.

"Should we get going then?" Zelnick asked after about half a minute.

"Let's go see if everyone is ready," Gruber suggested.

With that said, they stood up and Gruber, who was closest to the door, opened it. Suddenly the noise and commotion of the hangar struck them like a hit in the face with a frying pan. The booth was well soundproofed so it was easy to forget the noise outside. Some of the people near the booth noticed the three key players exiting the control booth in a suspicious, attention attracting manner. By the time they were half-way through the crowd, all eyes were on them and the noise had turned into loud silence.

They finally reached the shuttle and saw a few dozen people standing separately from the crowd. It looked like everyone enlisted for the ships was there.

"Alright, It's your show from now on," Hayes said to Gruber and Zelnick. After a few glimpses of farewell, he joined the crowd.

Gruber and Zelnick were left in front of their subordinates who quickly straightened up their rows.

"Shall I make a roll call, sir?" Gruber asked Zelnick in a formal manner.

Zelnick nodded in agreement.

Gruber started calling out names as listed in the roster and the crew answered the call one by one. The crew of the starbase was already the best humanity had to offer and these men and women were the best of the best – even O'Donnell who, to Gruber's surprise, replied formally when his name was called out. All 52 were present. The rest of the crew was on the ships already. Many of the original crewmembers of the Tobermoon were qualified and eager to continue on their post, so the Tobermoon got only 10 replacements. The rest were assigned to the Vindicator. In addition to Zelnick, seven of the Vindicator's original crew remained. They were as qualified as anyone else to operate such an alien piece of machinery and they had had time to get familiar with the ship on their trip to Earth.

"Everyone is here, captain," Gruber informed Zelnick.

"Good," Zelnick said and took a few steps to address his crew.

"Most of you know me already, but allow me to properly introduce myself," he said in an audible voice. "I am Robert Zelnick, captain of the Vindicator. Captain Matthew Trent of the Tobermoon is on board his ship already. I shall lead our voyage to Vela, where we try to get the Precursor factory running again, evacuate everyone who wishes to be evacuated, and then return here. We shall arrive at the second planet of Vela, also known as 'Unzervalt', in approximately nine days. We will remain there for as long as we have to, and then take the nine day return trip."

Everyone was listening to the speech, standing straight, not making a single sound or nose scratch. Most of them were veterans from the Great War so it was easy to re-adopt old military habits.

"But, ladies and gentlemen," Zelnick continued, "don't forget that we, as representatives of the New Alliance of Free Stars, are officially at war with the Ur-Quan Hierarchy. This is a dangerous mission. We can't let the Ur-Quan know about us just yet. We will try to reach Vela unnoticed, but if we by chance encounter the enemy, we will have to destroy them before they can report of us."

So it's The 'New' Alliance of Free Stars now, Gruber thought. It sounded inspiring enough. He wouldn't make a point about it to Zelnick, who was about to finish his speech.

"It's time to get going," Zelnick said. "To those boarding the Tobermoon: I'll see you on Unzervalt."

Zelnick gave Gruber a signal to indicate that he was done talking. Gruber nodded and stepped forward.

"Everyone into the shuttle!" Gruber commanded. "Those boarding the Tobermoon will enter last!"

Zelnick and Gruber watched everyone board the shuttle.

"This is it then," Zelnick said.

"Indeed it is, captain," Gruber replied. "Let's make this one shot count."

After the last crew members were inside, Gruber and Zelnick entered. The crowd in the hangar was cheering and waving. In his final glimpse at the crowd, Gruber saw that one particular woman from the supply division and their eyes met. The woman seemed sad. Gruber didn't do anything, just stepped inside the shuttle and buckled himself up.

The shuttle was crowded. There were seats for only 12 people, but there was just enough room for everyone to stand. It was no problem in space, but they wouldn't squeeze in like this if they were entering an atmosphere.

After a while they arrived at the docking port of the Tobermoon. The seven people assigned there entered through the hatch and then there was a little more room in the shuttle. A while later they entered the shuttle hangar of the Vindicator.

The hangar was located directly below the cockpit section, which was, as everything else on board, huge. The rear ramp was lowered and Gruber stepped inside the Vindicator for the first time, right after Zelnick. It was a sight. He had seen lots of alien ships in the Great War, but nothing compared with this one. Everything looked highly advanced and was at least five times bigger than on human constructs.

What was left of the original crew of the Vindicator was waiting for them in the hangar. They worked as guides, showing the important parts of the ship to the new recruits, although everyone had received a virtual layout of the ship for study. Gruber had memorized all the key locations and was walking with Zelnick.

The crew module, where the living quarters were, was on the fourth module slot. They made their way through the approximately 10 meter wide hallways to the center of the cockpit module, from where they could enter the 'Spine' of the ship. The Spine was, once again, enormous. It was a hundreds of meters long and a few dozen meters wide cylinder.

"With all this empty space," someone from the group asked, "what did we need the storage module for?"

"They must expect us to scavenge enough materials to build a whole fleet," someone else suggested.

They soon reached the fourth slot and entered the crew module. It was like an Earthling Cruiser inside the Vindicator. Dr. Fredrikson's team had modified the plans to make the module more suitable for humans.

Gruber and Zelnick soon found their own quarters. Gruber didn't familiarize himself with his room yet. Instead, he just tossed his bag onto the bed and rejoined Zelnick.

"It's time to show you where the action is," Zelnick said. "Let's go to the bridge and get this operation started."

"Yes sir," Gruber eagerly replied.

The bridge wasn't far from where they had entered the Spine. Gruber knew what to expect, but still he was amazed to actually see it. The controls were simply too big for humans. The room had a large window which gave a 180 degree field of vision forward. At the center of the room there was a formation of chairs and consoles. Clearly they weren't a part of the original design, since they were made for humans. In front of the chair in the center was a strange piece of equipment, which, Gruber thought, had to be the control computer Zelnick used to operate the ship. Now Fredrikson's team had distributed the controls so that everything was not in Zelnick's hands anymore, although he could still fly it all by himself.

Zelnick sat on the chair and Gruber took his position next to him. Soon other bridge officers entered the room and, after a quick look around, took their seats close to Zelnick.

"Is everyone ready?" Zelnick asked.

"Status check!" Gruber ordered.

The operators responded one at a time, starting clockwise from the far left.

"Radar ok", said Danielle Dujardin with a moderate French accent.

"Communications ok", said Ekaterina Ozerova, a Russian red-haired woman who was commonly referred to as Katja.

"Engines ok", said Otto Steinbach, who had the stereotypical look of a German man, whatever that means.

"Weapons ok", said Samuel McNeil, the youngest of the officers, who also had an interesting natural talent: His hands were rock-steady.

"Hull ok", said Shigeo Iwasaki, a small black-haired man with a ridiculously strong Japanese accent.

"Navigation ok", said Gennadi Samusenko whose looks and personality were so nondescript that he could blend in any crowd anywhere.

"Great," Zelnick acknowledged the reports.

He then looked at the star map which was displayed in front of him. Vela was 166 hyperspace units away and they could travel through hyperspace about 25 units per day, if Fredrikson's calculations were accurate. But first they would have to get out of the solar system with true space engines. The trip to the edge of the system would take approximately one day. And before jumping to hyperspace they would have to check the outskirts of the system for the source of the alien transmissions.

“Set course for Uranus,” Zelnick ordered.

CHAPTER 4

ONE WITH THE SHORT TA PUUN STICK

March 5th 2155, somewhere between Mars and the asteroid belt

Gruber had plenty of time to familiarize himself with the ship since it would still take hours to reach the orbit of Uranus. For the beginning of their mission they had agreed that either Zelnick or Gruber would always be on the bridge and Zelnick was there now. They were constantly listening to locate the source of the alien signal, but so far they hadn't had any luck.

Zelnick had tried to explain the functionality of the ship's computer to Gruber, but since Gruber wasn't a Precursor prodigy, the attempt was futile. The new controls allowed others to navigate the ship adequately for long journeys, but without Zelnick their combat potential would be close to zero. It was a weakness and Gruber knew it. As much as he would have liked to take the ship out for a spin by himself, it just wasn't going to happen.

Gruber took the long walk through the Spine, past the last module slot and into the engine room. A few engineers were there; doing their thing, constantly checking that everything was in order. Gruber wasn't much of a technical guy so he wasn't as interested in the advanced anti-matter thrusters as the technicians, who barely noticed his arrival. He soon went back to the Spine.

It was quiet. Most starships had some kind of a background hum, but the Vindicator had none. Gruber's footsteps echoed in the long, spacious hallway. He thought how different things would have been if the discovery on Vela would have been made a few years earlier. Out of old habit he half expected to find O'Donnell sleeping on the job somewhere, even though he had shown a lot better attitude ever since the Vindicator had arrived.

Gruber finally reached the front end of the Spine and entered the bridge section without incident. He then made his way to the hangar, where he saw a group of twelve people around the shuttle. Soon he noticed that it was the landing team lead by Joseph Fritz. They were doing some kind of training. The pilot, Jane Jenkins, was checking something under the shuttle's wings. Gruber hadn't paid much attention to the landing team's roster, but he did remember that O'Donnell had volunteered for it. Most of the team was still the same as during the mission to the moonbase.

Gruber considered himself a bad person because of it, but he couldn't help being amused by the Liebermann triplets. They had a habit of using literary language and continuing each other's sentences with a strong British accent. As he was watching the team, one of the triplets suddenly approached him.

"I beg your pardon, sir, but I understand that you are an expert in alien cultures?" he asked.

Gruber was ready for the speech style, so he was able to keep a straight face.

"I know a thing or two about alien races, yes" Gruber answered.

"Is it true what they say," the man asked, "about the Black Spathi Squadron?"

There was a rumor during the Great War that a rogue band of courageous Spathi broke away from the main starfleet, painted their ships black with bright red stripes and formed the `Black Spathi Squadron', dedicated to performing brave and hostile deeds.

"Now that's something I don't know for sure, but I highly doubt it," Gruber answered. "I have encountered the Spathi numerous times and not once have I seen a brave individual."

"I'd have to see it to believe it, Alex," O'Donnell suddenly said from behind the man, putting his hand on the man's shoulder and making a point about knowing which one of the triplets the man was. "Don't bother the chief with such plebeian questions."

The man, presumably Alex Liebermann, walked away. Gruber was a little impressed at O'Donnell telling the triplets apart.

"Listen, chief, I've been meaning to talk to you," O'Donnell began. "I just wanted you to know that I'm not going to cause trouble here. I know that I've been a pain in your ass and I apologize for that. I had lost all motivation on the starbase, but now I've gotten it back and I was hoping we could put such unpleasant memories behind us and… you know…"

He scratched the back of his head and was obviously having a hard time finishing what he wanted to say.

…I'm sorry… please? No hard feelings?"

He reached out his hand, hoping to shake it with Gruber's.

During the past two weeks Gruber had seen that O'Donnell was working hard so he had no reason to bear malice.

"No grudge," he said and shook O'Donnell's hand.

After that there was an awkward silence.

"I'll get back to work then," O'Donnell finally said, saluted, and walked away.

Gruber ended his tour of the ship and returned to the bridge. They were just passing the asteroid belt.

"Have we picked up the signal yet, captain?" Gruber asked Zelnick who was sitting in his chair.

"Not yet," Zelnick replied, "but Katja thinks that if the origin is not further than Pluto, we should pick it up before… Jupiter, was it?"

"Sir, as a matter a fact," Ekaterina 'Katja' Ozerova said, "I'm picking up something right now. It is definitely coming from beyond Uranus – probably even beyond Neptune."

"You sure know when to enter a room," Zelnick commended Gruber. "So we've met the Ilwrath… What can you tell me about the Spathi?"

Gruber was glad that Zelnick was interested in learning about the enemy.

"Imagine facing a cowardly, mobile clam armed with a howitzer," Gruber said. "Then you'll get a good idea of what it's like dealing with a Spathi."

Zelnick looked a little puzzled, but Gruber continued:

"During the Great War, the Spathi seemed to avoid combat as much as possible. A fleeing Spathi Eluder ship was a common sight on the battlefield, although they never fled when the Ur-Quan were around. One of the biggest mistakes one could make was to chase them. The Spathi Eluder seems to be primarily designed for running away. Their speed is far superior to our Cruisers and their missile tubes are mounted backwards. Luckily for us, a single missile packs a moderately light punch, so our point-defense lasers offer good protection."

Gruber paused for a while and checked that Zelnick was still listening. He seemed to be, so Gruber continued:

"Of course, the Spathi soon realized that their normal tactics don't work very well against Earthling Cruisers. It came as quite a surprise to everyone when the Spathi ships suddenly stormed our Cruisers and attacked with forward cannons, which we didn't even know they had. It was in the first years of the war in Alpha Herculis, when we were raiding a Spathi base together with the Mmrnmhrm. I was there that time and barely made it out alive. We were not prepared for their offensive tactics and had to retreat. So in conclusion… Once in battle, a Spathi Eluder is one tough cookie."

Zelnick saw that the story had ended and it was time for questions.

"That is all very good to know," he said. "I have only one question."

Gruber was ready for anything.

"What's a clam?" Zelnick asked.

…

Gruber tried to be understanding. Of course Zelnick wouldn't know about clams. But still, he couldn't help but feel annoyed that **that** was what the captain clung on.

He took a breath and then explained, with very much detail, what a clam was. Zelnick seemed fascinated about Gruber's description.

"There was nothing like that back on Unzervalt," he said.

"Sir, I've pinpointed the signal's source," Katja reported. "It's coming from Pluto."

"Very good… Mr. Samusenko, set course for Pluto," Zelnick commanded the navigation officer.

"Aye-aye, captain," Samusenko replied. "ETA nine hours," he continued.

Gruber and Zelnick observed the virtual model of the solar system. Pluto was just a small chunk of rock and ice orbiting the sun almost 40 times farther than Earth. It had very weak gravity, its orbit was noticeably elliptic and sometimes it even crossed the orbit of Neptune. Currently Pluto was almost at the furthest point of its orbit.

"Captain, you should take this chance to get some rest," Gruber suggested. "I can watch over things here."

Zelnick considered this for a while.

"Maybe I should," he thought out loud. "Very well, I'll leave you in charge."

He then stood up.

"I'll be in my quarters," he said and started walking towards the door. The bridge was very spacious so it took him a while to get out.

After Zelnick had left, Gruber thought for a while whether he should sit in the captain's chair or not. He finally decided not to.

After about nine hours, they reached Pluto without incident. Gruber had expected Zelnick to return to the bridge well in advance, but he still hadn't shown up. He didn't want to push Zelnick around right from the start, but it seemed he had no choice. The captain was needed on the bridge.

Gruber called Zelnick's communicator, but there was no response. He was disappointed. He had gotten the impression that Zelnick was a responsible captain. Gruber couldn't leave the bridge himself, so he had to order one of the officers to fetch him. He chose Iwasaki, the hull officer.

Five minutes later Iwasaki returned with Zelnick, who was zipping up his uniform while he walked.

"Sorry about that," Zelnick apologized, "I was sleeping and the communicator didn't wake me up."

Gruber nodded with a disapproving look, but Zelnick either didn't notice it, or ignored it very skillfully.

"It's a strange thing," Zelnick said as he sat down in his chair. "I haven't slept well after we left Unzervalt, but this time I slept like a log."

"It is good that the captain feels comfortable aboard his ship," Gruber stated.

"So what's the situation?" Zelnick asked.

“I can narrow down the transmission source to an area of about one square kilometer on the surface,” Katja explained.

“There’s nothing out there, captain,” continued Danielle Dujardin, the radar officer. “I can’t see anything out of the ordinary.”

“Get the landing team ready,” Zelnick said to Gruber.

Gruber contacted Fritz and soon the landing team was ready for dispatch. Then Zelnick contacted Trent, who was flying the Tobermoon right behind the Vindicator.

“We’ll send the landing team to investigate the source,” Zelnick said. “I’ll send you the coordinates of the search area.”

“Roger that,” Trent answered. *“Shall we stay here and be ready to shoot at the surface?”*

“That’s what we’ll do,” Zelnick agreed.

After relaying Zelnick’s orders to the landing team, Gruber watched from the main window as the shuttle accelerated towards the surface. Landing on Pluto was easy because of the low gravity. When the shuttle was out of sight, Gruber returned to Zelnick’s side. Soon they heard Jenkins’ voice say that they had reached the surface. A scan of the planet’s surface revealed that the search area was in a small valley, which was actually a crater. The shuttle was a few kilometers away.

“We can’t see anything from here,” Jenkins said as the shuttle reached the edge of the crater.

“Make your way to the center of the search area,” Zelnick ordered.

The shuttle was getting near the target when Jenkins suddenly reported.

“Are you seeing this?” she asked anxiously. *“There’s some kind of a pit here – a huge hole in the ground”*

Dujardin checked her map and zoomed in on the location. He showed the site to Zelnick.

"Creepy," Zelnick said. "Take a look inside, but proceed with caution."

The shuttle slowly approached the pit. Gruber and Zelnick were watching a telescope view of the site and on another screen they could see video feeds from cameras mounted on the helmets of all landing team members.

"It's too dark, we can't see anything," Jenkins reported as the shuttle was directly above the pit. *"I don't dare to take the shuttle down inside. We'll have to step outside."*

The shuttle then touched down near the edge of the hole. Fritz gave the necessary orders and soon most of the landing team took their first steps on the surface of Pluto.

"One small step for meeeee," O'Donnell proclaimed and, because of the low gravity, took a much larger step than he probably intended to.

"Bring the flares over here," Fritz commanded as he walked towards the hole.

Soon almost all of them were looking down the dark pit. Only Jenkins, Robinson and Witherspoon were inside the shuttle.

"Rigby, get the bug, will you?" Fritz suggested, referring to their radio controlled mini-robot.

Rigby walked back towards the shuttle while O'Donnell lit the first flare and threw it down the hole to see how deep it was.

"For the record," Rigby began, *"I think that the—"*

Rigby's line was suddenly cut short. Eight of the helmet camera screens had turned black in an instant and the image on the remaining four flickered and shook. They could see from the telescope view that a huge dust cloud was now covering the entire site. There was enormous static in the audio link, but it sounded like more than one person was screaming.

"What the hell happened?" Zelnick demanded and jumped up from his chair.

To Gruber it seemed like there had been an explosion.

"There's too much noise in the signal," Katja reported. "I can't make out anything."

"We do **not** have a visual on the shuttle," Dujardin continued.

"I lost the signal from eight of them!" Iwasaki reported. He was keeping an eye on the heart rates of the landing team members. Gruber checked the monitor and indeed it showed a normal pulse only for Jenkins, Robinson, Witherspoon and Rigby, with Rigby's heart rate over 200. For the rest of them it showed a flat line.

Then the extra static disappeared as suddenly as it had appeared and they could hear Jenkins frantically shouting over the radio:

"Mayday! Mayday! We are under fire!"

"Everybody, report in!" Witherspoon simultaneously demanded.

"I'm all right," Robinson immediately reported.

Rigby then moaned something over the radio.

They waited a few more seconds, but nobody else reported themselves alive.

"What happened?" Jenkins asked.

Witherspoon went outside and looked in the direction where the rest of the team had been just seconds ago. Rigby was lying on the ground close to the shuttle, but there was nobody else in sight. In fact, there was a big chunk of ground missing where the rest of the team had stood.

Suddenly they could see something large emerge from the pit. At first they saw just a circular shape, then several spherical objects with protruding slender beams and, finally, a larger sphere to which all the beams were connected.

"Oh shit, it's the Spathi!" Witherspoon screamed. *"We have to get out of here!"*

Indeed the thing that was emerging from the hole was a Spathi Eluder starship.

Witherspoon quickly dragged Rigby into the shuttle.

"Should we fire?" Trent asked.

"Wait just a second," Zelnick commanded.

"Jane, Can you get back here?" he then asked Jenkins, addressing her by her first name as he usually did with women.

"I don't know, maybe," Jenkins replied, still with a little panic in her voice. *"We are leaking oxygen and have only one functional engine."*

"Assume that the rest of the team is dead," Zelnick commanded. "Return here as quickly as possible."

"Yes sir," Jenkins replied. *"We are initiating emergency launch procedures."*

Gruber looked at the landing team roster.

"Captain," he reported, "Kowalski, Fritz, Chin, O'Donnell, Luigi and all three of the Liebermann triplets are currently MIA."

Zelnick kicked his chair in frustration.

"Trent," he ordered, "fire immediately when the shuttle has reached safe distance."

"Will do," Trent replied.

Just then the Spathi ship hailed them.

"Should we answer?" Zelnick asked Gruber.

"Yes we should," he suggested.

Zelnick ordered Katja to answer the call and soon the familiar face of a Spathi was displayed on the main screen. It had one big gooey eyeball on top of a green slimy neck without any torso and two small but sharp looking claws at the end of thin arms.

"Attention big, mean, hostile alien vessel hovering overhead in an obvious attack posture," the Spathi said. *"This is Spathi Captain Fwiffo. I know you are going to torture me, so let's just get this over with right now. The*

coordinates of my homeworld, Spathiwa, are 241.6, 368.7 and the ultra-secret Spathi Cypher, which is known only by me and several billion other Spathi is Huffi-Muffi-Guffi."

Then the Spathi seemed to notice who he was talking to and changed its tone:

"Surprise and Terror! I am greeted by the smooth and hostile face of our old enemy, the Hootmans... no... the Huge-glands? no... I remember, the Hunams! Sorry about that little mistake on the surface! I was so startled when you threw something bright at my ship that ...er... my automated defense systems fired on it. I hope nobody got hurt!"

Zelnick looked like he wasn't going to accept the apology. Gruber tried to calm him down.

"Captain," he said, "if we remain calm, we can benefit from this. He could give us lots of valuable information. Try to reason with him."

Zelnick took a deep breath a few times before starting to talk.

"I am Captain Robert Zelnick of the starship Vindicator." he said. "We came in peace and with good will, but you attacked our landing team and killed our crew. If you want to live, you'd better continue talking."

"Of course, of course," the Spathi submitted. *"As I said, I am Spathi Captain Fwiffo of the voidship Star Runner, placed here in this planetary system as part of the powerful Earthguard star force which our masters the Ur-Quan established here to make sure the Earthlings don't do anything tricky."*

"Why are you here on Pluto instead of your base on Earth's moon?" Zelnick asked.

It was a nice move, Gruber thought, not revealing that the base has already been dealt with.

"Originally," the Spathi explained, *"we were stationed on Earth's moon, which made us Spathi a bit uneasy because with each passing day we grew more and more*

worried about the sneaky Earthlings making a surprise attack. The Ilwrath kept telling us that it was impossible since the Earthlings had no ships or weapons whatsoever. That made us feel a bit better, but when the Ilwrath left, again we grew fearful and decided to make a strategic redeployment to Mars.

We decided that if the Earthlings figured out we had abandoned the base on Luna, they would be more likely to try something sneaky. So we rigged up some old service androids and ordered them to drive around on the lunar surface in bulldozers, endlessly pushing around the same piles of dirt. In addition, we connected the base's local radio transmitter to an audio Melnorme FunRom called Winky's Happy Night, hoping that the Hunams would think we were still there."

Rigby's interpretation of the message seemed to have been a little off, but not too much.

"As days passed," the Spathi continued, *"we once again grew worried and later on we decided it would be prudent to relocate to Jupiter's moon, Ganymede then later Saturn's moon, Titan and finally here to Pluto."*

"So how many of them are there?" Gruber thought out loud. There couldn't be many, judging from the actions of this particular Spathi, Fwiffo, as he called himself.

"You mentioned the Ilwrath leaving. What happened to them?" Zelnick asked.

"The Ilwrath contingent was supposed to be the toughest ridge-crest, er, the most rigid flipper, no, ah yes - the BACKBONE of the Earthguard force. But they departed the system en masse not long after the last Ur-Quan Dreadnought vanished from this region of space. They claimed to have received a direct order from their Gods of Evil and Darkness, who had grown dissatisfied with the Ilwraths' passivity and wanted them to kill or at least torture

someone soon. Personally, I believe they just got bored and went off to have some fun."

"Where are the rest of your ships?" Zelnick asked. "How many of you are there on Pluto?"

"Over the past years," Fwiffo explained, *"it became necessary to redeploy strategically some of our Earthguard forces to our homeworld in case of a sudden surprise attack by a vicious, unrelenting alien race which we Spathi call The Ultimate Evil."*

"This Ultimate Evil," Gruber remembered, "is Spathi superstition. They believe that there is some undetectable evil entity and the fact that it is undetectable is evidence of its nefarious intentions."

"So, Fwiffo, how many of you ARE there on Pluto?" Zelnick asked, making a point about Fwiffo not answering his previous question.

Fwiffo seemed to ignore the point.

"Since it was our most powerful and unforgiving masters, the Ur-Quan, who stationed us here, we knew it would be grossly stupid to disobey them completely. But we decided that it would be okay to send just one ship home. We used one of our most ancient and solemn rituals, Puun-Taffy, to pick the lucky ship. Then... some months later, we decided that it wouldn't REALLY hurt if we sent one more ship home. And then later we sent another, and then another...well, you get the idea. Alas, as fate would have it, when the final ritual was performed, I, Fwiffo, was left here alone, for as even the most immature encrustling knows: There must always be one Spathi who picks the short Ta Puun stick."

Fwiffo seemed sad. If crying were a part of the Spathi physique, he probably would have shed a few tears.

"Captain," Gruber said, "now it should be safe to start searching for survivors on the surface. Shall I give the command?"

Zelnick nodded and Gruber instructed Dujardin to scan the surface.

"Now would also be a perfect time to get information on the Ur-Quan's movements and the situation of the other old alliance races," Gruber then suggested.

Zelnick's eyes quickly met Gruber's. He clearly agreed.

"Did you know," Zelnick asked Fwiffo, "that the resupply vessel for the starbase orbiting Earth was supposed to have arrived three years ago, but it never did? If we hadn't saved them, everybody in the starbase would be dead now. What do you think the Ur-Quan would have said about that?"

"Er..." Fwiffo paused for a while. Then he raised his arms up and did something strange with his eye, as if he was trying to scare someone. Then he changed his voice and did a pretty good impression of the Ur-Quan: *"Your insubordination seals your own devastation!"*

Fwiffo's face and voice then returned to normal: *"No, I didn't know."*

"Speaking of the Ur-Quan," Zelnick said casually, "where are they and what are they doing?"

Everyone on the bridge was very eager to hear the answer and they all looked at the communications screen.

"Our masters don't really keep us very well informed about their goings on," Fwiffo answered, sounding awfully sincere, *"so all we know is that immediately after the subjugation of the last Alliance race, the Yehat, I think, the Ur-Quan gathered their Dreadnoughts and departed towards the edge of the galaxy, commanding us to obey the slave laws or face their wrath when they returned."*

So the Yehat were the last ones to fall, Gruber thought. It was hard to imagine the Ur-Quan fleet running over Gamma Serpentis, the Yehats' home star. It was a well-known fact that the Yehat had never been defeated during the 1000 year reign of the Veep-Neep dynasty. There goes their perfect score…

"What about the other alliance races?" Zelnick inquired.

"We know only bits and pieces of what happened to each race," Fwiffo explained. *"For instance, when defeated, the Yehat joined the Hierarchy as combat thralls, while the Syreen, the Chenjesu and the Mmrnmhrm did as you Hunams and chose to be slave shielded. We don't know what happened to the Arilou. The last time we saw them was the final battle with you Hunams. That's it, I think... Oh yes, the Shofixti! They were utterly wiped out in a gigantic 'blaze of glory'!*

Gruber found it impossible to believe that the Yehat would have joined the Hierarchy. They were proud warriors and would have fought to the death, never surrendering, much less joining the enemy.

"What do you mean, 'blaze of glory'?" Zelnick demanded. "What happened to the Shofixti?"

"As you know," Fwiffo began, *"the Shofixti were half feral, having been uplifted by the Yehat just a few decades before the start of the war. Given their habit of detonating those suicidal, so-called 'Glory Devices' in combat, it came as no particular surprise to me when, upon the arrival of the Ur-Quan primary task force at their homeworld, the Shofixti caused their sun to explode in a colossal supernova, destroying the entire planetary system and, not incidentally, dozens of Ur-Quan Dreadnoughts!"*

Fwiffo let out a series of strange snorts, which probably was the Spathi way to laugh.

This was shocking news. If what Fwiffo said was true, all those little Shofixti fur balls were dead – extinct – gone forever. It was a lot worse than being slave-shielded. Although, such a desperate kamikaze action surely sounded like the Shofixti way to go.

Dujardin then reported that the biological scan found nothing from the surface of Pluto. It was safe to assume that the missing landing team members were indeed dead. Zelnick acknowledged this piece of bad news and moved on.

"Can you think of anything else?" he asked Gruber as he had run out of questions.

"Nothing important, Captain," Gruber replied. "I think we should kill him now."

Zelnick tapped his fingers on the arm of his chair.

"I have a better idea," he said to Gruber. Then he faced Fwiffo again:

"The galaxy teems with threatening monsters… Are you happy here – alone and vulnerable?"

"How true, captain, how true!" Fwiffo cheerfully agreed. *"In truth, just between us, during the past seven years, I have been quite ill at ease and yet now I find myself enjoying your company – this witty dialog and the presence of your huge, powerful, death-dealing starship which, being my friend, you would certainly feel compelled to use in order to save me from any hostile life forms who threatened me with death."*

"I'm sure you'd feel a lot safer if you were with us," Zelnick said with a smile on his face. "Come on, Fwiffo, join our fleet!"

Gruber's jaw dropped. His captain was a kid after all, asking the enemy to join him… an enemy who had just killed several members of the crew.

But the Spathi thought differently than Gruber. Fwiffo raised his arms up and started jumping around in joy.

"Happy days and jubilation!" it squealed. *"I discard all prejudice and hesitations and accept and celebrate your offer of protection and your undying commitment to my well-being!"*

Then the alien calmed down a bit and continued seriously.

"Although, I hope you understand that other Spathi individuals might not be as responsive to your friendly gestures. They have not been rotting alone in cold and dark for seven years as I have. But anyway, welcome me aboard, captain!"

"Good," Zelnick said. "Let me introduce you to the captain of the Tobermoon."

He relayed Trent's communication link to Fwiffo. As soon as Fwiffo saw Trent's face, his pupil, or whatever the black part inside his eyeball was, dilated and several drops of white liquid spouted from his mouth.

"Demon!" Fwiffo shouted, lost his balance and fell backwards, out of the sight of the communications screen.

"Nice to meet you, I'm Matthew Trent, captain of the Tobermoon," Trent said casually. He seemed amused by Fwiffo's reaction; in fact, he seemed to have expected it.

Zelnick and Gruber decided it would be best to wait and see what would happen. Soon Fwiffo's eye came into view from the lower edge of the screen, followed by the long, green neck.

"Sorry," Fwiffo said to Zelnick, *"it's just that this particular Hunam has quite a reputation amongst my people. But now I feel even safer! I am protected by not only your huge star ship, but also the Demon himself!"*

"Nice to meet you too, Demon!" Fwiffo joyfully said to Trent. *"I'll try to remember your real name."*

CHAPTER 5

THE WAY HOME

March 6th 2155, outskirts of Sol

As Gruber had expected, not everyone welcomed Fwiffo with open arms.

In the days of Star Control, whenever one was about to set sail under the command of a new captain, one was required to swear absolute obedience to the captain. Before their current mission began, they decided to readopt most of the Star Control practices, including the aforementioned oath. That was all that had kept Fwiffo alive, since it was Zelnick's decision to make an ally out of him. They were already under-crewed after the deaths of the landing team members and now some had to transfer aboard Fwiffo's Star Runner. Gruber was in charge of the roster so he had to assign a few trustworthy individuals to serve under Fwiffo.

Some of the crew members had been very close to the deceased, so there was a lot of mourning. Everyone had known the risks involved and they were officially at war, so several deaths weren't all that surprising. Telling that to someone who had just lost a friend or a relative wasn't much of a comfort though.

A few hours after the incident the three ships were already far enough from the Sun to make a safe and economical jump to hyperspace. The weapons operator, Samuel McNeil, was nervous since it was his first time, which came as a surprise to everyone. McNeil had more fighting experience than anyone when simulated battles were included, but in real life he had only participated in the final battle of Sol. Thanks to his precise firing, the ion cannon at Ceres held the invading armada back a little longer than had been expected.

The jump itself wasn't a spectacle. If you kept your eyes closed you wouldn't even notice it. But if you looked out of the window, you would first see the stars stretch into long thin lines before disappearing and finally space would seem to turn red.

When observed from far away, any object in hyperspace looked like a black sphere whose radius depended only on the mass of the object. They were actually true space bubbles inside hyperspace, so the ships themselves technically never entered hyperspace. However, such nitpicking was ignored in normal speech.

The Vindicator's hyperspace engines were so massive that the Tobermoon and Star Runner could just idle inside the same hyperdrive bubble and let the Vindicator drag them along.

After a few hours of flying through hyperspace, Zelnick wanted to arrange a meeting with Fwiffo and Trent. Since the other captains weren't needed at the bridge at all times, they could have a face to face conference aboard the Vindicator.

The Tobermoon's intact shuttle was used as a transport between the ships. The Vindicator's shuttle had been damaged so badly that it could only be repaired at the starbase.

Gruber was at the shuttle hangar waiting for Fwiffo, to escort him* to the conference room. The Spathi could breathe the same air as humans, which made everything a lot

* For simplicity, they had decided to refer to Fwiffo as 'he' for now.

easier. Soon the shuttle arrived, the entry ramp was lowered down and a frightened Spathi individual emerged from inside. Fwiffo took very small steps down the ramp, his eye slightly behind his raised arms. When he finally was off the ramp, the shuttle immediately took off to pick up Trent.

Fwiffo slowly approached Gruber. There was a notable difference in height. The top of Fwiffo's head was at the level of Gruber's belt.

"Welcome aboard the Vindicator," Gruber said, not looking down at the Spathi as he thought was best. "I am First Officer Adam Gruber."

Fwiffo was still nervously looking around.

"The air is thick. Are you sure it is safe?" he asked and looked up to meet Gruber's eyes.

"According to our knowledge there should be no problems," Gruber assured him.

"Well, if you say so," Fwiffo said with a trembling voice.

"Let's go to the conference room," Gruber suggested. "Follow me, please."

They were a comical pair walking down the huge corridors of the Vindicator. Fwiffo had to jog with his tiny leg-equivalents to keep up with Gruber, who was walking normally.

"It sure is big," Fwiffo commented, presumably meaning the Vindicator.

They used an originally vacant room next to the bridge as a conference room. There were chairs, a table and a screen. Zelnick was already standing there when Gruber and Fwiffo arrived.

"Ah, Captain Fwiffo, welcome!" Zelnick cheerfully greeted the Spathi and pointed at a chair, implying that Fwiffo should take a seat right there.

Fwiffo seemed to relax a little and made his way to the chair. The chair was designed for humans though, so Fwiffo had to climb up to it. He did it surprisingly nimbly.

"Hello, Captain Robert Zelnick," he said once he had successfully sat down. "In exchange for your protection, I will gladly do whatever you want me to do."

"Good, that's what I'm counting on," Zelnick replied and took a seat next to Fwiffo. "While we wait for Captain Trent, I'll tell you what you need to know about ourselves."

Zelnick was still in the middle of the story when Trent arrived and took a seat on the other side of Fwiffo, who was so attentively listening to Zelnick that he didn't even notice Trent. Zelnick soon wrapped up the story.

"Very touching," Fwiffo said, still not noticing Trent. "I am glad to be on your side."

"Hello," Trent surprisingly said, clearly intending to scare Fwiffo. He succeeded, since Fwiffo let out a scream, fell from his chair and dove under the table faster than lightning.

Trent laughed a little, but Zelnick shook a finger at him, meaning that he shouldn't make the creature any more frightened than he already was.

"Ah, demon," a voice said from under the table. "Nice to meet you in person."

Fwiffo jumped back to his chair.

"Now that we are all here," Zelnick declared, "we can get down to business. But first, Fwiffo, tell us a little about yourself."

Fwiffo seemed unprepared for such a question and his eye opened more than Gruber had thought possible.

"Me? You mean me, personally?" he asked with joy and disbelief in his voice. "How nice of you to ask!"

Fwiffo switched position and started talking enthusiastically.

"I was born a poor, green encrustling, the youngest child of a family of 18,487. My male parent had to work hard to support us - very hard - but each of my brothers and sisters and I tried to help out to make ends meet. The female parent was kind and sweet to all of us. Why, she once even called me by NAME! She said `Fwiffo! Fwiffo darling! Would you please answer the door? I think someone's there.' What a treat - a golden memory!"

Fwiffo proudly looked at the obviously not impressed faces of his audience before continuing.

"I swiftly matured into a fine example of my species and, with my parents' assistance, achieved independence. Specifically, they pried me from the doorjamb, and rolled me into the street. Thus prepared, I set out to make my fortune. I had great dreams in those days, yes, great dreams! I knew that someday I would be vastly rich, wealthy enough to afford a large, well-fortified mansion. Surrounding my mansion would be vast tracts of land, through which I could slide at any time I wished! Of course, one can never be too sure that there aren't monsters hiding just behind the next bush so I would plant trees to climb at regular, easy to reach intervals. And being a Spathi of the World, I would know that some monsters climb trees, though often not well, so I would have my servants place in each tree a basket of perfect stones - not too heavy, not too light - just the right size for throwing at monsters."

Fwiffo checked that his audience was still listening and then continued.

"I was thinking about what color the stones would be painted - aqua, mauve or magenta - when a vegetable cart came careening down the street outside my house, and knocked me unconscious. When I awoke, I was aboard the voidship Star Runner, headed for Earth. Apparently I had been out of my head for quite some time after the accident and with the assistance of some kind strangers had been relieved of my funds and convinced to join the navy, where I have been unpleasantly employed for the last 25 years."

"Very touching," Zelnick summed up his thoughts of the story as it had clearly come to an end.

Fwiffo seemed rather proud of his lifetime achievements. In Gruber's opinion he seemed so far like a nice enough fellow.

"Now then," Zelnick began after a short while, "let's talk strategy. Trent?"

Zelnick and Trent had obviously agreed earlier that Trent would be in charge of combat tactics.

"Fwiffo, tell me everything about your ship," Trent said directly, managing to sound non-hostile.

"Uh, okay," Fwiffo agreed, "but I'm not a tech person. I'm just the one holding the control sticks."

"Do your best," Trent encouraged him.

After six days they were getting near the hyperspace vortex leading to Vela. Time had passed without incident and most of the crew had accepted Fwiffo into the team.

Vela was a yellow dwarf star right next to Zeeman, a white super-giant star. When approaching the two stars, they could first only see the huge vortex to Zeeman. The star was so enormous that it would take hours just to circle around it in hyperspace.

Zeeman's vortex already blocked almost their entire view when they finally saw a tiny black dot next to it. It wasn't really that tiny, but next to Zeeman it looked almost like you'd have a hard time hitting it. Soon they realized that they actually were almost an hour away from it. The difference in the size of Vela and Zeeman was like that of Earth and the Sun.

Common sense would say that such a static twin star couldn't exist, since the big one would swallow the little one immediately. But common sense didn't work in hyperspace. Even though they were right next to each other in hyperspace, in true space the distance between Vela and Zeeman was nearly one light year.

When they passed the border into Vela's vortex, the effect was just like jumping into hyperspace, only backwards. Long thin lines of light emerged from the red background and shrank into stars. At the same time, the red color faded away and the familiar blackness of space returned. The dominant white light of Zeeman had disappeared and the super-giant was now just a star amongst billions of others, although exceptionally bright.

The Vela system had seven planets with the second one from the star being Unzervalt. The vortex from hyperspace always leads to the outskirts of the solar system so reaching Unzervalt would take approximately a day, just like the trip from Earth to Sol's outskirts.

"How do you feel about returning home, captain?" Gruber asked Zelnick.

"Good," Zelnick quickly replied. "This really is my home, isn't it? There are a lot of people I want to meet and we have lots of news to tell them."

"Mostly bad news, though," Gruber pointed out. "Right now they are probably still hoping that you return to tell them that the war is over, which it is… Just not the way we wanted."

"During these past few days I have constantly been thinking about how to tell them," Zelnick explained.

There was a moment of silence.

"I wonder if my dad has finished constructing that new shed," Zelnick pondered.

From a distance Unzervalt was supposed to look just like Earth. Sensors were tuned to search for an Earth-like spectrum. They had already passed the orbit of the third planet, but still didn't see Unzervalt.

"Danielle, shouldn't we see it already?" Zelnick asked the radar operator who was also in charge of the optical sensors, calling her by the first name again.

"Yes we should, captain," she answered with a puzzled voice. "It should be right… there."

She made a small circle appear on the sensor display. There was a red dot at the center.

"What the f…" Zelnick mumbled. "Is that a planet? IS THAT UNZERVALT?"

Dujardin quickly adjusted the sensors and got a reading of the planet.

"It's a planet all right," she said. "And there's definitely a slave shield over it."

"But that means that the Ur-Quan…" Zelnick tried to reason, but his voice failed him.

"Captain," Gruber said calmly but firmly, even though he was shocked as well. "Where there's a slave shield, there's Hierarchy presence. We have to consider getting out of here before they notice us. Actually, I'll be damned if we haven't been detected already."

"It's too late," Dujardin commented. "There's a ship orbiting the planet. I'll get a reading of it in a sec."

Trent's face appeared on the communications screen, soon followed by Fwiffo's.

"Captain, should we both align ourselves behind the Vindicator?" Trent suggested. *"That way we give them as little silhouette as possible."*

Zelnick hadn't recovered from the shock yet and was unable to respond.

"Captain!" Gruber said firmly and Zelnick snapped out of it.

"Yes, absolutely," he said to Trent.

"I got it!" Dujardin reported. "It's an Ur-Quan Dreadnought and it's coming this way."

"It's hailing us," Katja remarked. She was always called by her first name.

"Answer it," Zelnick ordered and immediately an image of an Ur-Quan lord appeared on the communications screen.

Just like in the stories, the Ur-Quan was a huge green caterpillar hanging from the roof. Its many eyes blinked one after another and its four sharp tentacles were moving back and forth in a threatening manner.

"SO, THE OFFSPRING HAS RETURNED TO ITS NEST!" the Ur-Quan said with a deep voice. Actually, the one talking was a small brown creature at the corner of the screen – a weird mixture of a frog and a brain.

"When you left this system, our ship was near enough to detect your translation into hyperspace. Though we lost your hyperspace spoor, we were able to backtrack your path here to this star system. And what did we FIND? An outlaw culture! Humans outside of a slave shield! You will note that this oversight has been rectified."

"Uh, am I talking to you or… you?" Zelnick asked, pointing at the Ur-Quan and the small brown creature.

"You are talking to me, but I am not talking to you," the little creature said. *"My talking pet speaks to lower life forms."*

"Why did you have to put a slave shield over planet?" Zelnick asked angrily. "What did they ever do to you? Why do you wish to enslave us?"

"Although you consider us the enemy, these conclusions are flawed," the little creature answered. *"We are your salvation. We bring you peace - a peace built upon OUR social framework, imposed upon your planet - a new world order in which your prosperity and security are assured by the Ur-Quan. We will protect you from the hazards of this hostile universe, from dangers so hideous your simple minds cannot imagine their dark scope. Today, we are the enemy. In time, this will change. Soon, you will come to understand*

the boon of slavery we force upon you and then, you will revere and even love us for this gift."

"Do you have a problem with us defending ourselves against these 'hideous dangers'?" Zelnick aggressively asked. "Don't you think we'd rather be free and try to make it on our own?"

"In our twenty thousand years along the Path of Now and Forever we have dominated thousands of species, yes, but we have saved hundreds from extinction. You imagine the threat of unknown invaders, or alien pestilence borne on the solar wind. We have seen these. But you do not acknowledge your own worst enemy, yourselves. We have found dead worlds without number, planets ravaged by atomic fire or gaian collapse. These planets were not rendered sterile by outside forces. They bear sad testament to the effects of unrestrained instinct and emotion or simple ignorance."

The creature talked with a monotonous, but convincing voice.

"We will prevent such mistakes. If you surrender immediately, we will spare the lives of your crew. But you, as the commanding officer of your renegade vessel, will have to bear the full extent of the punishment for your disobedience, which is death."

"We won't surrender," Zelnick answered, obviously not having to think about it. "Do you really think we'd believe for a second that you'd just let the rest of us off?"

"Human. We Ur-Quan never lie. It is a weakness to lie. And the Ur-Quan are not weak."

For some reason Gruber was ready to take the word of the Ur-Quan for granted. It somehow felt completely pointless to question their honesty. Of course that didn't mean that he would want to surrender.

"Sorry, but the answer is still no," Zelnick declared. "It is we who can't let you get away from here, so **you** should surrender to **us** or we will be forced to destroy you."

To put it simply, the Ur-Quan was not amused.

"Your insolence knows no bounds! You will be punished."

The transmission was cut immediately after the Ur-Quan's last comment.

"They have launched four… no, six… eight fighters!" Dujardin reported.

"Steinbach, full throttle!" Zelnick ordered.

Otto Steinbach, the engines operator, set the thrusters to maximum.

"Trent, you stay here and launch your nukes when I say," Zelnick instructed. "Fwiffo, follow us and circle around the Dreadnought."

Trent seemed to understand Zelnick's plan, but Fwiffo was panicking so much that all he could do was to do exactly as he was told.

Gruber wasn't sure what Zelnick was planning either.

"Captain, what's your plan?" he asked.

"I trust that they are not prepared for a massive ship like this to have such a high acceleration and speed," Zelnick explained.

"So you plan to fly past them?" Gruber continued.

"Not just past them," Zelnick said with a grin. "We will ram some of the fighters as we go, then use Unzervalt's orbit to sling shot us back and do another run."

Gruber was surprised. He didn't expect Zelnick to come up with such a daring tactic – and so fast.

"A good plan, Captain," Trent commented. *"You will clear the way for our nukes, but I don't think that will be enough to destroy the Dreadnought. The Star Runner will*

have to do its part or we will be left defenseless in the Dreadnought's line of fire."

"I'm picking up a blast of energy from the Dreadnought!" Dujardin exclaimed. "It is targeted at us."

"Steinbach, turn us two degrees outward and keep full throttle," Zelnick ordered.

"Aye-aye, Captain," the officer replied.

The Vindicator slowly turned, but its great speed made the slight turn significant. They watched from the tactical display how the burst of energy just barely missed them.

"Trent, fire now!" Zelnick ordered.

Two nukes from the Tobermoon came into the tactical display. Their speed was far greater than the Vindicator's, but the Vindicator had a good head start.

The fighters quickly came into view. The acceleration of the Vindicator had completely caught the enemy by surprise and the fighters had nowhere to run. Three of them were crushed under the Vindicator like bugs on a windscreen.

The turning rate of the Dreadnought wasn't enough to fire a second shot at its target. The nukes had almost caught up with the Vindicator and the fighters were still too busy scrambling to fire at them.

In the blink of an eye, the Vindicator had flown past the Dreadnought. At their speed, circling Unzervalt wouldn't take very long. Before going behind the planet, they saw from the tactical display how all four of the nukes landed on their target. One fighter had desperately tried to fire at the nukes and was caught in the blast. The Dreadnought's hull was intact, but it had to have taken severe damage.

"It's all up to you now, Fwiffo," Zelnick said.

Fwiffo was trembling and mumbling something to himself, but at least he held the control sticks in his claws. It wouldn't take long until the Tobermoon would be in the Dreadnought's firing range.

“Fwiffo, get the Dreadnought’s attention and fire at it as much as you can,” Zelnick commanded. “We’ll return in a few minutes.”

Fwiffo was too terrified to answer.

Soon they reached the far side of Unzervalt and the communication link was cut off.

Zelnick did something with the computer and held his hands on a console.

“Once we’ve circled the planet, I’ll steer us off the orbit and into the right direction,” he said.

Gruber wasn’t sure whether he meant that he would thrust them off orbit directly towards the Dreadnought at this speed. It wasn’t something a human could do.

After a few minutes they saw the other ships again. Zelnick tapped the console wildly and the Vindicator did a series of thrusts forward and sideways. Soon they were once again heading straight for the Dreadnought.

“How’s it going?” Zelnick asked after the communications link was re-established.

Fwiffo was waving the control sticks wildly and the Star Runner danced around the Dreadnought accordingly. But he was still too terrified to say anything.

“We have only a few seconds,” Trent reported. *“You have to take it down now!”*

The Vindicator approached the Dreadnought from behind, which made the scene like shooting fish in a barrel.

“McNeil, fire five shots in a row!” Zelnick ordered. “Fwiffo, concentrate your fire on the Dreadnought immediately!”

Simultaneously five ion bolts were shot off from the Vindicator and three Backwards Utilizing Tracking Torpedoes* from the Star Runner. In a few seconds they hit

---

* For convenience, the missiles were normally referred to by only the first letters of the words.

their target and the Dreadnought's hull finally cracked. First the starboard engine compartment was torn off and then the rest of the ship exploded.

Ur-Quan Dreadnoughts always exploded in a theatrical way. Many believed that they had a self-destruct circuit which prevented other species from learning the Ur-Quan's technological secrets.

The remaining two fighters were easily picked off when the Tobermoon got in range to use its point-defense laser system. By then, the Vindicator had already been carried far past the combat area by its momentum.

"It will take us a while to turn around," Zelnick said to Trent and Fwiffo. "Well done."

Fwiffo was still gripping the control sticks like mad. He wasn't trembling anymore, though. Instead he was stiff as a statue.

"That was a close call," Trent said. *"You sure came up with a nice strategy... ballsy, but nice."*

In about half an hour the Vindicator had managed to return to Unzervalt's orbit where the Tobermoon and Star Runner were already waiting. Now they had time to look at the inconsolable view of Zelnick's home. The planet really did look like Earth. Through the slave shield they could make out the lines of seas and continents. Zelnick showed them where their village and the Precursor factory were – the factory which was supposed to build a fleet of ships to oppose the Ur-Quan Hierarchy.

"So that's it then," Zelnick said in a sorrowful voice. "So much for our fleet... and hope."

"Things are looking bad right now, I agree," Gruber said. "I can understand how you feel personally, seeing your friends and family imprisoned like that."

Zelnick didn't respond. He covered his face with his hands. Gruber put his hand on Zelnick's shoulder.

"You showed great combat potential today," Gruber comforted him. "Without you, this would indeed be a hopeless situation."

"I can't believe I'm alive," Fwiffo suddenly said. He hadn't said anything since he was ordered to attack the Dreadnought.

"That was some A-class flying, Captain Fwiffo," Trent complimented. *"I completely misjudged you. With this team we are a force to be reckoned with."*

"Should we start scavenging the wreck, captain?" Gruber asked Zelnick with a very soft voice.

Zelnick nodded, still covering his face.

"I'll leave the command to you for a while," he mumbled to Gruber and left the bridge.

They took their time going through the debris of the Dreadnought and its fighters.

When they were finished, they held another meeting aboard the Vindicator.

"So, what are we going to do now?" Zelnick asked commonly.

"This trip wasn't a complete waste," Gruber said. "We got lots of useful materials from the wreckage."

"I guess the only thing we can do for now is return to Earth," Trent pointed out. "Then I think we should check up on the Chenjesu at Procyon."

They talked for a while, but nobody had any better ideas so they decided to return to Earth as quickly as possible.

It was Gruber's turn to be on the bridge when they jumped to hyperspace. Zelnick was resting in his quarters. Now they faced another six days of monotonous cruising through hyperspace.

They had the tactical genius Matthew Trent with a trusty Earthling Cruiser, a cowardly, but skillful Captain Fwiffo with a Spathi Eluder, and a Precursor prodigy Robert Zelnick with a powerful Precursor vessel. Luck had also been on their side. Things could be worse. Gruber let a slight thought of hope slip into his mind.

The captain is a good lad, he thought.

CHAPTER 6

PEACEFUL ENCOUNTER

March 16th 2155, hyperspace, 275.9 : 173.9

The atmosphere aboard the Vindicator had suffered a great blow after the incident in Vela. It was the third day of their return trip and they had just passed the Raynet star cluster when Gruber suddenly realized that he hadn't seen a single smile after their last jump to hyperspace. Zelnick had also been a lot more quiet than earlier. Gruber was under the impression that Zelnick left the bridge only to rest in his quarters and from there he only came straight back to the bridge.

It was now Gruber's turn to take control of the ship. The operators saluted him as usual as Zelnick took off. Gruber still wasn't comfortable sitting in the captain's chair, but he did it anyway. His original plan was not to sit in it, but on the first day after leaving Vela he was deep in his thoughts and suddenly noticed that he had, at some point, sat down. After that he saw no point in avoiding it anymore.

The operators didn't talk very much. Dujardin, Steinbach and Samusenko were currently on duty. The rest of them were on a three minute stand-by. That was enough time for them to wake up, put on their uniform and run to their posts from the crew quarters.

They all had their own ways to pass the time. Dujardin was interested in what happened outside the ship. She was constantly checking the star map and the telescope. Steinbach was more interested in the ship itself. He read all possible reports and operation manuals and wrote some himself. Samusenko on the other hand was playing some kind of role-playing game. There was no reason to deny him that when they were just cruising through hyperspace.

Gruber's own thing was a simple memo system integrated into their communicators. With it he could easily write down all his thoughts whenever he felt like it. And when he was overseeing the Vindicator, he had plenty of time to write. At some points his mind wandered off and he found himself reading the stories he had just written down. Some of them were quite interesting in his own opinion and he was processing them into a collection of short stories. Nobody but himself had ever read them. He was planning on making the collection public when their mission was over.

"Sir, there's something on the radar," Dujardin suddenly said.

Gruber snapped out of his thoughts. He stood up and walked to Dujardin's side. Indeed there was a dot on the hyperspace radar, indicating that they were flying straight towards a gravity well, most likely a ship. The radar's range was about five hyperspace units, so if the target was stationary, they would reach it in roughly five hours.

"Shall I alert the crew?" Steinbach asked.

"No," Gruber answered. "Just notify the captain for now."

If a ship wanted to intercept another ship in hyperspace and was aligned in its path, the other ship would have to take a very long detour to avoid interception. The difference of speed was essential. With their speed, the Vindicator would have to use about an extra day to circle around an Ur-Quan Dreadnought, which had the fastest known hyperdrive in the Great War.

Gruber was standing next to the captain's chair when Zelnick arrived. They all saluted him and he sat down.

Judging from Zelnick's appearance he had just gotten out of the shower.

They had to wait a while to determine the speed and direction of the object ahead.

"We should avoid all confrontations now," Zelnick reminded them. They had all agreed on that upon leaving Vela.

"Uh, captain..." Dujardin started her report. "It's flying straight at us at a speed of approximately 1000 milliunits per hour."

That was equal to the maximum cruising speed of the Vindicator.

"Check it again," Zelnick ordered.

"I already re-checked it two times before reporting, sir," Dujardin replied. "There's no mistake. Whatever it is, we will meet it in a little more than two hours."

"What the hell is that thing?" Gruber angrily said. "I thought we could outrun anything."

"I know what it is..." Zelnick stated in an ominous voice.

They all looked at him, waiting for an explanation.

"...It's the thing that killed Burton."

Zelnick told them what had really happened to Captain Burton and, in Gruber's opinion, it was about time.

Tobermoon was indeed the ship they had used on their original voyage to Vela. The ship had later on left to help defend Sol against the invading Ur-Quan armada. They had expected it to return in a few months, but it never did. Decades later, when Zelnick and the crew, led by Isadora Burton, left Unzervalt with the Vindicator, they found the Tobermoon derelict and tumbling through space. It hadn't even gotten out of the Vela star system.

The command of the Tobermoon had been given to First Officer Chi, who had been engaged to Burton. During the years of waiting for the Tobermoon to return, Burton had never given up hope on seeing Chi again. That said, finding Chi's body on the Tobermoon would have given her some closure.

But it got worse. There were burns along the Tobermoon's hull, as one might expect, but most of the important ship systems were intact. And there were no bodies – nothing to indicate that the ship had ever been manned. Burton was left mourning in dubiety whether Chi and the rest of the crew had been taken prisoners. And not just she, most of the current crew members had had people close to them on the Tobermoon.

With a few days' work the engineers had brought the Tobermoon back to life. And with Burton being the only one qualified to captain a Cruiser, Zelnick was left in charge of the Vindicator. Together they had set course for Earth.

About a day after their jump to hyperspace they detected a very fast hyperspace spoor – similar to the one that was coming at the Vindicator right now. In a few hours it had gotten close enough to pull both ships into true space. The ship looked like a pair of spinning red globes surrounded by a crackling energy field. Some kind of glowing rod or energy beam connected the red globes.

The ship had immediately stormed for the Vindicator with great speed. Burton flew the Tobermoon in between them and signaled the Vindicator to warp out of the area. As the Vindicator was warping out, Zelnick could see a crackling bolt of energy lancing out from the alien vessel and striking the Tobermoon. Then the enemy ship suddenly changed direction and left the area.

Soon Zelnick radioed the Tobermoon and learned that Captain Burton had been killed in the unexpected attack. Zelnick was left in full control of their mission as there was nobody left to captain the Tobermoon.

They managed to return to Earth then, but now they were facing the same unknown threat again – although this time they were much better prepared.

"So how fast was that ship exactly?" Trent asked. He had been listening all the time.

"Very fast" Zelnick answered. "What surprised us the most was its acceleration. And it was very close to the Tobermoon when it attacked so we should assume its main weapon is short-ranged. We need to try to keep our distance."

"If it is the same kind of ship," Trent pointed out. *"It would be best for us if we could entice it into chasing Fwiffo."*

Fwiffo was also listening in.

"Not to worry," Fwiffo said surprisingly confident. *"Running away is what the Spathi Eluder has been designed for."*

Two hours later everyone was at battle stations as the spoor was near enough to interfere with the hyperdrive at any moment.

"We're as ready as we'll ever be," Zelnick announced. "Keep your claws on the throttle stick, Fwiffo."

"That is how I live my life," Fwiffo answered.

Their plan was that Fwiffo's Star Runner would storm the enemy as soon as combat started, but then change direction and fly away at maximum throttle. If they were lucky enough, the enemy would then chase the Star Runner and Fwiffo would have valuable time to launch a wave of Backwards Utilizing Tracking Torpedoes. Tobermoon would then have plenty of time to support Fwiffo with homing nukes if necessary.

"Here it comes!" Zelnick said to alert everybody as the unknown ship entered the Vindicator's hyperdrive's operative range.

As soon as they were in true space they received an incoming message:

"We are not hostile and seek to establish friendly relations with your species."

There was no picture - only that one message. Dujardin put a view of the ship on display.

"Is that what you saw attack the Tobermoon?" Gruber asked Zelnick.

"That's definitely it," Zelnick said. "It's just as I remembered it."

"We are also on a peaceful mission," Zelnick then responded to the alien craft. "I am Captain Robert Zelnick of the starship Vindicator from the New Alliance of Free Stars. Identify yourselves."

They received a response immediately.

"This is probe 2418-B. We are on a peaceful mission of exploration. Mission description follows: Traverse space recording data. Seek materials for replication. Replicate to expand scope of mission. Contact life forms in peaceful manner. After ten replications return to point of origin. End of mission description."

"So it's just a probe," Gruber thought out loud. "We should still gather information and try to make contact with whoever sent the probe."

Zelnick agreed.

"Who sent you?" he asked the probe.

This time there was no immediate response.

"Captain, the communication link has been terminated," Katja reported.

"Captain!" Dujardin then cried out. "The ship is flying straight at us with incredible speed!"

Zelnick jumped up.

"We'll go with the original plan," he ordered. "Fwiffo!"

The Star Runner immediately took off looking like it would intercept the probe head-on. The probe was approaching so fast that Fwiffo didn't have much time before he had to turn away.

"If it starts chasing the Star Runner, we'll know for sure that it's attacking," Gruber pointed out.

The Star Runner changed direction and was now flying away from both parties. The probe immediately changed its heading to chase Fwiffo's ship.

"Now we know," Zelnick stated. "Fwiffo, lure it a little further away and then fire."

Fwiffo seemed a little more relaxed than in the battle with the Ur-Quan Dreadnought. Apparently this was the kind of tactic he was trained to utilize. The Star Runner was now flying roughly in the direction where the probe came from.

"Alright, Fwiffo, you're far enough. Fire at will," Zelnick said and Fwiffo immediately launched three missiles.

What happened then shocked everyone.

In the blink of an eye the probe was now flying towards the Vindicator and Tobermoon again. There was no noticeable turning or acceleration.

Gruber thought of how stupid it would sound to explain that at one moment the ship was flying at one direction and an instant later the ship was flying in the opposite direction, at the same speed. But that's what happened. The only way to believe something like that was to see it with one's own eyes. It was just a probe so there probably wasn't a living organism inside the ship, but still, there was no inertia-nullifier that could negate such seemingly infinite acceleration.

"Trent, fire!" Zelnick hastily ordered.

Two nukes were shot off from the Tobermoon, but there wasn't enough time to calibrate them to the new trajectory, so their guidance system didn't work. They were on a trajectory that would make them miss their target just barely. The probe seemed to ignore them. This gave Trent the option to remote-detonate the nukes when they were somewhat close to the probe.

It all happened in a few seconds, but Trent knew what he was doing. He set off the nukes at exactly the right time and the probe got its share of the shock wave. It was thrown off course somewhat, but it didn't slow down. Soon it was coming straight at the Vindicator with full speed again.

"Sir, we don't have time to reload!" Trent reported to Zelnick.

"McNeil!" Zelnick shouted as the probe was getting too close for comfort.

"I've got it, sir," McNeil responded while holding a handle that looked like a joystick.

The Ion-Bolt Gun fired three shots and then the probe had flown past the field of fire. The first shot hit the probe right in the middle and the second one hit one of the spinning spheres. The third one barely missed. The probe was still in one piece and now neither the Vindicator nor the Tobermoon could use their primary weapons against it.

"Fwiffo, get back here as fast as you can!" Zelnick nearly shouted.

A moment later a shaft of lightning from the probe hit the Vindicator.

"Sir, it's burning through our hull," Iwasaki reported. "It will soon cause structural damage if we can't take it down."

The probe then flew past the Vindicator, but they didn't have any time to catch a breath. Any normal ship would soon be far away and facing the wrong direction, but the probe had turned incredibly fast again and was now spinning around the Vindicator.

"We'll use the point-defense laser!" Trent said and steered the Tobermoon as close to the Vindicator as possible.

The probe was still giving electrotherapy to the Vindicator when the Tobermoon brought its lasers to bear. The lasers were primarily designed to intercept enemy missiles so they were fast and accurate enough to hit the probe even though it was right next to the Vindicator.

Several laser beams were shot off from the Tobermoon. Slowly they started to make cuts to the probe. Suddenly the shaft of lightning disappeared and the probe took off in the direction of Fwiffo's Star Runner which had managed to turn around and was now getting close to the other ships.

McNeil was ready. As soon as the probe entered the Ion-Bolt Gun's field of fire, McNeil fired rapidly. The first hit was enough to detach one of the spheres from the rod connecting them, making the energy field around the probe disappear. It probably meant that the probe was already neutralized, but the following two hits blew it into pieces. The two last shots passed through the explosion and narrowly missed the Star Runner which was just about to fire at the probe as well.

"Iwasaki, report," Zelnick commanded.

"We're good, sir," he replied. "The lightning melted parts of the shielding, but it didn't get through."

"The Tobermoon would have received serious damage if the probe had attacked us instead of you," Trent commented to Zelnick.

"Or me," Fwiffo continued. *"This is the first time I've encountered a ship I couldn't run away from."*

"Start the scavenging right away," Zelnick ordered. "The wreckage could turn out to be interesting."

They learned a lot in the next few hours, but at the same time they didn't really learn anything.

“We can conclude that this probe’s design and origins are unfamiliar to us,” Gruber reported. “There are signs of highly advanced technology, but also pieces of surprisingly standard machinery. I’d say it’s clearly above human level, but slightly below that of the Chenjesu. There is nothing left that could be reverse-engineered. In that sense the wreckage is similar to the Dreadnought’s as it appears that there is some kind of a self-destruct system.”

Zelnick was disappointed like everyone else.

“But here is the good news,” Gruber continued. “If there is a self-destruct system, it is not as thorough as those the Ur-Quan have. I’d say these scavenged materials are even more valuable than the ones we got from the Dreadnought.”

“I guess that’s something,” Zelnick said, still sounding disappointed. “Wrap it up and let’s get going.”

Gruber spent a great deal of the next few days in the storage module, trying to learn something from the wreckage of the probe.

Something about the attack didn’t seem right. Who was the probe looking for? It went through a great deal of trouble to intercept them, but it couldn’t have been seeking just them out. Then why would anyone send out a probe to attack randomly encountered ships? Maybe the probe was on a friendly mission like it stated, but it somehow considered them a threat.

Gruber thought back to the moment the probe cut transmission. He knew that the Vindicator didn’t do anything at that time, but he wasn’t so sure about the Tobermoon and the Star Runner. Could some functions on them have caused the probe to activate a self-defense protocol? He had to check the black box of the Tobermoon. He had no idea whether something similar even existed on the Star Runner.

He called Trent for a permission to access the Tobermoon's databanks. Trent didn't ask any questions so Gruber didn't give any answers. Gruber was very familiar with Earthling Cruiser's design so he knew what to look for and where.

There were no entries at the exact time of the transmission being cut. The probe had already been set as a target for the nukes, but that was standard procedure and there was no way – or no known way in Gruber's knowledge – to extract that information from outside the ship without specified clearance. Gruber wasn't more of a software person than he had to be. He would have to ask someone else whether it would be possible for the probe to detect the nukes targeting it. There was nothing else of interest in the logs of the Tobermoon so this was the only thing to cling on to.

He asked around the ship and soon learned that he would have to wait until they got back to the starbase. Apparently the only one who 'really' knew about the system's security was Richard Matthewson, the man in charge of programming the starbase's alien computer.

Richard Matthewson was one of the very few people who weren't substituted in the last resupply eight years ago. The Ur-Quan had originally given the required knowledge for programming the computer to only one person. That decision lead to the obvious outcome which Edward A. Murphy had figured out already in 1949. That particular man died after two years of serving on the starbase.

The pleas for another programmer were not answered by the Ur-Quan. They said that knowledge of the computer wasn't a necessity for survival so they wouldn't teach anyone else.

Things got interesting when the first resupply came and the starbase crew learned what had happened on the surface during those past five years.

About a year before the resupply every computer in the world had suddenly been infected by a certain virus. The virus was seemingly harmless to law-abiding citizens, but extremely harmful to certain organizations. It prepared the computers to be used in a highly advanced AI botnet. The AI thought up strategies on its own, disabled surveillance systems across the world, determined if a specific government was a threat to privacy and tried to overthrow it by leaking information.

The virus was perfect and its origins were completely untraceable. However, there was one thing its creator had overlooked. He didn't infect his own computer with it.

When the entire world wide network was transmitting the virus over and over again, one particular node lit up like a black Christmas tree, not transmitting anything and not getting infected. Two weeks after the epidemic had begun, a certain 25-year-old Richard Matthewson, who had been officially dead for 10 years, was brought to trial.

His amazing life story was all over the media for months. He was born and raised in London in a good family, but he had dropped out of school at the age of ten. By then he had already broken into several local corporations, uncovering unlawful and unethical business methods. He started getting himself in trouble with the law by disabling security cameras and other surveillance systems, which he saw as a major privacy issue.

At the age of 14 he was being prosecuted for unlawful entry to Star Control systems, where he uncovered details about several secret operations deep within Ur-Quan space. The official word was that he was later released due to lack of evidence, but there were countless theories on what kind of a deal he had made with Star Control.

Soon after that he died. Or that's what everyone thought. He had hacked into several major government institutions and staged his own death before fleeing to Tokyo. There he made a living by blackmailing corporations after – once again – hacking into their systems. His own life eventually went down the drain, but he still wanted to do something he thought was good. The AI was supposed to be his "final gift to humanity" as he called it.

Again, there are theories that getting caught was part of his plan. Some say the whole operation was just his way of calling for help. Maybe it was or maybe it wasn't, but in any case the only help he got was being sentenced for 20 years in prison.

Soon after that the first starbase crew returned and immediately announced that a new programmer was needed. After a short but intense turn of events, Matthewson was given the option to serve the rest of his sentence on the starbase, to which he agreed.

As soon as he arrived on the starbase, he began scheduling regular discussions about privacy, the war, ethics, humanity and philosophy. Soon enough, most people realized that he had lost all faith in humanity and many accused him of loving the Hierarchy, though he managed to silence most of those by leaking security videos.

When the Vindicator arrived, Matthewson had served 13 years of his sentence. He had been doing his job adequately. He actually had learned the ways of the central computer and had made himself useful, but on the other hand, he was a pain to deal with as a person. That changed soon after everyone realized that now was their only chance of overthrowing the Ur-Quan.

Matthewson suddenly revealed that he knew a lot more about the computer and the whole station than what he had made everybody think. He started co-operating and was a key player in making the Precursor software work with the starbase's ship repair fabricators.

Gruber never really knew Matthewson, but then again, he was pretty sure that neither did anyone else. After thinking about it, Gruber wasn't so sure anymore that the Cruiser's databanks were safe. Matthewson might just as well already have a hack for it.

Gruber's communicator beeped. Iwasaki notified him that his watch on the bridge would start in three minutes. They would reach Sol in a few hours.

CHAPTER 7

INTERMISSION

March 20th 2155, Sol, 175.2 : 145.0

Gruber was still at the helm when they passed the asteroid belt. He had had a really hard time getting Fwiffo to understand that he needed to know exactly what the Star Runner's systems were doing at the time of their encounter with the probe.

Fwiffo had kept repeating that he hadn't done anything. There might have been translation problems as it turned out that the Spathi way of thinking differs greatly from the human way. Their ships do absolutely nothing if not given the command. Apparently the same goes for all their machinery. Eventually Gruber dropped the subject as it was evident that the Star Runner really didn't have any hidden threatening functions.

Of course the Vindicator was an unknown factor. There's no telling what the ship exactly does. It wouldn't come as a big surprise to Gruber if the ship itself would turn out to be sentient. But right now all he could do was check the Cruiser's system security with Matthewson.

They all saluted as Zelnick arrived on the bridge. Gruber decided to stay there for the rest of the trip since they were about two hours away from Earth. They had been gone for only 15 days, but Gruber felt the same kind of warmth that you feel when you open the front door of your house after a long holiday – with the difference that he hadn't been on a holiday and didn't have a door to open. Judging by the suddenly cheerful and open atmosphere on the bridge, he wasn't the only one who felt that way.

They passed the orbit of Mars and soon they saw a small red-glowing planet which looked exactly like Unzervalt. Orbiting the red planet was a grey moon and when they got even closer they saw a familiar starbase in orbit. They would have a lot to report to Hayes.

Right after Zelnick gave Katja the order to send a message to the starbase, the Vindicator received an incoming transmission. They answered it and Hayes' familiar face appeared on the screen.

"Welcome back," he said cheerfully. *"We have a lot to tell you and judging by that Spathi Eluder I dare say you have as well."*

"Yeah, you could say that," Zelnick answered.

Right then Gruber saw one of the most welcome sights of his post-war life: There was another Earthling Cruiser being built on the starbase's dock. It was still far from completion, but its hull was recognizable. Maintenance robots moved swiftly from one working point to another and the hull was almost covered in welding flashes. The work that would take years by human workers at the Detroit shipyard was accomplished in weeks by the Hierarchy shipyard technology.

"Now ain't that a sight for sore eyes," Trent commented. *"I wonder who the unlucky son of a bitch of a captain will be."*

"Ahh, I see you noticed the Amateras." Hayes said proudly. *"We are well ahead of schedule on pretty much everything. We are already receiving a steady supply of base metals from the Moon – enough to finish the hull of Amateras. But we lack some more rare materials needed to complete some parts of the ship."*

"Our storage module is filled with all kinds of valuable materials," Zelnick boasted. "But let's not get too carried away. We lost some crew and we couldn't get to Unzervalt. There's a lot to discuss."

"I see," Hayes said calmly. *"We'll go through every detail when you get here. We'll meet in the conference room as soon as possible."*

They went through the usual routines and the service robots started patching up the Vindicator. When Gruber, Zelnick and a shuttle full of other crew members left the Vindicator, they finally saw what the ship actually looked like after their battles.

There were lots of dents and burns in the prow. With a little imagination one could picture the Ur-Quan fighters making them while being overrun. A long burnt scar in the side of the hull reminded them of the battle with the probe.

Even with the dents and burns it was a beautiful ship. There was something in the design which made it look unreachable – far above human level. And there weren't even that many modules yet. Gruber thought of the brilliance of the modular design and how humanity would benefit if the idea was implemented in Detroit. Modules could be manufactured all over the world and the shipyard could focus on its strong points, not wasting time on anything that could be done somewhere else.

Gruber thought back to his years in the academy. Getting familiar with the manufacturing process was a part of the starship officer's training so he had spent a lot of time in Detroit. Or maybe the real reason was that his sweetheart also lived there.

Lily was a sweet girl - not the kind that would win a beauty contest - but still very nice to look at. Back then Gruber was just a stupid young man who enjoyed alcohol and fast cars, but she was one of the brightest minds of the university. Luckily for Gruber, there were common gatherings for the cadets and university students. And even more luckily, that only time she had gone to such an event was the time when Gruber was on driving duty so he was able to start a rational conversation.

All those years in the academy seemed like an eternity at the introduction lecture, but at the graduation ceremony he suddenly realized that it was all over. Gruber had shown potential, but there were some who were better than him. The very best were made captains and Gruber was given the role of a first officer.

The war had just begun and he had only two days between graduation and his first mission aboard the Cruiser Artemis under Captain Yallah Rangoon. Lily was still in the process of writing her graduation thesis, but she had already been recruited to Star Control. Further details about her assignment were classified.

Gruber had made sure that those last two days were something to remember. When Lily saw Gruber off at the spaceport, they had an understanding that they'd settle down when the war was over. The first mission of the Artemis was scheduled to take only three months and after that they would still have had time to meet before Lily was shipped off.

But, due to certain circumstances, the mission lasted for two years and Gruber never saw Lily again. She had left him a message saying that her work involved highly classified research in an unknown location and that she couldn't be any more specific than that without violating her non-disclosure agreement. Gruber knew enough of Star Control to understand that he couldn't do anything to contact her.

Zelnick shook Gruber awake as they had reached the starbase. Other crew members were already making their way out of the shuttle. As Gruber returned to the present day, he realized that the hangar was once again full of people.

Gruber and Zelnick were the last ones to exit the shuttle and Hayes was waiting for them at the end of the ramp. While they were heading towards the conference room, Hayes told them that he hadn't made any announcements yet.

"There were eight casualties," Zelnick said once they were out of the hangar.

Gruber gave Hayes a list of the deceased, which Hayes silently read through.

"We need to have a memorial," Hayes concluded.

They reached the conference room and waited for Trent and Fwiffo to arrive. Hayes passed the time by reporting news about the starbase.

Fredrikson and Chu soon joined them. A few minutes later Trent opened the door and Fwiffo followed him to the room.

"Captain Fwiffo," Hayes said in a polite manner.

"Hey, I know you!" Fwiffo joyfully declared. "I've seen your face on the wall of fear."

Hayes was just as surprised as everyone else.

"Our Earthguard force had a wall where we put pictures of the most dangerous Hunams," Fwiffo explained.

"Good to know," Hayes replied. "Now then… Everyone have a seat and we'll listen to your report."

Zelnick did most of the talking. When he was describing what happened in Pluto, Fwiffo confessed that he shot at the shuttle himself and that there was no automated defense system. It came as a surprise to him that nobody had believed his lie in the first place.

"That was some trip," Hayes said after Zelnick had concluded his report. "I have some news too."

He touched a console and the star map of the quadrant appeared on the wall.

"For six days we have been bathed in broad-beam hyperwave transmission from the direction of the Rigel star system. Due to the broadcast's wide dispersion, we cannot discern its content. I suggest you check it out if you happen to be in that area in the near future."

Rigel wasn't far, but it was in a different direction than Procyon. Gruber waited for Hayes to continue by saying 'also…' which was what he always did. Sometimes it got really annoying when he had lots of bulletins.

"Also…" Hayes said on cue. "As you all know, the Alliance hyperwave network was destroyed at the end of the war. Even if you brought us an endless supply of materials, it would take years to reassemble the network. But despite that, Fredrikson's team has been cooking up a little surprise… doctor?"

"It's not a surprise, though," Fredrikson replied and stood up. "Some of you may be too young to know this," she started explaining while looking at Zelnick, "but we were technologically ahead of most species in terms of communication when we joined the Alliance. Since the Chenjesu communicated naturally via hyperwave, they gave the technology to every species they met. Few species ever had to come up with a way for interstellar communication by themselves."

She pointed at the screen and some kind of design plans appeared there.

"For the past few days we have been building one of these from the scratch. Do you know what it is?" she asked everyone in the room, although it was clear that Hayes and Chu already knew.

"Well I'll be damned," Trent said in amazement. Gruber was about to say something similar, but since Trent got ahead of him, he didn't have to, and just nodded his head instead.

Not counting Fwiffo, Zelnick was obviously the only one who didn't recognize it.

"Well? What is it?" he asked in an annoyed tone.

"It's an ansible transmitter," Gruber explained. "With it, you can send instant one-way messages to a specified receiver no matter where it is."

"Exactly," Fredrikson said, "although it only works in true space. Since the hyperwave network allowed two-way communications and it also worked in hyperspace, the ansibles were very soon forgotten. But now that we don't have use for a whole network and we want to remain undetected, this is exactly what we need."

She took out a small box she had been hiding under the table. Zelnick looked at the box. It was made of metal and it was roughly the size of a meal tray. It had a small screen and a speaker.

"What's that?" he asked.

"It's the ansible receiver," Fredrikson explained. "It doesn't need any external power. When it is linked, it will instantly display any messages written or spoken into the transmitter."

"Wow," Zelnick said. He didn't sound very impressed. "How does it work?" he asked.

"If you are interested I'd be happy to explain it to you in detail," she answered cheerfully. "But for now, to make the story simple, let's just say that the transmitter creates a micro wormhole between itself and the linked receiver. Then the transmitter sends an optic signal which the receiver decrypts. It is 100% untraceable."

She tapped her console and another technical drawing appeared on the screen.

"Creating the wormhole requires a great deal of space and energy, so that's why ships were never equipped with transmitters. But we are confident that the Vindicator is massive and powerful enough to have a transmitter of its own. We have already started working on designs for an ansible module."

"Wow," Zelnick said again, this time a little more impressed. "Could it be used to stream videos?" he asked surprisingly serious.

Fredrikson took a second to contemplate whether she should answer seriously.

"It could be," she decided to answer. "But it would exhaust our power cores in a matter of minutes."

"Darn," Zelnick mumbled. "That fat guy at the hangar had some nice ones."

"Well I'm sure he had," Fredrikson angrily said. "Can we get down to business now?"

"Yes ma'am!" Zelnick answered and sat up straight.

There weren't many other important matters to discuss so the meeting soon came to an end. A very large part of the materials they brought back had to be synthesized for fuel. Another large part was used to finish the turning jets of the Vindicator. Some remaining valuables were to be used in the construction of the Amateras.

Gruber took a while to watch the multi-purpose construction robots. They moved swiftly, always knowing exactly what their job was. He took note that they were optimized to the max. He tried to find an idle robot but he couldn't. After a while he was pleased enough to leave the robots to their work.

It was time to pay Matthewson a visit. His lab was on level 9, next to the central computer. Gruber was confident that Matthewson would be at his desk as always.

He entered the central elevator and waited for it to reach the desired level. Soon the doors opened and he saw a narrow corridor with office rooms on both sides behind a glass wall. At the end of the short corridor was the central computer console. The office on the right seemed like nobody had ever used it.

But the office on the left looked more like a flea market. Between towering piles of junk Gruber could see a desk and a figure behind it. It was a man with long brown hair and long beard as if he had been forsaken on a deserted island for years. Matthewson hadn't changed one bit since Gruber last saw him.

Matthewson didn't take any notice of Gruber as he entered the office. He was tapping his keyboard wildly. The space in front of the desk was inaccessible because of all the junk so Gruber walked to the side. He saw that Matthewson was coding something.

Gruber decided to be polite.

"Excuse me," he said.

"Mhm?" Matthewson mumbled.

"I need to ask you something," Gruber stated.

He got no response.

"It's about the security of the Cruiser's systems," he patiently explained.

Matthewson stopped typing, but didn't turn to look at Gruber.

"What about it?" he asked.

Gruber tried to make his point quick and simple. He was already feeling quite uncomfortable.

"Is it possible for another ship to detect the moment when a Cruiser's nukes target it?" he asked.

"Not with human technology," Matthewson answered without having to think about it. "But with infinite computing power… absolutely."

"What do you mean?" Gruber asked.

"Does the name Gordon Moore mean anything to you?" Matthewson answered with a question.

"Doesn't ring a bell," Gruber admitted.

"In 1965 Gordon Moore predicted that computing power would double roughly every two years for at least ten years," Matthewson explained. "The funny part is that the prediction, also known as Moore's law, has been pretty accurate even to this day."

Gruber waited for Matthewson to make a point.

"When the Cruiser system's security was being made, they came up with an algorithm that was unbreakable. It is as secure as it can be without being completely isolated. But here is the problem... The security is limited to human imagination."

Gruber started to get interested so he decided to keep silent.

"If Moore's law continues to be more or less accurate, we can crack the Cruiser's system ourselves in about 4000 years. But that is a very short time when looking at the big picture. There probably are races that have evolved far beyond our imagination in this aspect. To them the Cruiser's system could be like an open book."

"Is there anything we can do to prevent that?" Gruber asked.

"Sure there is," Matthewson said plainly. "Simply put, you just have to disable the Cruiser's antenna."

A few minutes later Gruber was explaining his theory to the captains. Fwiffo didn't understand anything, but Trent and Zelnick agreed to test the theory if they ever met with a similar probe again.

After a short discussion Gruber went to his quarters. He wasn't feeling at all tired until he had sat down on his bed. Suddenly all the pressure and emotions of their trip struck him. His pillow was calling to him like a Syreen captain. He answered the call immediately after taking off his boots.

The next thing he realized was the knock on his door. He felt like telling the person to go away, but he was too tired to raise his voice. The lights were still on and he checked the time. It took him a while to understand that he had only slept for a few minutes.

Groaning loudly in protest, he stood up and made his way to the door. Suddenly he got a head rush and he had to take support from the wall. For a second he thought about going back to sleep, ignoring the person knocking on the door.

The person knocked again.

Amidst all the cursing, Gruber finally managed to grasp the door handle. The one behind the door would most likely become the victim of his unjustified burst of anger. He knew it, but didn't have time to do anything about it. He quickly came up with a snappy and aggressive line to begin with. Feeling pleased with himself he opened the door.

"You'd b—" he started his line, but was interrupted by a woman leaping to embrace him.

He was taken by surprise and fell backwards to the floor – painfully. The woman fell with him.

He took a while to lie there watching the ceiling, waiting for an apology and an explanation.

He didn't receive any.

Judging by the sounds, someone walked by his room and stopped for a while to see what the ruckus was all about. Gruber didn't bother to do anything about it. After the observer had left, the woman stood up and closed the door.

"I was worried," the woman said, leaning towards the door as if preventing anyone from entering.

She was Veronica Williams, a younger-than-she-looks woman from the supply division. Gruber had had something vague going on with her in the past, but she was still on his case.

Gruber was surprised that his primary emotion at present was anger – for the missed chance to say his snappy line.

"Weren't we all," he replied and took his time getting up.

He sat down on his bed again and looked at Veronica, who looked right back at him. For a few seconds they just stared at each other.

"Can I help you?" Gruber finally asked.

She replied by starting to take off her clothes.

Gruber decided to tell her that he really wasn't in the mood right now, which was the truth. He tried to tell her, but the words didn't come out of his mouth.

She stepped out of her boots and Gruber saw only one possible outcome for the situation.

Then she removed her shirt with one swift move and threw it into a corner. After that she took a few seducing steps towards Gruber.

He tried to remember why he wasn't in the mood.

And there flew her pants.

Soon it would be too late to tell her off and he knew it very well. He was on the edge. He needed a distraction and he needed it right now.

But why would he need a distraction? He could just go with the flow – take the path of least resistance. He was sure he had a reason not to, but had no idea what the reason was.

Next was the bra.

He had passed the point of no return. Some vague memories of doubt remained in his head, but he had stopped resisting.

"Your attention please," suddenly echoed from the speaker system.

At that moment Gruber cursed Hayes and his timing to the lowest parts of hell, although a few seconds earlier he would have welcomed the distraction with open arms.

Veronica sighed very deeply. Apparently they both targeted their frustration at Hayes as if he had done it on purpose.

"There will be a memorial in the hangar at 20:00," Hayes announced. *"Attending is not mandatory, but we will*

have a moment of silence in all sectors at 20:05. A list of the deceased can be found in the news feed. That is all."

Hayes' mood-killer made Gruber remember how tired he was. He stood up.

"I'm sorry," he said while picking up Veronica's clothes. "Let's not do this now."

She dressed quickly and silently – disappointed, not angry. Gruber thought about things to say, but he concluded that all possible lines would only have a negative effect.

After Veronica was dressed again, she opened the door and stepped outside. Before closing the door behind her she gave one last look at Gruber. He didn't know what the look meant.

Without hesitation Gruber put his head on the pillow and instantly fell asleep.

After hours of semi-pleasant sleep with strange dreams, his subconscious made him finally wake up at 19:50. He had sweated so much that the bed was soaked. He hastily got up, took a clean set of clothes and a towel from the closet and dashed out the door towards the showers.

Like anyone well experienced in the army, he was fresh, clean and dressed in less than five minutes. Entering the elevator showed him that he wasn't the only one going to the memorial. He greeted some of the men and then took his place next to the elevator door, where there still was a little space left.

As the elevator moved, his mind wandered off.

What would it look like if someone in the elevator faced a different direction than everyone else? It would surely make the atmosphere uncomfortable. Or if the elevator was empty, one could go stand in a corner – facing the corner – and wait for someone else to enter.

The thought amused him. He could try it out at a more appropriate time.

Just then the elevator reached the hangar floor.

The hangar was crowded. There were as many people as when they were getting ready to board the Vindicator for the first time. Hayes was standing before everyone else.

Without a specific command, the crowd organized itself and stood up straight. Suddenly there was complete silence and Gruber took his place in the formation.

After the silence had lasted long enough, Hayes started to call out names of the deceased.

"Minka Kowalski… Joseph Fritz… Jin Chin… Jonathan O'Donnell… Luigi… Fred Liebermann… Paul Liebermann… Alex Liebermann…"

He took a very long pause before continuing.

"These soldiers… These brave individuals gave their lives for the freedom of the human race. They were brothers, sisters… fathers, mothers… sons, daughters… and friends… our comrades… No matter what our personal feelings were, we all had the same goal – to liberate Earth. These were the first casualties and I dare say there will be more in our struggle."

Hayes turned to face the stand where they had gathered pictures of the fallen.

"Farewell," he continued in a loud voice. "You will be remembered. Let it be known that you did not die in vain."

He turned to face the crowd again.

"We will now have a moment of silence to honor the dead."

Everyone bowed their heads down. Gruber noticed someone sobbing. Soon someone else broke down completely.

Death comes with great emotions, Gruber thought. That is why the enemy must remain faceless and demonized. If soldiers on the opposing side were considered as individuals, pulling the trigger when necessary might become too difficult.

The emotional shock of killing usually comes years after the war. Veterans suddenly realize that all their victims were not just mass and statistics, but sentient beings just like they themselves. It was observed after the Great War that the ones responsible for killing Androsynth and Spathi were much more traumatized than those who had killed Ur-Quan or Mycon. The theory was that the closer the victims resembled humans, the harder it was to deal with killing them.

Gruber looked around. Fwiffo was wisely somewhere else.

Hayes lifted his head.

"Thank you," he said to point out that the moment of silence was over.

People began to scatter. Gruber made his way to Hayes and saw that Zelnick was also there.

"I've been trying to contact you," Zelnick said to Gruber. Gruber instantly checked his communicator and noticed several unanswered incoming calls during the time of his sleep.

"We are technically ready to leave, but I prefer to wait until tomorrow," Zelnick explained. "I think the crew needs a little more time."

Gruber couldn't agree more.

"A sound plan, captain," he commented.

"How does 12:00 sound to you?" Zelnick asked.

"It sounds reasonable," Gruber answered.

In a little less than 16 hours Gruber found himself on the bridge of the Vindicator again.

He had had a talk with Veronica and they agreed to think things over until the Vindicator returned again.

The deceased crew members were replaced and new personnel were assigned for the Star Runner. All three ships were now fully staffed.

The Amateras would be ready for testing in a few days. Deciding the captain would be Hayes' problem, but at least there were plenty to choose from.

Their current plan was to first fly to Procyon and make contact with the Chenjesu, then stop by in Epsilon Gruis and negotiate with the Spathi, and finally drop by Rigel to locate the source of the transmission. Fwiffo was confident that his kind would not attack on sight, but he was also confident that there was zero chance of success in the negotiations. For some reason Zelnick insisted on trying and since he was ultimately in charge of everything, that's what they agreed on.

Gruber was very eager to meet the Chenjesu again. If anyone knew what to do, it was them. They probably would even have something nice up their sleeves.

He looked at the ansible receiver which was placed next to the captain's chair. Fredrikson estimated that they would have the transmitter up and running in about a week. The key for this receiver was already known so they could establish the link whenever the transmitter was ready.

Procyon was roughly 129 hyperspace units away so the trip there would take about six days. They had agreed that they would try to test the ansible on 29th of March at 09:00 so the Vindicator would have to be in true space then – and if everything went according to their plan, they would be in Procyon at that time.

"Are we good to go?" Zelnick asked Gruber.

Gruber did the usual checks with the operators and then reported to Zelnick that everything was ready.

"Samusenko, full speed out of the system," Zelnick ordered.

"Yes sir," Samusenko replied, "in what direction?"

"That direction," Zelnick said, pointing directly to port, away from the Sun.

The ship began to turn really fast. Finishing the turning jets seemed to have paid off.

"How do the Chenjesu move around?" Zelnick suddenly asked. "To my knowledge they don't have any moving parts."

Gruber had learned to be pleased with Zelnick's thirst for knowledge.

"They use a hovering platform of some sort," he explained.

"Yeah, but I mean naturally… before they invented hovering platforms," Zelnick specified.

Gruber realized that he didn't know the answer and had never thought about it.

"Let's ask them," he suggested.

CHAPTER 8

MESSAGE FROM BEYOND

March 28th 2155, hyperspace, 080.9 : 218.0

They were only few hours away from the vortex leading to Procyon. So far the trip had gone without incident.

Procyon was a somewhat isolated orange dwarf over 40 hyperspace units from its nearest neighbor. It had five planets; all of them far outside the habitable zone.*

The sapphire world second closest to the sun was the Chenjesu's home planet. It had a surface temperature of barely over -200 centigrade on a hot day and it had no atmosphere. But the Chenjesu's silicon-based life flourished in those conditions.

"Captain, look," Dujardin suddenly said just as they were about to enter the vortex. She pointed at the screen showing the hyperspace radar.

Several contacts had just entered the radar's range. The technology was pretty straightforward and even the Vindicator didn't have any special kind of radar. It was presumable that the other contacts would also take notice of the Vindicator at the same time.

---

* In the beginning of the 21st century, scientists believed that life could only exist on a narrow zone in a solar system – where water would remain in liquid form on a planet's surface. But liquid water turned out to be the key element only for carbon based life.

Soon even more contacts started to appear on the edge of the radar screen. It looked like a whole fleet of ships was on the move.

"Captain, are you seeing this?" Dujardin made sure.

Zelnick nodded, but sat in pondering silence.

"Shall we proceed?" Samusenko asked.

"If we go to the Chenjesu homeworld," Gruber explained, "those contacts, whoever they are, might have time to surround the vortex… IF that is what they want."

"Who could they be?" Zelnick asked. "With the Chenjesu gone, there should be nobody around here, right?"

True enough, according to the 20 year old star map, the closest sphere of influence for a non-enslaved race was that of either the Ilwrath or the Spathi, but they were both over 100 units away. There was no apparent reason for one of their fleets to be this far out.

The Vindicator glided forward towards the vortex. If they were going to turn around, they would have to do it within a few minutes.

"Captain, our window is closing," Samusenko pointed out.

"Proceed," Zelnick ordered. "There's nothing we can do about it and we don't have time to turn around and return to Earth."

Gruber agreed. They were practically on a sneaking mission with lots of things to do and time was against them. They had to gamble if they were ever going to succeed. He explained his thoughts to the captain.

"We'll hope that those contacts are either non-hostile or uninterested in an unknown ship entering the system. Or in the best case – they could even be the Chenjesu themselves."

"Or really slow," Samusenko continued. "As a last resort, we can always close our eyes and step on it."

"Step on what?" Iwasaki asked.

"You know, pedal to the metal," Samusenko said while trying to show with his foot what he meant. "Full throttle," he tried to explain while grabbing an invisible handle on the console and pushed it forward.

"Engines to the maximum?" Iwasaki suggested.

Samusenko gave him a thumbs up gesture with a friendly smile.

Just then they were sucked into the vortex and they found themselves in the blackness of true space. Their destination was far closer to the edge of the system than Earth was in Sol so the trip would only take about six hours.

"Well, let's go see how the crystal ones are doing, shall we?" Zelnick suggested.

Procyon seemed just like a bright star among many others when they were on the edge of the system, but after a few hours it began to look noticeably bigger than the rest. When they passed the orbit of the third planet, the atmosphere became somewhat tense again. It had been 20 years since they heard anything from the Chenjesu and Gruber found himself just hoping that the Chenjesu were alive.

Soon they made out a red dot. There was definitely a slave shield over their world as well. Some of the operators were disappointed, but to Gruber it was a relief. At least their planet hadn't been incinerated.

After a few minutes they saw a familiar looking starbase in orbit.

"Looks like they made the same deal," Zelnick stated. "Katja, send out a greeting on the common frequency."

They waited for a while, but got no response.

"Try again with a constant signal," Zelnick ordered.

A terrible thought came into Gruber's mind and he kicked himself on the butt for not thinking about it earlier.

"Maybe the Ur-Quan have neglected the resupply of this base as well," he said. "And maybe the Chenjesu weren't as lucky as we were."

There was no response from the starbase.

"Don't tell me that station is filled with dead crystals," Zelnick said with disbelief in his voice.

Katja zoomed in on the station. There were no internal lights visible through the windows, but then again, the Chenjesu didn't have eyes. The station rotated slowly, just like the one orbiting Earth and there were also similar external lights.

"Send a team to investigate," Zelnick told Gruber.

The shuttle crew had eight new recruits. Gruber hadn't memorized their names yet. The only ones who survived from the last mission were Jenkins, Robinson, Witherspoon and Rigby, Thomas Rigby being the new leader.

Gruber notified Rigby to get the team ready. They were on a three minute stand-by.

"We're all here," Rigby immediately responded. *"We can take off whenever you say, sir."*

"Alright, good," Gruber responded. "Your mission is to dock at the starbase and examine its interior. Currently it looks like there's nobody home, but be careful."

"Aye-aye, sir," Rigby said.

Soon the Vindicator came to a halt near the starbase and the shuttle took off. Once again, all Gruber and the rest of the bridge crew could do was watch and wait.

It took no more than ten minutes for the shuttle to reach the docking bay.

"The docking sequence is complete," Jenkins reported from the shuttle.

The team put on their helmets and took positions near the air lock. Rookie Viktor Belov looked through the small window in the air lock door.

"It's dark," he said, *"I can't make out anything."*

"Open the hatch," Rigby ordered.

With a faint steamy sound, the door opened as the atmosphere cycle was complete. The monitors aboard the Vindicator showed nothing but black.

"All the lights are out," Rigby reported. *"Helmet lights on,"* he then commanded.

The cones of light hit the interior walls. Everything seemed intact and the team moved forward.

"Squad B, make your way to the control room," Rigby ordered. *"Squad A will secure the dock."*

Claire Witherspoon was the leader of squad B. She took the team with her and carefully advanced towards the central elevator.

"Somehow this place doesn't look dead," she thought out loud. *"I mean, there's no dust at all for one thing."*

"I don't think that dust appears around the Chenjesu," Rene Cuvelier commented. *"They don't use fabrics and don't have hair."*

"Is that so?" Witherspoon replied. *"First officer Gruber, what do you think?"* she then asked.

"I've never thought about it," Gruber said to the microphone, "but I think Cuvelier is partially right. There should be nothing that could form dust."

"Shh, everybody quiet!" Witherspoon suddenly whispered.

They all froze still and listened. Cuvelier made a "What is it?" gesture with his hands to Witherspoon.

"Listen!" she said with a very small voice.

They waited. Nothing could be heard at least on the Vindicator.

"I'm sure I heard something," she explained. *"I think we're not alone here."*

"Proceed with extreme caution," Rigby ordered.

Squad B started to slowly advance again. Suddenly Cuvelier gasped loudly.

"Dammit, Claire," he said, *"you got me all jumpy. I thought that pillar over there was a Chenjesu."*

"Cuvelier's heart rate is increasing, now at 140," Katja reported.

Squad B soon reached the central elevator without incident. Meanwhile, squad A had secured a perimeter around the docking bay.

The starbase was identical to their own, so they knew exactly where everything was.

"We're opening the service hatch," Witherspoon reported.

Through the hatch they could make their way into the elevator shaft. There was no gravity in the shaft and they could easily float up to the control room level. They were just about to enter the shaft when a sound alerted them.

ding

The elevator arrived and the doors opened. There was nothing inside. They all looked at each other. Tatsuo Shoji then raised his arm.

"Sorry, it was me," he said. *"I pressed the elevator call button out of old habit. I didn't think it would actually work."*

Now the elevator blocked the entry to the shaft.

"Well, get in then," Witherspoon ordered and the squad entered the elevator. She set the dial to level 16.

Soon they reached the control room level and the doors opened. The room was just like the one back in Sol, except that there was a mechanical construct of some kind in the middle, right where Hayes stood when using the communication link.

"Wait a minute," Gruber interrupted, "get closer to that thing in the center."

Witherspoon approached the construct. It looked like it didn't belong there.

"That's Mmrnmhrm design," Gruber concluded. "It's a communication relay of some sort."

"Why would the Chenjesu have Mmrnmhrm equipment here?" Cuvelier asked. *"Or better yet... HOW can they have it here? Surely the slave laws prohibit that, right?"*

Gruber knew the slave laws better than his own pockets and indeed all communication with other fallow slave races was unambiguously forbidden.

"Maybe that's why there's nobody home?" Zelnick suggested. "Maybe the Ur-Quan found out about it and punished them."

Zelnick then spoke to Witherspoon.

"Proceed to check the data banks with haste."

"Will do, captain," she answered.

Tatsuo Shoji was the last one to be assigned to the shuttle crew, to the role of the "computer guy" as some called him. After Matthewson he probably had the best knowledge of the starbase's computer systems. He was now searching the data banks for some information on what had happened.

"This is pretty heavy stuff, captain, very heavy indeed" Shoji reported directly to Zelnick with a very strong Japanese accent.

"Anything you'd care to share?" Zelnick asked slightly annoyed as Shoji hadn't said anything during the ten minutes he had been working on the control room's main console.

"There definitely is a good reason for that Mmrnmhrm relay to be here."

"Well?" Witherspoon hurried him.

"This data is encrypted in a strange way. I can tell you the details later, but I believe that they wanted us to find this stuff. And I do mean us, humans. I'm pretty sure that no other race could have decrypted this.

Anyway, here's the most interesting part of the data: Once defeated, the Chenjesu and the Mmrnmhrm chose to be slave shielded on a single world together. Apparently the Ur-Quan didn't have a problem with that. And here's the big news... After the Ur-Quan had left, the Chenjesu and the Mmrnmhrm set up mindless robots to run this place and the ones assigned here returned to the surface."

Gruber and Zelnick looked at the red glow of the slave shield over the Chenjesu's home world.

"So when was the slave shield erected?" Zelnick asked.

"That's my point! According to this, it was already there. There's no mistake about it. It says here that they penetrated the slave shield. I couldn't tell you how they did it, though."

Just as Gruber had hoped, the Chenjesu really did have something up their sleeves.

"But if they knew how to get through a slave shield," Zelnick continued, "wouldn't they have gone out of their prison rather than gone in?"

"This is interesting," Shoji said, *"according to this, they were exploring synthesis schemes to create a hybrid race, half Mmrnmhrm and half Chenjesu."*

"Huh? Why?" Zelnick asked.

"Beats me."

"Well, anyway, we'll conclude the analysis here," Zelnick said. "Copy the data and scavenge anything valuable."

Rigby had also been listening.

"When you're done with the copying, get back to the dock level and we'll begin search and scavenge."

After a while the two squads were reunited at the dock.

"Let's start our search at the material storage," Rigby said.

The storage bay was at the hangar level. Back in Sol it was just a big, empty room since they never had any spare materials. The Chenjesu had access to some invaluable exotic crystals which they used in their Broodhome vessels, so there was a slight chance of hitting the jackpot. In addition, the crystalline Chenjesu bodies also contained valuable materials, so finding a pile of dead Chenjesu would be like the silver lining in a dark cloud.

The team made its way to the elevator in darkness again. Now that they knew the elevator was working, they used it to reach the hangar level.

Once inside the hangar, they saw a beautiful sight. The view of the red-glowing planet was similar to the one back home, but since all the lights were out, it had a tremendous contrast. The glow even provided them with a little light.

"Beautiful," Witherspoon thought out loud.

"Stay focused, Claire," Rigby reminded her. *"You can return here with a set of oil colors when the mission is over."*

Soon they reached the vault door, which separated them from the material storage. The door looked like it could take a direct shot from the Vindicator.

"Well, we're here," Belov said. *"Now how are we supposed to open this thing?"*

"Like so," Rigby replied and theatrically pushed a button on the door console.

Nothing happened, except that a very faint red light started to flicker next to the button Rigby had pressed.

"Well?" Belov insisted.

"I don't know," Rigby answered. *"There's some kind of a lock activated."*

They all looked at the door. It seemed almost as if it was welded into the floor and ceiling.

"Uh, sir?" Witherspoon said.

"What?" Rigby bluntly responded.

"There's something moving on the ceiling," she reported with a frightened voice.

When they all looked up, several objects suddenly fell from the ceiling very close to them. Surprisingly, they landed softly. Then the objects stood up and drew out weapons.

It took a few seconds for everyone to realize that the team was now being held at gunpoint by armed mechanical guard robots.

"Rigby, do exactly as they want," Gruber quickly instructed.

Rigby slowly raised his hands in the air.

"Hands up, people," he suggested.

The robots immediately opened up a path between them towards the central elevator.

"They are Chenjesu droids and will not harm non-hostile targets," Gruber explained. "They probably have been programmed to guard the material storage."

"I think they want us to leave," Witherspoon guessed.

The droid closest to the door slowly moved forward, indicating the team to start moving.

"I think you're right," Rigby agreed and started walking, still holding his hands in the air. The rest of the team followed his example.

The robots carefully escorted them to the elevator. They themselves were too big to fit inside. When the doors closed, everyone lowered their arms.

"Phew," Cuvelier sighed, *"For a second there I was sure we were done for."*

"Captain," Rigby said, *"what do you want us to do?"*

"Take your initial positions at the dock," Zelnick ordered. "We'll come up with something and keep you informed."

The elevator reached the dock level and the doors opened. Several more droids were waiting for them there with guns drawn. Everyone raised their hands up again.

Now the droids opened up a path towards the shuttle.

"Uh, captain?" Rigby reported. *"I don't think we can fulfill that last order of yours."*

"Disregard that," Zelnick said. "Get back here. Abort the mission."

"Roger that," Rigby replied.

The droids then escorted the team all the way to the shuttle hatch. When everyone was inside and the hatch was closed, Belov looked through the air lock window again and noticed the droids still pointing their weapons at the door.

"I don't think they want us to return," Witherspoon deduced.

"Jenkins, get us out of here," Rigby ordered.

"I think we can assume that the robots won't allow us to scavenge any materials," Zelnick concluded.

"At least we got the data," Gruber said. "Maybe we can learn what exactly happened here."

Gruber, Zelnick, Rigby, and some science geeks were analyzing the data at the briefing room. Being a xenotech, Rigby had the best understanding of the assumed synthesis scheme of the Chenjesu and the Mmrnmhrm. Gruber had the best general knowledge of the races and several others were needed to go through the alien data. Zelnick merely wanted to keep tabs on things and was waiting for someone to explain their findings to him.

After the data was extracted and converted to human file structure, Rigby and Gruber very soon realized what the Chenjesu and the Mmrnmhrm were planning.

The process involved diffusing the Mmrnmhrm and using their advanced circuitry to enhance the Chenjesu bodies. The Chenjesu would also have to go through a series of very thorough surgical procedures. But no matter how they looked at it, it basically seemed like the Mmrnmhrm were sacrificed to turn the Chenjesu into some kind of cyborgs.

And what's more, the process was somehow designed to be completely passive, fueled only by the radiant energy of the Procyon star.

"So the Chenjesu make themselves into some kind of super-beings?" Zelnick processed the information out loud. "How is that going to help against the Ur-Quan?"

"It appears they have a new ship design as well," Gruber said. "The information here is sketchy, but if these numbers are correct, this new ship could have the potential to defeat any kind of ship in combat – although only in extremely competent hands. I'm not an expert in this, but I get the impression that controlling a ship like this requires a superhuman mind."

"And that is probably why they are doing the synthesis," Rigby concluded. "Sentient mechanical response and natural hyperwave communication merged together makes anything possible."

"However, there is no mention of how they are going to penetrate the slave shield," Gruber noted. "The only way to learn more is to ask them... And I don't see that happening unless we find a way to boost the power of our hyperwave transmitter by a huge factor."

Zelnick didn't follow.

"Because the Chenjesu can communicate naturally with hyperwave, they would hear our call if we could send it through the shield," Gruber explained. "Obviously, it doesn't do us much good to defeat the Ur-Quan if we can't figure out how to get rid of the slave shield around Earth."

"I see," Zelnick said. "Looks like we're going to have to manage without the Chenjesu for now. Do you have any idea how long their synthesis process is going to take?"

"It would have to be years, maybe even decades" Rigby speculated.

After a few hours they were on their way out of the system and it was time to test the ansible. If it worked, they would receive a message from Hayes in a few seconds…

And they did.

Without warning, a wall of text appeared on the ansible screen.

We have gotten the ansible transmitter up and running. From our end it seems to be working. Here's a report on what has happened here during the past week:

A previously unknown alien race has recently made contact with our base. They call themselves the Melnorme, and they are anxious to initiate trading relations with us. They seemed friendly, but were unwilling to deal with us here, claiming that we have no data they consider valuable. If you are interested, they suggest making contact with them in any super-giant star system.

The construction of the Amateras was finished yesterday. Christian Halleck has been assigned as its captain.

We are still receiving the signal from Rigel and have concluded that it is a distress call.

As discussed earlier, we will send a brief report every day at 09:00 and a more thorough report weekly, starting seven days from now.

That is all for now. Good luck to you.

"At least that works," Zelnick said in relief.

Gruber checked the star map.

"The only super-giant in our path is Alpha Illuminati," Gruber observed, "but it's in Spathi territory."

"I'd like to check the signal from Rigel first," Zelnick said. "Samusenko, what does our fuel reserve look like?"

"If we fly straight to Epsilon Gruis," Samusenko calculated, "then we would still have enough fuel to check both Alpha Illuminati and Rigel on our way back to Sol. If we go to Rigel next, we won't be able to make it to either Epsilon Gruis or Alpha Illuminati. If we go to Alpha Illuminati first, we might barely have enough fuel to make a stop both at Epsilon Gruis and Rigel, but that would be cutting it close, captain."

"I see," Zelnick replied. "I guess we'll go with the original plan then and visit Epsilon Gruis first. Relay the ansible message to the Tobermoon and the Star Runner."

Now they could only hope that the fleet they caught a glimpse of hadn't surrounded the Procyon vortex. They would soon find out since they were now ready to make the jump to hyperspace.

"Here goes…" Zelnick said. "Make the jump, Mr. Samusenko."

Stars stretched into long, thin stripes and space turned red. Then the stripes disappeared and they checked their surroundings.

The radar showed dozens of contacts, some of them closer than an hour away from the Vindicator.

"What the hell is this?" Zelnick demanded. "Samusenko, get us out of here! Steinbach, give her all you've got! Towards Epsilon Gruis!"

"Captain, the route is blocked," Samusenko reported.

"Give me manual control," Zelnick ordered.

Zelnick checked the radar again. A normal ship could never squeeze through the blockade. But the Vindicator wasn't normal. The fleet couldn't be prepared for their speed. Now they would just have to find an opening and fly through it before it closes.

Zelnick touched the controls and the Vindicator accelerated ferociously.

"There," he said and pointed at a small sector where there were no contacts.

Very soon the ships noticed where the Vindicator was heading and started to close the gap. But it looked like they were too late. The Vindicator was already storming forward at maximum velocity and the unknown contacts were rather slow. It might be close, but they should be able to break free.

"Captain," Dujardin said, "their speed matches that of the Ilwrath Avenger. It looks like they are all of the same type."

In a few minutes the Vindicator had cleared the blockade and the Avengers soon realized that chasing it was futile. The whole fleet then started moving in the direction of Epsilon Volantis, directly away from the Vindicator.

"Why would the Ilwrath be moving a fleet of this size so far out?" Gruber thought out loud.

"Didn't the Ilwrath whose ass we kicked in Sol say something about some, er, preying they were doing?"

"Ah, yes," Gruber remembered. "They mentioned the name Pkunk. Maybe we should look into the matter in the future."

"Fwiffo, is there anything you could share with us?" Zelnick asked.

"I haven't heard from the Ilwrath ever since they left Sol," Fwiffo explained. *"Maybe the high council at Spathiwa or some other fellow Spathi know something else."*

"We'll know in ten days," Zelnick replied.

CHAPTER 9

THE EVIL ONES

April 4th 2155, hyperspace, 148.3 : 309.1

After five days of flying through hyperspace they reached the border of Spathi territory. Compared to other species in the region the Spathi had a noticeably large sphere of influence with a diameter of nearly 200 hyperspace units.

"Ahh, home," Fwiffo said in an overly relaxed voice, even though nothing really changed as they entered their territory.

"Do you expect there to be lots of patrol ships?" Zelnick asked Fwiffo.

"Well, there are lots of ships," Fwiffo began. *"After all, we are trying to prepare for The Ultimate Evil making a sudden sneak attack. But I think that most of the patrols have chosen to stay close to home. Usually the world of Spathiwa is completely covered by orbiting Eluders."*

"What about yourself?" Zelnick continued, "What would you like to do?"

"Are you worried about me deserting?"

"It would seem logical."

"I see...You know, I HAVE thought about it, I admit. But then I saw the whole episode before my eyes: I would gloriously break away from your fleet and hide behind a wall of Eluders. You would shout at me for a while and I would pretend not to hear you. That part would definitely work. But then I would have to report to the officials back home. If I were to escape a gruesome punishment for leaving my post, I would at best be sent back to the mighty

Earthguard – to be alone and vulnerable again. So you see, Captain, I am much more comfortable with you."

"I'm glad we understand each other," Zelnick concluded.

They soon passed between the Herculis and Illuminati star clusters. In addition to those and their destination, Gruis, there were three other constellations inside Spathi territory: Squidi, Ceti and Vitalis.

They still had about three days' worth of travel left. Just as Fwiffo had anticipated, there were no patrols in sight.

Epsilon Gruis was a giant star, but since it was orange and the only planet was far from the sun, the system wasn't too hot. Spathiwa orbited the star well inside the hospitable zone. According to Fwiffo, it was a water world very much like Earth or Unzervalt.

Such a long cruise through hostile territory was wearing even though nothing seemed to happen – or maybe that was exactly why. They had to keep a high alert at all times and the crew had less time to relax.

Gruber had taken a habit of walking up and down the Spine as a way to pass the time and get some exercise. At some point he had realized that he was often being passed by joggers. Jogging had suddenly become popular. There hadn't been a chance for that back at the Starbase.

After the same person passed by him the fourth time – and saluted the fourth time – Gruber gave a permanent command not to salute while running in the Spine.

The space they had on the Vindicator seemed luxurious compared to the small hallways of the Earthling Cruiser. Fwiffo's Star Runner was still a mystery to Gruber, but the word was that it was no sugar and rainbows there either – although there was a ball pool on the bridge, probably used as a hiding place for the captain in case of boarding.

Reaching Epsilon Gruis without incident didn't seem to come as a surprise to anyone. Fwiffo kept reminding them that the system itself wouldn't be as quiet. And it's a good thing he did, because the sight came as a shock even though they knew about it in advance.

There were Spathi Eluders everywhere. It was like a swarm of insects on a calm summer evening at the terrace of a lakeside cabin. Spathiwa was barely visible under several layers of ships. Curiously there was an even more dense concentration of Eluders all over Spathiwa's moon.

The Vindicator had warped in somewhat close to the planet and a squadron of Eluders was already making their way towards them.

"They're hailing us," Katja soon reported.

Zelnick motioned to put them on screen.

Soon the link was established, but the screen was pitch-black. The Spathi might have used some kind of advanced encryption technology, but to Gruber it seemed more like they just kept their lights out.

"What is the secret cypher?" was asked from the darkness.

Thanks to Fwiffo, they knew about the cypher and were prepared.

"Once I've given you the Cypher, what do I get?" Zelnick asked the black screen in front of him.

"You get to live a bit longer," was the imminent and ominous response.

"Huffi-Muffi-Guffi," Zelnick then said in a confident tone.

The darkness didn't disappear immediately. Instead the lights were turned on very smoothly. They obviously weren't talking to just some random starship captain, but a roomful of important looking Spathi individuals.

"We are The Safe Ones –" one of them said, *"– the Spathi High Council. You have given us the correct Cypher and so you will not be destroyed immediately."*

Some of the council members seemed to be a lot more interested in their hats rather than the conversation.

"Now, if you please, tell us how you acquired our most Secret Spathi Cypher which every Spathi swears never, never to reveal, even when threatened with considerable pain."

"I suggest being honest with them," Gruber advised.

"I agree," Fwiffo butted in. *"They will not like you, but they probably won't attack either if you don't try anything tricky."*

Zelnick nodded.

"We met a Spathi in Sol and, uh… We became good friends!" he semi-truthfully said.

Another council member stepped up.

"And just where is this Spathi 'friend' now?"

"We have Captain Fwiffo right here, look," Zelnick proved and relayed the communication link to Fwiffo. "He can vouch for our good intentions."

Fwiffo was taken by surprise and didn't seem to understand that the link was already relayed.

"No! Don't put me on with THEM!" he frightfully screamed, but got no response from Zelnick.

Fwiffo trembled a while and looked everywhere for help. Then he suddenly froze and gazed directly at the camera.

"Fwiffo – is – not – here – right – now – please – leave – a – message."

It might have been convincing if he had done the act straight from the beginning. It was rather impressive really.

Zelnick gave Fwiffo a look which clearly indicated that if he didn't start co-operating in a matter of seconds, Zelnick would take the shuttle, board the Star Runner and give Fwiffo a painful smack on the head.

"Er..." Fwiffo hesitated, still not out of character.

The first council member took the 'microphone' again.

"If you held a weapon to Fwiffo's head, he would say anything you wanted him to say."

A third member of the council took off his hat and spoke.

"In fact, if you held a vegetable to his head, he would probably say anything you wanted him to say."

Then the councilman put on his hat again. It had to be admitted that the hat was indeed a thing to look at. It was so impressive that if you wore a hat like that at a bank, you could probably get your transaction processed without even showing your ID.

After it became evident that Fwiffo was going to be of no use, Zelnick took the stage again.

"We come in peace and with good will," he proclaimed.

There was a series of strange snorts.

"No doubt," the initial spokesman said.

"Do you find something amusing?" Zelnick asked in a slightly threatening way.

"'Peace', as you call it, is an illusion," the spokesman said. *"If you have 'peace', you simply haven't yet seen the thing that's trying to kill you. And 'peaceful missions' rarely require weapons large enough to punch holes through a small moon."*

"Whatever," Zelnick said, shaking his hands. "We got off to a bad start, so I'll try again from the top..."

He then straightened himself up and made a more serious face.

"We offer our hand in friendship. Join us and our **many allies** in the New Alliance of Free Stars... Together we can break free from the Ur-Quan's slavery!"

The council members looked at each other.

"We are too afraid of the Ur-Quan to consider such an alliance. They would most certainly punish us with extreme tortures."

Zelnick had just gotten in the zone and rode ahead with his momentum.

"We're stronger than the Ur-Quan. You're better off with us."

This time the reaction from the council was stunned silence for a while as they obviously contemplated whether Zelnick was serious or not.

"Hello?" One of them finally said. *"Hello! Awaken from your dreamy state, Hunam. Now is the time for realism, not wild fancy."*

There were a couple of snorts again, which seemed to annoy Zelnick.

"Yes we ARE strong enough!" he insisted. "Look at our Precursor vessel. Is it not unique?"

"Yes," the same individual sighed. *"Your vessel is unique. And here is the crux of the problem."*

The one talking twisted its claws as though it was trying to explain the problem by making a model of it from invisible wire.

"A `Unique', meaning 'singular', starship is not equal to the task of destroying the entire Ur-Quan armada."

Another fellow continued:

"If you had, say, ten thousand similar starships, we could take your boasts more seriously."

"Look," Zelnick tried, "what do I have to do to prove this to you – destroy your entire fleet?"

Many of the Eluders surrounding them made a series of reverse thrusts. The council members were whispering to each other. Soon one of them stepped up again:

"Well, that would probably work, but we have a better idea – a test"

One Spathi from the back leaned forward.

"One of those questy kind of things," it said.

A silence followed. All of the council members were watching Zelnick very closely.

"Well?" he asked. "What kind of a test did you have in mind?"

"You must wipe the ***'Evil Ones'*** *from the face of Spathiwa!"* the one from the back said, changing its voice much lower and clearer at the bolded part.

"Huh?"

"Oh, I forgot to tell you! We-" Fwiffo began, but Zelnick had to cut him out because the council continued.

"Let us explain the sad history of our species... Once upon a time, many thousands of years ago, we inhabited the warm, safe surface of our home planet, Spathiwa. We were happy and content. During those golden centuries, we evolved from a primitive nomadic culture into a complex, agrarian society. We learned to write on clay tablets and we were well on to being able to read those tablets when the Darkness fell upon us – when the ***Evil Ones*** *came!*

Creatures from the darkest pits of hell they were. They hunted our people – devoured them like tasty nodules and we had no defense against them. Suddenly, our culture became once more nomadic. We fled across the oceans, from continent to continent, but the ***Evil Ones*** *always followed. Spurred by our great need, we advanced from bronze to atomic technology in less than one of your centuries, but none of our innovations was a match for the* ***Evil Ones'*** *natural cunning and ferocity.*

Finally, with no other option available, we fled our world and took up residence here on our own moon where we have resided, most uncomfortably, for the last three hundred years."

Now that they looked at it, the Eluders really were actually protecting the moon rather than the planet itself.

"Okay, we accept your test," Zelnick agreed right off the bat. "We of course need all the information you have on these 'Evil Ones'."

"There isn't much," the same Spathi said. *"We have never quite figured out where they came from. The few specimens we collected, who had mostly died of tooth decay from eating sweet Spathi flesh, were physiologically unlike any other species from Spathiwa."*

"Send the information over," Zelnick requested

"Sure, sure, and there's no doubt that your 'friend' Captain Fwiffo can answer all your questions. Now then, if you'll excuse us, come back when the world of Spathiwa is free from the clutches of the ***Evil Ones****. Then we'll believe that we are safer with you than we are as a battle thrall of the Ur-Quan AND we will join your alliance."*

The one from the back spoke again:

"We wish you good luck in your courageous, yet foolish attempt. We will await your return with great anticipation."

The other one continued:

"Simultaneously, we will prepare a short, poignant eulogy to mourn your demise."

Immediately after that, they cut the transmission.

"Did they send us anything?" Zelnick asked Katja.

"Yes, the data is all here," she checked

"Get Rigby to analyze it," Zelnick said to Gruber.

"Aye, sir," he replied.

"Fwiffo, get over here," Zelnick commanded.

"I don't really know anything, but ok."

"Fwiffo, you could have TOLD US that your kind doesn't actually inhabit Spathiwa anymore," Zelnick said in an accusatory tone as soon as Fwiffo had entered the conference room.

"Yikes, don't hate me!" Fwiffo screamed and took a step back. "It never even crossed my mind! Living on the surface of Spathiwa is ancient history for a young Spathi like me. I didn't deliberately withhold anything from you, BELIEVE ME!"

“I forgive you,” Zelnick said understandingly, “if you tell us everything you know about these ‘Evil Ones’.”

Fwiffo retracted into his shell a little bit.

“You don’t expect me to face them?” he said with genuine fear in his voice, “…do you? I’d be much happier playing with Waffy-cards here, safely in orbit. In fact, I’m sure I’d be a lot more useful to you if I played with my Waffy-cards.”

With trembling arms Fwiffo took out a strange card deck from somewhere inside his shell and started shuffling.

Just then Rigby entered the room and saluted.

“That was fast,” Gruber said, meaning that Rigby had only had about an hour to go through the data on the Evil Ones.

“Aye sir,” Rigby replied, “first look at the data was enough to come to an important conclusion.”

“What conclusion?” Gruber asked.

Rigby displayed an autopsy report on the screen.

“Just like it says about a dozen times in this document,” he explained, “this species really is completely unlike any other species native to Spathiwa. And I don’t have to know the species of Spathiwa to tell you that.”

“What is that supposed to mean?” Gruber inquired.

“I’m telling you that nothing can naturally evolve into something like this,” Rigby explained. “This species is clearly hand-crafted for one purpose and one purpose only – hunting Spathi.”

The body in the autopsy report didn’t really look like anything. To Gruber it was just a pile of brown hair and some slimy substance.

“So let me get this straight,” Zelnick began. “Someone wanted to get rid of the Spathi so they made these creatures and dumped them on the face of Spathiwa?”

“We can only guess why,” Rigby answered. “But yes, that’s what I’m saying.”

"Who could be so cruel?" echoed from within Fwiffo's shell.

"Maybe we'll find out some day," Zelnick concluded the topic, "but for now let's concentrate on how to get rid of them."

"About that..." Rigby continued, "I am absolutely sure that this species is completely harmless to humans."

"Very interesting," Zelnick said, "please go through the data in detail and keep us informed."

"Yes sir," Rigby replied, "that was all I had so far."

He saluted and left the room. Zelnick turned to address Fwiffo.

"Fwiffo, how many — *what are you doing?"*

Fwiffo was completely retracted into his shell and the cards he was previously holding were being thrown out to the floor at a steady pace. A silent and frightened voice from within the shell answered:

"I can't look at the picture."

"What picture – oh – Gruber, would you mind?"

Gruber took the autopsy report off the screen.

"Now then, Fwiffo," Zelnick tried again, "how many of these 'Evil Ones' are there? Thousands? Millions? Billions?"

Fwiffo relaxed a little.

"The ancient texts describe a wave of pure evil covering the sun and wiping villages into nothingness in the blink of an eye," he explained. "Of course there might have been some exaggeration in the old clay tablets. The Evil Ones were never seen in two places at the same time so there probably was just one herd. I'd guess a hundred individuals."

"I see," Zelnick pondered. "Is there anything else you can tell us about them?"

"Well, they are a bit smaller than you Hunams," Fwiffo managed to say.

Zelnick was making up his mind about something.

"Fwiffo, wait outside for a minute," he then ordered.

"Okay," Fwiffo quickly replied and left the room. Now there was only Zelnick and Gruber.

"Maybe we should give Fwiffo a vacation," Zelnick suggested. "What do you think?"

"Do you mean like a 'shore leave'?" Gruber specified.

"What's a 'shore leave'?" Zelnick asked.

Gruber thought for a while how he would best explain it.

"It's a vacation."

"…That's what I suggested," Zelnick said.

"I think that he would not return," Gruber speculated. "But since we don't need deserters anyway, there's no real harm in trying."

"That's a good point," Zelnick agreed. "Fwiffo! Get back here!"

Fwiffo entered.

"I've got good news for you," Zelnick began and intentionally kept a long pause afterwards. "You'll get a shore leave – starting right now and ending when we are done with our business here."

"What's a shore leave?" Fwiffo asked.

"It means," Zelnick explained, "that you can go home and do what you want for a short while. We will contact you when you have to return to duty."

"Oh, okay…" Fwiffo processed the information. Then he raised his arms up, cried "yippee!" and ran out of the room.

Zelnick smiled.

"I hope he does come back," he said.

"Me too," Gruber agreed. "There's one thing I've been thinking."

"Just one?" Zelnick asked in a comical way.

"We have very sophisticated life form analysis features on board and we can keep captured specimens in suspended animation for a very long time."

"What's your point?"

"Do you trust the Spathi?" Gruber asked.

"I don't know, do you?" Zelnick replied.

"I trust them about as far as Eddie could throw them.* And that's why instead of killing the Evil Ones, I think we should consider capturing them. Then we'd have leverage against the Spathi if they choose to betray us."

"I like the way you think," Zelnick commended him.

The next day Rigby had retrieved all relevant information from the data pack. It was evident that the simple gun of the shuttle and small stun arms were all the armament they were going to need IF the Evil Ones weren't scattered all over the planet.

"Danielle, scan the surface for this particular life form," Zelnick ordered.

The Vindicator had very advanced surface scanning equipment capable of pinpointing life forms, energy sources and even mineral deposits from orbit in just a few seconds.

A 2D projection of the planet was displayed on the main screen. Soon several green dots appeared in a specific location on the shore of the biggest continent.

"That's all there is, sir," Dujardin reported. "There are 23 individuals, assuming there's no more on the other side of the planet."

"I presume the landing team is ready?" Zelnick asked generally.

"Yes sir," Gruber replied. "They are waiting for landing coordinates. Rigby is with them so we'll just have to give them targets."

"Very well," Zelnick said, "proceed with the operation."

---

* Eddie "Rocket Man" Wright was a promising javelin thrower in the late 21st century. Everyone expected him to win gold in the London Olympics in 2088 on his home turf, but due to a series of mishaps, his best throw was 12,82 meters.

Several alien containment units were loaded into the shuttle. The team was already aware of their simple, but unusual mission: Stun every 'Evil One' pinpointed by the Vindicator, drag their unconscious bodies into the shuttle, return to the Vindicator and place the specimens into the containment area.

Gruber gave the team their launch command and soon they watched the shuttle enter Spathiwa's atmosphere on a trajectory towards the bio-scan hits. When they were getting close to the ground, the view from the shuttle's cameras was relayed to the Vindicator. They were right on target.

Jenkins landed the shuttle near the shore. According to the bio-scan, the herd was under a kilometer away inland.

Rigby led the team out of the shuttle to establish a perimeter around it. Jenkins was constantly ready to take off and give air support. They weren't using their helmets since the air of Spathiwa was breathable for humans as well, although the oxygen level was somewhat higher than back on Earth. The planet was like another Earth, only with different inhabitants. There were plants, animals, and some weird apparently living organisms which couldn't very well be classified as neither.

The team walked in a line through thick woods. Most of them hadn't received any proper combat training. Those who had, had mostly died on Pluto. At least everyone knew how to use a gun – that was included in every training program in Star Control.

Soon they emerged from the woods into a clearing and saw their targets, right where they were supposed to be. They took a while to observe the Evil Ones from the forest line.

"Sir, are you seeing this?" Rigby asked.

"We are seeing it," Zelnick replied. "Proceed with the mission as planned."

Witherspoon had later described the mission as shooting teddy bears in a stuffed animal store, which was not far from the truth. The 'Evil Ones' didn't react to the approaching humans in any way. Rigby gave everyone their targets and in a few seconds they had stunned every one of the critters.

Specifically female members of the team had had a hard time moving the sleeping care bears into the shuttle - not because they weren't strong enough, but because they kept scratching the furry creatures and taking pictures.

Jenkins relocated the shuttle closer to the target area and all bodies were hauled inside in less than an hour. Then they took off and returned to the Vindicator.

"That wasn't hard," Zelnick stated. "Hundreds of years' worth of Spathi tragedy was solved in a few hours."

"I think it would be best not to tell the Spathi the details of this operation," Gruber suggested.

A few hours later the Evil Ones were in containment and the Vindicator was ready to give the high council a call. This time they didn't have to give the secret cypher – the lights were on from the beginning and the council room looked exactly the same. Everyone seemed to be present, except for the one who had the fine looking hat – or he had just taken it off. The council didn't seem too excited to converse again. However one of them politely stepped up and got straight to the point:

"How go your foolishly courageous and noble efforts to rid the ***Evil Ones*** *from our beloved Spathiwa?"*

Zelnick and Gruber had agreed to give only a very short version of what had happened.

"Although we lost many crew," Zelnick said very convincingly, "we have eliminated the scourge."

All talk within the council ceased.

"Can this be true?" The spokesman said. *"This is too good to be true! We will immediately check your statement*

in the traditional way. We will honor our encrustlings and the infirm elderly by sending them to the surface first. Please come back later when we have checked."

"How much later?" Zelnick asked, but the transmission was already cut.

Eight hours later they were ready for negotiations and Katja opened the communication link to the Spathi high council.

There was a party. Only one of the council members seemed to notice the incoming transmission. He wiped some indeterminate body fluids off his neck and shouted into the microphone:

"Oh joy! Oh happiness! We rejoice and make merry in celebration of our imminent return to our homeworld. You are most heroic and helpful - thank you, thank you, thank you! But now I must return to our festivities. It is my turn in the Ja-ja pole, you see. Please feel free to come back any time!"

He looked like he was about to cut the transmission again.

"Now wait just a moment!" Zelnick sturdily said and the Spathi froze. "I gather you have checked that Spathiwa is indeed cleared of the 'Evil Ones'?"

"Oh, well, yes. We are currently in the process of transporting Spathi from this unpleasant moon down to the safe surface of our beloved Spathiwa. We are grateful."

"So what about our alliance?" Zelnick asked.

The party came to a halt and everyone was now paying attention to the conversation.

"Why don't you just wait a while, until after we are resettled on our homeworld? We can discuss details at that time."

"And how long do you expect that to take?" Zelnick inquired.

The spokesman looked around.

"Ten, fifteen years tops."

Zelnick facepalmed.

"Just as you expected," he said to Gruber.

"Am I correct in understanding that you refuse to live up to your end of the bargain?" he asked the council.

A council member from the back answered this time.

"No, no, no! We are simply taking a more adult, `welcome to the real world' view of the situation. We cannot simply say, `Hurrah!' and form an alliance with you this very moment. Surely you see that?"

"You know what?" Zelnick began, "Those Evil Ones aren't actually dead. We have them in suspended animation. If you go back on your word, we would be forced to return the creatures to the surface. Surely you see that?"

The council members looked at each other in silence.

"Er... no, please," the one in the back finally said. The original spokesman continued with a sigh.

"Exactly what kind of a relationship were you thinking of?"

"You will join the New Alliance of Free Stars," Zelnick declared. "You will help us in our struggle to free the galaxy from the slavery of the evil Ur-Quan. You will be a part of a mutually beneficial alliance of minds and might! – a part of an egalitarian fellowship of sentient life forms!"

"Huh?" was heard from the crowd.

"Er... what?" the spokesman asked.

"The kind of a relationship," Zelnick put it simply, "where you do everything **exactly** as we say!"

"Oh... ok... we're quite familiar with that arrangement." the spokesman said. *"Very well... I bet we will regret this decision later on, but you leave me with no choice. We shall join your alliance of mutually egalitarian... and beneficial... might. I'm sure you will provide us with details."*

"That we will," Zelnick said and stood up smiling. "Welcome, allies!"

CHAPTER 10

FAIR TRADE ALIENS

April 10th 2155, Epsilon Gruis, 241.6 : 368.7

After long discussions with the high council, the Spathi finally understood all their new tasks and obligations. They claimed they didn't have much information or resources to spare, but agreed to send a delegation to the starbase in Sol with the blueprints for Eluders and a few qualified captains. They would receive an ansible at some point in the future.

The little information they did have on other races in the Hierarchy turned out to be rather valuable. They knew of a new battle thrall in the Draconis constellation that didn't participate in the Great War: The Thraddash, which they described to be weak and obnoxious. In addition, the Spathi noted that the Androsynth had been absent for some years now.

Although it didn't seem to have much strategic value, Zelnick was obsessed with the Spathi information on the Precursors. They believed that the Precursors hadn't really gone anywhere; they just used their superior technology to make them appear gone (a 'perfect invisibility shield' as the Spathi wistfully speculated). But more importantly, the Spathi said that they had been able to translate one ancient Precursor text which mentions a sequence of 10 artificial 'waste disposal sites' they built somewhere around this part of the galaxy. It was safe to assume that even the waste of the Precursors was invaluable.

When all formal things were said and done, Fwiffo was called back. To everybody's surprise, he actually showed up.

"Hello again, my Hunam friends," Fwiffo greeted them as he took his place on the bridge of the Star Runner. *"I am proud to be in your team. I don't know about the Safe Ones, but the commoners love you and, thanks to that, I was able to get the contact info of a highly fertile and extremely female individual."*

"Way to go, Fwiffo!" Trent cheered in a surprisingly friendly and familiar manner.

"So, Fwiffo," Zelnick began, "why **did** you come back? Surely that… female… would've been better company than us?"

"How true!" Fwiffo agreed. *"But alas, my sweet Snelopy didn't share my confidence in your good will. Being a perfectly raised Spathi, she suspected that if I deserted, you would punish me in a way which would result in collateral damage to her and her pretty garden."*

"She sounds like a good catch," Zelnick commented.

"She's also the offspring of someone who is close to the high council. Although I didn't want to hear it, she told me a rather disturbing rumor about the Androsynth... Have you heard?"

"Yeah," Zelnick said. "They told us."

"Oh, good. Being eaten alive is not something I'd like to think about – much less talk about."

"Eaten?"

"By the fish-folk."

"Fish-folk? What are you talking about?"

"Well I don't know if the Orz actually ate anybody, but they sure as hell did something creepy."

"Fwiffo," Zelnick said in a serious tone, "that's all news to us. Start from the beginning."

"Do I have to? It's scary!"

"Just take your time."

Fwiffo was obviously not happy about it, but nevertheless started explaining with a fearful voice.

"Snelopy told me that some fishy race called the Orz invaded the Vulpeculae star cluster a few years ago and that the Androsynth haven't been heard from since."

"Well that's worth looking into," Gruber stated.

"Is there anything else, Fwiffo?" Zelnick asked.

"Not from Snelopy. Oh, but I did hear something interesting from Phlendo, who also used to be in the Earthguard! He was sent to patrol near Umgah space after we learned that the Grand Master Planet Eaters, Jud the Ineffable Vug and Killmaster 18 had all been Umgah pranks.

But anyway, while in the region, Phlendo saw a new star appear between the Chandrasekhar and Circini star clusters! He said that it just appeared out of nowhere and three days later disappeared into nowhere again. And then he saw the Arilou."

Fwiffo seemed to have finished his story.

"The Arilou?" Zelnick asked. "What do you mean?"

"He told me that he hadn't told this to anyone else, but while he was waiting to see if the star would come back, an Arilou Skiff suddenly appeared in front of him. He said that he had panicked, set course for Spathiwa, jumped into his ball pool and remained there for the entire trip. That's all he told me."

"That's also worth looking into," Gruber said.

"Nice going, Fwiffo," Zelnick commended him. "We should send you out on recon more often."

The Vindicator didn't have much fuel to spare, but they still agreed that meeting with the Melnorme was worth a few extra fuel units and one day. After all it was pretty accurately on their way to Rigel and Sol.

After about a day in hyperspace they were getting near their target, a spectacular vortex leading to the super-giant star Alpha Illuminati. Just like at Zeeman, the huge star blocked their entire view when they still had a good hour to reach the edge of the vortex.

Alpha Illuminati was a red star so the contrast looked rather different in hyperspace when compared to the white light of Zeeman. Without the black outline of the vortex, you could miss the star entirely, although it wasn't exactly the same shade of red as the background in hyperspace.

Jumping to true space at a super-giant star was also an experience. First, in hyperspace, the huge star would slowly get closer and closer and then, when you reached the edge of the vortex, the star suddenly rocketed far into the horizon and you found yourself at the edge of the solar system in true space.

"Well, we're here," Gruber stated. "Now to find out if anybody's home."

They examined the system. There were seven planets whose orbits were at somewhat even intervals from the sun. Nothing seemed to indicate the presence of a ship seeking contacts… excluding the ship they just noticed hurrying towards them.

"Scan the ship," Zelnick ordered.

Soon a view of the ship's silhouette appeared on the main screen.

"That ship type is not in our data banks," Dujardin reported.

The silhouette was circular with a gray spectrum on visible wave-lengths and there were small rectangular parts on both sides of the ship. It was moving at a decent speed and seemed non-threatening.

"Katja, accept their transmission when it comes," Zelnick said.

"Aye, sir," she replied. "Actually, it's coming right now. I'm putting it on main screen."

They watched the screen, waiting for the visual link to be established. Meeting a new alien race would have been a huge event at the time of peace, but they had been so focused on their mission that they hadn't thought that much about this encounter.

According to the ansible message, the 'Melnorme', as they called themselves, wanted to establish trading relations. But right now the primary target was to make an ally out of them. The New Alliance of Free Stars would need all the strength they could get, and an unknown race could always be a black horse.

"Hello, Captain Robert Zelnick in command of the starship 'Vindicator'," a voice suddenly said. At the same moment visual link was established.

Gruber didn't want to think rudely, but the apparently living organism on screen didn't look like anything. It was an orange lump of what seemed to be organic material. In its defense one might say that it did have a mouth... and an eye – singular. In any case, it was far from being humanoid.

"I am Trade Master Greenish in command of the starship 'Inevitably Successful in All Circumstances'."

The translation computer either didn't have a sense of humor or had too much of it.

"Uh, hello," Zelnick managed to say. "I heard you were looking for us at Sol."

"Yes," the alien said. *"We are looking forward to an extended profitable relationship with you."*

"As are we!" Zelnick proclaimed. "We represent the New Alliance of Free Stars and are looking for allies to join our just cause to free the galaxy from the clutches of the evil Ur-Quan! What is your response?"

"I note your friendly gesture," the Trade Master said, *"but first you need to understand where we stand. We don't take sides in politics. Our goal is to gather information – primarily through trade."*

"This is not politics!" Zelnick tried. "The Ur-Quan will enslave you like they have done to a thousand species already. The only way to stop them is to forge a strong alliance!"

"I believe you, Captain Zelnick," the alien assured him. *"Our metachron has always been white, but when we recently entered this region of space, it started turning light grey. It is a device which predicts its own destruction. The darker it gets, the nearer its demise. If nothing changes, the metachron will be destroyed in about five years, give or take a few months."*

"So, there you have it!"

"I'm sorry, but we have no interest in this matter. Please, don't worry yourselves about our well-being. We have our ways of protecting ourselves."

"Well couldn't you help us in some other way then?" Zelnick innocently asked. "Like, do you have some information that would be valuable to us?"

The alien cheered up.

"Absolutely – for a price. Here everything is for sale. Since this is your first time doing business with us, let me explain how our system works. There are certain things we are interested in. If you are in possession of them, you can sell them to us. With the credits you accumulate, you can purchase something of equal value from us."

"That sounds simple," Zelnick said, having given up on recruiting the Melnorme. "So who judges the value of the commodities?"

"I do," the alien said in a matter-of-fact tone. *"I **am** the Trade Master."*

Gruber had had his suspicions about Zelnick when they first set off for their mission, but he had already learned to trust him. The captain seemed to be on top of things and his honest and innocent, but not gullible character had already proven to be effective. Gruber felt that there was no need to intervene.

"What if we don't trust your judgment?" Zelnick asked and crossed his arms, making himself look stubborn.

"Then you don't have to make the transaction," the Trade Master replied plainly, not at all annoyed. *"We are looking for a long-term relationship, because it is more profitable – for us both – than a quick rip-off deal."*

Gruber was taken aback by how convincing the trader was. Zelnick also seemed to buy it.

"So what are these 'certain things' you are interested in buying?" he asked.

"Our primary trade g—"

"Hey!" Zelnick suddenly exclaimed. "How did you know my name and the name of this ship?"

It hadn't occurred to Gruber either, but the alien had indeed known those names right from the beginning.

"Even before our first meeting, we knew of you," the alien mysteriously replied.

Somehow the self-proclaimed Trade Master constantly managed to keep an extremely friendly and non-threatening 'face'. It was a respectable feat with only a mouth and one eye sticking out from a lump of cheese-like substance.

"We gather information from a thousand secret sources in space and time. Our charge for revealing even one of these sources would be so high that your species would be in debt to us for centuries. Because of these superior sources, we are less interested in information about current events. We are mostly interested in biological data on alien life forms. However, we have recently learned that this region of space contains... 'strange' worlds... whose radiant energy defies all scanners, producing a rainbow-like image. These worlds are of great interest to us and thus we value highly the information on their coordinates."

"So if we find these 'rainbow worlds' and tell you where they are, we will get…?"

"You will get 500 credits. With 500 credits you could get, for example, 500 units of fuel, lots of highly useful information, or even modifications for your ship.

I'm sure your ship's data banks have information on some basic modules, but we have the blueprints for every module the Precursors ever used – including, but not limited to – much more powerful weapons."

"Alright," Zelnick said eagerly. "Shall we begin trading then?"

"Yes, let's get down to business," the trader joyfully replied, obviously entering its comfort zone. At the same time his bridge, or whatever the space around the alien was, turned from red to purple.

"Why did your bridge turn purple?" Zelnick asked.

The alien kept on 'smiling'.

"That's a good question with a very interesting answer! The fee for this information is 12,000,000 Credits."

"Well, we have these creatures we captured at Epsilon Gruis," Zelnick explained. "Does that count as 'biological data'?"

"Absolutely!" the Trade Master cheerfully said. *"We know where the creatures came from and that is why we are very interested in opening them up. If you give all their bodies to us, you will receive 150 credits."*

"How much is tha— Hey! How did you know what creatures I was talking about?"

"Once again, a very good question, Captain. Unfortunately, that information is worth more than 150 credits."

"So how much IS 150 credits?" Zelnick asked slightly annoyed. "What can we get with that?"

"Incidentally, 150 credits is the cost of designs for a new type of module for your ship. A piece of information relevant for you would cost around 75 credits on average. We also sell fuel for one credit per fuel unit."

"I see," Zelnick pondered. "We shall prepare the specimens you desire for transfer. If you can wait a while, we shall discuss our options here in detail."

"Of course, Captain. Please call us when you are ready for the transaction."

"Alright, thank you," Zelnick concluded. "Katja, cut the transmission."

Now they were by themselves again and Zelnick turned to Gruber for opinions.

"Judging by their characteristics," Gruber started making his point, "I'd say their prices are not negotiable. Since we have no particular use for the creatures, we should definitely sell them to these traders. As for our purchase… I think we should ask their opinion. If they know what information is relevant, they should also know what would be the best deal for us. If not, we should prioritize info on the Ur-Quan's current movements. Fuel and technology is something to think about in the future, but not now."

Zelnick nodded and then asked Trent for his opinion.

"I mostly agree with the First Officer," Trent explained. *"Ever since humanity's first wars, scouting has been at least as important as building an army. We can't fight our enemy if we don't know what they're doing."*

"What about that rumored 'super weapon' you once mentioned?" Zelnick asked.

"If it exists," Trent replied, *"we need to know what it is, where it is, and how to deal with it."*

Zelnick tapped the armrest of his chair.

"I have an idea," he proclaimed.

After the 'Evil Ones' were loaded into the shuttle, Zelnick ordered Katja to contact the Melnorme again. They answered immediately. Details of the docking procedure were given and soon the shuttle returned with an empty hold.

"Your balance is 150 credits," the Trade Master said. *"Do you wish to make a purchase?"*

"Yes," Zelnick answered and stood up. "Please tell us the most relevant piece of information about the current situation of races in the old alliance – and also the most relevant piece regarding the Ur-Quan."

"With pleasure! I will give you information on both of those subjects for 75 credits each. Do you agree?"

"Yes," Zelnick said, "please proceed."

"After you humans were defeated in the Great War, the Shofixti weakened the Ur-Quan armada by destroying their sun, Delta Gorno, while the invading fleet was inside the system. The resulting solar flare destroyed about 30% of the Ur-Quan forces and the Shofixti's home planet as well.

The Shofixti are thought to be extinct, but the truth is not so simple. Due to their short gestation and maturation time, only one individual of both genders is needed to resuscitate the species in a matter of years. And there still exists one male and several females alive.

You will find the last male orbiting their late homeworld Kyabetsu in a barely functional ship, whereas the females are a part of the menagerie of Admiral Zex at Alpha Cerenkov I."

The Trade Master kept a short pause and then continued with the other piece of information.

"The Ur-Quan are presently at war with a race called the Kohr-Ah. They are fighting within a large spherical region of space centered around the Crateris star group. Although it is probably too early to tell, it would appear that the Kohr-Ah are winning – largely due to the Ur-Quan losing so many ships at Delta Gorno."

The Trade Master fell silent and it didn't seem like it was going to continue.

"So who are these 'Kohr-Ah'?" Zelnick asked.

"Captain," the Melnorme paternally explained, *"your credit balance is at zero. The information I gave you is equally valuable to you as studying the creatures is to us. If you wish to purchase more information, you need to acquire more credits."*

"Can't you give as an advance?"

"No."

"But our cause is just!" Zelnick desperately tried. "Isn't altruism the highest pinnacle of morality?"

The bridge of the Melnorme ship turned blue.

"No, it is not." the trader said in a calm and scary, but still non-hostile way. *"In fact, in our culture, `giving' with no fair exchange of goods or services, is considered vulgar and inappropriate. Please do not mention this subject again."*

Gruber motioned Zelnick to drop it and he did.

"Okay," Zelnick wrapped things up, "so I understand that we should return when we have found these 'rainbow worlds' you mentioned, or have captured some other interesting species?"

The Melnorme bridge turned back to red.

"Yes, you definitely should! It has been a pleasure dealing with you, Captain Zelnick. We look forward to your next visit. Remember that you can find us at any super-giant star in this region."

"Goodbye then," Zelnick said and signaled Katja to cut the transmission.

"That was some heavy information," Gruber stated after screen had gone black.

"So who ARE these 'Kohr-Ah'?" Zelnick asked thinking out loud.

"There's an old Chinese saying…" Gruber began. "It's good to strike the serpent's head with your enemy's hand."

Zelnick had a blank expression which forced Gruber to try again.

"It means that the enemy of my enemy is my friend," he explained. "No matter what their motives are, uniting against a common enemy serves the interests of both parties. Anyway, the Ur-Quan fighting a losing battle is good news."

Trent joined in on the conversation.

"We should make contact with this 'Kohr-Ah' our top priority," he said.

"You're not suggesting we fly straight to the Crateris constellation, are you?" Zelnick asked in disbelief. "It's pretty damn far. We would need additional fuel tanks – full – just to get there."

"Not right now," Trent specified, *"but if we have a chance in the future and don't find any other way to contact them."*

"If we are to fly towards the Ur-Quan armada," Gruber speculated, "we have to be prepared for a quick getaway. That's why it would have to be done with this ship and none other."

"I agree", Trent said.

"So that didn't change our short-term plans, did it?" Zelnick pointed out. "What about the Shofixti? Are we in a position where we should worry about their resurrection?"

"Absolutely," Trent replied. *"The tactical significance of the Glory Device is beyond compare in battle."*

"And I can agree with the trader there," Gruber said. "If we can bring together two Shofixti of different sexes, the carnal gymnastics proceed and we'll have thousands of them in years – a lot faster if there are several females originally."

"And if that 'barely functional ship' the trader mentioned is a Shofixti Scout," Trent pointed out, *"it'll have its own designs in its data banks and we can start mass production."*

"So what was it about the menagerie where the female Shofixti supposedly are?" Zelnick asked.

"I don't know about any menagerie," Gruber began, "but Admiral Zex was the commander of the Vux fleet in the

Great War. It is said that the Alliance would have overrun the Vux without his ingenious tactics."

"I can confirm that," Trent continued. *"The Fortress Square and the Dynamic Triangle were his creations."*

Just then the ansible lit up and displayed a message – right when it was supposed to, only nobody had remembered to wait for it.

Captain Halleck and the Amateras are guarding the starbase. Our production rate is climbing and we have already begun constructing a new Cruiser.

The design plans for an ansible transmitter module for the Vindicator are ready. Dr. Fredrikson is eagerly waiting for your return so she can test the prototype.

We are still receiving the distress call from Rigel. That is all.

"Looks like we're ready to go to Rigel," Zelnick said. "Mr. Samusenko, get us out of here."

"Affirmative," Samusenko replied and steered the Vindicator towards the edge of the system. They were pretty far from the star already so they soon managed to jump into hyperspace.

"What's that?" Zelnick asked as soon as the scenery had turned red. He was pointing at the radar screen which showed a contact quite close to their position.

Dujardin watched it for a while and reached a conclusion.

"Its speed matches that of a Spathi Eluder," she reported. "It is moving on a direct trajectory from Epsilon Gruis towards Sol."

"Ah," Zelnick realized. "It's probably the delegation heading for the starbase."

"We can only hope," Gruber said.

CHAPTER 11

THREE-WAY INTERACTIONS

April 15th 2155, hyperspace, 226.1 : 292.9

Thousands of Ur-Quan Dreadnoughts were guarding something in a tight spherical formation. The fleet of the Alliance was forced to make a desperate attempt to break through. Every race of the old Alliance was there in their best ships: Yehat Terminators, Chenjesu Broodhomes, Mmrnmhrm Transformers, Earthling Cruisers, Syreen Penetrators, Arilou Skiffs and a swarm of Shofixti Scouts.

Just when the firing was about to start, a squadron of Spathi Eluders warped in and bravely stormed the Ur-Quan forces. The confusion broke the formation and Gruber saw a way through. He found himself flying a Shofixti Scout vessel which was, for reasons unknown, painted red.

The Ur-Quan formation scattered in front of Gruber like a school of herrings evading a predator. Gruber tried to activate the Glory Device, but couldn't move the last one of the three levers. Soon he had passed the Dreadnoughts and now saw what they were guarding. It was the Vindicator.

So that's their rumored 'super-weapon', Gruber thought and suddenly realized that he was all alone and actually flying underwater. The Vindicator didn't have any modules, but instead all the module slots were taken by an artillery battery. It all made sense now. The Vindicator wasn't unique and the Ur-Quan had modified it to fit their own needs.

Gruber surfaced and opened the cockpit hatch. He was on Unzervalt and his village hailed him as a hero. He entered his house and there he saw his wife, Lily.

An alarm went off. It was making a loud *BEEP* *BEEP* noise. Gruber felt like he had only seconds to live and Lily was suddenly almost a hundred meters away. He tried to run towards her, but his legs were too heavy to move. The sound of the alarm was getting louder and the world was falling apart.

Then he saw a bright white light which dazzled him. He noticed that the air was a lot cooler and the alarm wasn't as loud as he thought – it was actually quite a gentle sound. He was lying on his back in a room with walls made of metal.

His awareness was returning. The confrontation between the Alliance and the Ur-Quan felt too real to be dismissed as a dream. He tried to remember what had happened before the battle, but couldn't. He hadn't had any training for flying a Shofixti Scout, but the controls seemed so intuitive that no training was necessary. Surely a Scout could also fly underwater, right?

He wanted to accept that he had only been dreaming and tried to reason his way out. A long time ago a certain dream-psychologist had said that when backtracking your way in a dream, you'll either end up in an impossible situation or realize that you don't know how you got there.

Gruber remembered the Spathi Eluders making a brave offensive on the Ur-Quan forces and stood up. He took a shower, got dressed and made his way to the bridge. He was to relieve the Captain in less than ten minutes.

Rigel was an orange dwarf about 70 hyperspace units from Sol. It had one rocky planet close to the sun, one gas giant a little further and another gas giant almost as far as Pluto. The system was famous for the battles that took place there in the Great War.

After the Indi-Mira defense line had fallen, Rigel became the most important star of the coreward front. The Chenjesu made a valiant effort leading the remains of the Alliance to stand their ground much longer than had been expected.

The trench warfare at the Indi-Mira line had lasted for years, but the Ur-Quan clearly had other plans when Rigel was being besieged. When their march was brought to a halt, they immediately sent a large force to attack Procyon – probably after realizing that the Chenjesu were the key in the resistance. How Rigel finally fell remained a mystery. Nobody from the Alliance made it out of there alive.

"That was roughly 20 years ago," Gruber explained, "I don't see how there could be any survivors. Even if the life-support still functioned, they would have run out of food in a matter of months – a year or two at best."

"Humanoids, maybe," Zelnick pointed out. "But what about the Chenjesu and the Mmrnmhrm? How long can they survive without… food? Do they even eat?"

Zelnick had a valid point, but Gruber still didn't feel like accepting the possibility of rescuing Great War veterans.

"It is theoretically possible," he reluctantly agreed, "but I'm putting my money on coincidence. I assume that this distress call doesn't have anything to do with the history of the system."

"We'll soon find out, won't we?" Zelnick concluded the topic. "But hey, if there were so many battles, could there be something for us to salvage?"

The thought hadn't occurred to Gruber, because normally the victorious forces would salvage everything from a battle. The end of the war was far from normal, though. If the Ur-Quan were in a hurry, they might have just left the system full of debris.

"Now you've got my hopes up, captain."

They entered the vortex and emerged only a short distance away from the orbit of the furthest planet – which incidentally happened to be less than an hour away.

"Captain," Dujardin called out, "there is a significant amount of debris around that planet. I can't make out details from this distance, but there's a whole mess of objects of different sizes."

"Captain," Katja reported after Dujardin had finished, "we are receiving the signal now. It is definitely coming from the inner parts of the system."

The second planet was roughly 10 hours away.

"Let's go check the debris first," Zelnick ordered. "Mr. Samusenko, take us carefully to a safe observation distance in outer orbit."

The grim truth revealed itself little by little as they got closer to the planet. The orbit was like a starship graveyard. Most of the mass consisted of pieces too small to be identified, but there were some bigger parts as well.

"See those crystalline dodecahedrons over there?" Gruber pointed. "Those are parts of a Chenjesu Broodhome's propulsion system. And that long piece of metal? That's a part of a Cruiser's hull."

Dujardin zoomed in on the aforementioned piece and they could make out the word 'Minerva'.

"I remember Minerva and its captain Jacob Ismail," Trent commented. *"Ismail was a good man – someone you could count on."*

They kept on scanning for a while and found parts from Yehat Terminators and Arilou Skiffs as well. The more they searched, the more disturbing became the fact that they couldn't find any wreckage of Ur-Quan Dreadnoughts. There was no evidence that the Ur-Quan had even been there.

"Take a look at that," Trent pointed out and marked a rather large piece of what used to be a Broodhome vessel.

The part didn't look like it had been ripped off in an explosion. Instead, it looked like it had been sawn off. The edge was burned neatly in a cylinder shape.

"It's like a giant ball of fire went straight through that ship!" Fwiffo commented with an alarmed and trembling voice.

"Fwiffo is right," Trent said. *"Whatever did that was no Dreadnought."*

"Look there!" Dujardin blurted out probably a lot louder than she intended.

There was an intact bridge of a Cruiser. Dujardin zoomed in and they could see through the windows – and soon wished they couldn't. There were frozen corpses floating around. At least some of the crew were probably still alive after their ship had been defeated.

Zelnick turned to Gruber.

"What should we do?" he asked.

"I don't mean to be blunt," Gruber said, "but some of this scrap we've seen is highly valuable – especially that part of the Broodhome's thrusters. We should take our time and fill our storage bay with these wreckages."

"Should we check the source of the signal first?" Zelnick suggested.

"Maybe," Gruber speculated, "whichever you consider to be of higher priority."

"I think we should do business first and salvage later," Zelnick said. "Afterwards we'll have plenty of time and no other agenda than returning to Sol."

"That sounds reasonable," Gruber agreed.

After a few hours of flying inwards in the system, they could tell that the signal's source was beyond the second planet, probably at the first one. The signal itself was a common invitation or distress call, depending on how you viewed it. The content could be deciphered to something like "Anyone who hears this, please come here."

There was also some debris around the second planet, but not nearly as much as they had previously seen around the third one. Now they could pinpoint the signal to the first planet which was only an hour away from the second.

Slowly the innermost planet came into view. Compared to the other two it was very small, as terrestrial planets usually are when compared to gas giants.

"There's a ship on the radar," Dujardin reported. "It's orbiting the first planet."

It was still too far away to see what kind of a ship it was, but very soon it became evident that they were once again meeting a previously unknown species.

The ship's design didn't resemble anything they had previously encountered. It was small and round and had several parts that looked like robotic arms. It actually made it appear a little like a spider, but it only had those arms in the front.

"Well it wasn't a derelict Chenjesu," Gruber stated, maybe even slightly disappointed.

"Try to contact them," Zelnick ordered and Katja hailed them on a common frequency.

"They responded right away," Katja reported and opened the link.

On the screen were three small creatures, each more strange than the last.

"Attention starship,"

the one in the left said. It was green and looked like a cross between a swan and a grasshopper without legs.

"Make no hostile actions!"

the one in the right continued. It was blue and looked slightly like a jack in the box without the box. It had a spring and a head, nothing else.

The third one, in the center, was brown. It had one big eye in its round head and a mane of some sort. If you had to venture a guess, it probably moved similarly to a snail.

"We had already given up hope of anyone responding to our call."

"Some of us had."

"We are the Zoq-Fot-Pik. We come in peace and with good will."

"But if you make one false move, you're vapor."

"Don't worry; my companion is just a bit nervous."

"No I'm not!"

"and argumentative"

"No I'm not."

The brown one kept quiet. His eye was constantly fixed on the one who was talking.

"Why did you send the distress call?" Zelnick asked.

"We seek help."

"We only need a LITTLE."

"We are in a desperate situation."

"'Desperate' is too strong a word. I think 'troublesome' is more like it."

"We represent The New Alliance of Free Stars," Zelnick proclaimed. "I am Captain Robert Zelnick of the starship Vindicator. We might be able to help you."

"Hurrah! Then we've finally found our saviors!"

"Maybe."

"At last, our search is over! It is just as the great Crystal ones promised!"

"They look sneaky. I think they're lying."

"Quiet, fool! Can't you see our nightmare is over? This ship is from the Great Crystal One's fabled alliance – The Alliance of Free Stars!"

"Maybe."

"Are you talking about the Chenjesu?" Zelnick asked.

"Yes! They told us about the alliance a long time ago."

"But when we finally decided to join, the Chenjesu had already vanished."

"We couldn't contact them anymore and were left alone."

"So now we finally came here ourselves to look for their alliance."

"This was the only place they had mentioned. We didn't know where else to go."

"And then we saw all that wreckage."

"We didn't know what to do so we just stayed here and broadcast an open invitation."

"I wanted to go home a long time ago, but SOMEONE insisted that we stay here for

'just a little longer' – weeks ago!"

"Is that 'someone' supposed to be me?"

"Yes, and if these guys hadn't shown up today, I would've jumped on you and taken us home with or without your consent."

"What 'nightmare' were you talking about earlier?" Zelnick rather hastily asked, not wanting to see the aliens fight with each other. "What's the matter?"

"Our planets are under attack from an invading horde!"

"We do not know who they are, or why they are here."

"Some of the vessels are huge, green battleships which launch wave after wave of small fighters."

"The other ships are black as space and their hulls are carved with strange alien writing."

"We are being blown to bits."

"Fleets of these ships appear out of nowhere and unleash terrible destructive energies."

"Fortunately..."

"...they release these energies on each other."

"Unfortunately..."

"...they favor combat near strong gravity wells. Their stray shots regularly strike the

surface of our planets, often with tragic results."

"Fortunately..."

"...they have never found our homeworld, only our colony planets."

"Unfortunately..."

"...all of our colonies have perished as a consequence."

"Those green ships are Ur-Quan Dreadnoughts," Zelnick explained. "The Ur-Quan are our enemy as well. You should join the New Alliance of Free Stars immediately."

"These are the words we have prayed for!"

"Hey! This trip's not a waste after all!"

"But we are only emissaries. You must meet with our leaders. They are wiser... more powerful beings!"

"They look just like us, though."

"So where do we find your leaders?" Zelnick asked.

"We hail from the green dwarf star at coordinates ziggerfau-gerrrnuf, Ah-ah, Pahoy-hoy."

"No, you idiot, in their coordinate system!"

"Oh! Er... Coordinates 400.0 : 543.7."

"The planet closest to the sun is our home."

"That's Alpha Tucanae," Samusenko checked. "These guys have come a long way to ask for help."

Zelnick checked the star map and had to agree. No human had ever been that far towards the galactic core.

"You fellows are far from home," he commented.

"That is true."

"We have travelled far through hostile, uncharted space."

"To find you."

"Don't take this the wrong way," Zelnick began ominously, "but are you part of the same species or… er… are you three different species?"

"I'm just curious!" he quickly added.

"Ah, a good question."

"The crystal guys were also interested in that!"

"In our ancient past, four species evolved intelligence on our homeworld."

"Simultaneously."

"They were the Zoq…"

"…the Fot…"

"…the Pik…"

"…and the Zebranky."

"We three, the Zoq, Fot, and Pik evolved in such a way as to acquire sustenance from many sources..."

"...from airborne zooplankton..."

"...from solar and ambient energies..."

"...and from rocky fungal clingers."

"Our favorite!"

"The Zebranky also consumed a variety of foods – namely: the Zoq, the Fot and the Pik."

"To survive the predations of the Zebranky, we banded together, annihilated the Zebranky..."

"...and formed the cooperative union you now encounter."

Zelnick seemed to be very interested.

"Who's who?" he asked.

"He is Fot–"

"No, she is!"

"No I'm not!"

"Yes you are."

"Cripes! We've been through this a million times!"

"That doesn't change anything. You're the Fot."

"Faugh! Well, Captain, as you can see, this is a point of some contention."

"Fot!"

The brown one still hadn't joined in on the conversation.

"Does that guy in the back ever say anything?" Zelnick asked.

"Nope."

"Not a word."

Zelnick couldn't seem to think of anything to ask right away so the aliens seized their opportunity to ask questions.

"Captain Robert Zelnick of The New Alliance of Free Stars, could you please tell us

what happened in this star system?"

"Yeah, and why did the crystal ones disappear?"

Zelnick told them the whole sorrowful story.

"So this is not the same alliance the Chenjesu represented when they contacted you," he concluded his explanation. "But our goal hasn't changed! We are still standing to defend the galaxy against the slavery of the Ur-Quan."

"That is dreadful news."

"Yeah, and a real bummer what happened to the Chenjesu. I really liked those guys. And if we ever see them again, they'll be some weird cyborgs!"

"If only we had acted sooner, we could have helped the alliance."

"OR we would now be enslaved as well."

"In any case, we need an ally to help us survive in this hostile universe."

"We are having some problems of that general nature."

"So what are YOU going to do now?" Zelnick asked.

"I guess we'll return home and tell them to expect you."

"Are you crazy! If these guys are going there anyway, we should join up with them."

"We can't do that! We'd only slow them down."

"Hey now," Zelnick interrupted, "we would gladly take you on board, but we can't fly to Alpha Tucanae right away. We must first at least return to Sol and figure out where to get enough fuel for such a trip."

"We understand. I'm sure your huge vessel uses a lot more fuel than our small Stinger."

"It's not THAT small."

"But if it really is okay with you, we would like to join your fleet and assist you in any way we can."

"Yeah, I'm pretty darn mean in a fight! There ain't nobody better than me with a thrusting stinger tongue attack!"

"Ha-ha, I'm sure there isn't!" Zelnick laughed in a sincere way. "We are very interested in hearing about the capabilities of your Stinger starship. Welcome aboard! We'll just do some scavenging here before setting course for Sol. I should now introduce you to the other captains of our fleet."

Zelnick added Trent and Fwiffo to the conversation.

"Hello, I am Matthew Trent, captain of the Tobermoon."

"I am Fwiffo, captain of the Star Runner."

"Hello! I am Dip."

"I am Pak."

"And he is Por. We are in command of the starship Voyager."

"Pffft," Gruber barely managed to hold his laughter which Zelnick noticed.

“What’s so funny?” he asked.

“Sorry, sir,” Gruber apologized. “It’s just that history knows of quite a famous starship by that name. I’ll tell you about it later.”

CHAPTER 12

THE THIRD MISSION

April 20th 2155, Sol, 175.2 : 145.0

The starbase was more alive than ever. In addition to the reluctant Spathi volunteers, the crew of the Voyager was also exploring the corridors in their flying saucers. Apparently the green members of the Zoq-Fot-Pik union were the only ones who needed assistance moving around, but, in the name of equality, they all moved using their floating platforms, which Junior Scientist Edward Hawkins had named flying saucers.

Gruber's task at hand was to figure out the right questions to ask the Spathi. The Spathi didn't speak much unless spoken to and they mostly spent time in their own group. Whenever Gruber needed to find them, he first checked the hangar, because that's where some of them always were – admiring the view as they said. And they always seemed quite busy doing it.

The Spathi delegation consisted of their spokesperson Snurfel, several starship captains and a few individuals whose purpose remained unknown. Currently Gruber was interviewing Snurfel in a conference room with no others present. He had already learned that the 'Bugsquirt' system, where Fwiffo remembered the Syreen to be imprisoned, was actually Betelgeuse and that the Syreen were indeed slave-shielded like humans.

"There's just one thing that has been bugging me," he began. "If you, as a species, are such cowards as you say, why did you fight for the Ur-Quan?"

Snurfel was enjoying the hospitality of the humans to the fullest. He* had specifically taken a liking to apple juice, which he was currently slurping.

"We didn't fight THAT much," he pointed out. "We tried to avoid combat as much as possible, but the Ur-Quan didn't take it very well. They gave us three warnings, each more strident than the last. After the third one it became evident that there would be no fourth warning – simply annihilation – so we **reluctantly** assumed our new role as one of the Ur-Quan's thugs."

"I believe that you didn't like it," Gruber assured him, "but that's not what I was after. Why did you choose the role of a battle thrall and not imprisonment like we did?"

"Oh, I see," Snurfel replied. "That is a sad tale, so don't even try to contain your tears."

He took one last sip from his juice, sat back and started his explanation.

"After the Ur-Quan demolished the Ilwrath, they turned the force of their Armada against us Spathi. The term 'rapidly subjugated' would best describe what happened next.

When the Ur-Quan arrived at Spathiwa, there was a great ceremony. Part of that ceremony involved blasting portions of our planet's surface into radioactive dust and this part we did not enjoy.

But the worst was yet to come. Our leaders were called into the command chamber of Ur-Quan Lord 1's

---

* Further examination of their species revealed that the Spathi didn't have genders in the same way as humans. Thomas Rigby simplified the concept with a model where each individual was 0-100 % male and 0-100 % female, sometimes, but not always, adding up to 100 %. It was then decided that if an individual was over 60 % of either gender, they would be called 'he' or 'she' respectively, and if neither gender reached 60 %, they would be called 'it'.

Dreadnought where they were read a long and complicated document explaining the choices given new slaves. When our leaders heard the term ‘forever encased’ and ‘impenetrable shield’ they grew over-excited, I'm afraid, and made a fatal error.

The decision was to be transmitted to the Ur-Quan via one of two rods, one colored black and the other one white. Our leader handed the white rod to one of the Ur-Quan's servants, signifying `Fallow Slavery', but the servant somehow exchanged rods and handed the Ur-Quan Lord a black rod indicating our desire to become fighting slaves!

By the time we learned of the switch, it was too late – the Ur-Quan would not permit a change in status. Oh, how I remember that day all too well. Worst day in the history of our species that one was. We had already begun tearing down our starship factories and were in the middle of a 6-day festival when the news was broadcast.”

Snurfel was barely holding himself together. Gruber almost felt guilty for not crying.

“Did you ever find out anything about the rod exchange?” he asked. “Was it a mistake or intentional?”

Snurfel was leaking some white body fluids from the corner of his eye.

“Well, the servant who made the exchange was an Umgah,” he explained. “Since they have always tricked us… I mean **tried** to trick us with all kinds of pranks, we could only assume that they switched the rods on purpose.”

“That sounds like the Umgah all right,” Gruber agreed.

“Not too long ago we managed to catch them in the act,” Snurfel proudly said, wiping his fluids with a handkerchief. “They were using an extremely powerful hyperwave caster to impersonate a being of higher existence called Jud the Vug. We were already, in horror, doing rituals in its name when it suddenly said something in a different voice and then repeated the same with the original voice. It went something like this:

**Harharhar* tell them that only half of them may live.*

Only half of you may live!

*And that *hee-hee* they have one day to decide which half.*

You have one day to decide who lives and who dies!

Then one of our bright minds realized that Jud the Vug was actually Umgah in disguise and that the pranksters had forgotten to turn off the microphone in their caster in the mean time! We were able to locate the device and take it from them, thus ending our torment. The Umgah haven't bothered us since."

"So do you—" Gruber began, but then realized that an exceptionally powerful hyperwave caster was exactly what they needed to contact the Chenjesu through their slave shield.

"Do you still have the caster?" he asked.

"Yes, why?" Snurfel replied.

"We might have a use for it. We need you to deliver it here to this starbase as quickly as possible."

"Oh, okay… Just don't let the Umgah get their hands on it again."

Zelnick and Hayes were watching the maintenance robots when Gruber joined them after his interview. The robots were being configured for building Spathi Eluders. Hayes was overseeing the process and Zelnick was with him merely because he couldn't think of anything better to do.

"Betelgeuse, huh?" Hayes commented after Gruber had given his report. "It's conveniently on the way if you stop by at Vulpeculae first and Tucanae afterwards."

"We'll be needing a lot more fuel," Zelnick pointed out. "One full fuel tank module won't be enough."

They looked at the star map on Hayes' mobile device.

"I doubt even two will be enough," Hayes calculated. "If you take this route here…"

Hayes drew a route into the star map.

"…Eta Vulpeculae – Betelgeuse – Alpha Tucanae – and then the Arilou sighting somewhere between Circini and Chandrasekhar clusters… That trip would take about 120 units of fuel."

"So we'll need three tanks, preferably full," Gruber concluded. "Do we have the resources for something like that?"

"I'm pretty sure we have," Hayes estimated, "but then we would have to postpone our plans for building a fleet."

"Not more than a week if we send the Amateras on a scavenging mission to Rigel right away," Gruber said. "I'm sure Captain Halleck is eager to get something to do."

"Scavenging, you say!?" Halleck exclaimed without even trying to cover his disappointment.

Christian 'Unsinkable' Halleck was very much like Trent, except that he was neither a tactical genius nor a very pleasant man. However he had a respectable skill for survival, thus the nickname, so he wasn't a bad choice for a captain.

Hayes had summoned Halleck to the conference room where Gruber and Zelnick were giving him details on the mission to Rigel.

"I guess I'll have to cope with that for now," Halleck continued. "Is there anything else?"

"There's one other thing you could do," Gruber said, thinking about what he had agreed on earlier with Hayes and Zelnick. "We have learned that a single Shofixti male can be found in orbit around their homeworld in a barely functional ship. You should rescue him as soon as there are enough materials for another Cruiser. And keep him alive at all costs."

"That's quite a trip for rescuing one individual," Halleck said with suspicion in his voice. "Who is that guy?"

"We don't know," Gruber answered truthfully, "probably just some old warrior with a death-wish. But if we ever acquire Shofixti females, he's going to have a busy time."

"So you're expecting me to go near a Shofixti Scout whose pilot is tired of living?" Halleck clarified while making a 'boom' effect with his hands.

"Yep," Gruber replied. One should always give an answer whose level is equal to the question. "I dare say you are exactly the right man for that job."

"No, I am the man who doesn't do jobs like that."

"You g—" Gruber began, but Zelnick butted in.

"Don't worry," he said. "If the Shofixti wants to die AND has a functional Glory Device at hand, I doubt he—"

"I know, I know," Halleck interrupted. "The Amateras is ready to take off whenever you want."

Two hours later Gruber watched the Amateras set sail dragging a hastily assembled barge for the scavenged materials. The service robots were constructing the additional fuel tanks and the ansible transmitter module was being installed into the Vindicator.

The installation of the ansible module had taken a lot more time than anticipated since it wasn't Precursor design. Although they didn't have to worry about integration with the ship's computer, because it was a 'dumb' module, as Fredrikson had explained, some improvisation was still required. It was basically a modified storage module filled with ansible equipment. The link from the module to the bridge was made with human technology – by routing a cable through the corridors.

Gruber didn't have any more pressing matters to attend to, so he decided to find Veronica and talk things over. As he entered the main elevator, he realized that he hadn't thought about the upcoming conversation at all and that he wasn't any wiser than the last time they met. After he got out of the elevator he had about 20 meters to figure out his own thoughts.

At the door to Veronica's quarters he merely hoped that she would have some answers.

Seven hours later Gruber woke up. He tried to figure out where he was and how he had got there. His right arm was numb as someone was sleeping on top of it.

After a while he knew where his dreams ended and reality began. For a second he thought about getting up, but he decided to just release his arm instead. He found himself comfortable. He hadn't been at all interested in a relationship on the starbase earlier and wondered what had changed.

It was hope.

Before the arrival of the Vindicator they'd had none. Even a small glimpse of it makes a person do so much more. And that's what they had now – infinitesimal odds, but still more than zero.

The person next to Gruber mumbled in her sleep. Soon she turned around and put her arm over Gruber's chest. He continued to feel comfortable. It had been so long since he had felt the warmth of a woman. He decided to lie there and enjoy the moment while it lasted. He didn't plan on sleeping anymore.

Two hours later he woke up again and Veronica's face was right above his.

"Good afternoon, Chief of Staff and First Officer of the Vindicator Adam Gruber," Veronica said with a smile.

Indeed it was afternoon. Time seemed to pass a lot faster here, in this room, compared to aboard the Vindicator when monotonously cruising through hyperspace.

“Afternoon, ma’am,” Gruber replied and reached for his communicator, which wasn’t in its usual place since he wasn’t in his own room. He realized that it must still be in his pants’ pocket, so the obvious next task would be to locate the pants.

“I’d better check if I’m needed somewhere,” he said as he got up and spotted his pants in the corner of the room.

“You are needed somewhere,” Veronica seductively said and it took a few seconds for Gruber to get the hint.

For once the communicator didn’t show any new messages. And since he was asking for it, he got a message just then. For a split second he cursed the sender, but then he actually read the message. It was just a notification about a briefing which was to take place in five hours. There was no need to rush and since Gruber still didn’t have anything to do, he put the communicator on the table and went back to bed.

The briefing room was more crowded than usual. In addition to those who were there the last time, there was now a delegation of Spathi and the commanding trio of the Voyager.

The Vindicator looked different. The original fuel tank in the fifteenth slot was now accompanied by two more of its kind in slots 13 and 14. Since they were all at full capacity, the ship now held 160 units of fuel. Gruber wondered if any ship had ever had that much fuel in its operating tanks.

The ansible was installed in the fifth slot, behind the crew module. They preferred to mount it in the first available slot, but since they wanted to leave the first three open for weapons, it had to be the fifth.

Hayes did most of the talking after Fredrikson’s lecture. A star map was projected onto the screen and Hayes drew the planned route of the Vindicator there. It was as they had agreed earlier.

First – they would fly to Eta Vulpeculae to investigate what had happened to the Androsynth. Second – they would fly to Betelgeuse and make contact with the Syreen. Third – they would proceed to Alpha Tucanae to make a formal alliance with the Zoq-Fot-Pik. And finally – they would check the area between the Circini and Chandrasekhar star clusters where the Arilou had supposedly been sighted.

It was a very long trip. The flight time in hyperspace alone was nearly two months. Reaching Eta Vulpeculae would take 10 days alone.

"The only thing we know about the Androsynth is what our Spathi allies have told us," Hayes explained and Snurfel was looking rather pleased with himself. "There have been no sightings of the Androsynth in a few years and their space is currently occupied by a race calling themselves the Orz. While it's in our best interests that the Ur-Quan battle thralls are fewer in number, we advise caution when dealing with a race that has so quickly and silently invaded Hierarchy territory."

"Shouldn't we consider them potential allies for now," Zelnick pointed out, "like the Kohr-Ah, who are fighting the Ur-Quan directly?"

"And while we're on the subject," Trent commented, "the Crateris constellation is not too far from Alpha Tucanae where we are heading. I think while we're that far out already, we should try to seek out these Kohr-Ah."

These matters had been discussed earlier behind the scenes, but now was the time for everyone to join in and give their opinions.

"You both have a point," Hayes agreed. "Allying with the Orz is of course a priority, but you are the ones who will have to make a judgment call about that."

He looked directly at Zelnick before turning his attention to Trent.

"And about the Kohr-Ah… I still feel we are too vulnerable to risk confrontation with the Ur-Quan. I think we shouldn't take that risk until we are strong enough to stand our ground."

Dip and Pak of the Voyager joined in on the conversation.

If the black ships fighting the Ur-Quan near our worlds are these 'Kohr-Ah', I'd like to point out that they are just as bad.

Yeah, they don't care for our well-being at all!

In fact, I'm pretty sure that the green ships have never fired at our planets on purpose.

*But the black ships destroy everything in their path, including – but not limited to – the grand frungy stadium of our first colony *sob*.*

A gush of steam came out of Pak's nostril-equivalents. The brown one, named 'Silent-Por' by Zelnick, closed its eye at the mention of the stadium.

"Okay…" Hayes uncertainly began. "Whatever you decide to do is ultimately up to Captain Zelnick. I'm sure you'll be a lot wiser when you have contacted the Zoq-Fot-Pik homeworld."

It's the best place!

"With our current strength," Zelnick said, "I still wish to avoid all confrontations. We will stick with the original plan unless something unexpected happens."

Trent accepted Zelnick's decision. Gruber thought that if it was Halleck, they would spend hours arguing. In fact, ever since the beginning, Halleck seemed to have had a problem with a young man such as Zelnick being in command of the whole operation. Gruber was glad that the Cruiser flying with the Vindicator was the Tobermoon and not the Amateras.

"If there are no questions," Hayes said while looking around, "we can bring this meeting to an end. The time of your launch is up to Captain Zelnick."

"We shall leave in two hours," Zelnick immediately announced.

Gruber had all his stuff already packed so he went straight to the hangar to wait for the shuttle. The Spathi delegation was looking at Earth very carefully again. Gruber approached them.

"Why are you always observing Earth like that?" he asked the Spathi closest to him with nothing but curiosity.

"Eek!" the creature squeaked. "Don't sneak up on me like that!"

Gruber patiently waited for an answer.

"Did you need something?" the Spathi asked, which made Gruber slightly annoyed.

"I asked…" he said and took a deep breath, "what is it that you are always looking at here?"

Now every Spathi froze and turned to look at him.

"What are we looking at?" the Spathi closest to him repeated. "Are you implying that we are up to something? – That we have some kind of a secret plan? Well you're wrong!"

He waved his claws around and the pitch of his voice got higher.

"Our feelings are injured by your unwarranted accusation! Apologies would be appropriate at this time."

He intensely looked at Gruber's surprised face, trying not to tremble, which made him tremble even more. Gruber was at a loss for words.

"Er… okay?" he eventually replied. "I wasn't accusing you of anything, though. I'll just leave you to it."

He turned around and started to walk away. Soon he heard a quiet "phew" behind him. *The Spathi are weird, yes, but Hayes should still probably know that they are keeping some kinds of secrets.*

"Hey, Gruber!" Zelnick suddenly called out from a little further away than seemed appropriate. He then quickly approached Gruber.

"Captain," Gruber responded.

"You don't have anything to do here before we leave, right?"

"Not really."

"Good, I was thinking you could tell me about the Syreen and maybe a little about the Androsynth and the Arilou as well."

"Of course, Captain. What do you wish to know?"

"I'm sure that during our trip there will be plenty of time to tell me everything, but for now let's start with the most important stuff. All I know is that the Syreen are blue humans with psychic powers, the Androsynth are high quality humans without psychic powers and the Arilou are little green men in flying saucers – mental powers unknown."

"I see you already know the basics. We still have over an hour so should we go sit down somewhere?"

"Sure. How about there?"

Zelnick pointed at the hangar control booth.

"Oh, hi Bob… and chief," Dave greeted them as they entered the booth. At least this time he was where he was supposed to be. "Is there something I can do for you?"

"Not this time," Zelnick said in a friendly manner, "we're here merely to sit down and tell stories."

"To me?" Dave laughed, but clearly hoped that this was the case.

"Nah, Gruber's going to tell me about the Syreen and stuff."

It seemed to Gruber that Zelnick and Dave were quite well acquainted, probably thanks to Dave's infamous video collection.

"Well then," Dave began, "have a seat and don't let me bother you. Imagine I'm not here."

They sat down and Zelnick was obviously waiting for Gruber to start, so he did.

"Did you know that originally women weren't allowed aboard ships – sea ships that is? Even in the late 20th century, when women were starting to get accepted to serve in the military, they weren't very welcome on ships or submarines."

"Why?" Zelnick asked.

"Because the presence of a woman in a closed off manly environment had a drastic negative impact on efficiency. In later studies it was shown that there had to be around 30 percent women for the negative effect to disappear."

"Ah, so that's where the 30 percent quota comes from," Zelnick realized. "I thought it was just some equality mumbo-jumbo."

"Well, originally it was," Gruber admitted, "but the outcome was good, even if the decision was made for the wrong reasons."

"Is this somehow related to the Syreen?" Zelnick asked.

"Yes, because all of the Syreen starship officers – and most of the crew – are female. In fact, I think I have never seen a Syreen male face to face."

"Yeah, now that you mention it, I have heard about that."

"And here are the interesting facts:" Gruber began. "The Syreen are genetically so close to humans that we could even have children across species – a friend of mine actually proved that. The Syreen are also more fertile and value breeding more than humans. And to top it all, the Syreen prefer to live in a higher temperature than us, in about 30 degrees centigrade, which they compensated by using less clothing. AND, I tell you, I have never seen an unattractive Syreen."

It was difficult to imagine Dave wasn't there, since he was listening so intently.

"Okay, I see how the story was related," Zelnick agreed. "You had a bunch of baby-craving pin-ups with mental powers – in bikinis – walking around, probably in high heels, while there was work to be done?"

"Actually," Gruber specified, "they mostly walked around barefoot and they only used bikinis in their own ships, but you got the idea."

"Is there anything else?"

"They live a bit longer than we do," Gruber explained. "I understand their average life span is a bit over 100 years."

"Does that extension come to the beginning or to the end?"

Gruber took a second to ponder what Zelnick meant and then took a guess.

"All I know is that their 'teen age' starts a few years later, so I guess it's spread evenly."

"I see… so a Syreen who's 'my age' would be… in their early twenties?"

"Something like that," Gruber said and wanted to conclude the topic. "But anyway, you can think of them as humans. Their culture doesn't differ that much from ours, so you don't have to watch your words any more than usual."

"I wish you'd said 'watch your **tongue**'", Dave snickered.

Gruber grabbed Dave by the neck and held him under his chair until he cried uncle, apologized, and went back to his work.

"That was really bad, wasn't it?" Zelnick commented. "One of the worst this month."

"Shall we move on to the Androsynth?" Gruber proposed.

"Yes, please."

"In 2019 a certain scientist called Hsien Ho discovered a way to clone humans and tinker with their genes. With good intentions he created a line of clones with the best genes human body could handle – 'the perfect humans' as many called them.

He saw his creation as a 'tool' for humanity and wanted the clones to do highly sophisticated research due to their exceptional intelligence. He was so obsessed with their training programs and such that it took him a few years to start thinking about human rights issues. He actually saw the error in his ways soon enough and arranged the clones to have a chance of living a normal life. I don't know all the details, but apparently some human rights association or something like that had a big part in it. Anyway, the future of the clones looked bright back then."

"I can see a 'but' coming", Zelnick commented and Dave hastily gestured that he wouldn't make a pun of it.

"Indeed trouble lay ahead," Gruber continued, "thanks to a certain individual. You might remember that there was a nuclear war in the Middle East in 2015?"

"I remember there was a war, but I wouldn't have remembered the year," Zelnick admitted.

"As you know, the bombs blasted most of the 'holy lands' in the region into oblivion. This caused a huge 'religious vacuum', which was soon filled by the cult of a charismatic former car salesman, Jason MacBride. The cult was known as 'The Godly Men', whose main belief was that the world would end at 'The Great Millennium' on March 11 in 2046 and then everyone who 'believed' would be granted divine status."

"And someone actually believed that?" Zelnick wondered.

"Millions, I'm afraid, maybe even billions," Gruber speculated. "Don't forget that half of the population has intelligence below average."

Zelnick's face clearly indicated that right now he was ashamed to be human.

"So how is this related to the Androsynth?" he asked.

"I'm getting to that," Gruber replied. "How do you figure 'the perfect humans' would fit in MacBride's plans?"

"Doesn't every religion always see everything new as a threat?" Zelnick guessed.

"And 'The Godly Men' were no exception," Gruber answered. "The word 'Androsynth' was actually first used by MacBride, or 'Brother Jason' as he was called then. It was first meant as a degrading term, but soon everybody was using it in a neutral sense. The same thing happened with the term 'big bang' in the 20th century.

So anyway, MacBride used his influence and the vast resources of his cult to strip the clones of their human rights. As the years passed, the Androsynth became nothing more than slaves."

"But what happened to the cult?" Zelnick asked.

"Oh, it disappeared soon after their promised Millennium, leaving another religious vacuum. As you can see, the world did not end and MacBride insisted it was because people lacked genuine devotion. He soon withdrew from public life and his followers scattered, though there were an awful lot of suicides that year."

"Okay," Zelnick said. "So then, being treated so badly, the Androsynth revolted, escaped Sol, set up a colony on Eta

Vulpeculae, joined the Hierarchy, and started exacting their revenge on humanity?"

"That's pretty much it," Gruber agreed. "I hope you understand that the Androsynth are all individuals, even if their genes are identical. Just as there were lots of humans – maybe even a majority – who wanted to treat the Androsynth well, there were Androsynth who didn't want an armed revolt. The most extreme views are always the ones that get the most coverage and followers."

"How did you feel about the revolt?" Zelnick asked.

"Hey now, I'm not that old!" Gruber mentioned, slightly offended. "I wasn't even born at the time."

"Sorry, I didn't mean it like **that**," Zelnick apologized. "It's just that you sounded like you had something personal related to it."

Gruber was surprised. He hadn't noticed saying anything that would hint to the past of his family.

"In a way my grandmother was an Androsynth," he confessed.

"Huh?" Zelnick wondered. "I thought the Androsynth were incapable of producing offspring."

"Indeed they were," Gruber began. "My real grandmother had died when my father was very young. My grandfather then remarried – to an Androsynth – and his new wife became like a mother to my father. Then, at the time of the rebellion, when my father was only 11 years old, he had to lose his new mother as well."

"Ouch, that's pretty heavy," Zelnick commented, trying to be compassionate. "So how did your grandpa take it?"

"I only know what my father has told me," Gruber explained. "He said that his father had somehow aided the Androsynth and that the military police took my grandfather away the day after the revolt – and that he was never heard from again."

Zelnick didn't say anything.

“So my point is,” Gruber concluded, “the revolt probably wasn’t easy for many of the Androsynth either. I’m sure that in the right circumstances we could make peace.”

“If these ‘Orz’ haven’t eaten them all,” Zelnick pointed out.

“Well, there’s that, too,” Gruber had to agree. “I’m not sure whether it would be a good thing or not.”

“Let’s hope for the best,” Zelnick said to say something.

Gruber was done talking about the Androsynth. He was in the process of remembering why they were having that conversation when Zelnick interrupted his thoughts.

“So what about the Arilou?” he asked.

“Oh, right, the Arilou,” Gruber said absent-mindedly. “They’re a mysterious bunch.”

He gathered his thoughts.

“Have you heard about the Roswell incident in 1947?”

“Should I have?” Zelnick answered unintentionally impolitely with a question.

Just then the voice of Heidi interrupted them.

The shuttle to the Vindicator leaves in ten minutes. All crewmembers please report at the hangar.

“Wow, time sure passed by fast,” Zelnick remarked.

“I’ll tell you about the Arilou later,” Gruber promised and stood up.

“So you’re going out again,” Dave commented. “Good luck to you and try not to get gruesomely killed.”

“We’ll try,” they both said in unison.

CHAPTER 13

DIMENSIONAL FATIGUE

May 1st 2155, hyperspace, 356.4 : 255.3

"Five minutes to jump," Samusenko reported.

They had flown through hyperspace for ten days without log events and were now about to enter the vortex leading to Eta Vulpeculae.

Many of the crew had grown nervous upon entering the Androsynth's old sphere of influence. Some had experience of the constant feeling of terror the Androsynth hit-and-run squadrons had made humans feel in the Great War. The Spathi assumption that the Androsynth were dead was not enough to calm people down.

As anyone with fear of flying knows, reason cannot overcome fear. Also, knowing that there are no monsters* doesn't mean that there couldn't be one under your bed. Although for some people anything that could fit under their bed couldn't be scary.

They managed to jump into the outskirts of Eta Vulpeculae seemingly undetected.

The system looked deserted. There was nothing to indicate that the system was the home of a Hierarchy battle thrall, and there were no signs of the Orz the Spathi had mentioned.

---

* Before encountering the Ur-Quan and the Ilwrath this really was the case.

“Well, we’re here,” Zelnick stated. “We might as well go to the Androsynth homeworld. Gruber, where was it again?”

“The Alliance never found out exactly where,” Gruber began,” but we do know that there is a telluric world in this system so that would be the obvious place to check first.”

“Okay, so which planet is that?” Zelnick asked.

There were eight planets arranged somewhat similarly to Sol. There were two rocky worlds close to the sun and the rest of the planets were quite evenly scattered much farther. The fifth planet was the only gas giant.

“There are two planets within the hospitable zone, Captain,” Dujardin checked.

“The one closest to us is eight hours away,” Samusenko continued, “it’s the second planet from the sun.”

“Very well, set course there,” Zelnick ordered.

Just as Samusenko promised, they reached the planet in eight hours and it was like arriving at Earth, only without the slave shield. It had one moon and about a half of the planet’s surface was covered by water. Closer inspection revealed that its mass, radius, gravity, day length and tilt were all within 10% deviation of Earth’s.

The sun looked small because it was twice as far as Sol was from Earth, but since Eta Vulpeculae was a green star and thus warmer than Sol, the planet’s surface temperature was well above 20 degrees centigrade in day time.

Given all that, it didn’t surprise anyone that the air was also breathable, according to the Vindicator’s scanning equipment.

“So is there any sign of the Androsynth?” Zelnick asked. “Or the Orz?”

“The bio and energy scans will be ready in a few seconds,” Dujardin replied. “…There.”

A 2D projection of the planet's surface was displayed on the screen. It was covered in green dots and one specific area near the equator was highlighted in red.

"The planet is filled with all kinds of life-forms," Dujardin continued. "And there appears to be a city of some sort… here."

She pointed at the highlighted area which covered about 100 square kilometers. In the center was a single building notably larger than all others. It was built on the side of a river which snaked through the entire area.

The bio scan couldn't find any trace of the Androsynth.

"We'll have to go down there," Zelnick said.

"Aye, sir," Gruber replied, "I'll notify Rigby right away."

"What do you make of the city?" Zelnick asked Gruber.

Gruber took a moment to think. He was interested in taking a closer look.

"Captain," he said, "I think it would be best if I went down there with the landing team."

"Oh?" Zelnick was surprised. "Well, okay. I guess if there's something to make sense of, you'll have the best chance at it. You'll be in command of the whole operation then. Talk it over with Rigby."

"Will do, sir," Gruber replied. "I'll take my leave then."

He saluted and made for the door.

"But keep me informed!" Zelnick shouted after him right before he was outside.

"That sure makes my job easier," Rigby commented on the news. "And we'll have to leave someone out."

There were seats for only 12 people in the shuttle, so when landing on a planet with an atmosphere, no more passengers could be safely carried on board.

Soon the team was having a short briefing in the hangar. Gruber had selected a clearing near the central building as their landing zone. Their mission was to investigate what had happened and scavenge anything valuable. And at the same time they would have to be on high alert in case the Orz showed up.

"But how do we tell these 'Orz' apart from other life forms down there?" Witherspoon asked.

"All we know is that the Spathi called them 'fish folk'," Gruber explained. "But don't count on that too much, just focus on what we're doing. We will not remain too long on the surface. We shall land here," he pointed at the landing site on a map, "set up a perimeter for the shuttle and enter this building here," he pointed at what looked to be the main entrance of the central building. "What happens afterwards depends on what we find. It is unlikely, but we must also consider the possibility of getting involved in an armed conflict, so be ready to use your weapons."

The team rather nervously checked their gear and put their handguns on their belts. Gruber reported to Zelnick that they were ready to leave and got an instant clearance for take-off. Jenkins welcomed Gruber on board and he took a seat next to Rigby.

Entering the atmosphere was bumpy. It was over 20 years since Gruber had done it last and he didn't remember it being this bumpy then. Maybe he had just gotten old. The bumpy part didn't last for long though and soon they had slowed down enough to descend to observation altitude at about 200 meters and take a look at the city.

Or rather, the ruins of a city. It wasn't that obvious from orbit, but all the buildings were shot to pieces. When they closed in on their target they noticed that, unlike the rest, the central building was mostly intact.

They managed to land on site as planned. Gruber had left the tactical command of the squad to Rigby, so currently he was just waiting for orders.

"Witherspoon, Belov, Ahmed, Cuvelier, secure the perimeter," Rigby ordered as they stepped outside the shuttle. “Kilgore, Bukowski, Hawthorne, Robinson, Shoji, you come with me and The First Officer.”

The shuttle made an awful lot of noise. If there was anyone home in the whole city, they would have to be deaf not to notice the shuttle landing. When Jenkins finally shut down the engines and Gruber’s team was a good 100 meters away from the shuttle, Gruber could start thinking clearly and observe his surroundings.

Most of the buildings were one or two stories high. They were currently in a central street of some kind. The devastated buildings around them looked like they had been shops, or whatever places where the Androsynth distributed food and other supplies. It would have been interesting to see what kind of a society the Androsynth had – did they even use currency?

There was something wrong with all the destruction. The city looked like there had been a huge land war, probably within the previous five years, but there were no signs of orbital bombardment or invasion from space. And there were no bodies anywhere to be seen.

“This is weird,” Kilgore said. “It’s like something appeared out of nowhere, blasted everything with nuclear bazookas, then grabbed all the Androsynth and disappeared.”

They were getting near the central building. It was five stories high and about the size of a football field. Also, being mostly intact made it really stand out next to all the destroyed buildings.

There was nothing to indicate what the building was. Apparently the Androsynth population was so small that they could rely on everyone knowing every place. And also, knowing the Androsynth and their situation, the big building probably was related to science and research.

It was now quiet. Maybe there really wasn't a sound anywhere, or the contrast of the shuttle's engines falling silent made the effect, but it made the atmosphere uneasy.

Shoji apparently couldn't handle the silence so he started to whistle an unfamiliar but catchy tune.

"Stay alert, people," Gruber reminded them. "If you were a survivor in a place like this, where would you set up your nest?"

The crew looked at each other.

"Probably in this intact building here," Shoji admitted.

They reached what looked like the main entrance. It had modest looking double doors.

"When breaking into a house," Rigby began, "do you know what you should always do first?"

"Check if the front door is open," Kilgore replied almost too quickly.

"Right," Rigby agreed and motioned towards the door.

Kilgore tried the handle and the door opened.

The interior was intact, but still a mess. There had probably been some kind of struggling, rioting or looting, even though shots might not have been fired. There was also less dust than one would expect. Kilgore pressed the light switch but nothing happened. The building had lots of windows both in the walls and in the ceiling in the front hall so it wasn't that dark.

"This was their research institute," Gruber stated.

"What makes you say that?" Bukowski asked.

He looked at Gruber and saw him standing next to a big placard that said 'Research Institute' and the same in German. There was also a map. The building was at the center of the city and at the center of the building there was a round room labeled 'central computer'. There were also countless laboratories specializing in different areas and at the end of the laboratory wing there was another big round room – this one labeled 'DF testing chamber'.

“Does this ‘DF’ mean anything to anyone?” Gruber asked.

They all shook their heads.

“Dynamic… Fusion?” Bukowski suggested.

“Disruptor Field?” Hawthorne tried.

There seemed to be no winning guesses.

“We should split up,” Gruber told Rigby. “Take Shoji with you to work on the central computer and I’ll take two men with me to check the testing chamber.”

Rigby nodded and gave everyone their orders. They all had radios so they could keep in touch. Soon Gruber was walking through the laboratory wing with Robinson and Kilgore.

“This place gives me a spooky feeling,” Robinson said as they passed yet another office room turned upside down.

They had to rely on their flashlights to see their footing.

“Wait, stop!” Kilgore suddenly cried out.

He pointed his flashlight at the floor right where Gruber’s foot was.

“I think I saw a footprint in the dust,” he explained, “but you stepped on it before I could be sure and now I can’t see it anymore.”

They all checked their surroundings with their flashlights, but saw no more footprints – which wasn’t a surprise since there was so much debris.

“I could be mistaken,” Kilgore added and they continued walking.

Gruber checked their own footprints and even they weren’t that visible.

“Rigby, how are you doing?” Gruber asked over the radio.

zzzttt* “We’re good. We’ve just reached the entrance to the central computer, but haven’t been able to open the door yet. *zztttt

“Copy that, out.”

In the last room before the testing chamber entrance they saw a seemingly intact computer console. It really stood out in the middle of all the wrecked furniture and trash. At the same time Gruber noticed a sign in the wall of the testing chamber saying 'Dimensional Fatigue Testing Chamber'.

"So that's what the 'DF' stands for," he said to the other two and they both checked it. Gruber reported it to Rigby.

zzttt* "That sounds pretty hardcore." *zzztt

Gruber, Robinson and Kilgore checked the computer console. It wasn't just intact, it was powered and on standby. The operational system seemed strange, but efficient. They tried to make something of it for a while, but then gave up and decided that they needed Shoji. Gruber contacted Rigby again.

zzztttt* "A computer console on standby you say? That's interesting. We'll come over there right away. There doesn't seem to be any means to open this door from here, at least not with the power off." *zzttt

In a few minutes the team was together again and Shoji started working on the computer.

"What's that?" Hawthorne asked, pointing at what appeared to be smudge on a wall.

Gruber lit it up with his flashlight and almost wished he hadn't. There was graffiti written in at least meter-high red letters saying 'DON'T LOOK'.

Hawthorne let out a little scream.

"Tell me that isn't written in blood!" she cried out.

"It's not written in blood," Gruber told her and pointed at a can of red paint under the graffiti.

"Captain, are you seeing this?" Gruber checked.

"I'm seeing it," Zelnick replied. *"Looks like we didn't take the advice."*

"I've got it," Shoji suddenly said. "This is quite simple, really."

Shoji then taught Bukowski to use the operating system and soon Bukowski also got the hang of it.

"There's lots of stuff about the DF here," he reported. "Give me a minute and I'll fill you all in."

Hawthorne was investigating the graffiti and noticed a piece of paper under some scrap. She took it in her hands, read it and then showed it to the others.

'CAN'T BE UNSEEN' was written several times on it.

"Creepy," Rigby said.

They all started to search the room more thoroughly. Hawthorne soon found another piece of paper just like the previous one.

"Bingo," Robinson suddenly declared, but, instead of a bingo-board, he held out a notebook from which the scraps obviously were taken. There was similar text on every page.

'CAN'T BE UNLEARNED'

'CAN'T ESCAPE'

'KILL THOSE WHO HAVE SEEN'

'JUST KNOWING IS ENOUGH TO A—' The sentence ended there since there was no more space on the paper. It didn't continue on the next page.

"I hope we can just get out of here soon," Hawthorne thought out loud.

"Alright, are you ready for this?" Bukowski asked them.

He had looked at neither the notebook nor the scraps of paper. Since he had everybody's attention, he continued.

"The Androsynth began studying this 'Dimensional Fatigue' phenomenon over ten years ago after they had found some Precursor artifacts at Alpha Lalande. As far as their scientists could tell, these devices generated some kinds of waves that would allow the user to see into… uh… other dimensions I guess. Maybe I'll just quote: *realms of existence which share position with our own universe, but have a different reality phase.*"

There was a natural silence, during which everyone pretended to understand what had been said.

"So anyway," Bukowski continued, "they were planning on doing experiments in that testing chamber right there. They had hoped to use the DF technology to create new, faster forms of hyperdrive and hyperwave. I'm pretty sure they didn't succeed, because according to this log here, they only made one test. After that the log gets out of control. There's only one more entry and it's just rambling about ghosts and such – for 113 pages – and most of it seems to be in Latin. I don't know Latin so I'm not sure, but I assume it's nothing important. Do any of you know Latin?"

They all shook their heads.

"Is there anything about their reproduction problems?" Gruber asked.

"I'm pretty sure there isn't," Bukowski replied. "Everything in this console seems to be linked to the DF."

"There was a section in the map of this building regarding reproduction," Rigby pointed out. "It was in the other wing."

"If we can find a functional computer there," Bukowski said, "I might be able to learn something about that."

"What about the central computer chamber?" Rigby asked. "Can you do something from here to open the door?"

"I can try to turn on emergency power," he answered. "Should I?"

Rigby looked at Gruber, who nodded, so Rigby gave Bukowski permission to try.

Soon a few lights were turned on – basically the ones that were still intact – and they saw what a mess the place really was.

"So where did the computer get its power?" Hawthorne asked.

They all looked at each other. Shoji checked the cables and they saw that there was no power cable connected. It probably ran on batteries of some kind.

"Let's go check the door now," Rigby said and they all left the room.

There were only a few functional lights in the corridor, which made strong shadows and therefore something was always flashing in the corner of the eye. Now they also saw several more graffiti on the walls. All of them said the same thing:

'DON'T LOOK'

"This is starting to get old," Robinson declared. "Judging by the strokes in the letters I'd say these were all done by the same person."

"What about that one?" Gruber asked, pointing upwards as they reached the front hall.

High in the ceiling was one more message written with the same red paint and same kind of letters:

'CAN'T HIDE'

The ceiling was at least five meters from the floor.

"How the hell did they manage to write that **there**?" Robinson commented.

"Apparently there is something we can't hide from, can't run away from, and shouldn't see," Hawthorne concluded. "Should we close our eyes?"

"Let's just figure out what happened here," Gruber said. "We can leave this DF research to Dr. Chu and his pals."

Soon they saw the previously inaccessible central computer room. There was a faint green light over the door.

"That looks promising," Rigby stated. Apparently there was no such light last time.

There was no handle on the door, but a touch-sensitive button next to it. Rigby put his finger on it and the door opened. At the same time, lights in the room were switched on. Unlike in the hallways, the lights in this room were all in good condition and the room was very brightly lit, making everyone cover their eyes for a while.

The computer had the same operational system as the one near the testing chamber. Bukowski sat in front of it.

"There's a message here," he immediately said.

An icon of an unread message was blinking on the screen.

"Twenty bucks on it saying 'don't look' again," Robinson made a wager.

"You're on," Kilgore took the bet.

Bukowski opened the message and Kilgore got twenty bucks richer.

liberate tuteme ex inferis

"Is that Latin again?" Gruber asked.

"I'm pretty sure it is," Bukowski answered. "I'm not sure what it means, but if 'liberate' is the same as in English and 'inferis' has something to do with 'inferno'…"

"Liberate hell?" Robinson suggested.

"Whatever," Gruber ended the speculation. "Bukowski, try to find out what has caused the destruction here and also, if you find something on their reproduction capabilities, let me know."

"Yes sir," Bukowski replied and got to work. "This might take a while."

After about a minute he continued.

"Hey, this is interesting."

Everyone gathered around him again.

"Here's the history of everything that has been searched from the computer's data banks. As you can see here, it's mostly scientific stuff at a steady pace up until January 27th 2151. This other number here must be a new time system they created. I think the number was the same at the log entry of the DF test."

"So what happened after that date?" Gruber asked and Bukowski showed them.

On that day, there were hundreds of searches for ghosts, poltergeists, haunting and even exorcism. There were also some for reality aberrations and similar phenomena. The last entry was a search for 'mosquito mange'.

"What does that mean?" Hawthorne asked.

After a while of pondering, Kilgore opened his mouth.

"I have heard that term somewhere – maybe in an old book. I think it has something to do with strong gravity, but I'm not sure."

The first search for ghosts was at 07:21. The search for mosquito mange was at 19:10. There were only three such searches during the first hour and around four hundred during the last.

"What **does** the computer say about the mosquito mange?" Rigby asked and Bukowski opened the data.

'DON'T LOOK'

"I should've known," Rigby stated with a disappointed voice.

"I think I should get ten bucks for that," Robinson pleaded to Kilgore, but got no compassion.

"So currently we could assume that..." Zelnick suddenly began. *"On January 27th 2151 at about 07:00 the Androsynth did a dimensional fatigue test, which resulted in them being haunted to death in 12 hours."*

"So these 'Orz' the Spathi mentioned," Hawthorne deduced, "are ghosts?"

"In a way, I think so," Bukowski joined in. "According to this data here, they made contact with some kind of a life form immediately when they tested their DF equipment for the first time – a life form on 'the other side' – a creature from an alien dimension. And that's when the requests for information on ghosts and such began."

"Try to find out how exactly the destruction happened," Gruber suggested. "We'll leave you to it and start searching and scavenging this place."

Gruber then contacted the squad outside over the radio. "Witherspoon, how's it looking out there?"

zztttt *"It's a sunny day and the air is clean."* *zzzttt*

"Good," Gruber responded. "Search the nearby buildings if you can."

zzztttt *"Roger that."* *zzttt*

They split up into two teams again and this time Gruber was with Robinson and Shoji. They made their way towards the reproduction labs as Rigby, Kilgore and Hawthorne explored the area near the central computer.

There wasn't much worth looking into. The frequent 'DON'T LOOK' warnings decorated the walls. After a while they reached their destination. There were double doors with a sign saying 'reproduction' and also 'maturation' both in English and German.

The doors turned out to be locked and they agreed to try force. They simultaneously kicked at the center of the doors which, as a result, didn't just open – they fell to the ground, making an awful noise which echoed through the hallways.

zzzttt *"What the hell was that?"* *zztttt* Rigby justifiably asked.

"We broke through some doors," Gruber explained. "No need to worry."

The area formerly behind the doors was completely different from the rest of the building. It was clean. There were no signs of destruction and it was well lit. In fact, it was a bit too clean – like it had been swept recently. They looked inside the nearest room.

It was a laboratory. There were multiple transparent water tanks in a row, some of them filled with water. What was more, some of them contained human – or Androsynth – embryos.

"Looks like they managed to breed after all," Robinson stated.

"Are they alive?" Shoji asked while looking at one of the embryos.

"No," Gruber was able to say right off the bat.

Gruber then found a hand-written journal in one of the drawers. It contained at least a hundred pages of text in German. He took the journal with him and decided to read it at a more appropriate time.

Just then they heard a commanding voice from the doorway:

"Hände hoch! Still bleiben!"

Skipping several heart beats they turned around and saw a teen-age girl pointing a maser rifle at them. Gruber assumed that neither Robinson nor Shoji understood German so he translated for them.

"It's German. Hands up and don't move."

They all slowly raised their hands.

<<Who are you?>>[*] Gruber asked.

<<Who are YOU?>> the girl asked in return.

<<We mean you no harm,>> Gruber explained. <<We came here to find out what has happened to the Androsynth. I am Adam Gruber and these men are Tatsuo Shoji and Harry Robinson. We represent the New Alliance of Free Stars.>>

<<The Alliance is evil,>> the girl replied. <<Are you going to alert the demons?>>

<<What do you mean?>>

<<Don't look. If you see them, they see you. You can't hide and they will eat you.>>

What the girl was saying seemed somehow expectable.

<<Is that what happened to everyone else here?>> Gruber asked

<<Not everyone. Only the smart ones.>>

<<Are there others who are still alive?>>

---

* << in German >>

<<Not anymore.>>

So far Gruber had said the first thing that came into his mouth. Now he was getting over the initial shock and started to think.

<<What’s your name?>> he asked.

<<The smart ones called me Seventy-Two, but my name is Lydia. You don’t look smart. Which are you?>>

<<We are humans from Earth. If by ‘smart’ you mean the Androsynth then no, we are not smart ones. Are you?>>

<<I am a normal. That’s why I wasn’t eaten.>>

*zzztt* “Sir, we found something!” *zzzttt* Witherspoon suddenly reported in an anxious voice.

<<There are five of us outside,>> Gruber patiently explained. <<One of them just said they found something. Can I answer?>>

The girl nodded, but still pointed the gun at them.

“What did you find?” Gruber asked.

*zztttt* “One of these buildings is filled with rotten corpses.” *zzztt*

*zzzttt* “They must have been here for years. There are even small children.” *zzzztt*

“Copy that, I’ll get back to you, over,” Gruber replied.

<<What happened to the other ‘normals’?>> he asked the girl.

<<Most of them died in the haunting. The rest of them died afterwards.>>

Gruber decided to test the girl.

<<What happened to their bodies?>> he asked.

<<I… We dragged them all to a shed. And I can understand English.>

<<Could we speak English so my friends would understand too?>>

“Yes,” the girl said in English. “But my English is not very good.”

Robinson and Shoji had no idea what was happening.

"Lydia, could you lower your gun, please?" Gruber politely asked.

Before she could comply, a voice appeared on the radio again. This time it was Hawthorne.

zzztt* "Gruber, sir, we have a situation here!" *zzztt She sounded frantic.

"What is it?" Gruber replied without asking for permission.

zzzttt* "It's Bukowski, Sir. He's gone berserk. He locked himself in the central computer room and is now trashing the place." *zzzzttt

<<He looked,>> Lydia said in terror and lowered her gun, probably inadvertently. She started to tremble and breathe heavily.

"Can we go see him?" Gruber asked.

Lydia let go of her gun and it fell to the ground close to Robinson, who picked it up. The girl had an empty gaze.

"Hold on to that gun," Gruber told Robinson. "Shoji, take her with us to the central computer."

Shoji was a lot smaller than Gruber and Robinson and he clearly didn't know how to take her. He seemed to think whether he could carry her, but then decided to lead her by the hand. She came along nicely.

"We're coming there," Gruber responded to Hawthorne on the radio. "And we found a survivor. We're bringing her with us."

Soon they met up with the others. The formerly green light over the central computer room door was now red. Rigby, Hawthorne and Kilgore were watching Bukowski through a window which was apparently unbreakable.

"He's been like that for a while now," Hawthorne explained.

Bukowski was moving around the room, shouting. He used everything he could get his hands on to hit the computer with. There was fear in his voice. Actually, there was nothing but fear. He was screaming in terror.

"When I got back here," Hawthorne continued, "he was talking to himself pretty loudly. When he saw me, he screamed that we can never learn what he had learned – that just knowing was enough to alert 'them'. I got scared so I took a few steps back and then he locked the door."

Bukowski kept on screaming. Suddenly words could be made out:

"THEY'RE COMING! OH MY GOD THEY CAN SEE ME AND ARE COMING FOR ME!"

Then he ran to the window and hit his head against it pretty hard which made everyone jump back.

"They were right!" he said in a slightly smaller voice. "You shouldn't look!"

Now they could see that his face was covered in cuts. He hit his fist against the window and they saw that his arms were cut up equally badly.

<<It's happening again,>> Lydia said in an absent voice.

Bukowski fell to the ground and started screaming for his life. The computer seemed damaged beyond repair.

Bukowski was now twitching on the floor. He then rose up again and blindly took a few swipes at the air with his arms. When he turned towards the window, they could all see that his face was cut up a lot more badly than just a few seconds before.

"Get out of there," Zelnick commanded. *"Return to the ship."*

"Yes, sir," Gruber replied. "What about Bukowski?"

"Leave him. That's an order. Return as quickly as possible."

They looked at each other.

"Everybody to the shuttle!" Gruber then ordered.

"But sir," Hawthorne began, "we can't just… leave him!"

"You heard the captain!" Gruber sternly reminded her. "Now move it!"

Gruber then relayed the orders over the radio.

"Abort mission, repeat, abort mission… Everybody to the shuttle at once."

They started to run towards the exit, but Lydia wouldn't move very quickly and Shoji wasn't good at making her. Gruber then lifted the girl to his shoulder and they picked up the pace. As they covered more distance, the terrifying screams of Bukowski got quieter. When they got outside, the only thing they could hear were the engines of the shuttle again.

Since Bukowski wasn't with them, they had a secure seat for Lydia.

"What happened in there?" Witherspoon asked as they hastily boarded the shuttle.

"We'll go through every detail when we get back to the ship," Gruber replied. He strapped Lydia to Bukowski's seat and when everyone was inside, he gave Jenkins the order to take off and return to the Vindicator.

The noise and trembling were so intense that it was pointless to explain anything before they were out of the atmosphere. When the blue sky slowly turned black, the ride smoothened and he gave the short version of things to the shuttle crew.

"Captain, we're bringing over a guest," he then told Zelnick over the radio.

"I noticed," Zelnick replied. *"And I'm assigning you to take care of her."*

Gruber thought whether he had just committed a kidnapping.

"Aye, sir," he said.

CHAPTER 14

FISH FOLK

May 2nd 2155, Eta Vulpeculae, 358.7 : 256.6

When they stepped outside the shuttle Gruber told Jenkins, who was the youngest woman available, to keep Lydia company for a while and take her to the crew quarters. He would have to talk to Zelnick as soon as possible.

When he entered the bridge, Zelnick was waiting for him with an answer to the question he was about to ask.

"I didn't want to put the entire crew in danger," he said. "It seemed to me that Bukowski was already gone and I didn't want us ending up like the Androsynth."

"It was a tough decision," Gruber said. "I have no objections."

"Captain!" Dujardin suddenly cried out. "A whole fleet of alien ships has surrounded us!"

"WHAT?" Zelnick exclaimed.

"I don't understand where they came from," Dujardin continued, "it's like they appeared out of nowhere!"

"What kind of ships? How close?" Zelnick inquired.

An image of the ship type was displayed on a screen. It was an unfamiliar design.

"They are already in conventional firing range," Dujardin checked. "All of them!"

"Fwiffo, are those the Orz?" Zelnick asked.

"They resemble arrowheads with a turret in the middle," Fwiffo said. *"It is like Snelopy described them."*

"Prepare for emergency warp!" Zelnick ordered. "If they show hostile action, we have no choice but to try to get out of here."

A red light flickered and an emergency siren echoed through the halls. A warp inside a star system and this close to a planet wasn't a joyride. There was also a slight delay in charging the hyperdrive so if the surrounding ships wanted to, they could inflict heavy damage to the Vindicator, not to mention the Tobermoon, Star Runner and Voyager, before they could jump to safety.

Just then they received a signal from one of the supposed Orz. But no image was displayed on the screen and no message was shown either. Instead, the ship's computer had something to report.

"There seems to be a problem with the translation," Zelnick deciphered.

One of the first adjustments made to the Vindicator at the starbase was to implement the standard translation subsystem on the computer.

"The computer says that the message is extremely unusual in composition," he continued. "There are gaps in the translation and... it appears that the computer has tried to somehow guess the missing parts, but can give no guarantee of the accuracy of the translation."

"That's the first time I've heard of anything like that," Gruber said.

"Let's see what it looks like," Zelnick decided, and gave the computer permission to continue.

An image was linked. What was seen on the screen was a light-green fish-like creature submerged in a transparent liquid. It seemed to have gills and four mixtures between an arm and a fin.

"Hello extremely!" the creature said. *"I hope you like to *play*. Some *campers* are not so good for *games*. Is it time for *playing* yet?"*

It was difficult to decide whether the message made any sense or not.

"Greetings," Zelnick responded anyway. "I am Captain Robert Zelnick of the starship Vindicator. We represent the New Alliance of Free Stars. We are having some difficulty translating your message."

*"Yes, of course. Difficulty. Problems are difficult. Let's be *special* together. *Spicy games* are always fun."*

Zelnick feigned ignorance.

"Our charts show this as Androsynth space. Do you know what happened to them?"

At the mentioning of the Androsynth, the face of the creature somehow changed.

"Androsynth are not here," the creature plainly said. *"Orz are here. You are not the same too much like Androsynth. You are *happy campers*. Do you want to see our surprising *toys*? No!! Do Not!!*

The creature sank a little deeper, narrowed its eyes and blew out a few bubbles.

*Androsynth are so silly. We do not *tell stories* a lot about them. No more Androsynth *stories*."*

"Er…" Zelnick hesitated. "Now don't take this the wrong way, you don't have to tell any details, but… did you DO something to them?"

The creature got more serious and its voice got deeper and somehow darker.

*"I am say best word *frumple*. Maybe you do not know. *Frumple* be *round* yet *lumpy*. So bad!!! The asking about Androsynth is so *frumple* we are not happy.*

*Do not asking it so much. It is better to not *frumple* or else there is so much problems. No more Androsynth is better. If you are say the question another time it is *frumple* too much and Orz are *dancing* for *dissolving* the *campers*.*

*I am clear!! You are not so *silly*!"*

Zelnick seemed to be pondering how to place his words. Gruber hoped from the bottom of his heart that he would drop the subject.

"Alright, well, this isn't really a question, but—"

He looked at Gruber for help. Gruber shook his head slightly. Zelnick then turned back to the Orz,

"I mean, that's okay," he said with a convincing fake smile. "I didn't really care about the Androsynth so much anyway."

The creature loosened up and its voice became joyous.

*"Ahaa! I am told other Orz *cousins* you are *connected* for *camping*. I am so right! It is happiest days to not care about Androsynth anything. So now we can be *together* for friendly *dessert*. I am so right. I will tell them again."*

"So, uh," Zelnick uncertainly began, "we came here to check out the ruins on that planet there. What brings you here?"

*"The Orz came to *play*. We are *squeezing* the *juice* in our *house* when *silly cow* *look through window*. And there we find *slippery place*! It is too much fun. It is same as before, but *smell* different. We *pull through window* the *silly cow*. Then find more *silly cows* in *heavy space*.*

"Did you get any of that?" Zelnick asked Gruber.

"If you think of Bukowski as the 'silly cow'," Gruber pondered, "then it would, in some strange and disturbing way, make sense."

"That sounds… fun," Zelnick said to the Orz. "We are struggling to free the galaxy from the clutches of the evil Ur-Quan whom you might have heard of. We are looking for allies and you seem like friendly fellows so could you maybe help us in our mission?"

The Orz seemed to get excited, maybe a little more than what felt comfortable.

*"Yes. Yes. We are too friendly. Extremely happy *sisters* should correct each other for *celebration*. So much enjoyment! Shall we come to your *house* so that we can be *relatives*?"*

"Uh…" Zelnick seemed to be at a loss for words. "Let's think about it for a second. You seem very… trusting. Why is that?"

*"We are not trusting. We like to be *together*. Do you want to be *together* with us?*

*Always the other *sad animals* go away, but first we have lots of fun. Too many fun is not enough!! Do you agree? I think you *smell* like you do. This is the story about trusting.*

*It is sad and makes many Orz *dissolve* or burst into several. Why is it that you are trusting? What a funny question. I am tired."*

"Well, hey, no sweat," Zelnick said. "If you want an alliance then yes, we are very interested. We invite you to join the New Alliance of Free Stars and—"

He was interrupted by the Orz who was now swimming around in ecstasy.

*"*Jumping* *peppers*!! This is smiley time! I am *squirting* more *nice colors*. It is the best way! You are *campers* after all.*

*We will be happy *together*. Do not be *terrified*. You must going to my *house* to start *alliance* *parties* for better enjoyment! It is *silly* name Gamma Vulpeculae I.*

*We will have fun *party* at the new *slippery place*. Do not forget to *enjoy the sauce*!"*

"Okay," Zelnick said with a little confusion in his voice. "We will go to the first planet of Gamma Vulpeculae to discuss the alliance formally. It was nice seeing you."

The Orz seemed to find something amusing in Zelnick's comment.

*“That is *funny*. You think you *see* Orz but Orz are not *light reflections*. Maybe you think Orz are *many bubbles* too. It is such a joke. Orz are not *many bubbles* like *campers*. Orz are just Orz.*

*I am Orz. I am one with many *fingers*. My *fingers* reach through into *heavy space* and you *see* *Orz bubbles* but it is really *fingers*. Maybe you do not even *smell*? That is sad.*

**Smelling* *pretty colors* is the best *game*. But now the *game* is goodbye.*

And with that, the transmission was cut. Zelnick sighed very deeply and slumped into his chair.

“That was exhausting,” he stated.

“You did well,” Gruber said. “At least it looks like that for now. If they meant what they said, we could have a new ally soon.”

“A scary ally,” Zelnick pointed out. “I’m not sure what they did to Bukowski, but it sure as hell was something creepy.”

“Bukowski ‘looked through window’,” Gruber speculated, “and the Orz ‘pulled him through the window’ from a ‘slippery place’. The ‘looking through window’ must be what all the warnings were about.”

“So when you look,” Zelnick continued the thought, “the Orz see you and take you. But why haven’t they ‘taken’ us then?”

“I think what Bukowski saw was something different,” Gruber suggested. “We haven’t looked at the other dimension and I advise against it in the future as well.”

Zelnick tapped his fingers on the armrest of his chair.

“Mr. Samusenko,” he commanded, “get us to Gamma Vulpeculae.”

“Aye-aye, sir,” Samusenko replied and the ship accelerated towards the edge of the system. “We should reach the system in approximately 30 hours.”

"Their ships look powerful," Trent commented as the Orz ships were gathering in orbit over the Androsynth ruins. *"The visible gun turret in the middle rotates freely, their acceleration is fast and smooth, and they are highly maneuverable."*

"Let's hope they're on our side when we find out their full capabilities," Gruber said.

Samusenko seized the opportunity to share a little bit of trivia:

"Gamma Vulpeculae is actually so close to our current location in true space that we could fly straight there without jumping to hyperspace."

"Really? How long would that take?" Zelnick asked.

"Only about two years," Samusenko replied.

Gruber went to the crew quarters to find Jenkins and Lydia. He had no idea what to do with the girl and tried to figure out why exactly he had taken her with them.

He checked the common room first and there they were, along with several others. Jenkins was teaching some kind of a hand slap game to Lydia, who seemed to be pretty good at it. She looked cheerful. When Gruber approached them, Jenkins got up, clearly indicating that she had done her part.

"What have you talked about?" Gruber asked.

"Nothing but the rules of this game," Jenkins replied. "May I go?"

"Yes," Gruber replied, "and sorry for keeping you from your normal duties this long."

Indeed, as the pilot of the shuttle, Jenkins had a lot to do after a landing mission – especially after landing on a planet with an atmosphere. She saluted and left the room, and Gruber awkwardly sat down and tried to start a conversation.

<<How old are you?>> he asked in German.

<<That's not something you should ask a lady,>> Lydia sternly replied. She might have meant it as a humorous

statement, but Gruber wasn't sure and didn't dare to assume. He was about to apologize when Lydia continued:

<<I'm six and a half.>>

There was no way that was the truth, Gruber thought. She looked more like she was around 15. He was about to say something about it, but then remembered that the Androsynth culture had their own time system, which was probably related to the rotations of their own planet rather than Earth. He hadn't paid that much attention to the general info of the planet when they had first approached it, so he couldn't tell how long the orbital period was. He did remember though that the planet was a lot farther from the sun than Earth, so a full circle had to take at least two years.

<<Does that mean six and a half circles of your planet around the sun?>> he asked to make sure.

<<Yes, and one circle is 8187 ruoh.>>

<<What's a ruoh?>> Gruber asked.

<<A ruoh is 100 nutes,>> Lydia explained and seemed to be enjoying herself.

<<Nutes?>>

<<A nute is 100 conds.>>

Gruber took out a notebook.

<<So how much is a cond?>>

<<There!>> Lydia said. <<That's a cond – and that – and that. There are 100 000 conds in a day.>>

Gruber wrote the numbers down.

<<By 'day' do you mean one rotation of your planet?>>

<<Yes, and there are 10 ruoh in a day.>>

<<Let's see if we can find a way to understand our time systems,>> Gruber said. <<I'll call the bridge.>>

He then reached Dujardin on the communicator and got the information from her: A day on the Androsynth colony was 25.68 hours.

<<Your way of telling time is similar to ours,>> he told Lydia. <<We have 365 days in a year – that's a circle around

the sun – 24 hours in a day, 60 minutes in an hour and 60 seconds in a minute.>>

Lydia laughed at him.

<<Those numbers make no sense!>>

Gruber found himself slightly offended, but had to admit that Lydia had a point. Although he had never thought about it before, the number of hours, minutes and seconds in a day sounded dumb when explaining it to someone. The Androsynth way indeed seemed better.

<<So it seems that,>> Gruber continued ignoring his uncomfortable feeling and the fact that he was laughed at, <<10 ruohs equal 25.68 hours. How old would th—>>

<<Ahh!>> Lydia interrupted him. <<So I'm about 15.6 **years** old.>>

Gruber was stunned.

<<Did you just calculate that?>> he asked.

<<Yes, I'm very good with numbers,>> Lydia proudly proclaimed. <<Even the smart ones said so. So one cond is 0.9245 seconds and… it's like this:>>

She took Gruber's notebook and started to write something down. All Gruber could do was observe. Soon she showed Gruber what she had written. It was what Gruber had hoped to write by himself, given a little time and a calculator.

1 cond = 0,9245 seconds
1 nute = 1,5408 minutes
1 ruoh = 2,568 hours
1 my day = 1,07 your days
1 circle = 2,400 years

<<This is fun!>> she rejoiced. <<How old are **you**?>>

Before Gruber could answer Lydia, his communicator beeped and he had to answer Zelnick.

"Let's go over the recordings of the messages the Orz sent us," Zelnick half-suggested, half-ordered. *"Come to the*

conference room and bring our guest with you. Some of the stuff we miss might make sense to her."

Gruber agreed. It was a sensible plan.

<<Let’s go meet the captain,>> he proposed to Lydia after he had put his communicator away.

<<I thought you were the captain,>> she said, not disappointed, only surprised.

<<What made you think that?>> Gruber asked curiously.

<<Because you are older than anyone else,>> she answered sincerely. <<I thought captains are always the oldest ones on board. Is the captain of this ship even older than you?>>

<<You’re in for a surprise,>> Gruber hinted.

They entered the conference room where Zelnick was already waiting along with Rigby and Katja. They all stood up as they saw Lydia.

<<They’re all younger than you,>> Lydia whispered to Gruber.

Katja was the closest one to the door so she introduced herself first.

“Hello, my name is Ekaterina, but you can call me Katja,” she said and offered her hand to Lydia.

Lydia shook her hand in an exaggerated vertical path.

“My name is Lydia,” she replied in basic English.

Rigby was next in line.

“I’m Thomas,” he said. “You can call me Thomas.”

Lydia laughed at him slightly, which probably was Rigby’s goal, and shook his hand too. Zelnick was sitting further away.

“What can I call you?” Lydia asked Zelnick from across the table.

Zelnick smiled at her.

“You may call me captain,” he replied. “But my name is Robert.”

Lydia burst into laughter.

"You are young!" she managed to say.

Zelnick seemed offended.

"So are you," he said.

Lydia pulled herself together.

"Are you really the captain?" she asked. "Can you give him orders?" She pointed at Gruber.

"Mr. Gruber," Zelnick then said formally, "please raise your right hand."

Gruber felt extremely uncomfortable having to help the captain prove something to a little girl. He still reluctantly did as was ordered.

Lydia seemed impressed and let out a silent "wow" which made Zelnick look rather pleased with himself. Rigby and Katja seemed to be enjoying the show.

"Well then, **captain**," Gruber began, "shall we get down to business?"

Zelnick nodded and they all sat down.

After they had watched the recording, they all looked at Lydia who didn't seem very interested.

"Did any of that mean anything to you?" Zelnick asked her.

"I didn't understand," Lydia said. "My English is not very good."

"Did you recognize the alien?" Gruber then asked.

"No," Lydia replied, "but I had a strange feeling. There was something familiar about it."

Gruber didn't know what he had expected, but he couldn't help feeling disappointed.

"Can you translate it to German?" Lydia asked.

Gruber realized that he didn't know. He looked around and soon everyone was looking at Katja.

"Not directly, no," she explained. "The standard 'human-language' in the programming is English and we can't change that. We could translate the translation then to German, but that would make the accuracy suffer even more."

"Well then," Zelnick said to get on with their business, "do any of you have something clever to say about the Orz?"

Rigby showed a sign of wanting to speak and Zelnick gave him permission.

"This might be stating the obvious," he began, "but to me it looks like the Orz killed all the Androsynth and probably Bukowski too. I'm afraid that understanding how they did it would result in the same fate for us. At the end I think it described their relation to our dimension or something like that… But as I said, I think it is not wise to figure it all out. If we are really going to ally with them, I'd prefer to keep some distance."

"I got the impression," Katja said, "that the creature doing the talking was a part of a hive mind. Maybe there is a 'queen bug' or something on Gamma Vulpeculae and these creatures are somehow all part of it."

"We'll find out soon enough," Gruber concluded.

Zelnick clearly wanted the meeting to end already.

"This has been useless and interesting at the same time," he proclaimed. "Take the recording with you and if you think of anything else, let me know."

The flight time in hyperspace to Gamma Vulpeculae was less than half a day. Lydia was given a bunk in a room with three crew members and Gruber found himself relieved when she finally went to sleep.

They entered the star system and made their way to the first planet which was notably closer to the sun than all the rest. There were three rocky planets quite close to each other at about the same distance from the sun as the asteroid belt is in Sol and roughly twice as far was a solitary gas giant.

The first planet was a water world inside the habitable zone, very much like Earth. The planet was heavily guarded by the same kind of ships they had encountered at the Androsynth homeworld. The ships ignored their arrival, though.

There were no signs of civilization on the surface. The bio-scan detected lots of life-forms, but they saw no constructs whatsoever. One spot in the middle of the ocean was a little more crowded with life though.

Zelnick decided to make a call on a common frequency and it was answered immediately.

The answering creature that was displayed on the screen was identical to the one they had talked with earlier. According to Zelnick the translation program gave the same warning as last time. Then the creature spoke:

*"This is my *house.* Did you come to *play*?. Do not be sad if you are *other*. We can still have a *party*. There are never enough *campers*."*

"Captain," Katja reported, "I can't pinpoint the source of the signal. It seems to be coming from everywhere."

Zelnick nodded in acknowledgement and then responded to the Orz.

"Hello, we came here to talk about an alliance between our species. We met some of you at Eta Vulpeculae and they told us to come here."

The creature swam closer to the 'camera'.

*"*Silly* name Eta Vulpeculae is funny *gravity center*. My *fingers* go there to *party* at *slippery place*. Even better than *campers*, they find *relatives* I am guessing. Are you *family* with Orz?"*

"I, uh, hope to be," Zelnick said uncertainly. "We represent the New Alliance of Free Stars and would like you to join us."

*"I am *smile*! *Alliance* *parties* are best *snappy fun* every time. We come to your *house* and you come to*

*my *house*. But wait! You already *visiting*. I am in hurry. What is your *house* *silly* numbers?"*

The creature was waiting for a response and Zelnick didn't seem to know what it wanted.

"What do you mean… silly numbers?" he asked.

*"My *silly* numbers are 371.3 : 253.7. I am *happiest* at your *house*, but *heavy space* is *slow* and *dark*. Your *silly* numbers show the way *in darkness*."*

The Orz was waiting anxiously, its face nearly touching the 'camera'.

"Oh, the coordinates, you say?" Zelnick realized. He then turned to Gruber.

"Should I tell it the coordinates to Sol?" he asked.

Gruber wasn't sure.

"It's a gamble," he said.

Zelnick pondered it for a second and then reached a conclusion.

"If your plan is to save the world," he told Gruber, "you've got to push a few old ladies down the stairs."

"Huh?"

"It's something my dad used to say. I don't know what it means, but I think we need to gamble."

Zelnick turned to face the creature again.

"The Alliance headquarters is at 175.2 : 145.0 orbiting the third planet."

The creature started to swim in circles.

*"I am *expanding*! Do you know? Orz can *dance* very well. Now you are a *happy camper* and Orz can give *heavy space* ships for *dancing*. Orz will give. Orz ships have the GO! GO! Do you know? These are best for letting go near *heavy space* planet bodies. Then GO! GO! can going fastest to enter ships of the *other*. Then it is *happy time*."*

"That sounds great!" Zelnick said. The good mood of the Orz seemed to be contagious. "Would you like to join us on our current mission? We could use your… GO GO."

*"*Fun* times! *Dancing* is best when not *dissolving*. I will *accompany* your *heavy space* ship in *slow time*."*

"Captain," Dujardin reported, "one of their ships broke away from the formation and is heading our way."

"Let it come," Zelnick said. "Our ever-growing fleet is becoming quite variegated."

He then talked to the creature again.

"I'm afraid I'm still not exactly clear on who you are and where you're from."

The Orz seemed amused.

*"You are a *silly* *camper*."* it replied. *"I am always Orz. If I was not Orz, then I would not be, but of course I am Orz.*

*We are from the *outside*. Also the Arilou *quick babies* are from *outside*. It is the same, but not. Orz are from *below*, Arilou are from *above*.*

*Orz does not like Arilou. Arilou are too much trouble. We cannot have *parties* when Arilou always *jumping in front*. It makes Orz *frumple* so much.*

*These are *fat* words. Do you want to play this some more?"*

This was an interesting piece of information, Gruber thought. Contacting the Arilou would be one of their highest priorities, but at the same time it would be a problem if they didn't get along with the Orz.

"Do you know where we could find the Arilou?" Zelnick asked.

The creature looked slightly angered again, like when the previous one was asked about the Androsynth.

*"You are asking *silly* numbers. Orz do not know. The Arilou are not here. They are *outside*. You are too*

**sticky* to *slide* to them. If they come to *heavy space* in *slow time* like Orz, even you can *smell* them."*

The approaching Orz ship had now formed up with the Star Runner, Tobermoon and Voyager.

"Are you in that ship that just came to us?" Zelnick inquired.

The creature was once again amused.

*"I am many. My *fingers* move the *heavy space* ship *silly* name Nemesis. If you want to come, that is okay."*

"Well then," Zelnick concluded, "we should get going. I'm sure we'll have lots to discuss on the way. Do, eh, **you** have a name?"

*"*Deep*"*

"Uh… Should I call you Captain Deep of the Nemesis?"

*"*Silly* *no function* makes *campers* happy. Orz want to make *campers* happy every day. I am *Deep* of Nemesis, but also not. I am only joke. Hello!"*

CHAPTER 15

EDEN

May 8th 2155, hyperspace, 400.4 : 341.3

Four days have passed since we left Gamma Vulpeculae and set course for Betelgeuse, to where we will arrive shortly. It is hard to decide which male crew members are more excited – the ones who have met the Syreen before or the ones who haven't.

The Orz are still not making much sense. I am pretty sure that when they say 'camper', they mean 'friend' and to them combat in space is 'dancing'. But so far they have been very friendly and Trent has been over-excited about their Nemesis ship. It is fast, maneuverable, durable, and can fire in all directions. The Orz can also send out individual soldiers in special combat suits to board enemy ships during battle. They call it the 'GO GO'.

...

They still make me uncomfortable. I have a feeling we've always talked to the same creature. Katja suspected that they are a hive mind, but I think they are not individuals at all – rather, a projection of a creature from a higher dimension.

The thing that puzzles me the most is... Why are we still alive? Why haven't the Orz done to us what they did to the Androsynth? Rigby and Zelnick believe it's because we don't really 'understand' them – that interactions on the next level require certain knowledge. I don't believe that. I'm afraid that we are just a part of their ultimate plan, whatever that might be. We might be unable to comprehend. This must be how religious people sometimes feel.

...

I suppose we should focus on earthly matters since those are the only ones we can affect. A friend of mine once told me that there's no use in preparing for divine judgment. It is like making sure that you are well rested and have lots of money when you die.

...

It amazes me how joyous Lydia has been. Or at least that's the front she puts up. It is interesting to learn of the Androsynth society – how they have repeated so many of the human mistakes. Their distinction between "normals" and "higher ones" resembled almost too much the racial separation of the early 20th century.

According to the journal I found in the reproduction labs, the Androsynth never managed to procreate naturally, but were able to use human ova they had brought with them during their escape from Earth. They had to decide whether to 'create' normal humans who could reproduce, or more of themselves, who were smarter, but sterile.

Creating more oppressed people would have the same result as their own revolt in 2085. The writer of the journal saw that and wanted equal rights for the 'normals'. I got the impression that he was in either a minority or a silent majority, but in any case nothing was done about the matter.

Gruber's communicator beeped. Zelnick notified him that they had reached the vortex leading to Betelgeuse, so Gruber put away his personal log and made his way towards the bridge.

Zelnick looked worried.

"What if the Ur-Quan neglected their resupply as well?" he asked. "And they weren't as lucky as you— we were?"

That was a good point. As with the Chenjesu, Gruber felt stupid for not thinking of it earlier.

"At least Betelgeuse is a lot closer to the Ur-Quan than Sol," he tried to comfort either himself or Zelnick.

"We are about to enter Betelgeuse," Samusenko reported. "Entering true space in three… two… one…"

The thin bright lines outside shrank into dots and the surrounding red color faded out, leaving nothing but the blackness of true space.

"By the way," Samusenko continued, "we are now further away from Earth than any man has ever gone before."

"I don't feel any different," Zelnick stated. "And this system looks like any other."

There were three planets, all quite close to the sun. The two innermost were inside the habitable zone.

"It will take us about seven hours to reach the planet closest to the sun," Samusenko calculated. "The other planets are behind the sun from where we're standing."

"Let's get going then," Zelnick ordered. "Set course for the innermost planet."

Someone had dug up an old picture of a Syreen starship captain and it was now being passed around in the common room. After several men had spoken aloud their unpleasant and unsurprising remarks, the picture was inadvertently passed to Lydia.

"She's pretty," she summed it all up at first glance. Then she observed it more closely for a while.

"I'm not pretty," she continued miserably, still holding up the picture.

Gruber walked behind her and looked at the attractive blue face which he immediately recognized.

"She was a fine captain," he thought back out loud. "I fought alongside her once at the coreward front. Her psychic potential was among the highest, and when I saw her, her ship was crewed almost entirely by Hierarchy forces."

He looked around and felt he had dampened the joyous mood of the (male) crew members.

"And how could I forget a face like this?" he joked, trying to lighten up his previous comment.

It worked. There were a few chuckles and he gave the picture to the closest man who, Gruber now realized, hadn't paid any attention to the topic. To avoid further uncalled for actions, he took a second to look around.

All (male) crew members were tidier than usual. Their uniforms were clean and they had shaved thoroughly. Some even seemed to be proud of their smell, which Gruber didn't care to inspect. Even though he had no particular sexual interests (currently) towards the Syreen in general, something primitive inside his head made him go to his quarters and take out his comb for the first time on the trip.

"I see you're ready," Zelnick perceived as Gruber returned to the bridge.

"Captain," Dujardin reported just then, "there's a ship on the radar."

"What ship?" Zelnick asked and straightened up.

"It's fast and not recorded in our data banks," Dujardin checked, "but wait… We have encountered this type of ship before. It is the same kind of probe we met on our last trip from Vela to Sol."

"Well, Mr. Gruber," Zelnick said, "looks like we can test your theory now."

"It's not a theory, sir," Gruber pointed out. "I just think we should try ruling out the possibility of—"

"I know, I know," Zelnick interrupted him. "It is a sound plan. We will keep all offensive systems turned off until the probe makes a threatening move."

"At least we now know that these probes don't just wander around in hyperspace, but enter star systems as well," Gruber noted.

"What about… 'Captain Deep'?" Zelnick asked. "Do you think… 'it' has understood the rules of this engagement?"

"We can only hope, captain," Gruber replied. "Of course since we now have the alien technologies of the Nemesis and the Voyager, there are quite a lot of unknown factors in this plan."

Zelnick opened up the communication link to all ships in their fleet.

"Fwiffo, Trent, Dip-Por-Pak*, Deep, we will follow First Officer Gruber's plan for this encounter. But in the meantime, just in case, assume Trent's probe-crushing formation."

Trent had calculated that the summed fire power of all five ships was enough to stop the probe before it reached its own firing range. They just had to be in a concave formation with the Tobermoon at the center, Vindicator and Nemesis by its side, and Star Runner and Voyager at the ends of the row.

"It's hailing us," Katja reported.

"Patch them through," Zelnick said.

They received a message without a picture just like last time:

"We are not hostile and seek to establish friendly relations with your species."

Zelnick stood up in a formal manner.

"I am Captain Robert Zelnick of the Vindicator. We represent the New Alliance of Free Stars. We also wish to establish friendly relations with you. We met one of your probes earlier and it attacked us. Please explain why."

---

* This is how Zelnick addressed the commanding trio of the Voyager. They seemed surprisingly comfortable with it.

The response was instant again.

"Behavior follows dictated priorities. Priorities set at point of origin. Priorities are as follows: replication – data gathering – contacting alien life forms in peaceful manner."

"Where is this point of—"

"Captain," Katja interrupted him, "the link has been terminated again."

"It's coming at us just like last time, Captain," Dujardin reported.

Zelnick sighed.

"Prepare to fire," he said to the other captains.

Gruber couldn't figure out the probe's behavior at all.

"This is a strange line of probes," he said. "I can't see why any species would choose this course of action."

"At least we get something to salvage," Zelnick looked on the bright side.

The probe was targeting the Voyager so the formation moved accordingly. As soon as the probe was about to enter the Voyager's firing range, a single nuke was fired from the Tobermoon. As it sped past the Vindicator and the Nemesis, they both fired at the space directly in front of the probe, using proper deflection. A few seconds afterwards, the Voyager and the Star Runner both fired their short-range main guns.

The probe didn't make any evasive maneuvers and so all the shots hit it at the same time. The resulting explosion shone like a small star for a short while.

"Do you think we overdid it a little?" Zelnick asked.

When the dust cleared, they could see that the probe was indeed neutralized, although 'pulverized' could have been more appropriate.

"The salvage team is going to like you," Gruber remarked.

In a few hours they were approaching the planet closest to the sun with a probe wreck in the storage bay. They could see the all-too-familiar red glow of a slave shield over the planet. When they got closer, they spotted a starbase in orbit – a starbase exactly like the ones at Sol and Procyon.

Zelnick looked different than usual. He wore his uniform exactly by the book and his hair was combed very neat. The colors in his uniform seemed a lot clearer and stronger, which probably just meant that he had washed it.

"Katja, hail the starbase," Zelnick ordered as they had reached appropriate distance.

There was a standard reception sequence and then, in a few seconds, the link was active. Even though Gruber knew what to expect, he still found himself swallowing and blushing.

The image on the communications screen was like something out of a fantasy. They were talking to a Syreen, that was for sure. She had a tall, well-stacked blue body whose most strategic parts were only barely covered by a golden bikini and a purple loincloth.

"Attention, unidentif—" the Syreen began, but fell silent in the middle of her sentence. Zelnick coughed a little, probably to clear his throat. He opened his mouth, but didn't manage to say anything. Then the Syreen saved him by continuing.

"You're human!" she said in amazement. *"How can you be here?"*

"Er…" Zelnick tried to begin, squirming in his seat. "We, uh… the Vindicator— this ship, the Vindicator, we— Zelnick! I am Captain Robert Zelnick of the Vindicator and uh… I'd be speechless if I'd keep my mouth shut."

Zelnick's face was red as a rose and he had to catch a breath. He wiped his forehead with his arm, gathered his thoughts and tried again:

"We represent the New Alliance of Free Stars," he managed to declare.

The Syreen was watching him very carefully.

"The 'new' Alliance, you say?" she replied, changing stance, making her divine hip-to-waist ratio stand out even more. *"Has the slave shield been lifted from Earth?"*

In Gruber's opinion she sounded a bit skeptical.

"Well, no," Zelnick answered truthfully, little by little getting over the initial shock, "but we're trying. We've got our hands on this Precursor ship and have already recruited a few allies. We will build our strength and then, all together, fight the Ur-Quan and win back our freedom."

"Wow," the Syreen said. *"You Earthlings are so brave. I am pleased to make your acquaintance, Captain Robert Zelnick."*

She ran her hand through her hair and put her other hand on her hip.

"I am starbase commander Talana of the slave planet Gaia. What exactly do you want from us?"

Yes, what exactly did they want from the Syreen, Gruber thought. When the Safe Ones at Spathiwa had explained that they couldn't just say 'hurrah' and form an alliance at the very moment, it sounded like they were only chickening out. But now that you looked at it objectively, it was really a rather sensible thing to say.

"We've come to free you," Zelnick gloriously laid it out, "—but we're also going to need your help."

This statement had some kind of an effect on her. She took a deep breath, probably to buy some time for thinking how to put her words.

"I'm sorry, my human friend, but we don't want your help," she replied with sad eyes. *"Even though we value freedom as much as anyone else, we are not going to do anything to antagonize the Ur-Quan. Even though we are*

slaves, we are now far better off than we were before being enslaved – before the Ur-Quan became our masters."

Zelnick looked empty. Even to Gruber this felt like being rejected – and it hurt even more since the one doing the rejecting was a gorgeous female.

"But… how?" Zelnick tried, "…and why?"

Talana made a comforting smile.

"I understand your disappointment," she said. *"You humans are so straightforward and you have come a long way just to be turned down. Please, come visit the starbase in person, captain. I will make time to explain our situation to you in detail."*

This seemed to cheer Zelnick up.

"That sounds reasonable," he agreed. "Can I bring a few men with me?"

"Ha ha, yes, Captain," she laughed. *"Yes you can."*

"Gruber, I need you to come with me," Zelnick said immediately after the transmission was cut. "Mr. Samusenko,"

"Sir!" Samusenko replied, probably hoping to join them.

"You have the command."

Samusenko did a poor job concealing his disappointment. Zelnick then hastily walked away, followed by a surprised first officer.

"Captain," Gruber began as they were outside the bridge, "do you think it's wise for us both to leave the ship?"

"I think it is necessary," Zelnick answered. "We'll also take Rigby with us. Can you think of someone else we should take?"

"A woman might be a good idea," he figured.

Gruber assumed that Zelnick needed him to give him some support and Rigby, being a xenotech, could make some objective observations. Also, a woman might be less susceptible to certain distractions they were bound to face.

"Good thinking – anyone in particular?" Zelnick asked.

Gruber thought of Lydia, but soon scrapped the idea.

"How about Witherspoon?" he suggested.

"Alright," Zelnick agreed right away. "Tell her to come to the shuttle on the double."

Zelnick seemed to be in a hurry. Gruber was just about to contact Witherspoon when they entered the hangar and saw that Witherspoon and Rigby, along with a dozen others, were gathered there. Zelnick strode towards the shuttle and Gruber ordered Rigby and Witherspoon to tag along immediately as they seemed to be adequately dressed.

Witherspoon didn't show any kind of a reaction, but Rigby was understandably ecstatic. They boarded the shuttle and soon were gliding towards the familiar looking starbase. Zelnick used the time to tell them all they needed to know.

All the procedures when entering the hangar were the same as at their own starbase. They gathered up at the rear ramp of the shuttle and when it was lowered, the three men stepped into paradise.

There were gorgeous Syreen females everywhere. Each and every one of them could have been a model back on Earth. Some of them had purple loin cloths, golden bikinis and golden head accessories – similar to what commander Talana was wearing, but most of them didn't have those pointy golden ear bijoux and their upper body was also covered in a purple cloth. Whether they had a golden bikini underneath remained a mystery, at least for the time being.

Commander Talana stepped forward from the crowd.

"Captain Zelnick," she greeted. "Welcome aboard this starbase. Please forgive my subordinates as some of them are quite anxious about meeting humans after all these years."

As she had said that, Gruber was surrounded by Syreen females and he noticed that Rigby got the same treatment. Zelnick was mostly left alone, probably because he, as the commanding officer, was the most formal guest. A handsome looking Syreen male, dressed only in a loincloth, was talking to Witherspoon, who was blushing like a little girl.

"Your ship is so huge," a female said to Gruber, grabbing his upper arm.

She sure is thin, Gruber thought. Thin, but voluptuous. They didn't make them like this at home.

Another one grabbed Gruber by his other arm.

"How did you get a ship like that?" she asked.

This one had the golden head gear and the bikini and, as Gruber just took notice, a very noteworthy bust.

It's hot in here, he thought. He was suddenly feeling overdressed for the occasion and tried to loosen up his uniform from the neck a little.

"I'm sorry," the one in his left arm said, "we are so excited that we just ask stupid questions."

"Come," the ~~busty~~ one with the golden bikini said, "let us take you to a place where you can sit down and have some refreshments."

As the two girls started to lead Gruber away from the hangar he noticed that he had lost sight of Zelnick. Rigby and Witherspoon, on the other hand, were escorted in the same direction as he was. He tried to say something about it, but the words didn't come out of his mouth. He felt too comfortable. He also realized that he hadn't said anything at any point, but there was nothing he could do about it.

After a short walk they arrived in a room which back at Sol was used to store random junk, but here it was a cozy room filled with pillows and strange plant-like objects. When they were being seated, Gruber managed to speak his mind.

"Where's the captain?" he asked his hostesses.

The women surrounding him all smiled reassuringly.

“Don’t worry,” the closest one to him said, “your captain is with commander Talana. She will take good care of him.”

“Would you like some naal nectar?” one of them asked, carrying a glass and a pitcher.

After an unknown period of time Gruber suddenly took notice of his surroundings. He had mostly gotten out of his uniform with only the leg parts still on. His shirt was missing, or rather, it wasn’t really missing, he just didn’t know where it was. There were Syreen all around the room, one sitting on his lap. He looked to his left and saw Rigby in a similar position. The amount of clothing covering his body seemed to be about the same and he was clearly enjoying himself.

Gruber then looked to the right and saw his own reflection in a plate that was, for reasons unknown, in a vertical position. His reflection was smiling. Such a wide smile he hadn’t seen on himself in a very long time.

There was a half-full* glass of liquid within his reach. It was probably what he had been drinking all the time. He took a sip and deemed it to be quite refreshing. It wasn’t until then that he realized the woman sitting on his lap was constantly talking to him.

“—mother of Alia and Teela, but it hadn’t been my time yet. After the cataclysm it was all strictly regulated to optimize the little gene pool we had left. After meeting you it took many years before human genes were tested enough to be added into the ‘big plan’, but by then it was already too late as we lost the war only months afterwards and then we also lost the *giggle* supply of human genes and when we saw you come here, we thought that maybe—”

Her speech was interrupted by Zelnick and Talana entering the room. All chatter was silenced in an instant.

---

* With the Syreen, the glass is never half-empty.

Zelnick was still formally dressed and while he was viewing Gruber and Rigby, there was definitely disbelief in his look.

"Sir!" Gruber and Rigby shouted in unison as they hurriedly stood up to stand at attention. This sudden movement made Gruber's uniform, or the part that was still on him, fall to his ankles.

"As you were, gentlemen," Zelnick said, allowing Gruber to fix his attire. "Commander Talana has given me all the information we could think of needing. She also said we could enjoy their hospitality for a little while, but I can see you've already started. Mr. Gruber, a word?"

Zelnick gestured to Gruber to accompany him to the hallway. Having tied the sleeves of his uniform together around his waist, Gruber quickly followed Zelnick out of the room.

"We have a major situation here," Zelnick said in an agitated tone after they were by themselves in the hallway. "There's much to tell when we get back to the Vindicator, but we have a more pressing matter at hand… The thing is that…"

Whatever the thing was, it was hard for Zelnick to say out loud. He kept reaching for words.

"All right, here's the thing…" he tried, but then lost it again.

For a few seconds his mouth opened and closed, but no words came out.

"The thing is…" Zelnick tried again and Gruber lost his patience.

"What is the thing?" he asked.

"They want us to 'impregnate' some of them. That's the word she actually used! It was something about their small gene pool."

"I see," Gruber replied. Getting out of that room clearly made it easier to think. "I think it's okay," he then continued.

They both looked inside the room from the doorway. It was only a matter of time before Rigby would be wearing nothing but his birthday suit.

"I guess we don't even have to tell Rigby," Gruber observed.

"Looks like that," Zelnick agreed. "Where's Witherspoon?"

They looked around, but Witherspoon was nowhere to be seen.

"She was with a male Syreen earlier," Gruber explained. "It was the first time I saw a male of their species."

"Well, I'm sure she's all right," Zelnick concluded. "So… Do you want to… do it?"

"Er…" Gruber thought for a second. "I'm not actually sure what happened while you were away. I might have done it already."

"Well then," Zelnick said, "we're going to be here a little while longer, so go for it."

"Sir," Gruber began, "are you ordering me to have sexual intercourse – while on duty – with unbelievably sexy temptresses – that's plural – and no strings attached?"

"I'm only suggesting, Mr. Gruber," Zelnick replied with a grin.

"Very well then," Gruber agreed and looked at the room again. "What about yourself, sir?"

"What about myself?"

"Are you going to participate in this mission?"

"I think I'm in love."

"Huh?"

"I'm saving myself for Commander Talana. I think she likes me too."

"Some standards you have," Gruber laughed. "Although she is exceptional, I'll give you that."

"You just worry about yourself, old man," Zelnick said and motioned to Gruber to re-enter the room.

Soon the shuttle brought a set of healthy reinforcements from the Vindicator.

Some hours later three blissful men and one woman met at the hangar.

"Witherspoon, where have you been all this time?" Gruber asked, not aggressively.

"Girl stuff," she answered. "It's none of your business, sir."

There was something new in Witherspoon's look, but Gruber couldn't put his finger on it and apparently neither could Rigby nor Zelnick. The rest of the men had already left and now they were the last ones there.

Commander Talana was seeing them off, along with many others of her kind. Gruber noticed Talana whispering something into Zelnick's ear right before they boarded the shuttle and waved goodbye.

"I'm glad we came here," Zelnick stated after the ramp had closed and they were on their own again. "We'll meet at the briefing room in one hour. I'll tell you everything Talana told me and then we can get moving again."

Exactly one hour later Zelnick began his explanation. The Syreen had two understandable reasons not to join the Alliance. The first reason was that they didn't want to and the second one was that they didn't have any ships.

The Syreen were in a different situation than any other race during the Great War. In the past they had lived on their homeworld, Syra, which was very much like Earth, only it was not covered in concrete and plastic. But then, in 2034, an asteroid hit the surface of their planet.

An odd thing about that asteroid was that it was not pulverized on impact. Instead, it penetrated the crust and went all the way to the mantle, creating a 'super volcano'.

The earthquakes caused by the impact were severe. The magma pumped out of the caldera wreaked significant damage on the nearby terrain, but within a few weeks it had cooled, forming a solid rock bandage over the wound. In a few months the mess was pretty much cleaned up and the caldera was calming down.

But later, just a year after the impact, all hell broke loose. Huge calderas were opening up everywhere – and not just around the meteor impact, but everywhere. Entire cities slid into oceans of molten lava. Kilometer-wide sections of land were pulverized by a cataclysmic explosion and clouds of poison gas and superheated steam created a death shroud around the planet. Within three days the surface temperature had risen above the boiling point of water.

The ones who survived were almost all from the Syreen's newly established Space Patrol, which consisted mostly of females. They managed to rescue only a handful of people from the surface. At that point the entire Syreen population was less than ten thousand, with only five hundred males.

With their planet completely inhabitable, they had no other choice but to take with them everything they could and depart to look for a new home.

For nearly 75 years they wandered through the stars and near the end their slow moving habitats got raided by the Vux. Then they met the old Alliance and had no other choice but to join.

"The next part you all know, right?" Zelnick checked. "During the following years of war they fought alongside the Alliance all the way to the bitter—yes, Rigby, do you have a question?"

Rigby had raised his arm.

"Where was this homeworld of theirs? This… Syra?" he asked.

"Oh, right, right…" Zelnick said and displayed the star map on the screen.

"It's right here," he showed them. "Beta Copernicus I."

"That's in Mycon territory," Rigby rightfully observed.

"Indeed it is now," Zelnick agreed. "Talana told me that the Mycon's sphere of influence was much smaller back then and that they had never met the Mycon until in combat in the Great War."

"So what exactly happened to the Syreen at the end of the war?" Rigby asked.

"I was just getting to that when you interrupted me," Zelnick answered. "But don't let that get you down. All questions are welcomed. So, as I was saying…"

When humans were defeated in Sol, the remains of the Alliance fell apart. The Yehat and the Shofixti retreated to their home stars and didn't want the Syreen to follow. The Arilou, on the other hand, mysteriously vanished. The Syreen were left alone, with nowhere to go, in the path of the oncoming Ur-Quan armada.

They surrendered and chose fallow slavery. But when the Ur-Quan ordered them to return to their home planet they had to explain that they had none.

"Now this is where it gets interesting," Zelnick stated in the middle of his explanation.

The Ur-Quan said that they had encountered a similar situation before. They wanted the Syreen to tell them what kind of a planet they needed and they would search their extensive astronomical databanks for a good match. And they really did provide. After the Syreen had given a full description of Syra, in less than an hour the Ur-Quan gave them a set of coordinates and ordered the Syreen to disembark there, to their new home.

"Is that the world right there," Rigby asked, "under the slave shield?"

"Yes it is," Zelnick replied. "They call it Gaia and according to Talana it is everything they wanted – a world as beautiful as their original home world, Syra."

“So they had been searching for a new home for nearly a century and in the end it was their enemies who gave one to them.” Gruber concluded.

Zelnick pointed at Gruber in a “right you are” kind of way.

“I can see why they don’t want to oppose the Ur-Quan,” Gruber added. “It would have been a different story if their resupply had been neglected as well.”

“I’m afraid that’s the case,” Zelnick agreed. “Anyway, they gave us documented material on the collapse of Syra. Feel free to look through it on your own time.”

Zelnick’s tone indicated that the meeting was over so people started to get up and make for the door.

“Oh, wait, one more thing,” Zelnick stopped everyone. “Talana did tell me an interesting detail about their fleet.”

Everyone sat down again.

“Their ships weren’t destroyed after they surrendered. Talana said that, since the Ur-Quan never waste anything, they had the Syreen captains fly their ships ‘blind-folded’ into some deep vault on an unknown alien world. The only clue was that based on how long it took them to get there, it couldn’t be farther than 200 hyperspace units from here… Oh, and the ‘only clue #2’ was that when the Syreen captains were being boarded into an Ur-Quan Dreadnought after flying their ships to the vault, they caught a very short glimpse of the outside world and as far as they could tell, the sun was either red or orange.”

Once again Zelnick’s ending tone indicated that the meeting was over, but this time nobody dared to get up right away.

“That doesn’t narrow it down much,” Gruber said.

“Yeah, I know,” Zelnick agreed. “But it’s one of those ‘nice to know’ kind of things.”

Now it was allowed to exit the room and the ones with the quickest feet were already outside.

"Mr. Gruber, one moment please," Zelnick said as Gruber was also leaving the room.

Soon everyone else had left and they were by themselves.
"How was it with the Syreen?" he asked and made a hand gesture which will not be described here.
"A gentleman doesn't kiss and tell," Gruber grinned.

CHAPTER 16

WORSE THAN ZEBRANKY

May 16th 2155, Alpha Tucanae, 400.0 : 543.7

Seven days have passed since we left the warmth of Betelgeuse and I'm still bewildered by the speed of this ship. We have this quickly travelled 167 hyperspace units and reached Alpha Tucanae a few hours ago.

With this ship, we could explore the entire quadrant in a reasonable amount of time, which we, sadly, do not currently have. If we survive this war – and by 'we' I mean myself, Captain Zelnick and this ship – I'd be delighted to participate in such a mission... to explore strange new worlds, to seek out new life and new civilizations, to boldly go where no... something like that.

Our visit at the Syreen starbase significantly raised the morale of the crew. During these troubled times a good recreation is necessary, although it was a bit disappointing not to be able to recruit the Syreen to our cause.

We are now far beyond the old coreward front and there's no telling what we'll find here. The Zoq-Fot-Pik have three planets in this home system of theirs, with the closest to the sun being their home. We will reach it in a few hours. Once there, we are likely to form an official alliance with the Zoq-Fot-Pik. Although their ships aren't too powerful, the location here beyond the old lines could prove itself invaluable in terms of intelligence.

The ansible displayed a message shortly after they had passed the orbit of the second planet. There were normal reports on the progress of different sectors, but the final paragraph of the message was something else:

We have been invaded by an alien race calling themselves the `Orz', though so far the invasion is a friendly one. The fishlike creatures don't make much sense and have been stomping around the base in their robotic walking exoskeletons which look like combat vac-suits, if you ask me.

They keep saying we are relatives and should party together, which Dr. Fredrikson is trying to figure out. So far we have very little common understanding.

We sincerely hope that they are new allies you've recruited because based on the summary reports I've seen on their `Nemesis' ship design I have but a single comment: I like it!

"I'm sure Hayes and pals will have a lot of fun with the Orz," Zelnick speculated. "…Wait a minute. So 'Nemesis' is actually the name of the ship type?"

"It seems so, captain," Gruber agreed.

"Well whatever," Zelnick wrapped it up. "I don't intend to make a point about it with Captain Deep. Do you?"

"No, sir."

Just then the commanding trio of the Voyager hailed them.

"We have a troubling report."

"The folks at home aren't answering our calls!"

"Neither are they greeting us upon entering the inner part of the solar system, which they should always do."

"Something must have happened to them!"

"Maybe the Ur-Quan have finally found their home planet," Zelnick guessed, not speaking into the microphone. "Ms. Dujardin, can you already determine whether there is a slave shield over the planet?"

"Yes sir," she replied, "and no sir. There is no slave shield."

"Don't worry," Zelnick reassured Dip-Por-Pak. "The Ur-Quan haven't enslaved your world. Maybe there's just a problem with their transceiver?"

"Maybe so."

*"*sob* maybe *sob*"*

"We'll soon find out," Zelnick continued, "but in any case prepare yourselves for anything."

As they got closer to the planet, they could see some kind of one-sided combat going on. There was one big ship in the center and a squadron of small ships circling around it like small birds trying to protect their nest from a fox stealing their eggs.

"Someone's attacking our home!"

"We must hurry!"

"It looks like one of those black destroyers."

"Our ships don't stand a chance against them!"

"They shoot spinning projectiles which tear our ships in two with a single hit."

"And if we ever get close enough to do the stinger tongue attack, they activate some kind of a fire shield."

"The blue ring of death. Our ships are incinerated in an instant."

Based on the movements of the smaller ships, a projectile was fired from the big black ship. It was mostly evaded, but a bright explosion at the middle of the fleet indicated that one ship wasn't fast enough.

"Katja, contact the black ship," Zelnick ordered. "Dip-Por-Pak, try to make contact with that fleet of yours. Tell them to withdraw. We'll handle the situation somehow."

Katja tried, but there was no response. After a while Dip informed them that the message was received and that the Zoq-Fot-Pik fleet would comply. Then, as suggested, the fleet scattered and escaped the combat area leaving the black ship all alone with nothing to stop it from bombarding the surface of the Zoq-Fot-Pik homeworld – nothing except the New Alliance of Free Stars.

"Sir, they're hailing us now," Katja reported.

"Patch them through," Zelnick said and stood up to address them formally.

If they were the Kohr-Ah, enemy of the Ur-Quan, a certain level of understanding would be extremely profitable. However, if shooting at helpless, non-threatening civilizations was on their agenda, they would be a less welcome party in the Alliance.

It would all become clear in a few seconds. The link was now established and they could see that the alien commanding the black destroyer looked familiar. To everyone's disappointment, it was an Ur-Quan, only its skin was black.

"We are the Ur-Quan Kohr-Ah," the creature said. It was hanging over a pit filled with what looked like bones. Its many eyes blinked in a seemingly random order making one feel unease when looking directly at it.

"We cleanse our destiny. You will soon die. Make whatever rituals are necessary for your species."

They got half of the routine right, Gruber thought.*

"I am Captain Robert Zelnick of the Vindicator," Zelnick replied, unshaken by the sudden hostility. "We have been informed that you are at war with the **green** Ur-Quan. Since we have a common enemy I ask you to cease hostilities. We can benefit from each other."

"We are self-sufficient," the creature immediately responded, or actually, just like with the green Ur-Quan, the one really doing the talking was the little brown frog-like creature. *"We need nothing. We want nothing beyond the total destruction of all non-Ur-Quan sentience. You are filth and require cleansing."*

"Want nothing? Filth?" Zelnick repeated the key points. "Then why did you even bother to contact us?"

"Before we destroy other thinking beings we share with them this comforting fact: This life of yours, which shall end immediately following this statement, is but one of many lives you will live. Perhaps in your next incarnation you will be born an Ur-Quan. You can choose to be grateful for this opportunity we make available to you."

And with that the transmission was cut.

"War-mongering idiots!" Zelnick shouted at the blank screen. "You're even worse than the green ones!"

He then sat down and contacted Trent.

"What's your take on this?"

---

* Shortly after the Chenjesu had contacted humans for the first time, a group of intellectuals were assigned to come up with a standard pattern to follow when encountering a new alien species. After six months and millions of dollars spent, they presented a simple set of guidelines:

1: Get to the point.

2: Be non-threatening.

"Clearly they cannot be reasoned with," Trent said. *"And since we don't know their capabilities, we should proceed with line formation and test their defenses by firing a single nuke at them."*

"Very well," Zelnick agreed and opened a link to all the captains. "Form a line and prepare for battle. We will formulate a strategy after we have tested their defenses."

"Captain!" Dujardin franticly cried out. "They're firing at us!"

"From that distance?" Zelnick said in disbelief. They were still well outside the maximum range of the cruiser's guided nuclear missiles, a weapon whose range was known to be bested only by the Chenjesu Broodhome's main gun.

"It's a projectile," Dujardin reported, "and it's coming at us fast. Thirty seconds to impact."

"Everyone, take evasive action," Zelnick told the other captains. "What are they thinking, firing from so far away?"

"It's probably just as Trent suggested," Gruber reckoned. "**They're** testing **our** defenses."

If the turning jets of the Vindicator hadn't been finished, they might have had a hard time evading the shot. But now all the ships were maneuverable enough to easily steer clear. A few seconds before the shot had reached their line, Zelnick asked Iwasaki to get a good look at the projectile. An image of it was soon displayed.

"That thing is huge!" Iwasaki exclaimed as the projectile flew past them.

It was a blade, somewhat similar to a throwing star, and it was spinning at an enormous speed. Its diameter was roughly equal to the bridge of an Earthling Cruiser. Just like Dip had said, it could probably tear apart most ships in a single hit and even the Vindicator would suffer serious damage.

"There's no way to launch something so massive at such velocity," McNeil almost shouted. "The recoil alone—"

"But they're doing it in reality," Gruber cut in. "Needless to say, we can't afford to take a single hit."

"They can't have too many of those projectiles stored on board," McNeil continued his analysis. "There's just no room."

"That may not be the case," Gruber pointed out. "Disc-shaped objects like that could be stored in a relatively small space. Iwasaki, how thick was the projectile?"

"I can't say, sir," Iwasaki checked. "I couldn't get a proper reading in that dimension, but it looked very thin."

Zelnick contacted Trent.

"When can you fire?"

"In about two minutes. From the missiles' maximum distance the Tobermoon still has enough time to dodge similar shots from the enemy... narrowly. The other ships should have no problems, so let's stick with the plan."

The enemy ship fired again, this time targeting the Tobermoon. Then it fired three more shots, one for every ship in the Vindicator's fleet.

"They're testing our maneuverability now," Trent observed. *"It looks like they have plenty of ammunition."*

After finally entering its effective firing range, the Tobermoon launched a single missile at the enemy ship.

"Let's see what happens now," Trent said.

The enemy ship turned slightly to face the Tobermoon and fired back. The missile would reach its target at about the same time as the projectile the enemy fired.

…Or so they all thought. Instead, the spinning blade hit the nuke half-way. From the perspective of the Vindicator's radar, the missile just vanished and the other projectile kept on going without even slowing down.

The Tobermoon managed to evade the shot, barely, just like Trent said.

"McNeil, tell me that was a lucky hit," Zelnick wistfully said.

"I don't believe in astronomical luck, sir," McNeil responded. "And the sheer momentum of that projectile… it's really scary."

"The Nemesis, Voyager and Star Runner must draw the enemy's attention to themselves," Trent stated, unshaken. *"It looks like our weapons are ineffective head-on."*

Trent's calm analysis came at the right time.

The Nemesis suddenly accelerated and broke away from the formation.

*"I am told GO! GO! sisters want *happy time*,"* Captain Deep said. *"Orz will show. It is the best *dance*."*

"Fwiffo and Dip-Por-Pak," Zelnick commanded, "follow the Nemesis, but fly past the enemy from the other side."

"I was afraid Captain Deep would go solo," Zelnick then told Gruber.

"At least they're flying in the right direction," Gruber replied. "Let's hope Deep does something useful, but we shouldn't make any plans that count on it."

The Star Runner, being the fastest ship in their fleet, soon passed the Nemesis and made its way to the port side of the Kohr-Ah vessel. The Nemesis approached from the starboard side.

A shot was fired at the Star Runner, but Fwiffo seemed to dodge it with ease. Soon Fwiffo was at the side of the enemy ship and fired two B.U.T.T. missiles.

"There's no friggin' way it can turn around fast enough to shoot down those torpedoes," McNeil half hoped, half speculated.

And he was probably right, since they didn't even try. Instead, the enemy ship accelerated strongly. The Spathi missiles were easily left behind since they were designed to intercept enemies chasing the Eluder, not targets flying away.

The Nemesis was still in front of the enemy.

"GO!" Deep shouted in a scary **deep** voice. A small craft was detached from the Nemesis and it headed straight towards the oncoming enemy ship. If they had understood Deep correctly, the Nemesis had several 'one man' craft or rocket suits or whatever in which the Orz could board enemy ships and fight them from the inside. Apparently Deep had just launched one of its crew on such a mission.

A lot happened in the next ten seconds. The Kohr-Ah ship adjusted its heading slightly and right before the Orz trooper could get into position, it was wiped out by another spinning blade. The Nemesis flew past the enemy from the starboard side and sent another trooper out, this time well outside the Kohr-Ah ship's supposed firing sector. At the same time, the rotating main gun of the Nemesis was targeted at the enemy, taking it by surprise, and it managed to land two shots. The boarding party had almost reached the hull of the enemy ship safely from behind, when the thermal imaging camera of the Vindicator captured a distressing sight.

Just like Dip and Pak had described, a ring of blue super-heated flame was shot out from the black destroyer. The ring expanded and gradually weakened, but the Orz trooper got caught in it and was incinerated.

"So attacking from behind is no walk in the park either," Trent said. *"We must find out how often they can use a defense mechanism that powerful."*

"There has to be a time lag of several minutes at least," McNeil guessed.

"We need to focus our attack right after it has used that fire ring," Trent continued.

It would take a while for the Nemesis and Star Runner to turn around and join the fight again. The Voyager was just about to pass the enemy from the port side, but the Kohr-Ah seemed to ignore it. They probably considered the Zoq-Fot-

Pik Stinger vessel to be of little or zero threat. Instead, it set course directly towards the Tobermoon.

"Captain Zelnick," Trent said in a very serious voice, *"they will very soon get so close to us that we can't dodge their attacks anymore. You need to engage them right now or we're done for."*

"I see," Zelnick acknowledged and then addressed the operators. "I'll take control of the engines. Mr. McNeil, prepare to fire our batteries dry."

Zelnick started tapping his console and the Vindicator accelerated ferociously towards the enemy.

"Sir, we can't dodge their attacks at this speed," Gruber pointed out.

"I know," Zelnick replied, "but I'm counting on the ion-bolt gun having a better success than the nukes at intercepting the enemy's projectiles."

The Vindicator got in range of its main gun and Zelnick ordered McNeil to fire a single taunting shot at the enemy who, as expected, turned and fired a shot to counter it.

"McNeil, now fire everything," Zelnick commanded.

The incoming spinning blade blocked the firing sector, but the Vindicator fired rapidly anyway. The first shots hit the oncoming projectile and, as Zelnick had hoped, the third one was enough to render it harmless. The rest of the shots were on their way and McNeil continued to fire. The enemy ship managed to shoot one more time at the ion bolts, stopping the next three ones, but after that, the bolts started to land on their target.

Just as Dr. Fredrikson had calculated, after 15 shots were fired, the Vindicator's computer informed Zelnick that the combat batteries were empty. Now they could just wait and watch to see how much damage was done.

"There's the fire ring again," Trent observed. Before the last of the ion bolts had hit it, the ship activated its fire defense, swallowing the last shots from the Vindicator.

"Now's our chance," Trent continued. *"Hit it with everything."*

Two nukes were immediately fired from the Tobermoon. There were two missiles in the firing tubes at a time so the Tobermoon would have to wait and reload before firing more.

"We're empty," Zelnick replied.

"I can't get close enough in time," Fwiffo reported.

The Nemesis had already sent out two more boarding units and it was now tailing the black destroyer.

*"This time will be *happy time* I am sure,"* Captain Deep declared. *"I am help with *slow time particles*."*

The Nemesis fired three shots at the Kohr-Ah ship and they all hit.

"Nnnnngggaaaa!" Deep shouted in what appeared to be an annoyed tone. *"*Hard* *bubbles* not *dissolving*!"*

The Vindicator flew past the enemy from the port side and at the same time two nukes from the Tobermoon hit their target.

"The enemy ship is still intact," Dujardin reported.

"How can anything take a pounding like that and survive?" Iwasaki wondered.

"Would we have survived that, Mr. Iwasaki?" Zelnick asked.

"Er…" Iwasaki hesitated and did some calculations. "Yes, I think we would have, sir."

"Our window is closing," Trent said.

The commanding trio of the Voyager then spoke their mind.

"We are in position to do the
Stinger-tongue attack."

"But if we can't neutralize
those Zebrankies before they
release another blue death
ring, we're done for."

"We're going in."

The Voyager stormed towards the Kohr-Ah ship and right before ramming it right on, a red tongue-like lance was thrust forward from the Stinger vessel. It penetrated the hull of the enemy ship and made the Voyager stick to the port side of the black destroyer. Now they could properly see just how small the Zoq-Fot-Pik Stinger was in comparison.

"We can now fire again," Trent reported. *"Dip, Pak, Por, get out of there. Your ship can't take the shockwave."*

The Nemesis was now right behind the enemy, firing rapidly at its rear. The boarding units entered the ship apparently through the holes the Nemesis made.

The Voyager retracted its tongue and detached itself like a mosquito. At the very same moment, two more nukes were fired from the Tobermoon.

"We're too close now," Trent said. *"If it comes after the Tobermoon, we can't escape."*

The nukes hit their target.

"Captain," Dujardin called out, "I can detect temperature rising within the enemy ship."

"So it has finally had enough," Zelnick said in relief.

The Nemesis was still pounding on the enemy's stern like mad.

*"I am told *happy time* is too many fun,"* Deep 'reported'. *"So much *juicy* burst into several."*

"It looks like the enemy is neutralized," Zelnick told the other captains. "Stay clear in case they have a self-destruct system similar to the green Ur-Quan."

But the Nemesis stayed on the Kohr-Ah's tail, shooting at it.

"Captain Deep, withdraw," Zelnick ordered.

*"*Dissolving* is the *now game*,"* Deep answered. *"I am *squirting nice colors*!"*

There were explosions all around the Kohr-Ah ship. Any second now it would break completely…

“Oh no,” Zelnick said as he looked at the collapsing ship.

The ship managed to fire one more blue flame ring before its complete destruction. The flames devoured the Nemesis and after a few seconds nothing but debris was left of either of the ships.

“Dammit!” Zelnick shouted. “Damn that weird fish-frog!”

This was a whole new insult. Indeed they couldn’t afford to waste powerful starships in such a petty way. Captain Deep and the Nemesis had been in the fleet for only a short time so Gruber didn’t feel any personal sorrow for their destruction, but he still shared Zelnick’s frustration.

“Sir, there’s something moving amidst the shambles,” Iwasaki reported.

Zelnick looked at the image from the wreckage

“What is that?” he asked, pointing at the moving part.

Iwasaki zoomed in on the target, which turned out to be one of the Orz boarding troops.

“I wonder how they managed to survive,” Iwasaki said.

“Well let’s go pick them up,” Zelnick commanded. “Mr. Samusenko, you have the helm. And get the scavenging team ready.”

The commanding trio of the Voyager hailed them.

“You really are capable in battle.”

“Yeah, we really kicked their afterburner!”

“We were right to trust you. Now you need to talk to our leaders.”

“And maybe we’ll get a prize too, hmm? After all, we helped save our ENTIRE PLANET!”

"Fool. How can you think about personal gain at a time like this?"

"It's easy for you to say! You can just sit in the sun and wait for an umbrabee to pollinate you when I have to— YEOUCH!"

Dip detached a thorn out of itself and somehow rocketed it at Pak's face.

"I'm sorry you had to hear that, Captain. Now, please fly to our planet. Our leaders will surely contact you right away. If it's okay with you, we would like to leave your fleet now."

"Oh," Zelnick was taken by surprise. "Well, okay. Are you going to return when we leave this system?"

"It's not up to us, but I would personally like that. Flying with you has been very enlightening."

"Yeah, and maybe I'd get to do more Stinger-tongue attacks!"

"In any case we will contact you before you leave. Goodbye for now."

"Take care!"

"I hope to see you again soon," Zelnick responded and then the transmission was cut.

A few hours later their storage bay was filled with booty and they entered the orbit of the first planet in the Alpha

Tucanae star system. Just as Dip had predicted, they were contacted right away. Or actually, it was hard to decide whether it was just the Voyager contacting them again… all Zoq-Fot-Pik trios looked the same.

"Hello, human friends."

"You have amazing firepower. We are in your debt."

"We hope that during this visit we can make clear to your species the benefits of a mutual-assistance pact."

"If you hadn't shown up, that black Marauder would have killed us all!"

"Um, yeah, hi," Zelnick began. "Dip, Pak and Por of the Voyager told us that you are looking to join the New Alliance of Free Stars. This is the alliance's flagship Vindicator and I am Captain Robert Zelnick."

"Greetings and welcome to our world."

"Yeah, welcome to our world."

"I just said that."

"So? That doesn't mean I can't say it too. Besides, you always get to talk first!"

"Sorry, that's just the way it is."

"Faugh!"

"So, Captain Robert Zelnick, what do we get from the Alliance and what do we have to give?"

"What? We have to give something?"

"Hush now."

"As you may know, we oppose the Ur-Quan Hierarchy," Zelnick explained. "So we would give you protection against them. In return, we need your full co-operation. Regarding warfare, you would have to do what the Alliance command council says."

What command council, Gruber thought, but didn't say anything.

"We would also require you to send a delegation to the Alliance's headquarters at Sol. We can build your ships there too if you give us their plans and provide enough captains."

"That sound reasonable.
What kind of protection can
you give us?"

Zelnick didn't answer immediately. Gruber also thought what they could actually promise at this stage. They didn't have much to spare.

"The kind we just showed you," Zelnick wittily replied.

"Then we join your alliance!"

"Seriously, though," Zelnick continued, "we will send a small fleet to protect this system as soon as possible."

"Fair deal."

*"Bummer. I was hoping **you** would stay."*

"So then," Zelnick gloriously proclaimed, "you are now officially members of the New Alliance of Free Stars, along with us Earthlings, the Spathi and the Orz."

"Hurray!"

"Hmh... I'll celebrate more when the fleet you promised arrives."

"Let's get down to business," Zelnick continued. "For starters we should exchange information."

"Ah, good idea."

"Yeah, let's tell him about Frungy!"

"Be quiet, you fool! This is a serious matter. He doesn't want to know about Frungy."

The blue one jumped next to the green one in what seemed to be an angered way. A gush of steam came out of its three nostrils.

"How do you know? What makes you so smart? You never even asked him if he wants to know about Frungy. Why, I'll bet right now he's wondering `What is this wonderful sport, Frungy?', `How is it played?' `What kind of equipment do you need to play Frungy?' and `I wonder who's ahead in the Frungy Championships?'"

Now the green one extended its neck-equivalent and yelled at the blue one.

"AUGH! Will you SHUT UP ABOUT FRUNGY?! If you say another word about that STUPID GAME, I'm going to lose control and blow a cloud of spores at you!"

"Yech! Okay, okay. Don't blow your sac. I won't mention Frungy again, I promise."

"Now, Captain Robert Zelnick, in all seriousness, this space exploration stuff is kinda new to us so we don't know much about what's going on outside our solar system."

"Before you showed up, we had met four different alien species."

"Or at least that's what we think."

"First were the Chenjesu. The crew of the Voyager told you about that already."

"Then we met the Ur-Quan. They attacked one of our exploration vessels after its commanding crew refused to reveal the location of our homeworld."

"And shortly afterwards the black ones found one of our colonies – and destroyed it!"

"And lately we have seen strange red probes entering the system. They claim to be on a peaceful mission."

"But then they attack like slavering Zebrankies!"

"Actually, the probe visits have become much more frequent lately."

"They are multiplying!"

"—at what appears to be a geometric rate."

"Hey, maybe you could check out where they come from!"

"Ah, yes. My companion is referring to the fact that by back-tracing their course paths we have been able to calculate that the source of the probes is somewhere on a direct line that includes our star and Epsilon Muscae."

"As you surely understand, we haven't been able to leave home lately to check some possible locations."

"Wow, you've had tough luck," Zelnick stated. He then turned to Samusenko.

"Please check how many possibilities there are in this region."

"Aye, sir," Samusenko replied. He quickly drew a line on the star map and a few stars were highlighted. "It looks like there are six additional stars very close to that exact line; three in both directions."

The closest highlighted star was Beta Mersenne just a little off from their planned course to the Arilou sightings. Much further, at the edge of charted space, there were Vega and Beta Corvi, very close to each other. In the opposite direction there were Alpha and Gamma Kepler near Mycon space. The last hit was Alpha Sagittarii on the other side of the Mycon territory.

"You have given us valuable information already," Zelnick commended the Zoq-Fot-Pik leaders. "Allow me to tell you what we know of these races that keep attacking you."

Zelnick took his time explaining things to the Zoq-Fot-Pik. After an hour or two Gruber had to hint that all the historical information could be sent in a single data pack which the Zoq-Fot-Pik could study for weeks.

Since the Vindicator still had places to be, they didn't stay for festivities. They sent a message with the ansible to Hayes notifying him that a delegation of the Zoq-Fot-Pik were on their way towards the starbase.

"Captain," Gruber began, "we don't have ships to spare here, but what about the Orz? Since they have arrived at the starbase, we could send a message via Hayes and ask them to dispatch a squadron here."

"Hey, that's a great idea," Zelnick said, sounding a little bit too surprised. He typed the message right away. "Should I send regards to that woman of yours as well?"

"I'm fine, sir, thank you," Gruber replied. He didn't even know that Zelnick knew – or cared – that much about his personal affairs.

"What about the Spathi?" Zelnick asked. "Should they contribute as well?"

"I thought about that," Gruber said. "But then I figured that the Ur-Quan probably still don't know that the Spathi have turned against them. We should keep it that way for as long as possible."

"I see. I'm glad to have you as first officer."

Gruber swallowed. Receiving sudden praise is difficult for a modest man.

"Thank you, sir," he managed to reply.

The Vindicator was ready to leave.

"Should we just leave without Dip-Por-Pak?" Zelnick raised a question.

And speaking of the devil… They were hailed at the very same moment.

"Captain Robert Zelnick, may we come with you?"

"—us and three other ships that is."

"We figured that since in matters of war you are so much more capable than us, we would be of more use under your command."

"These, including the Voyager, are our best ships."

This was a pleasant surprise. With the Nemesis gone, they could use a few extra escorts.

"Yes," Zelnick replied, "you are very welcome to join us."

Then they received another signal, this time from the surface. The image was identical to the previous one so it was a little confusing to tell who they were talking to now, but they probably were the leaders again.

"Before you go, we wish to assign four of our finest starships and crew to your fleet."

"They are the Voyager, the Traveler, the Seeker and the Tracker. Try not to lose them all right away."

"We wish you best of luck and safe travels."

"Yeah! And one more thing..."

The blue one looked at the green one ominously.

"Frungy! Frungy! Frungy!"

"Ach!"

The green one opened a hole of some kind in its body and a cloud of spores gushed at the blue one. Then the transmission was cut.

Zelnick and Gruber stared at the empty screen for a while.

"We might have a less dull journey this time," Zelnick predicted.

"Aye, sir," Gruber agreed.

"Mr. Samusenko, set course for 050.0 : 650.0," Zelnick commanded. "Let's go see if we can find the little green men."

CHAPTER 17

INTO DARKNESS

June 1st 2155, hyperspace, 070.3 : 645.9

We are just passing the Columbae star cluster and thus entering the region where, according to Captain Fwiffo, a friend of his saw an Arilou Skiff a while back. While it's not much to work with, even a slim chance of finding the Arilou is worth looking into. If this last stop on our trip proves fruitless, we'll just fly straight back to Sol.

We have traveled 345 hyperspace units in 14 days, including four days inside Umgah territory. We might try to work out a diplomatic solution with the Umgah sometime in the future, but right now there's too much at stake.

Although everyone is in high spirits now, the surviving Orz trooper creeps me out – and I'm not the only one. Ever since we rescued it from the Kohr-Ah wreckage, it has just been standing in the shuttle hangar in its weird exoskeleton. It doesn't speak unless spoken to and, just like Captain Deep, it doesn't make much sense.

On that note, Lydia has taken a liking to talking with the creature. While there's nothing wrong with it, I can't help feeling a little uneasy... and worried. I should ask her sometime how she's doing. This is not the right place for her, although neither were the ruins of the Androsynth city, nor would the starbase be.

"Tell me again about the Arilou," Zelnick said to Gruber as he entered the bridge.

Gruber walked to Zelnick's side and used the few seconds to think where he should start.

"As the rumors say," he began, "the Arilou have indeed made many visits to Earth. The first reported sightings were found in some ancient hieroglyphs in Egypt, describing the construction of the early pyramids. Their last unofficial visit that we know of was in 1947. There were lots of tensions between the most influential countries at that time, so when the North-American air defense spotted an unidentified flying object above Roswell, New Mexico, they fired at it. The object crashed and the U.S. military hid it in a secret bunker where it stayed hidden for nearly two centuries. It wasn't until after the Arilou officially showed up on Earth's moon to declare their desire to join the old alliance that the Roswell incident was made public. The Arilou never really explained what they were doing on Earth and we never dared to press the matter... Do you find something so far rather hard to believe?"

"Yes," Zelnick replied. "How was it possible to shoot down an Arilou ship with the weapons we had over 200 years ago?"

"Bingo," Gruber said. "That remains unknown even to this day. The Arilou were a mysterious bunch. They appeared out of nowhere, fought alongside us, and then disappeared again. There never was any reason to question their loyalty, but I dare say there was something in their motives they weren't telling us."

"And how well **did** they fight?"

"As well as us, I'd say. But they had another notable asset."

"Hmm?"

"They had some means to travel between stars incredibly fast. They never shared that technology with us."

"Do you mean faster than the Vindicator?"

"A lot faster."

“Then I’m pretty sure they don’t use hyperdrive at all,” Zelnick deduced.

“You sound awfully sure about that, but that’s how I feel as well.”

“Think about what the Orz said,” Zelnick explained. “According to them, the Arilou are from the ‘outside’, although they mentioned that they themselves are from ‘below’ and the Arilou are from ‘above’. So I think it’s logical to assume that they use their position ‘above’ or whatever to move faster from star to star.”

Gruber pondered the theory.

“Think about it this way,” Zelnick continued. “Traveling between stars in true space takes an eternity. Then there’s hyperspace, a ‘higher dimension’ so to speak, where the travel time is only a fraction of that in true space. So maybe the Arilou similarly utilize a dimension higher than hyperspace?”

“That sounds very reasonable,” Gruber had to agree.

After a few hours they had reached their destination. There was nothing out of the ordinary in the region, but they were prepared for that. The fleet was split up into three: The Voyager and the Tobermoon would search the three stars of the Columbae cluster, the Tracker, the Traveler and the Seeker would search the five stars of the Chandrasekhar cluster and finally the Vindicator and the Star Runner would cover the six stars of the Circini cluster. They would be able to communicate with each other over such short distances even without the hyperwave network.

The trip to Gamma Circini, the closest star of the Circini cluster, would take only about a day for the Vindicator and the Star Runner. The others would reach their destinations a little later.

Zelnick was eating dinner and Gruber was at the helm when he suddenly noticed an anomaly right in front of them.

"What's that?" he asked Dujardin, the radar operator.

"I don't know, sir," she replied. "It looks like a star, but there should be nothing here according to the map."

Gruber contacted Fwiffo.

"Do you see the vortex right up ahead?" he asked.

"Yes I do," Fwiffo replied. *"It must be what Phlendo told me about."*

"No, wait," Dujardin interrupted them, "I don't think it's a star. The diameter of the vortex seems to be growing."

Whatever the anomaly was, it was getting bigger right before their eyes. Unlike normal vortexes, which were basically holes into the black true space, this one was completely green – a green hole in the middle of the red hyperspace.

"Let's keep our distance," Gruber decided. "Mr. Steinbach, stop the engines. Mr. Iwasaki, alert the captain."

"Aye, sir," they both replied and Iwasaki called Zelnick.

Soon Zelnick entered the bridge and they all saluted. Gruber vacated the captain's chair and Zelnick sat down.

"Why are we flying towards it?" Zelnick asked.

"We're not," Steinbach explained. "Our engines are shut down and we're holding our position. Look."

Steinbach pointed at the hyperspace radar which clearly indicated that they weren't moving.

"Then why are we getting closer to that green sphere if we're not moving?" Zelnick asked angrily. "Is **it** moving towards **us**?"

Zelnick's observation was justified. Indeed it looked like they were flying straight into the mysterious hole.

"The hole is not moving, sir, "Dujardin checked. "Wait… It has begun expanding at an alarming rate! It's going to swallow us in a few moments!"

"Turn us around and get us out of here!" Zelnick hastily ordered.

"It's too late!" Samusenko reported. "We won't make it."

"Send a mayday to the rest of the fleet," Zelnick commanded.

"Aye, sir," Katja replied and then broadcast a message to the other ships. "Mayday, mayday, this is the Vindicator. We are being sucked into an unknown green vortex at coordinates 043.8 : 637.3—"

Right then the edge of the hole reached them and the hyperwave transmitter stopped working. The ship was intact, but that was all they were certain of at that moment.

In true space you could see stars in all directions and the plane of the Milky Way was easily distinguishable. In hyperspace there were ghost lights which made it look like the ship was inside a thin red cloud. But here, there was nothing. They were in green emptiness.

Gruber's natural instincts told him that it was the perfect time to panic. His training on the other hand told him that that was the worst available option. The two opposing views fought it out for a second or two, but the latter one triumphed in the end. Gruber decided to remain silent and let the captain handle the situation.

Zelnick interacted with the ship's computer in his unique way and then reported his findings:

"The computer has no idea what just happened. How about any of you?"

You could almost hear the silence. It was finally broken by Gruber's beeping communicator. According to the name list, the caller was Bukowski, but Gruber knew that after Bukowski's death, his communicator was given to Lydia. Although it wasn't a good time, Gruber assumed that Lydia had a reason to call him, since this was the first time, so he answered.

<<*The Orz is gone,*>> Lydia said.

<<What do you mean?>> Gruber asked.

*<<It just disappeared. I was talking to it and in the middle of its sentence *poof* it vanished.>>*

<<When did it happen?>>

<<Just now! I called you right away. Not even a nute— a minute has passed.>>

"What is she saying?" Zelnick asked as Lydia sounded quite frantic.

"The Orz has disappeared," Gruber translated.

"Go check it out quickly and then get back here," Zelnick ordered.

"Aye, sir," Gruber replied and then talked to Lydia again:

<<Stay put, I'm coming over there.>>

Gruber entered the shuttle hangar and from a distance saw Lydia – and the Orz exoskeleton.

<<What do you mean it's gone?>> Gruber rather angrily shouted from across the hall. <<It's right there, isn't it?>>

<<The… animal isn't here!>> Lydia shouted back. <<This piece of metal is, but it's empty!>>

Gruber walked across the hangar, regretting sounding so angry. When he reached Lydia, he had to agree with her. The transparent liquid tank in the middle of the exoskeleton was empty and the level of the liquid was somewhat lower than before.

<<How did it disappear?>> Gruber inquired.

<<It just did,>> Lydia said. <<I asked it how old it was and it said it had no beginning and was about to say something more when it just… stopped existing. At one moment it was here and at the next moment it wasn't.>>

Gruber scratched his head.

<<Calling me was the right thing to do,>> he commended her. <<It's a good thing you noticed this happening.>>

<<I'm happy to be of some use,>> Lydia cheerfully said.

<<I have to get back to the bridge,>> Gruber explained. <<We've just entered an unknown place. The space is green and hyperwave doesn't work.>>

<<Oh, we must be outside then,>> Lydia said as if it was obvious.

Gruber didn't want to ask 'What do you mean?' all the time.

<<What do you mean?>> he asked anyway.

<<It's something the Orz told me – that they are from 'outside' and we are from 'inside'. And that the Orz are different on the inside.>>

<<That's interesting,>> Gruber said. <<Let's talk more about it when I can leave the bridge again.>>

He started walking to the direction of the bridge. When he was on the other side of the hangar, Lydia called out to him again.

<<Adam!>> she shouted and Gruber quickly turned around. <<There's some other creature in the tank!>>

Gruber ran back to her and saw what she meant. A small green frog-like creature was swimming in the tank of the Orz exoskeleton. It was about the size of Lydia's fist. Lydia and Gruber both looked at it very closely and it swam against the wall to look back at them.

"Er… Hello? Can you hear me?" Gruber asked the creature.

The creature stared at him, not showing any sign of sentience, which made Gruber feel stupid for talking to a frog.

"Well?" Zelnick asked as Gruber entered the bridge.

"The Orz has been turned into a frog," he answered and then explained.

"That is compatible with our theory," Zelnick began. "We think – or rather, Ms. Dujardin speculated that we are in a higher dimension of space – if you could still call it space. This… quasi-space… seems to have vortexes in it similar to hyperspace. Where they lead? Your guess is as good as mine."

"Captain," Dujardin then said, "take a look at this. I used the gravity wave sensor to calculate approximate locations of some anomalies, which 'might' be vortexes out of here. At least gravity seems to work here the way it does in true space."

She projected a rough map of their location relative to the nearest gravity wells.

"And we can probably navigate here using the true space engines," Steinbach reasoned.

"Then how about we fly there," Zelnick said and pointed at the largest dot on the map. The gravity waves were significantly stronger there compared to the other points. "And take us pretty close to that one point on the way… Let's see if we can get a glimpse of those targets."

"Aye, sir," Samusenko reported. "The big one is about a day from here and we should pass the smaller one on our route in a few hours."

Zelnick opened a link to the Star Runner.

"Captain Fwiffo, we ar—," but he had to stop in mid-sentence, because Fwiffo wasn't there. "Fwiffo!" he then called out in case Fwiffo was just away from his spot.

There was no response.

"I'll try to contact someone from the crew with the personal communicator," Gruber suggested and got to it. He called the first person he remembered to be assigned aboard the Star Runner.

"Mr. Gruber, sir," the man responded.

"Do you know where Captain Fwiffo is?" Gruber asked.

"Er… on the bridge, I think."

"Go check."

"Yes sir."

A few minutes later he called back.

"Sir, I'm at the bridge, but Captain Fwiffo is not here."

"Check the ball pool," Gruber ordered.

The crewmember then groaned for a while and the sound of plastic balls rustling could be heard.

"Found him!" the man soon reported.

"Good, drag him to the communication screen."

Soon Fwiffo's face appeared on the Vindicator's main screen. The poor fellow had seen better days. His skin color was a lot lighter than usual and he was, once again, trembling.

"Captain Fwiffo," Zelnick addressed him, "I know we are in a troubled and even frightening situation, but we need you to stay focused and follow us with the Star Runner."

Fwiffo twitched forward and Zelnick took that as an affirmative.

"Alright, let's go," he then commanded.

Three hours later they were passing their waypoint, a smaller gravity well. It was a red hole in the green background - a reverse of the green hole that had pulled them into the 'quasispace'. It was tempting to fly into it right away.

"That looks promising," Zelnick said. "If the bigger gravity well doesn't look better, we should enter one of those and hope that it takes us back to hyperspace."

They still had 20 hours to go, so Gruber had a chance to talk with Lydia. She was where he had left her, admiring the toad, and didn't notice Gruber approaching her.

<<Do you like being a frog?>> she asked the frog, obviously.

The frog stared at her in silence.

<<It must be nice when nobody tells you what to do.>>

Gruber kept silent and observed the ~~dialog~~ monologue.

<<I mean, I got that a lot so I could relate, but… That was a long time ago, back at my home planet. I used to live there with a bunch of people that weren't very nice, although Fifty-Three was. Then the smart and old ones all died when ghosts attacked the city, but you know all about that, right?>>

The frog didn't answer.

<<Fifty-Three, or Anna as I liked to call her, helped me through it. We hid in the vents, you know. We stayed there for three days and then had to crawl out to get water. The smart ones were all gone then and most of the normals like me and Anna were dead. I know you don't like me asking about the smart ones, but I know you took them. I kinda liked the first few months with Anna and some of the other normals we found, so I'm not mad at you. But then the normals started catching a fever and dying. It was tough dragging their corpses around and finally it was just me and Anna left… and then Anna caught it *sniff*. Do you know how hard it was for me? Anna was a few years older than me and she had taught me everything about survival. After I had dragged her body away too, I just waited for the fever to come, but it never did. I was all alone. Do you know what it's like to be all alone for nearly two circles?>>

The frog ignored the question.

<<I stayed alive only because I had nothing else to do. I had long ago stopped dreaming of ever meeting anyone anymore and then these guys suddenly showed up. I'm not saying they're the greatest, but at least this is now far better than what I had back then. I just wish I had someone my age to hang around with… someone who could understand me. There's this one old guy who tries and he can even speak my language… but he is… old and busy and… boring.>>

The frog blinked.

<<He's standing behind me, isn't he?>>

The frog blinked again and Lydia turned around.

<<So you’re certain that frog is the Orz?>> Gruber asked, thinking that it would be the least awkward way to begin.

<<Of course it is,>> Lydia answered, looking like she wasn’t at all ashamed. <<They are projected differently in different dimensions, just like we are.>>

<<Are we?>> Gruber asked, sounding surprised and at the same time looking at himself.

<<The smart ones were pulled into the Orz dimension and from our perspective ceased to exist. This frog here might see this whole scene in a completely different way.>>

<<You sound awfully certain.>>

<<It just seems logical to me.>>

<<Do you know why only the Androsynth were… taken?>> Gruber asked. <<Why didn’t the ‘ghosts’ take you too?>>

<<Because I didn’t look. And since I didn’t look, I didn’t see. And since I didn’t see, I wasn’t seen.>>

<<Did you write the graffiti on the walls back at the research center?>>

<<No, I was already hiding at that time, but I agree with their message.>>

<<So how would I ‘look’ if I wanted to?>> Gruber asked.

Lydia rolled her eyes and looked at him like you look at someone asking a very, **very** stupid question.

<<Ask me again tomorrow,>> she said. <<Then, if you still want to know, I’ll tell you.>>

She turned around, managing to make the movement look angry, and walked away.

Gruber watched her exit the hangar and then noticed the frog still staring at him.

“What are you looking at?”

“There it is,” Dujardin reported as they could see their target.

“So that’s the party place around here,” Zelnick said. “It looks a lot different than the rest.”

Indeed, unlike the red holes, this vortex was black, like the ones in hyperspace. As they got closer to it, they saw a planet at the center.

“That doesn’t look like a vortex at all,” Gruber observed. “Rather, it looks like it’s a true space bubble with a planet inside.”

Soon they saw that it was a terrestrial planet – there were blue oceans, green and brown continents, and white clouds. Orbiting the planet was a white rocky moon.

“Doesn’t that look a little too familiar?” Zelnick raised a question.

The shape of the continents somehow resembled those of Earth. Clearly they weren’t the same, but there were too many similarities for it to be a coincidence.

“Isn’t that there Africa?” Dujardin asked, pointing at one continent on the equator.

It could have been, but it was aligned a bit differently and the shape wasn’t an exact match.

“What should we do, Mr. Gruber?” Zelnick asked. “Shall we try to fly inside that sphere?”

“I can think of two good reasons,” Gruber began. “First, if we do indeed arrive at true space, we could check our location from the stars. Second, we might get an ansible link to the starbase.”

“That sounds reasonable,” Zelnick agreed. “Mr. Samusenko, fly us inside.”

The Vindicator slowly glided towards the black sphere, which covered more and more of their view as they got closer.

“We are reaching the border line,” Samusenko reported. “Five… four… three… two… one…”

Nothing happened. They were clearly in true space now, but couldn't feel any kind of transition like when entering a true space vortex from hyperspace. There was nothing to indicate that they had been in a strange green quasispace just before.

"What an anticlimax," Zelnick stated.

"There are no stars," Gruber observed. "And I mean none at all. This planet seems to be all alone. Where does the heat and light come from?"

"Sir," Dujardin began, "according to the radar, there's a swarm of ships all around us."

"What? Again?" Zelnick said in disbelief.

"Yes sir," Dujardin continued. "It's just like with the Orz. They just appeared out of nowhere. I'll get a scan ready right now… there."

She projected a view of one of the ships on the screen.

"Well I'll be damned," Gruber said. "It's an Arilou Skiff. How many are there?"

"About twenty," Dujardin checked.

A faint rustling of plastic balls was heard from the Star Runner's bridge.

"I guess this explains why they never told us where their homeworld was," Gruber remarked.

"Well let's contact them already!" Zelnick anxiously commanded and Katja immediately opened up a frequency for them.

They waited for the "awaiting confirmation…" text to disappear and the image to appear. After an eternity of three seconds, the link was established and they saw the familiar face of an Arilou – a little green humanoid who appeared to be hovering in a lotus position.

"Ha-ha!" the Arilou laughed. *"Our clever ward has found our nook in *time*!"*

"Arilou!" Zelnick exclaimed and smiled. "It's good to see you! We've wondered what happened to your people for a long time."

"Yes, I am Arilou Lalee'lay," the alien answered, smiling as well. *"You are the first, brave human! No others have made the trip. This is our homeworld, Falayalaralfali, nestled safe in this true space eddy."*

The Arilou kept turning a glowing sphere between his hands without actually touching the sphere.

"What happened to you at the end of the war?" Zelnick inquired.

"Oh, that is right..." the Arilou said with a hint of surprise in his voice. *"I suppose it has been a long time since you've met one of my kind. I imagine you humans are still very short lived. How sad. Ah well, to answer your question, we chose to cease our efforts with the Alliance of Free Stars when it seemed that there was no longer any threat to our Earthlings. I am pleased to see that you, from outside the slave shield, survived. You seem healthy."*

"Could you be more specific?" Zelnick pressed the matter. "Surely the Ur-Quan didn't allow you to just leave?"

"Forgive us if we forget the importance you attach to such events as this," the Arilou apologized, sounding sincere. *"Our... context is infinitely broader than yours in scope, both in space and *time*. Nevertheless, to please you, I shall try to recall."*

He shut his eyes for a moment and the sphere started glowing brightly.

"Yes, now I remember," he said after a while. *"Here is the sequence: The Ur-Quan fleets have moved through your solar system and you are defeated. Your people make the choice not to fight with and for the Ur-Quan. A shield is cast about your world. Your people are now safe. This makes us happy. The Armada departs your star system and moves toward the remaining Alliance members: ourselves, the*

Syreen, the Yehat and their adopted Shofixti. The Yehat and Shofixti withdraw to Delta Gorno, but they do not permit the Syreen to follow. We are content with the flow of events and leave the area to return here.

From our perspective, this sequence of events ends here."

Zelnick wasn't satisfied with the answer.

"But how did you manage to escape?" he demanded.

The Arilou kept on smiling.

"Your curiosity is promising. I shall try to explain it in a way you understand."

Again he fell silent and closed his eyes for a moment.

"You entered this dimension through a portal from hyperspace," he explained, eyes still closed. *"We live here. We are able to focus dimensional fatigue rays to create such portals of our own. Once you were defeated at Sol, we created these portals and used them to return home. I can see that from your and the Ur-Quan's point of view we vanished."*

"He mentioned dimensional fatigue," Gruber pointed out. "That's what the Androsynth were looking into right before they disappeared."

"So that's the secret to your speed!" Zelnick realized. "It was a great mystery how you were able to travel to distant stars so fast."

The Arilou seemed to be bathing in an indescribable pride, but not of himself.

"You are very clever. The portal you passed through is a rarity, a natural point of interdimensional fatigue. We use these phenomena to speed our transit through the realities."

"Wow," Zelnick said. "But hey, you said that you left the war once we Earthlings were safe… What did you mean by that? Weren't you concerned about the other races in the alliance?"

"You desire honesty," the Arilou replied, still smiling widely, *"and I shall give it to you."*

The sphere between his hands now illuminated the whole space around him. The Arilou kept his eyes closed and got somewhat more serious.

"You are the priority. It was no coincidence that we appeared in the open for the first time the day after humanity joined the Alliance of Free Stars. We have a long history with your species. You could say that we knew the very first human.

You have painted our pictures on cave walls, erected standing stones and pyramids for us. You have wondered at our signs to each other in your wheat fields and written books about our more personal endeavors when we allowed you to recall our examinations.

To call our interaction with your kind an experiment would be much too simple and impersonal. Let us just say that we have a vested interest in your... development. You are one of our... extended family, just as other sentients in other dimensions have their extended families. We are proud of you as you would be of your children, and some day..."

He stopped in the middle of his sentence, just like he was about to blurt out a big secret.

"Well, I must tread carefully now. You are not ready for everything. Premature exposure to some information would be dangerous. The most important thing is that all... modifications we have made in your past have been in your best interest.

There are parasites – creatures who dwell beyond. They would like to find you, but they are blind to your presence... unless you show yourselves. The Androsynth showed themselves and something noticed them. There are no more Androsynth now, only Orz."

"Yes, we've met the Orz," Zelnick explained. "They are weird, but they are currently helping us. But if you can tell us anything more about them—"

"No!" the Arilou suddenly cut in, losing his composure. *"Ignorance is your armor, your best protection. They cannot see you now. They cannot smell you. Much of our work with your people involved making you invisible... changing your smell. If I tell you more, you will look where you could never look before. And while you are looking, you can and* ***will*** *be seen. You do not want to be seen."*

"Are you saying we should stay away from the Orz?" Zelnick asked, sounding a little frightful and disappointed.

The Arilou calmed down.

"No... They are useful to you right now. But do not trust them. Remember that they are dangerous."

Zelnick calmed down as well.

"Well, I should get to the point now," he began. "We are still struggling against the Ur-Quan. Can you help us?"

The Arilou looked sad – like he was about to say something extremely disappointing.

"With ships and weapons... blood and bones... no. Too many shipmates were forcibly... discorporated... in the last conflict. Our cooperation is not necessary. You are the focus."

Zelnick was about to say something.

"However," the Arilou continued, *"we would be happy to give you our means to utilize this higher dimension to save you needless transit time."*

"Oh? You mean we could jump on and off from this quasispace place and travel as fast as you do?"

"Yes, but there is one problem..."

"How big a problem?"

*"****Big*** *is the right word, captain. Our portal spawners are designed to work with our small Skiff vessels. Your ship is so*

massive that our small units would be ineffective, however..."

"Yes?" Zelnick had to say, as the wait became too long.

"We do know of a way to make a powerful enough portal spawner. The key element is a warp pod, which needs to be extremely powerful to work on your huge vessel. A sufficiently powerful warp pod could be found in an Ur-Quan Dreadnought."

"Well that's a negative then," Zelnick said. "We can't salvage anything functional from a defeated Dreadnought. They always self-destruct after being disabled.

"You are of course right," the Arilou said with great pride once again. *"However, during one... how should I say... reconnaissance mission, we witnessed the crash landing of an Ur-Quan Dreadnought on the surface of the seventh planet of Alpha Pavonis. In this case, these self-destruct circuits must have failed, because the ship didn't disintegrate on impact. We suspect that you might find a functional warp pod there. If you can acquire it, we would be delighted to fit a portal spawner into your ship."*

"Where is Alpha Pavonis?" Zelnick asked the operators and Samusenko soon pointed it to him on the map. It was at 056.2 : 800.0.

"Alright," Zelnick told the Arilou, "if we get our hands on the warp pod, we shall bring it to you here… But how? The portal to quasispace appeared in front of us by chance. How can we find it again?"

"Ah, of course, how silly of me," the Arilou laughed. *"There is only one naturally occurring portal from hyperspace to quasispace that we know of. It appears and disappears periodically right where you saw it – at 043.8 : 637.2. In your time units, the portal is open for three days and then closed for 27 days.*

"What were the odds of us flying right over it when it appeared, huh?" Zelnick asked, making a point of the odds being astronomical.

"Yes, it is hard to believe it was a coincidence, am I right?" the Arilou creepily answered.

"Uh…" Zelnick was taken aback. "So… how do we get home?"

"Oh?" the Arilou said, sounding very surprised. *"That is a problem indeed..."* he then seemed to be deep in thought for a while and once again prepared to disappoint. *"I'm afraid that for you the only way to your... dimension... would be to choose one of the many natural portals out there. They all lead to different parts in hyperspace, but, alas, we cannot tell you where they take you exactly."*

"Huh?" Zelnick sounded offended. "Why the hell not?"

"Because we do not know."

"How can you not know if you use them all the time for traveling?" Zelnick rightfully asked. Gruber was also thinking the same thing.

"We do not use the natural portals," the Arilou patiently explained. *"We can focus the dimensional fatigue rays the other way around as well, to jump from quasispace back to hyperspace. The natural portals are... trivial to us. They do not interest us."*

"Oh, great," Zelnick replied, frustrated, "so we could end up at the far side of the galaxy if we choose the wrong portal?"

"No, not that far," the Arilou reassured him. *"If you use the portal spawner in this region of hyperspace, you will always end up at the same spot in quasispace. Likewise, if you go through a portal in this region of quasispace, you end up in the same region in hyperspace."*

Zelnick scratched his head and then wiped his forehead with his both hands.

"I can see that I have confused you," the Arilou said. *"I am sorry. This is what I had feared from the beginning."*

"No sweat," Zelnick lied.

"This must be hard for you to understand, because your mind cannot comprehend higher dimensions. That is also why, even with the portal spawner, you should use the natural portals back to hyperspace. The logic behind the transition is... incomprehensible to you."

"I see," Zelnick accepted the explanation. "It's a shame you won't join the new alliance. We could use your Skiff vessels."

"I understand your disappointment, but don't worry," the Arilou reassured him. *"We shall be there when you need us the most. We will be... watching."*

"Creepy," Zelnick remarked. "Can you help us in any other way or should we get going?"

Now the Arilou seemed sad.

"We cannot be of any more assistance right now," the Arilou sadly said. *"I would have enjoyed your company far over your... time... but that would've been inconvenient for you. Perhaps in the fullness of time we will let you visit the surface of our world. There are many beauties here unmatched anywhere... the Mountain Clouds of Thought, the Tangible Wish... the Dark... Unfortunately, you are not yet... acclimated."*

"Okay, well then, I… uh… will be seeing you?" Zelnick managed to say in an uncomfortable situation.

"Goodbye, friend," the Arilou replied and waved with a small gesture. *"But wait! Before you go, I would like to ask a favor from you."*

"Huh?" Zelnick was taken by surprise. "Well, if it's in my power…"

"Wonderful," the Arilou joyously said. *"When we witnessed that Ur-Quan Dreadnought crash, we of course inspected the wreckage by ourselves first and were surprised*

to find a survivor – the Ur-Quan's talking pet. As you may know, the Ur-Quan use these non-sentient creatures for interspecies translation, which the Ur-Quan themselves find ultimately demeaning."

"So what's the favor?" Zelnick asked.

"The poor creature was badly hurt. We did what we could, but it was evident that without superior measures the creature would die. So we turned to the Umgah, whom we have known for many centuries. Their bioscience skills are far above ours. They promised to do what they could and let us know how the talking pet fared."

"So let me guess," Zelnick began. "You haven't heard from them since and want us to go ask them?"

"Yes! You humans are so clever! The best place to ask would be at their home planet in Beta Orionis."

"I don't think the Umgah would take too kindly to us arriving there just to chat with them," Zelnick pointed out. "They're still Ur-Quan battle thralls, right? So we're technically at war with them."

"Yes of course. But if you get the chance anyway, please ask."

"Well, ok," Zelnick agreed.

"Thank you," the Arilou sincerely said. *"To repay your kindness, let me give you this little piece of information: To discover the nature of the red probes, seek creatures who inhabit a world with no surface."*

"Hey, how do you know that?" Zelnick pressed.

"I'm sorry, but I cannot be more specific than that. Now, farewell my clever child."

That being said, they cut the transmission.

"They must mean a gas giant," Gruber deduced. "I've never heard of anything living in one of those. They consist mostly of gaseous hydrogen and helium. If they have a solid core, it's so deep that the pressure would be ridiculous."

“That narrows down the search a lot,” Zelnick said. “If we get back home, we should start checking out the possible stars.”

“Home…” Gruber mumbled out loud. “We’re pretty far from it right now – two dimensions higher, who knows haw ‘far’ actually, and on the other side of an impenetrable slave shield.”

Zelnick laughed a little.

“And speaking of home,” Gruber continued, “let’s try out the ansible.”

“Oh, right,” Zelnick agreed, presumably having forgotten all about it.

Zelnick tried to make the ‘call’ to the starbase, but the ansible terminal said it couldn’t establish a link between the transmitter and the linked receiver.

“Bummer,” he said.

“Looks like there’s something wrong with the true space here after all,” Gruber stated. “…Or there is no receiver – a possibility we’d be better off not considering.”

“I hear you. Let’s get going then,” Zelnick decided. “Mr. Samusenko, take us to that nearest vortex over there. If we can’t know which one to take, we might as well take the one that is closest to us.”

Zelnick then contacted Fwiffo.

“Fwiffo, what’s your take on all of this?”

Fwiffo seemed unnaturally relaxed.

“I just want to go home,” he said plainly.

After a few hours they were right in front of a red sphere in a green background.

“Here goes,” Zelnick declared as they closed the distance.

The Vindicator and the Star Runner slowly crossed the border from green to red. Just like when doing it the other way around, nothing exceptional really happened. The space around them was now familiarly red again and they were clearly back in hyperspace.

"A walk in the park," Zelnick announced. "Now then, Ms. Dujardin, Could you tell us where we are?"

"Yes sir," Dujardin replied and worked on her console for a minute.

"Eh, sir," she began after a while, "you're not going to like this."

"Out with it," Zelnick ordered.

"That white giant star there," she said and pointed at the nearest star on the radar, "that's Groombridge."

"Groombridge?" Zelnick asked. "I've never heard of it. What are our coordinates?"

"It'll take a while to calculate our exact location," Dujardin explained, "but Groombridge is at 996.0 : 904.2 and we're only a few hours towards the negative Y* from it. There are no other stars for over a 100 units in any direction."

Zelnick kept silent.

"The distance from Groombridge to Sol is 1118 units," Dujardin continued her report.

Zelnick still didn't say anything.

"It would take us about a month and a half if we flew straight home from here," Samusenko calculated. "Not to mention the 110 units of fuel, **which we do not have**."

"He is right," Steinbach checked. "We have about 85 units of fuel left."

"It is June 2nd now," Samusenko continued, "so we would be home in the second half of July at best."

There was a slight sound of panic in Samusenko's voice. Zelnick then stood up.

---

* The hyperspace can, against common sense, be expressed as a two-dimensional plane. Thinking about it as a 20th century map, the positive Y axis is the north and positive X axis is the east.

"We need to contact the starbase as soon as possible," he stated. "Mr. Samusenko, fly us into Groombridge so we can use the ansible."

Zelnick's clear order was enough to calm Samusenko.

"Yes sir," Samusenko replied and set the course.

The following few hours were long. Gruber was thinking so hard about their troublesome situation that he didn't move at all from where he was standing. There wasn't any of the usual chatter either. From the looks of it, all decisions would be made after they had talked with Commander Hayes, **if** they could get the ansible link up again.

Gruber tried to write his log for a bit. He soon realized that he had way too much to say so he closed it and continued to do nothing.

Slowly they could see more and more of Groombridge. The star was a giant, but not a super-giant like Zeeman. It felt completely irrelevant what kind of a solar system Groombridge actually had. They just had to get to true space as fast as possible.

Gruber held his right hand on the captain's chair's back as Samusenko started the countdown to jump. All operators were at their posts and Zelnick was silently observing things in his own chair.

"Five," Samusenko said and they couldn't see hyperspace from the vortex anymore.

"Four."

If the starbase couldn't send out a tanker ship full of fuel, their only chance would probably be with the Melnorme.

"Three."

The Melnorme did say that they could be found in any super-giant star system. Even though there were none in the vicinity, at least their fuel reserves would easily allow them to reach one.

"Two."

Although the Melnorme did make a point about not giving anything away. Would they have anything to offer the Melnorme in return for the fuel?

"One."

And that was if they could even find the Melnorme. Ah well, in any case, Hayes would know if the starbase was able to help in any way.

"Jump."

They reached the border of the vortex. The star-lines started to shrink and the red background color gently faded to black.

The stars stretched into long thin lines and the black background of true space turned into the familiar red of hyperspace.

"What happened?" Zelnick asked. "Why are we back in hyperspace? Samusenko?"

Samusenko didn't answer. In fact, he had disappeared. Gruber realized that he was standing on the other side of the captain's chair, resting his **left** arm on the back. He had no memory of moving there.

"What the hell? Where's Mr. Samusenko?" Zelnick asked again. Gruber then noted that Katja wasn't there either. The rest of the operators looked around with a puzzled look in their eyes, but didn't have anything to say.

"Mr. Gruber," Zelnick then addressed him.

"Sir," Gruber replied.

"Try to contact Samusenko. There's something really strange going on here."

"Aye, sir."

Gruber took out his communicator and was about to call Samusenko when he noticed something.

"Captain," he reported, "there's something strange in my communicator as well."

"What do you mean?"

The shortcut to Gruber's notebook indicated that it had been significantly altered. Gruber checked it and found a huge number of new unknown entries. The last one was dated June 16th 2155. He tried to open it, but the entry was somehow encrypted. He tried several others, but they didn't open either. The one that opened was the last one he remembered writing – just an hour ago – whose date was June 2nd.

He closed the notebook and noticed that according to the communicator's calendar, it was now June 16th. He reported it to Zelnick who then checked his own communicator.

"I get June 16th as well," he said and interacted with the ship's computer for a while.

"Everyone check your communicators," he ordered.

Zelnick looked at the ship's log. It had one new entry on June 2nd and according to the ship's calendar, it was still June 2nd. He looked at the last entry, which once again didn't make any sense to Gruber, but since he wasn't a Precursor prodigy, he had gotten used to it.

"I don't understand this," Zelnick said after a while. "I mean, I don't know how, but I've always somehow understood the logic in this computer, but this… this is clearly Precursor stuff once again, but I have no idea what it's about."

"Captain," Iwasaki said, "according to my communicator the date is June 16th."

Dujardin, Steinbach and McNeil all nodded and agreed that theirs showed the same date.

"Did you call Samusenko?" Zelnick then asked Gruber.

Gruber had completely forgotten.

"Sorry sir, not yet," he replied and got to it.

Soon Samusenko answered. He seemed like he had been sleeping and had no idea why he was woken up in the middle of his off-time. Gruber told him to come to the bridge and then called Katja. It was the same deal with her.

"Mr. Gruber?" Zelnick got his attention. "You always write that log, right? Could you check if you have written something after June 2nd?"

"I already did, sir," Gruber answered. "There indeed are entries in my log book all the way to June 16th. But the entries are all encrypted. I can't open them."

"So…" Zelnick tried to make sense of things. "Have we all just forgotten about two weeks we apparently spent in Groombridge?"

Gruber didn't know what to say right away.

"At least I advise against entering Groombridge again until we know," he then said. "I think we should make our way to the nearest super-giant that is not too far away from the course to Sol."

He then checked the star map himself.

"That would be Alpha Eridani at 587.5 : 772.9. We should actually stop by at the first star on our way there for the ansible. And **that** would be… Epsilon Aquarii – a little over five days away."

Zelnick nodded at his suggestion.

"There's all kinds of weird things going on lately," he stated. "We have plenty of time to discuss them on the way. Mr. Samusenko, set course for Epsilon Aquarii."

There was no response.

"Sir," Gruber said, "Samusenko is on his way here."

CHAPTER 18

JUST CHECKING

June 3rd / June 17th 2155, hyperspace, 978.8 : 900.4

I'm writing to see if this thing still works...

...It looks like it does, but I'm also hoping that I can open this file again after closing it, unlike the two-weeks-worth of mysteriously encrypted entries...

...And it opened! I'm really curious to hear what Matthewson has to say about this encryption.

I don't think everyone has yet fully grasped the seriousness of our situation. Even if we did have enough fuel to fly straight home, we would have hundreds of units worth of unknown space to cover, not to mention that the Ur-Quan and the Kohr-Ah are probably fighting somewhere between here and Sol.

Although it was my suggestion, I now find it very unlikely that we'll be able to get fuel from the Melnorme for two reasons:

1: They said that we could find them in any super-giant star system, but that's a big promise to keep. I fear that there's nothing waiting for us at Alpha Eridani.

1b: Even reaching Alpha Eridani is a challenge.

2: The Melnorme seemed to have a strict policy. They considered it inappropriate to give anything away and I'm afraid we don't have anything to give them in exchange.

But I can't think of a better course of action, so we don't have much choice. At least when we reach Epsilon Aquarii we can ask Hayes what the date is.

And speaking of the date... The uncertainty has drastically lowered the morale of the crew. I can't say I blame them, but there has been some unwelcome muttering about the leadership of Captain Zelnick.

...In fact now that I think of it, it is rather surprising that it hasn't happened until now. Only those at the bridge see how Zelnick fares as a captain. Most of the crew only see him as a very young man who is quite unlike other captains they might have encountered.

I'm also concerned about the Tobermoon and all those Zoq-Fot-Pik that were left behind on the other side of the quadrant. Even if they had enough fuel to reach Sol, the trip would take them a very long time – at least a few months.

On a lighter note: the Orz has returned. Or should I say, it turned back to 'normal'. It probably happened when we returned to hyperspace, but there was nobody to witness it happening. The Orz itself doesn't seem to have anything to say about it. Lydia might have better luck at prying into that matter.

Gruber put down his log and stopped to look around. As usual, he had been walking around engulfed in his writing and now found himself at the rear end of the Spine. It was quiet. Only the footsteps and panting of one jogger could be heard. He was coming towards Gruber, just passing the foremost fuel tank.

Senior Medical Officer Karan Mehul was the most vigorous exerciser, always preaching about the dangers the slightly lighter gravity of the Vindicator posed to supporting muscles. Gruber didn't know him very well, but acknowledged his medical expertise. If he ever had to go to the infirmary, he would be in good hands.

As Mehul got close to the turning point, he made eye contact with Gruber, looking like he had something to say. He slowed down to a walk, checked his communicator and approached Gruber with his hands on his waist.

"First officer," he greeted.

"Doctor," Gruber responded.

Mehul then leaned on a railing next to Gruber and did some stretches.

"Where exactly are we going?" he asked in a tone that clearly indicated disapproval.

"What do you mean?" Gruber wanted him to specify.

Mehul stopped stretching. He came slightly closer to Gruber than what was comfortable in German culture.

"I mean this odyssey of ours. We are three times farther towards the galactic core than anyone has ever been before us, and we can't get back on our own."

Zelnick had announced that their next stop would be at Epsilon Aquarii, and everyone had been given a memo on their current situation. Gruber had hoped that Zelnick would soon address the entire crew personally, but he hadn't suggested it to him yet. Mehul's frustration was understandable.

"The captain thinks that contacting the st—" Gruber began, but was interrupted by Mehul's outburst.

"The **captain** thinks, huh? As far as I can tell, that kid you call captain has done nothing but make us crawl out of a hole just to fall into another. He even left Bukowski behind at the Androsynth homeworld without consulting any of the medical staff."

"There were circumstances," Gruber defended.

Mehul lowered his voice slightly.

"Why are we being led by a teenage boy when there are qualified and experienced captains available?"

He then switched to a more compassionate tone and looked Gruber directly in the eyes.

"Personally I think, and I'm not alone in this, you should be the captain."

Gruber didn't like where the conversation was going. Mutiny was the last thing they needed right now.

"That's enough out of you," he ordered in a very strict voice. Mehul was a short man so Gruber had to stoop down to face him at equal level.

"Robert Zelnick is your captain and you will respect that man. If you have a problem with it, you can take it to Hayes when we're back at the starbase, but in the meantime you **will** live up to your vow."

He was referring to the vow of absolute obedience, dating back to the early days of Star Control. Before setting sail under the command of a new captain, all crew members had to promise, amongst other things, to obey the captain under all circumstances.

"If we ever see the starbase again," Mehul remarked. He then turned around, tapped his communicator and started jogging towards the prow.

Mehul probably wasn't the only one feeling that way, so the situation had to be dealt with. Gruber thought he could spend the next few hours checking over every manned section of the ship, talking to crew members and finding out how they felt. Since he was already next to the engine room at the back, he decided to start there.

Most of the original crew members from Unzervalt who were still on board were engineers. Unzervaltians seemed to have above average respect for Zelnick, which was logical. When you're marooned for 20 years with only a few dozen people, you get to know everyone pretty damn well.

There were huge horizontally sliding double doors at both ends of the Spine. Every time Gruber walked through the doorway, which could fit a truck, he thought of the

Precursor's physique. Of all Earth creatures, the Vindicator was best suited for elephants. Most of the original 'furniture' was removed at the starbase, but some parts were either unmovable, not in the way or welcomed. Particularly one cushioned area sunken into the floor near the bridge was a popular space for wrestling. It was probably originally meant to function as a single bed.

When the Vindicator's integration at the starbase had begun, they had wondered about some events that seemed to occur randomly. Sometimes doors opened by themselves and sometimes they didn't. Sometimes lights turned on when you entered a room and sometimes not. After a long investigation on the matter it turned out that some functions were operated by weight sensors which were calibrated in such a way that it took two* humans to trigger them. Such mechanisms were eventually bypassed.

The engine room was a peaceful place, quite unlike the ones aboard 20th century diesel submarines, thanks to the stabilized antimatter technology. The engineer closest to the door put down her portable console and greeted Gruber upon his arrival. She was Anna Ivanova, an Unzervaltian, originally an engineer from the Tobermoon. She had been very enthusiastic about remaining on board the Vindicator.

"As you were," Gruber said. "Don't let me trouble you."

"Not a problem, sir," she replied. "I'm not doing anything important at the moment. What brings you here?"

Unlike most of the Russian-born crew members, she didn't have a noticeable Russian accent. Instead, there was something different you could never really put your finger on. All Unzervaltians had the same peculiar quality.

---

* Dave was enough on his own. His contribution to figuring out the puzzle shall be remembered.

"I'm just checking to see how you're doing back here," Gruber truthfully explained, "and if there's something on your mind."

"Are you referring to our troublesome situation here, way too far towards the galactic core?" she asked, understanding right off the bat the real reason behind Gruber's sudden visit.

"Well, yes," Gruber was taken by surprise. "There has been some… uneasiness."

Ivanova gave him a convincing smile.

"You don't have to worry about us, sir. I can speak for all of us Unzervaltians when I say that we've had worse. When we left Unzervalt, we were all cramped on the bridge, sleeping mostly on cushions made of wilehay – a plant native to Unzervalt. The worst part was not knowing what was waiting for us back on Earth. If it wasn't for Captain Burton's leadership, we would have fallen apart before even leaving Vela."

Mentioning Burton made her look slightly sad.

"Then we found the Tobermoon, which was terrible" she continued. "It was like a ghost ship. The crew, our loved ones, were gone. Not knowing what had happened to them was awful – it still is. And to make it all worse, we even lost Captain Burton soon after that. I can tell you that many of us were ready to jump out of the airlock then, but do you know what made us continue?"

Gruber hadn't heard this part of the story before.

"What was it?" he asked to make her continue.

"It was that shy little boy, Robert. He never wanted to board the Vindicator in the first place, but he did it because we needed him. And when we Earth-born were falling apart, he was the only one who seemed to know what needed to be done. And he was also the only one who didn't have any real reason to actually reach Sol. I couldn't tell you how exactly it happened, but he made us all believe in ourselves, our mission, and…"

She looked at Gruber like she was apologizing.

"...him. I believe in him. We all believe in Captain Zelnick. I don't know why, but I am convinced that there's nobody I'd rather have calling the shots on this ship."

Gruber was impressed and also relieved.

"I'm glad to hear that," he commented.

An awkward silence followed.

"I'll just leave you to your work then," Gruber said. "Carry on."

With that said, he made his way out of the room. A moment before the door closed behind him, Ivanova called out:

"We're far better off now than we were back in February."

Gruber had known that lobbying of the Unzervaltians played a big role in deciding that Zelnick would continue as the captain of the Vindicator. But he didn't know that they felt so strongly about him. It seemed that there was no need to worry about the engineering department.

He started walking down the Spine towards the prow and thought about his next move. There was a manned control room in each module so he decided to check all three fuel tanks while he passed them. The tank in slot 15 was empty, though, so he skipped that one; no need to have someone watching an empty tank.

The control room of the second tank was dark and cramped. The only source of light was the glow of a holoscreen set up on a table in the center of the room. Two men were ferociously arguing and examining a true space star map which was projected on the screen. They noted Gruber's arrival, but continued their discussion.

"—in a spherical universe, yes," the other man said. It was too dark to see his face properly, but based on the Scottish accent Gruber knew that it was Dougal Skeates. He was one of the very few all-around repair men that had always been extremely valuable. No matter what broke down, Skeates somehow knew how to fix it. Him and machinery were like Zelnick and Precursor equipment: They possessed insight that couldn't be taught.

"Oh, come on, not this theory again," the other man commented. His face was better lit and Gruber recognized him as a Filipino man whose name was impossible to pronounce without a violin. In his mind Gruber always referred to him as Tai.

"It's not just a theory if it's correct," Skeates insisted.

"Just because these few stars here fit your model of a hyperbolic universe, it doesn't nullify the 100 years' worth of opposite evidence," Tai argued. He actually knew what he was talking about since his area of expertise was true space cartography.

Skeates fell silent for a while and then turned his attention to Gruber.

"Can I help you, sir?" he asked. This room was currently his post and Tai's was the last fuel tank.

"No," Gruber put it simply, "I'm just checking to see how everybody's doing."

"Well we should be doing great," Skeates explained, "with us being this much further away than anyone has ever been, not to mention the visit to quasispace. This trip should be the scientific discovery of the century, but T… this man here refuses to question his old theories so I'm left alone to do the thinking."

"I **wish** they were my theories," Tai replied.

"Even worse," Skeates continued. "How come you're not more excited?"

Gruber decided that they were doing alright so he left, which the two barely noticed.

"You're dead inside!" was the last thing Gruber heard before he shut the door behind him. He knew Skeates well enough to understand that he bore no ill will. He just tended to get a little over-excited.

Gruber's next stop was at the crew module. He didn't intend on waking anyone up so he skipped the cabin section. As he passed a small meeting room, he heard a voice through the door that sounded somewhat familiar but out of place, so he listened for a while.

*"—Difficulty. Problems are difficult. Let's be *special* together. *Spicy games* are always fun."*

It was the voice of the Orz, but there's no way they could squeeze through this small human-door in their exoskeleton. Now there was a second voice.

"Our charts show this as Androsynth space. Do you know what happened to them?"

It was the voice of Zelnick. It all made sense now, so Gruber opened the door and saw their psychologist Eduardo Vargas listening to a recording of the first Orz encounter. He had headphones on so he probably didn't notice Gruber arriving and neither did he probably know that the sound was also coming from the speakers – loudly.

Gruber approached him to get his attention when he noticed a picture frame hanging on the wall. It contained the two rules of first encounters written in an artistic fashion.

At least he didn't have a shrine built around it, Gruber thought.

"Androsynth are not here. Orz are here," came from the speakers. Gruber remembered this enigmatic conversation all too well.

*"—You are not the same too much like Androsynth. You are *happy campers*.—"*

Vargas leaned closer to the screen, his nose almost touching it.

*"Do you want to see our surprising *toys*? No!! Do Not!!"*

He leaned back again and wrote something down. Gruber took this opportunity to tap Vargas on the shoulder, which almost made him jump through the roof.

"Oh, it's just you," he stated in relief and with an all too loud voice.

Gruber pointed at his headphones. Vargas took them off and noticed that the sound was still playing, so he paused the video.

"I've been doing some research," he explained. "I'm trying to start a whole new line of science in alien psychology."

This was news to Gruber.

"Interesting," he commented. "How's it going?"

"Rather good, actually," Vargas replied. "There's so much new material here that I've been busy just making some general remarks on non-verbal communication of different aliens – and also how they respond to our non-verbal cues."

It seemed to Gruber that Vargas was somewhat satisfied at the moment so he wouldn't have to worry about him either.

"Keep up the good work," he encouraged him. "Your research might come in handy in the future."

"That's the plan," Vargas replied as Gruber was already walking towards the door. "Was there something on your mind?"

"I was just checking," Gruber said before stepping outside.

So far it was looking good. The crew kept themselves occupied in a positive way and Mehul's frustration didn't seem to reflect the common mood. And thinking of the devil, Gruber was just passing the infirmary. He might have to have a deeper chat with Mehul in the future, but now wasn't the time for it. Instead, Gruber thought he could talk to Lydia next. He checked her room, but it turned out to be empty as usual. She was probably at the hangar, where Gruber could likely find some members of the landing team as well. He decided to go there next.

And he was right. They were all there – Lydia and the whole landing team. They were in the middle of what appeared to be a game of some sort. Witherspoon, Ahmed and Lydia were standing at the center of the hangar while others walked around the sides. Everyone was staring at their communicators rather than watching where they were going. The Orz was standing where it always was.

Suddenly Keller sprinted towards the center and Belov, apparently responding to Keller's sprint, made a similar dash. Lydia and Ahmed reached out their hands, Lydia towards Keller and Ahmed towards Belov. When Keller tagged Lydia slightly before Belov reached Ahmed, some of the ones remaining on the sides cheered.

They all put down their communicators and started walking towards the center, chatting. It looked like the game was over so Gruber joined in on the crowd.

"As you were," he said in a loud voice as some noticed him and were about to salute.

Shoji was the one closest to him so Gruber asked him the obvious.

"You seem to be in high spirits. What were you doing just now?"

Shoji smiled and glimpsed at the others.

"We were playing a game Lydia taught us," he explained. "It was really interesting."

"And exciting," Witherspoon added.

"And tough," Keller continued, still panting from the sprint. "I'm in terrible shape."

"Do you want to play too?" Lydia asked.

They all looked at him; some with a grin, and Gruber felt himself uncomfortable. He was somewhat curious about the rules of the game, but he didn't feel like running around the hangar.

"Uh… Could you tell me the rules first?" he said.

"I don't think I can do a second round," Keller commented.

Her view was supported by a few agreeing nods and thus Gruber was saved for the time being.

"I'll call you the next time we play," Lydia promised as the group started to scatter.

Soon Gruber and Lydia were by themselves.

<<So, how are you doing?>> Gruber asked.

<<I'm fine,>> Lydia assured him. <<That nice narrow-eyed man taught me how to program stuff for the communicator. The game we just played used my program.>>

Gruber had never bothered to learn the communicator's programming so he had a slight feeling of inferiority.

<<What's your take on the missing two weeks?>> he changed the subject.

<<I thought you weren't sure about that,>> she pointed out.

Lydia clearly was on top of things. There was something about her that always made it easy to talk to her.

<<We're not,>> Gruber admitted. <<But what do you think?>>

He found himself hoping that Lydia would have it all figured out. He wasn't sure why.

<<I don't understand it myself, but I think the Orz knows,>> she explained. <<I tried to talk to it about it, but…>>

She paused for a while, obviously wanting Gruber to ask "but what?"

<<But what?>>

<<…but I couldn't make any sense of it.>>

This was news. So far Lydia seemed to have had a common understanding with the Orz.

<<Maybe we could talk to it together?>> Lydia proposed.

Gruber glanced at the Orz which was still standing in place, staring straight forward.

<<Alright then,>> he agreed and they started walking towards the Orz. It noticed them approaching and followed them with a weird gaze.

They silently reached a comfortable talking distance and Gruber noticed that the eyes of the Orz had been focused on Lydia all the time.

<<Hello,>> Lydia cheerfully greeted, which made Gruber wonder.

<<Do you always talk German to it?>> he asked.

<<Yes,>> she replied with an innocent face. <<Does it matter?>>

<<Not that it matters,>> Gruber tried to explain, <<but the translator should only work with English.>>

<<I don’t use it,>> Lydia replied.

Gruber looked at the Orz, who was still staring at Lydia, and then looked at Lydia again.

<<Does it understand German?>>

Lydia shrugged her shoulders in an honest way.

<<Hello,>> Gruber greeted the Orz in German as clearly as he could. <<Do you understand me?>>

The Orz looked back at him, but didn’t respond.

<<We want to ask you about the lost time,>> Lydia said and the Orz looked at her again.

“*Old cows* play *time tricks* at your *silly* numbers 996.0 : 904.2,” the Orz said, sounding somewhat interested in the matter. “Your level of *camping* is fun, but not enough.”

<<Who are these ‘old cows’?>> Gruber asked.

The Orz looked at him, but didn’t respond.

“Who are these ‘old cows’?” he repeated in English, rather angered.

“The Orz do not know *silly* name,” the creature responded. “Other Orz *cousins* should be *invited to party*. It is best fun.”

“Have you seen the ‘old cows’ before?” Gruber tried.

The Orz looked at him in a strange way.

“They do not *reflect*,” it ‘explained’. “The Orz can *smell* their funny *colors* and not just *inside* at several *gravity centers*. Also *in between*. They are best *playgrounds*.

<<Tell us about these playgrounds,>> Lydia helped.

“Aha!” the creature almost shouted and turned to Lydia. “*Playgrounds* are not *fun* for *campers*, but for more fun than several you can visit. It is too bad you cannot *HYUIVBHJHG* there, but flying the *heavy* ship is okay.”

The Orz was waiting for its own punch-line.

“I am *joke*!” it joyfully proclaimed. “*Silly cows* want *silly* numbers. The *playground* for Taalo and Orz is 372.1: 261.9.”

Gruber wrote the coordinates down.

<<Who—>>… “Who or what are the Taalo?” he asked.

The Orz got more serious.

“Taalo can *slide* and play *time jokes*. Where are the Taalo?”

Suddenly the creature raised up the arms of its exoskeleton and screamed in ecstasy.

“There they are! It is too much fun.”

Gruber looked behind him in a futile attempt to see something. The Orz then lowered its voice as if telling a secret.

“Also Arilou can *slide*. *Old cows* have better *tricks* and more *slippery*, but Orz is best of course.”

Gruber thought back to the conversation with the Orz at their supposed home world in Gamma Vulpeculae and raised a question.

"One of your kind mentioned earlier that we can't 'slide'. Why is that?"

The Orz switched to a neutral tone.

"I will tell again the many *pieces*. You do not know *special things*. Here is some. *Time* is not one but many. *Space* is many. *Colors* are many. You are so *sticky*. You cannot *slide* like Orz from *outside* to *inside* and *in between*. It is sad, but Orz can *pull* the *campers* after being *connected*. This is soon."

Lydia grasped Gruber by the hand.

<<This is it,>> she said sternly, with fear in her voice. <<We mustn't learn this or we'll end up like the smart ones!>>

But the Orz continued, the lights inside its liquid tank dimming.

"Orz are trying to *pull* the Androsynth, but they are so *silly*, they do not want."

Lydia squeezed his hand harder.

"We don't care about the Androsynth," Gruber hurried. "Let's talk about something else."

It seemed to have an effect, since the lights inside the tank brightened again.

"Your *spit* is *making happy*," the Orz commented. "Do you want to play this some more?"

Gruber wanted to end this conversation and have a talk with Lydia.

"I think we're good," he responded. "You can continue your business; we'll just… go over there." He pointed at a random direction and started leading Lydia there.

"Yes!" the Orz cheerfully said. "Goodbye is better than *silly* word *game*. Do not forget to *enjoy the sauce*!"

They walked away with hasty steps.

<<That was the second time,>> Lydia pointed out. <<You've got to stop prying on that matter!>>

Gruber knew what she meant, but considered himself innocent.

<<That wasn't what I had in mind,>> he defended himself. <<But what do you know about the 'sliding'?>>

Lydia looked at him like an idiot again.

<<Well *duh* it obviously means going to other dimensions,>> she said.

Gruber tried to ignore the hostile tone.

<<So who are the 'old cows' or the Taalo?>> he asked.

<<That I don't know,>> Lydia replied. <<I've never heard either of those before, but we're all **silly** cows, right?>>

<<Right,>> Gruber agreed, acting as if he had known. <<I'll have to have a talk with the captain. Let me know if you find out something else, alright?>>

<<Yes, yes,>> Lydia said, and then suddenly cheered up. <<Hey, can I come to the bridge too?>>

<<Huh?>> Gruber wondered. <<Well, sure. But why?>>

<<No reason,>> Lydia suspiciously dodged.

The bridge was manned only by Zelnick, Samusenko and Iwasaki. Zelnick was playing a game on his communicator as they entered.

"You're early," Zelnick remarked.

Lydia stepped forward.

"I am pleased to make your acquaintance, captain," she said in an overly polite manner and made a curtsy, holding her hands as if she was wearing a dress.

Zelnick looked at Gruber for answers, but he didn't have any so he just gestured that he had no idea what Lydia was up to.

"I think you're using that phrase wrong," Gruber corrected her, which made her give him an exceptionally angry look.

After recovering from the surprising situation, Gruber tried to tell Zelnick the reason for his visit.

"May we have a word in private?" he asked.

Zelnick looked at Lydia who was now attracting attention pestering Iwasaki.

"Okay," he replied. "How about the conference room?"

"That will do," Gruber agreed.

"Samusenko, you have the helm," Zelnick said as they were leaving the bridge.

Once outside, Zelnick asked the obvious.

"What was the deal with the girl?"

"I have no idea," Gruber answered. "She just said she wanted to come to the bridge."

The conference room was close. Once inside, Gruber told Zelnick what he had learned, especially of Mehul's frustration and the conversation with the Orz – although while explaining the latter, he realized that it's hard to explain something you don't understand yourself.

"I see," Zelnick said after Gruber was done talking. "Well, you're the one with military education. How do you think we should handle mutinous individuals?"

Zelnick was right of course. Handling these kinds of situations was a part of every starship officer's training and Zelnick was self-educated.

"We should explain our decisions openly to the crew when possible," Gruber suggested. "Mehul is a good man so it would be a shame to throw him out the air lock."

Zelnick seemed to consider it.

"That was a joke, captain," Gruber hurried to clarify. "But in all seriousness, it would be a good idea to hold a gathering where you would explain to the entire crew where we stand and what our plans are."

"That sounds reasonable," Zelnick agreed. "It's just like my mother always taught me… You need to know what your goals are… Or why you were doing it… Or… something like that, and then you work harder."

"People move faster when they have a purpose." Gruber quoted.

"Yes! That's it," Zelnick remembered. "Where have you heard that?"

"Oh, it's just something a person I used to know said a lot."

"Who?"

Gruber felt uncomfortable, but had no real reason to evade the question.

"An old girlfriend of mine," he truthfully answered.

"You mean that old lady at the starbase?" Zelnick specified.

"No," Gruber replied in brief. He was slightly offended by Zelnick calling Veronica old, although now that he thought about it, she really was old… He himself was old – really old. He could see an age-crisis coming, but didn't have time for it right now.

"I meant someone I hooked up with back at the academy," Gruber clarified.

"So we're talking loooong ago," Zelnick commented. His joke had perfect timing and Gruber had a hard time ignoring it.

"How old are **you** exactly," Gruber asked, going for a comeback.

Zelnick smiled apologetically.

"Funny thing," he said. "That actually depends on what day it really is now. I'm either 18 or 19."

"Your parents didn't waste much time after being stranded on Unzervalt, did they?" Gruber pointed out and noticed himself sounding a lot more offensive than he meant to.

Luckily for him, Zelnick seemed to take it really well.

"Ha-ha, I guess not," he laughed. "I've never really pressured them on that matter, though, so I can't tell you any details."

Gruber took this chance to steer the conversation permanently away from his own long history.

"What kind of people are your parents?" he asked.

Zelnick seemed surprised, but not in a bad way.

"My dad builds stuff," he replied, "like houses and equipment. And my mom is in charge of farming."

"What was their role in your original mission?" Gruber continued.

"Oh… Er…" Zelnick clearly wasn't too familiar with the subject. "My dad was an officer of the Tobermoon and my mom was… some kind of a researcher, I guess. The way I understood it, she didn't do much of her original work at Unzervalt. She had her hands full with me and the cultivation."

"So you were a handful?" Gruber needled.

"So I've heard," Zelnick stated. "Of course not anymore."

"Of course."

They both nodded. There was a silence which clearly indicated that the next line would mean the end of the conversation.

"I don't think we're constantly needed at the bridge anymore," Zelnick figured as he got up.

"I agree," Gruber said.

"Four days to Epsilon Aquarii," Zelnick thought out loud. "You could start thinking what we're going to say to Hayes."

"Will do, sir."

CHAPTER 19

COSMIC DEPRESSION

June 7th / June 21st 2155, hyperspace, 882.9 : 866.8

In a few hours we'll be able to contact the starbase. It should put Hayes and the folks at ease somewhat, but strangely it feels like we are the ones who really need that ansible contact. It's not like they could help us in any way. Maybe it's just that it would make us feel less alone.

There really is an awful lot to tell: quasispace, Arilou, Groombridge... And last but not least, we could finally ask what day it is. Actually, that could be the first thing to ask.

The coordinates the Orz mentioned – "playground for Taalo and Orz" – point to Delta Vulpeculae. The Vulpeculae star cluster is very dense, so it's right next to the so-called "homeworld" of the Orz and also very close to the former Androsynth colony planet. But, sadly, it's just a curiosity for now and we have no real reason to check what kind of a "playground" it is. At more peaceful times I'd be thrilled to look into these kinds of things.

And still thinking about the playground... I vaguely remember reading about something ancient in the Vulpeculae cluster when I was at the academy. It was somehow related to some speculations of an old interstellar empire. I'll have to ask around to see if anyone remembers more.

"Entering Epsilon Aquarii in three… two… one…" Samusenko counted down.

The space around them faded from red to black and the stars appeared as dots again. A quick scan revealed that there were five planets in the system… It also revealed a large fleet of unknown alien ships in orbit of the outermost planet.

"Again?" Zelnick said in disbelief. "How many new races have we found already?"

The question was of course rhetorical, since they all remembered the Zoq-Fot-Pik, the Melnorme and the Orz very well. It was still somewhat under debate whether they could count the 'Evil Ones', the Kohr-Ah or the mysterious red probes as new races.

It would take them about an hour to reach the crowded planetary orbit.

"Let's do what we came here to do," Gruber suggested.

"Right, first things first," Zelnick agreed. "Katja, contact the starbase."

If the ship's clock was still in the same time as the starbase's, it was now the time of Hayes' sleep cycle. Zelnick took the ansible keyboard in his hand and waited for the ansible to be ready. Gruber had completely forgotten to worry about whether the starbase would still be intact. Maybe it was for the best, since the link was soon established. Zelnick got straight to the point then.

[outgoing] *This is Captain Robert Zelnick of the Vindicator reporting from Epsilon Aquarii at 875.0 : 864.5. Respond please.*

The answer took less than thirty seconds to arrive. Both parties used text messaging to save energy.

[incoming] *Alexander Leonov responding from the headquarters of the New Alliance of Free Stars. Commander Hayes has been informed. Please confirm your coordinates 875.0 : 864.5.*

[outgoing] *Coordinates confirmed. What is the current date and time?*

[incoming] *The time is 23:02 June 7th 2155. Please explain your situation.*

So the missing two weeks weren't really missing, or at least not in the starbase's time. Gruber didn't know whether he should be relieved or even more worried. He **had** to get someone to decrypt his log entries.

Following a structure Gruber had written in advance, Zelnick explained in detail everything that had happened after their last ansible message – which was over three weeks ago at Alpha Tucanae. After a lengthy typing marathon, Hayes arrived at the other end of the ansible.

[incoming] *This is Commander Hayes. Please give the exact last known location of the Tobermoon.*

Zelnick explained that the Tobermoon and the Voyager were exploring the Columbae star cluster at the time they got sucked into quasispace. There was no way to tell where they were exactly, but at least Columbae was a relatively small constellation.

Hayes agreed that there was nothing they could do. They had to trust that if the Tobermoon had any chance of survival, Trent would find it. It might be possible for them to round up their fuel and use a single ship to evacuate everyone back to Alpha Tucanae – which would take several months, but should be doable. Although they would have to cross Umgah space again, this time at a much more moderate speed. The Cruiser's hyperdrive wasn't among the fastest.

[incoming] *Focus on your current situation now. Make contact with the ships you see, be diplomatic, and try to recruit them into the Alliance if possible.*

[outgoing] *We will signal you again when we are done here. End of transmission.*

[incoming] *End of transmission received.*

They had gotten quite close to the planet already. Gruber coached Zelnick for the encounter and they simultaneously planned a way to escape in case the ships decided to attack. A closer inspection revealed that the whole fleet consisted of ships of a single type, with one exception. The majority of the ships were dark, somewhat cylindrical with two large wings.

The exception was nothing like the rest. It was green as spring, long, thin and streamlined. Based on the differing design it was evident that the ship types did not belong to the same species.

"In the worst case," Gruber analyzed, "they attack us on sight and we might or might not escape."

"In the best case," Zelnick continued the thought, "we get two new powerful allies. It's time to get diplomatic… How's my hair?"

"Short and blond, sir," Gruber assured him.

"Alright then… Katja, send an open invitation to chat."

For a few intense seconds, the main screen displayed text *waiting for response.*

"After this," Gruber began, "you'll definitely be the most experienced human in first encounters."

"Let the professors come to me for advice," Zelnick laughed and somewhere between the d and c of 'advice' an image of an alien appeared on screen.

They all watched it. Neither party said anything. Gruber tried to make sense of things and even tilted his head a little, but it was no use. No matter how you looked at it, they were conversing with a plant.

Zelnick finally snapped out of it – before Gruber.

"I am Captain Robert Zelnick of the starship Vindicator. We come in peace," he proclaimed.

The main stem of the plant moved slightly – or maybe it was just the wind. If you really wanted to, you could see eyes at the end of the stalk. In any case, it had all the characteristics of vegetation you could find anywhere on Earth. There were green leaves and green stalks coming out from brown dirt.

"I am Captain Ala-la'la of the starship Tender Shoot," the translation computer suddenly relayed. *"We come in peace."*

It was somewhat scary that nothing on the screen implied that there was a talking creature there.

"We represent The New Alliance of Free Stars," Zelnick said.

"We represent the Supox Utricularia," was an immediate response.

"Er..." Zelnick searched for words. "We're from a place called Earth – well, most of us are."

"We're from a place called Earth."

Zelnick addressed Katja.

"What the hell is the computer doing?" he asked.

"Everything seems normal, sir," she replied. "That must be what they're saying."

Zelnick turned to face the screen again.

"You're from Earth?" he asked in an offended tone. "Are you just copying whatever I say?"

"Oh yes, we apologize for the confusion. Our homeworld is also called `Earth', or more properly `Vlik', which means

`Perfectly Good and Nutritious Dirt'. `Earth' is pretty close, is it not?"

At least they seemed friendly. But they had an unusual way of introducing themselves – amongst their other unusual qualities.

"But why copy our speech and mannerism?" Zelnick asked.

"We learn and we adapt," ~~the creature~~ the thing explained. *"We are symbionts. Our first step in making friends is always to copy them. This is our idiom."*

"They want to make friends," Zelnick triumphantly pointed out to Gruber.

He then turned back to the screen.

"We want to make you our friends as well!" he joyfully said. "In fact, we invite you to join The New Alliance of Free Stars. We fight to free the galaxy from the clutches of the evil Ur-Quan and the Kohr-Ah."

The plant didn't show any reaction, as plants usually don't, but based on the latency of a few seconds in their response, it was probably contemplating the offer.

"We welcome your friendly gesture. However, we are but humble plants, mere saplings as a starfaring race. You should speak to the Utwig about such things. We have a strong cultural bond with them. They are not merely our allies, but our friends as well. In situations such as this we follow their advice."

"The Utwig? Are these all their ships?" Zelnick clarified and gestured with his hand to mean the space all around them.

"Yes, the Wearers of Masks. You ***should*** *talk with them."* There was an unnatural weight on the bolded word. *"They could use some excitement. You see, they are a little depressed and morose right now. Usually they are most festive and fun."*

It seems that every race has their own problems. You meet someone new, help them out with whatever they need help with, and you get a new friend. That seems to be the pattern, not only in first encounters, but also in everyday life.

"Why are they depressed?" Zelnick asked.

"They broke their Ultron," the plant sorrowfully replied.

"What's an Ultron?" Zelnick inquired, knowing very well that a story would follow.

The 'voice' of the plant got furious.

"The Druuge! The cruel, sallow trading race who sold the device to the Utwig, called the device the `Ultron' and claimed that it would give the Utwig super-powers," the plant raged. It then took a little break and continued more calmly.

"Unfortunately, the Utwig believed the Druuge and bought the Ultron. However, the device DID make the Utwig very happy. Of course, we didn't tell them what we REALLY thought of the Ultron – that they were vapid fools to buy a piece of junk for a planet's ransom.

We went along with the falsehood, and in doing so showed our own stupidity. Then, one sad day a few years ago, during a particularly energetic and festive ritual, the Utwig Proctor dropped the Ultron and it broke."

The plant got downhearted, or at least the translation computer thought so.

"Now the Utwig are morose and depressed. They feel they cannot ever achieve greatness because they lost the powers of the Ultron. They even gave the broken device to us, saying that they couldn't stand the sight of it anymore."

"A sad tale," Zelnick sympathetically said. "We could contact the Utwig right now and have you online as well. How's that?"

"Yes, please do."

Zelnick asked Katja to arrange a three-way conference call. She then hailed the closest Utwig ship.

"They're not plants like you, are they?" Zelnick asked as they were waiting for the Utwig to answer and join in on the conversation.

"No, they are more like you. We have never seen their faces though."

"Huh?"

Zelnick's wonderment was answered in the next few seconds as the link was established. The new alien, apparently Utwig, was a humanoid, but it was wearing a mask that covered its entire head.

"Ugh," it said with an extremely depressed voice. *"I suppose, as a courtesy, I should extend an appropriate greeting."*

"Well, greetings," Zelnick replied. "We represent the New A—"

"Normally," the Utwig interrupted, *"we would not bother to acknowledge your presence, but you find us in a state of moderate depression instead of our normal cycle of self-destructive tendencies."*

"Yes," Zelnick tried to be compassionate, "your Supox friends told us that you were feeling a bit down. As I was saying, we represent the—"

"We are A BIT down, yes," the Utwig interrupted again. *"We are so depressed that death by your hand would be welcomed."*

"Hey now, whoa," Zelnick tried to slow things down. "We just want to be friends."

He turned to Gruber.

"This isn't going as well as with the plant," he remarked.

He then turned back to the Utwig.

"Maybe we can help you, hmm? Could you tell us how you got so depressed?"

The only thing you could see behind the Utwig's mask were the eyes. They were so sad that it was hard to bear.

*"*sigh* What good would that do? I mean, why should we? After all, we have a famous Utwig saying: when one loses the reason for existence, one tends to get less motivated. This goes hand-in-hand with the painfully appropriate credo `We broke it so we are paying for it'. Of course, this isn't really accurate; the situation is so much more hideous! Imagine, if you can, holding within your hands The Answer! – Only to have it taunt you with its former potential! Ah, cruel irony! The loss of the Ultron grieves us all!"*

"What exactly is the Ultron?" Zelnick asked. Hopefully talking about it wouldn't depress the alien even more.

"Bah! It doesn't matter! Besides being of no concern to you, I find discussion of this matter, well, distasteful."

After a moment the Utwig continued the story anyway.

*"*Sigh.* The Ultron was not only the thing which assures total and complete meaning of life for you and I. It is Universal; I'm sure that you too are aware of this thing if only in legend! It granted us all limitless power and knowledge. It has been since, well, rendered inoperative. We agonized for hours wondering if it was a cruel twist of fate or simply a serious case of butterfingery..."*

It started to look like there was a hell of a long story incoming.

"...Ah, the lifetimes that have been spent in the pursuit of the elusive answer to this deceptively simple question has driven many of us down the dark road of self-destruction..."

They couldn't just interrupt now. The depressed alien might kill himself, or worse, attack and hope that he would find death on the battlefield.

"...Indeed, even as these words strike the ears of any who care to listen, the real question is, Does It Matter? I cannot say. I wallow in a quandary unable to determine what better atones for my part of the Great Sin..."

Zelnick inconspicuously whispered to Gruber:

"You should talk to the plant while I pretend to listen to this story."

Gruber obeyed and tried to shut-off the depressed ramblings of the Utwig.

"...Should I engage in slow and painful self-termination? Should I commit myself to a long life of painful self-flagellation...?"

"Hello," Gruber greeted the plant, "I am first officer Adam Gruber. You were right about the Utwig being depressed."

"...Should I throw myself with enthusiastic verve at the problem of collective annihilation? I do not know. Even now my mind writhes in anguish of indecision, lest the outcome be inadequate..."

"Oh dear," the plant replied. *"It is worse. We fear that they might really commit mass-suicide."*

"...You know, our past is one of a glorious and proud people coupled with a cataclysm that rocks the Universe to its very core! It all began when the Chimt rose from the Murky Bog and the Utwig emerged as well..."

"Have they mentioned the possibility in the past?"

"...In these primitive times we cavorted about our world oblivious to any sort of higher purpose. We took everything at face value..."

"Indirectly, yes."

"...Meanwhile, the tendrils of the Chimt infiltrated the vast sky canopies of Fahz and then the veils fell!..."

"What do you mean?"

"...Suddenly, the Utwig were stunned by a collective realization! All immediately and urgently donned veils of every description! Hides, leaves, shells, rocks even living drells were donned in the early days..."

"They have several times hinted towards their possession of an ancient relic – a Precursor device that they say has the potential to destroy an entire planet. Do you know of the Precursors?"

"...You see, the face is the mechanism that expresses many of the primitive qualities that hinder sentience. Now rid of constant reminders of greed, rage, hatred, and lust the wisdom of the Utwig was no longer hampered by constant reminders of the primitive urge..."

"We have heard of them, yes," Gruber put it lightly, deciding to spare the details for now.

"...Over many generations mask etiquette was refined to a rock-solid foundation of our society..."

"We know that they really do possess such an item. We have seen it ourselves and have every reason to believe that

it could easily reduce a planet – if not an entire solar system – to a particulate dust cloud."

"...Sure, the Morality Riots were expensive, both in lives and infrastructure, but the result was better mask regulation; specification from your basic Mask of Gruelling but Neccessary Activity to the most highly decorated Countenance of Stellar Representation. These were clearly defined..."

Suddenly Gruber felt a lot less safe.

"Should we be this close to the planet then?"

"...Recognizing the importance of flexibility, clear-cut and efficient procedures for revision and redesign dealt with the few anomalies..."

"Don't worry, the device is not in this solar system. This here is only a colony planet – the last colony the Utwig had set up before their... accident with the Ultron. As I'm sure you understand, colonization hasn't been a priority for them since.

"...From that moment when we covered the source of our intellectual oppression we knew that it was a grand purpose that defined our destiny. Are you still listening?! Our entire development as a sentient species was coordinated to coincide with the appearance of a remarkable device: the Ultron! We were oblivious to its tragic implication..."

"You mentioned that the broken Ultron is in your possession now. Have you had any luck fixing it? It sounds like that would solve a lot of problems."

"In order for you to truly understand the situation, you need to know more about the Ultron and its unique capabilities. You see, when the Druuge discovered the Ultron they knew that it was ours. The Druuge were compelled by intrinsic universal direction to take it to where it has always belonged..."

"Yes, we thought of that as well. And no, we haven't been able to fix it or even get any of the flashing bits working again. For you see, aside all the Druuge's falsehoods, the Ultron IS some kind of an artifact and we could not synthesize the necessary replacement parts."

"...They brought it to us. Oh, the Ultron! It assured total and complete meaning of life for All – the Universal! With the Ultron in hand I could sense not only your motivations and desires, but your purpose. I could act upon these things in ways that would most likely seem mysterious if not, well, daft..."

"May we have a look at it? We might see something that you have missed."

"...Years later, you would herald our participation in your development as the turning point for your species..."

"Yes! Please! But, alas, we have it currently at our homeworld. If you have the opportunity, please visit Beta Librae."

"...The Druuge were only one of the few to benefit in this way. Even now, they are puzzled by the way we rewarded them for the delivery of the Ultron to its correct place..."

Gruber checked the star map. Beta Librae was at 741.4 : 912.4 – 142 units away, but at least not too far from their planned course. It was a shame that they were so low on fuel.

"We'll see if we can make the trip. We don't have any fuel to spare right now."

Gruber then pondered for a while, before daring to ask the next question.

"I'm ashamed to ask, but do you have any fuel we could buy or borrow?"

"...In twenty-four years, two months and three days they will all dance the dance of Jubilation. Indeed, the Ultron has allowed us to fundamentally change the Druuge forever! The Supox too received many benefits from our use of the Ultron. They can testify to its power!..."

"No need to be ashamed. We understand. We would of course give you the fuel you need to reach our home, but I fear the, well, 'fuel' of our ships is of no use to you."

"...Things were perfect. What happened is, well, I... it is difficult to talk about. But I saw it happen. I witnessed the Chinz-Rahl celebration. I felt the Ultron fill the empty place that I did not know was there..."

"I see."

Gruber accidentally paid a little attention to the Utwig for a while:

"...I saw the Grand Proctor pass it to, well, they say that the Chief Groo did not know that it was so heavy and slippery..."

He then rallied his thoughts and decided to let his curiosity take over.

"I'm actually very interested to hear how you evolved into intelligent creatures. I mean, no offense, but our top scientists – not to mention science fiction writers – have proven that plants can't be intelligent."

"...Perhaps it was a combination of factors. Some who have reviewed the records claim it was actually a conspiracy! The commission investigation officially

stated that the Ultron was rendered inoperative by the fall to the ground, yet many feel that the whole story has not yet been told! As it struck the ground, I saw its glow fade, and then the painful void incapacitated all..."

"Yes. No offense taken. The same has been proven by our people as well. Strange, is it not? Many of our people regard this inconsistency as proof of our divine origin."

"...All Utwig immediately donned the mask of Ultimate Embarrassment and Shame with a vow to wear it forever!..."

Gruber laughed a little and was relieved to see that the plant laughed as well. He wrote down that thought.

"But in all seriousness, we evolved from single-cell organisms that originally lived in oceans. Then some plants got to dry ground, animals followed, and finally some evolved into biped creatures like us. We are the only species known to achieve intelligence on our home planet. Could you tell us your story?"

"...Bonfires all over Fahz consumed all but this mask; no other mask was spared! The Visage of Ceremonial Orations in all of its contexts and revisions, as I'm sure you understand, all of the courting masks from the clever and intriguing Veil of Flirtatious Prancing to the infamous Lewd Monacle... all consumed by the hungry flames..."

"Of course. I didn't mean to avoid your question. Our species has flowered and grown well from the canopy of the great jungles to the shores of the azure seas. Early in our evolution, we adapted to exist in symbiosis with other, hardier life, both flora and fauna, who supplied us with nutrients while we supplied them with reproductive assistance."

"...Even the most fundamental fixtures were committed to this irreversible fate. The Mask of Natural Bodily Excretions once hung in every lavatory! Most of the public facilities have removed the disposable mask dispensers but every once in a while I still see such a repository... always empty. In despair, we gave the broken device to our allies, the Supox..."

"That is very interesting. I wish we could discuss such matters sometime in the future with proper time. Do you know anything of the Ur-Quan and the Kohr-Ah the captain mentioned earlier?"

"...We just couldn't stand to look at it any longer. At that time, many suggested that we use the Precursor relic as a form of self-punishment. The proposal was that we collectively go to the second moon of the sixth planet of Zeta Hyades and use the ancient planeteering device to end our existence."

"Listen! The Utwig just mentioned their Ultimate Weapon."

Gruber paid full attention to the Utwig:

"...After much discussion, we decided that we deserved to suffer. We can use the Bomb if we ever decide the time is right. In the meantime, we atone for our grievous mistake with our collective misery. I suddenly sink into a chasm of depression. I must go."

And just like that, the Utwig cut the transmission. Zelnick winced in a way which made it obvious that he had not been listening at all.

"They're not attacking, are they?" Zelnick asked the operators and got a negative response.

"Do you want to take over here, captain?" Gruber asked.

"No," he replied, "it's better if you continue."

"Oh dear," the plant fretted. *"They really seem to be considering using the Bomb. Traveler of the New Alliance of Free Stars, please save the Utwig! We will help you in any way we can."*

Gruber felt sympathy, but had to face reality.

"I'm sorry, but I fear there's not much we can do. We're very far from home and we're currently at war with the Ur-Quan and the Kohr-Ah. The only thing we could do right now is to take a look at the Ultron, but we need fuel for that. Now if you'd happen to know the coordinates of some planets whose radiant energies defy scanners producing a rainbow-like image, we could buy fu—"

"Yes!" the plant cut in, overly excited. *"We know of such a world! On one of our mapping missions we found a strange world that generated a field of unusual radiations which scramble delicate circuitry. Just as you described, it reflected light on all wavelengths."*

Gruber and Zelnick both took a step forward at the same time.

"Ask where it was!" Zelnick hurried Gruber.

"Where was this planet?"

"Not too far from here. It is the first planet of Beta Leporis."

Gruber checked the map again and, indeed, it was only about 100 units away and, most importantly, almost directly on the route to Alpha Eridani.

"We could check it ourselves," Zelnick commented to Gruber, "and if there really is a rainbow world, we could then easily stop by at Beta Librae."

The distance from Beta Leporis to Beta Librae was only around 50 units. It wouldn't be a long detour.

"We will definitely check that out," Gruber told the plant. "If what you said is true, you have given us extremely valuable information and we could afford to stop by at your home planet."

"Marvelous!"

"On second thought," Zelnick said, "I'll take it from here."

Gruber stepped aside and Zelnick addressed the Supox. He thanked the Supox for the information on his behalf as well and explained about the threat of the Ur-Quan and the Kohr-Ah. The humble plant suggested giving all the important information at their home world, which Zelnick promised to do.

Soon there was nothing important left to talk about, and they said goodbye.

"Did the Utwig tell you anything significant?" Gruber asked Zelnick.

"I have no idea," he replied. "Do you think we should check the recording?"

"Aye," Gruber stated. "And we should notify the starbase and set course for Beta Leporis."

CHAPTER 20

LUCKY STREAK

June 14th 2155, Beta Librae, 741.4 : 912.4

We've been so lucky that it's almost scary. Thanks to the plant creatures known as the Supox, we were able to find one of the so-called rainbow worlds the Melnorme value highly. If I recall correctly, they said that they would give us 500 credits for a single set of their coordinates. We can now buy more than enough fuel to get home, not to mention the possibilities of purchasing technology and information.

And I must say the term 'rainbow world' fits perfectly. I've seen all kinds of weird and fascinating things in my life, but a rainbow-colored planet was something else [image]. It's a shame we couldn't explore the surface because of the unusually high radiation levels.

But before getting too carried away, we should remember that we have no guarantee of finding the Melnorme at Alpha Eridani. All we have is their word that they can be found in every super-giant star system in this region. If they aren't there, we get little comfort from knowing the location of a rainbow world. Our fuel reserves would barely take us to the Zoq-Fot-Pik homeworld where we would have to wait for a rescue probably for a very long time.

On another note: Unexpected progress has been made on decrypting my log. As I was hopelessly examining the files, Lydia happened to look over my shoulder and she said she saw some kind of a pattern. I still have no idea what she actually saw, but she has been very interested in it ever since. Apparently there are some numbers that 'stand out' or something. I'll let her play freely with this device after our business with the Supox is over.

And what business do we have here, exactly? We will look at the wreckage of an unknown alien artifact in hope of repairing it. Other than that, we seem to be on a diplomatic mission to get on good terms with a new alien race. I must admit that the Supox physique is highly interesting. Dr. Chu and his pals back at the starbase would pay anything to get their hands on an intelligent plant.

It was wearying to go through the recordings of the Utwig's depressed ramblings. Sure there were some interesting bits of abstract knowledge, but the only solid piece of information was the whereabouts of a Precursor planeteering tool – or a 'bomb' if you like. If we ever get on good terms with the Utwig, we could maybe examine the device.

On a final note: It felt pretty stupid to have been flying away from Epsilon Aquarii for a few days when someone realized we forgot to ask more about this 'Druuge' race the Supox and the Utwig both mentioned. Oh well, the Supox at their homeworld can probably fill us in on that. This time we might get to have a thorough exchange of information. We should reach the planet's orbit in a few hours.

There was only one planet orbiting the green star Beta Librae. A moderate fleet of ships similar to the one on Epsilon Aquarii was positioned around it. The planet looked similar to Earth, as the homeworlds of non-Chenjesu life usually do. There were few oceans and the land mass was more green, but the palette was pretty much the same.

It was unclear whether the Supox had a means of sending messages from one star system to another so the Vindicator's crew didn't know if they were expected. It wouldn't remain a mystery for long. They were already being hailed from the planet.

After responding to the signal, an image of the Supox was once again projected on the screen – if they indeed were the Supox. There were now several plants that all had their own characteristics. Two were somewhat similar to the one they encountered earlier, except that these two had flowers – red and yellow. Then there was a miniature palm tree, a spiky blob that could be considered a cactus, lots of green grass, and finally, in the background, a very large tree trunk.

"Greetings fellow carbon creature," someone said. *"May your roots always be well watered."*

It was impossible to tell who or what was doing the talking. The thought of hundred-meter-tall sentient redwoods was somewhat disturbing.

"Hello," Zelnick replied and got straight to the point: "We represent the New Alliance of Free Stars. We met some of your kind on Epsilon Aquarii and they asked us to stop by and take a look at the broken Ultron."

"Yes, we were expecting you," someone or something responded. *"If you look at our planet's surface, you will see one area turning red in a few seconds. That is where you should land."*

It was a strange suggestion, but they looked as was instructed.

"There" Katja remarked and pointed at one region near the equator.

Dujardin zoomed in with the optic telescope. They could see that all the green color came from a rainforest type terrain that probably covered most of the planet's surface. What was notable, though, was that it looked like watching a fast-forwarded video of a forest starting to glow with autumn tints. All of the vegetation smoothly turned from green to red right before their eyes. Looking without the telescope they saw that the red parts formed a circle with a dot in the middle.

"That circle must be a thousand kilometers in diameter," Katja pointed out. "How the hell can they do that? Even that dot must be nearly a hundred."

Zooming properly with the telescope revealed that the dot was actually a circle as well and there was an even smaller circle inside that one. Finally they could make out a clearing inside the smallest circle which had a diameter of a few hundred meters.

"You gotta hand it to them," Gruber began. "That's a pretty intuitive way of telling us where to land."

"I don't think so," Samusenko disagreed.

"That's because you're colorblind," Dujardin reminded.

She got a few laughs.

"Very impressive," Zelnick commented to the Supox. "We will send a team down to the surface right away."

"A nutritious spot in the sunlight is reserved for you," the plant said.

The translation computer pointed out that it wasn't sure whether to translate the words directly. On a footnote was a suggested idiom: *"Make yourselves at home."*

"Mr. Gruber," Zelnick addressed.

"Captain," Gruber responded.

"You will lead the landing team again. Katja, relay the coordinates to Jenkins."

"Aye-aye, sir," Katja replied.

"Gruber," Zelnick continued, "I trust your judgment. You will make the calls."

"Yes sir," Gruber said. "If I don't find it a complete waste of time, I will try to get the Ultron on board."

"Right," Zelnick agreed. "Go get 'em."

Gruber saluted and left the bridge. He summoned the landing team to the hangar and gave them a very quick briefing. When it was time for questions, Robinson raised a valid point.

"How's the atmosphere?" he asked.

"It's safe, but there's too much oxygen," Gruber explained. "We will use rebreathers. Pressure on the surface is 1,1 bar, gravity is 0,8 G and the current temperature at our landing site is 32 degrees centigrade. Are there any more questions?"

There weren't.

"Alright, it's time for us to make like a tree and get the hell out of here. Board the shuttle."

They all took their seats in an orderly fashion. When everyone was inside, Gruber gave Jenkins the launch command. Soon they were outside the Vindicator and preparing to enter the atmosphere.

Nobody talked so Gruber decided to lighten up the atmosphere just a bit.

"Witherspoon," he addressed the woman sitting opposite him.

"Sir?"

"Keep your vegetarianism to yourself on this trip."

There were a few chuckles which created just the right mood for a surface mission.

The ride down to the surface was once again bumpy. There was that normal five minutes or so during which the noise was too loud for conversations. After they had reached conventional airplane altitude, their speed had reduced enough for a steady ride inside the atmosphere.

"Finding a landing site has never been this easy," Jenkins remarked as she observed the innermost circles of red leaves passing by, showing them the way towards the center.

They soon reached the clearing and saw a number of ships, similar to the Supox ship they had encountered, hiding under tall and thick trees. There was also one tree, or at least it looked like a tree, that was ridiculously tall. Looking at it from a distance you could mistake it for the original space elevator.

"That thing must be tens of kilometers tall," Jenkins guessed.

"How did we miss that from orbit?" Gruber thought out loud. "Captain, take a look at that," he then suggested to Zelnick over the radio.

"I see it," Zelnick responded. *"It's not easily distinguishable from here. It appears to be perfectly vertical and we can't see any branches. It's like a hundred-kilometer-tall flag pole."*

It remained a curiosity for now as Jenkins took the shuttle down and the crew prepared to disembark.

"Rebreathers on, everybody," Gruber ordered and they all put on small masks that covered their mouths and noses. Other than that, their gear was the same as on the Androsynth homeworld.

After everyone was ready, Gruber lowered the boarding ramp and they set foot on the surface of a new planet.

"One small step for man," Robinson began, but didn't have to finish the sentence. It was something someone always said in such a situation.

There was nobody to greet them, although they had to consider the possibility that the grass under their feet was the welcoming party. The engines of the shuttle were soon shut down and it became quiet. They looked and listened for a while. At first the green light of the sun made all colors look funny, but their eyes soon adjusted.

After a minute or so they could see an animal of some sort approaching them. It had four legs and walked at a moderate pace. As it got closer, they saw something growing from its back. It looked like a row of the kind of plants that had greeted them upon their arrival into orbit – the kind that had flowers.

The animal finally reached them and they noticed that the plants weren't really growing from its back, but rather on its back. The creature's back was shaped like a shallow vat and it was filled with dirt, making it effectively a portable flowerbed. Other than that, the creature somewhat resembled a brown hairy crocodile without a tail.

"Hello, bipedal creatures without cell walls," the translator computer said. It was once again unclear who actually talked. "Welcome to Vlik. We hope our atmosphere suits your needs."

Gruber stepped in front in an indication that he was the leader.

"Greetings," he replied. "We are humans from Earth and represent the New Alliance of Free Stars. I am Adam Gruber, First Officer of the Vindicator. Your atmosphere is close to what we prefer, but because of the high oxygen levels we must use these masks."

He then took off his rebreather for a few seconds showing his face without it. The crocodilian creature paid no attention to anything that was said or done.

"We represent the Supox Utricularia," the computer translated. "We are deeply sorry for our polluted air. We have only recently awakened to the disaster that awaits us if we don't do anything about overpopulation and the excessive photosynthesis that follows."

Gruber knew history so he could relate.

"We understand," he sympathetically said. "We've had to overcome a similar problem in the past."

He then found himself curious about the 'animal' and asked what it was.

"We are on the back of one of our symbionts who provide us with mobility," presumably the plants explained. "He is not sentient. There is no non-plant intelligence on our world."

The hosts then wanted to get down to business:

"Please, follow us, and we shall show you the Ultron."

The creature turned around and started walking in the direction it had come from. Gruber signaled the team to follow. Jenkins and three others stayed with the shuttle as planned.

The forest line was about two hundred meters away. The Supox didn't look like they were planning on saying anything. Gruber took this chance to ask something that was on his mind:

"Do you have any predators here?"

"Don't worry," they assured the humans. "Our carnivores are all small and should be no threat to you."

"That's good to hear," Gruber said, "but I meant predators for you."

"Oh, right," the plants replied. "No, we developed a toxin against our leaf-eaters and uprooters early in our evolution. Nowadays we just battle for a place in the sun with different kinds of weeds."

"Are you the only kind of sentient plant-life here?"

"Yes, we are the only ones that have achieved intelligence. But we have made countless symbiont-pairs, with both animals and other plants. In some cases you could consider the pair as the unit that has sentience. Does that make sense to you?"

"I guess it does," Gruber answered.

They reached the edge of the forest and saw a line of ships hiding under the trees. They didn't notice it in space or looking from a hundred meters away, but standing right next to them made it evident. The ships were not constructs – they were organic. In fact, the ships seemed to be growing from the trees like fruit. And the ship-trees formed a chain that went in the direction of the hundred-kilometer-tall tree.

Then Gruber almost tripped over the crocodilian creature as it had suddenly stopped. There was an out-of-place construct the size of a pumpkin in front of them, placed on a stump. It was made of some kind of metal, but didn't really look like anything.

"Here is the Ultron," the plants said.

They observed the device more closely, but it still looked like nothing but a piece of junk.

"We hope you can fix it," the plants continued. "We fear it's the only thing that can save the Utwig now."

The crew gathered around it.

"Can you show us what it looked like before it got broken?" Robinson asked.

There was a rustling of leaves. Soon another creature similar to the one carrying the Supox emerged from the bushes. It also had something on its back – a small plant that had enormous multicolored leaves. The creature parked itself next to the other one.

"This is how we see it," the plants said.

Gruber was puzzled for a moment, but then realized that the leaves weren't just randomly colored. There was an image of the apparently unbroken Ultron printed on one of the big leaves… But no, the image on it wasn't printed. The leaf had undoubtedly grown solely for this purpose. The picture was detailed beyond belief. Robinson took a photo of the leaf.

"Take a closer look," Zelnick suddenly said over the radio. *"Put the camera closer to the picture."*

Gruber did as the captain asked.

"I know those shapes," Zelnick claimed after a while. *"I've seen something very similar."*

"Where?" Gruber inquired.

"I'm not sure... But I am sure that it is Precursor design. We should definitely get that thing on board."

"Roger that," Gruber replied and looked at the other crewmen. They were examining the device as if knowing what they were doing. Zelnick had obviously spoken to Gruber only.

"Good news," he told the Supox. "Our captain recognizes this design. If you'll allow it, we'll take it with us for further examination."

"Oh rapturous light of the green sun!" the plants rejoiced. "If there is any chance of you fixing it, please, take it."

Gruber gave the command and Belov and Hawthorne lifted the device up.

"It's heavier than it looks," Hawthorne commented.

"Can you handle it?" Belov asked in an annoying tone and got a murderous silence for an answer.

They started walking towards the shuttle, escorted by the Supox.

"You are a fascinating species," Gruber commented. "I hope we can find time in the future to get to know each other better."

After saying that, he hoped that the translation wouldn't relay any suspicious hidden meanings.

Soon they were boarding the shuttle again and it was time for Gruber to say final words to the plants.

"Hopefully we can return soon with the Ultron fixed," he stated and raised his hand to wave goodbye. "Farewell."

There was a gush of wind and the plants all raised one of their stalks.

"May the light always reach your leaves and your seed distribute widely," they said.

Zelnick was waiting for them at the hangar when the shuttle's ramp was lowered. Belov and Hawthorne carried the wrecked Ultron out of the shuttle and laid it on the floor. Robinson then showed the picture of the unbroken Ultron to Zelnick.

"Yup, it definitely has some familiar features," he said, sounding very sure of himself. "This has Precursors written all over it."

Gruber wasn't completely sure whether it was just a metaphor or if there actually was such text.

"Get Skeates over here," Zelnick said to Gruber who called the man on his communicator.

"He'll be here in a few minutes," Gruber reported.

"Good," Zelnick replied. "While you were gone, the Supox told us a little more about the Druuge – mainly where we could find them."

"The evil traders," Gruber put it simply.

"Right… Well, their trade world or whatever is supposedly at Zeta Persei."

Gruber didn't remember where it was so, noticing this, Zelnick continued.

"946.9 : 280.6"

"Ouch," Gruber commented. "I guess we're not going there any time soon."

"I can't see why we'd ever go there," Zelnick agreed, "but then again, I couldn't see this trip coming either."

"And who knows what awaits us on our journey to Alpha Eridani," Gruber continued the thought.

"Hopefully some less evil traders," Zelnick remarked.

CHAPTER 21

MAKING MONEY

June 21st 2155, hyperspace, 620.1 : 802.6

Zelnick and Skeates have made commendable progress on figuring out the Ultron-thingy. If there's someone who can fix something, it's Skeates, and if there's someone who knows about Precursor equipment, it's Zelnick.

According to them, it is evident that a hammer-and-wrench approach is impossible. The device lacks some important parts which we obviously can't replicate. Zelnick has a pretty good idea on what kind of spare parts we need, but of course there's no telling where – if anywhere – we could find them. The factory at Vela would probably be a contender... In reality though, I can't think of any other place to start looking except the so called Druuge who sold the thing to the Utwig in the first place. Of course we could ask the Melnorme, but I dare say we have much more important matters at hand and better ways to spend our credits.

Speaking of which, Zelnick agreed that we should leave some 50 credits unused in case of an emergency like this. Other than that, and fuel tanks full, we should prioritize new weapons for the Vindicator – if the Melnorme really have such plans.

And another note: Lydia tinkered with my communicator for a few days and somehow found a pattern of specific numbers in the encrypted entries. They didn't look like anything at first, but I tried rearranging them and just found out something interesting. The numbers are actually hyperspace coordinates, 10 of them. The full list is as follows:

039.5 : 745.8
283.6 : 785.7
543.7 : 827.0
766.6 : 866.6
853.4 : 879.7
996.0 : 904.2
862.5 : 700.0
741.6 : 508.3
602.0 : 297.9
468.1 : 091.6

That's right, Beta Leporis and Groombridge are among those coordinates. It's not surprising that the coordinates to Groombridge are in the list since we were there at the 'time' of that log entry, but we hadn't even heard of Beta Leporis and its rainbow world then. I can't wait to find out what lies within the rest of those coordinates. I should check them on the map as soon as possible. In fact, I should do that right now—

There was a polite knock on Gruber's door, but before he could respond to it, the door was less-politely opened and Lydia invited herself in. Gruber was too grateful for Lydia's help with the log to make a point of the rude behavior.

<<The numbers you found are coordinates,>> he told her right off the bat.

<<That makes sense,>> Lydia said, looking like it actually made sense. Before Gruber could ask why, she continued. <<They were arranged in such a way.>>

<<I was just about to look them up on the star map,>> Gruber explained and opened the map on his communicator.

Lydia sat next to him on the bed. Gruber copied the numbers and made the map point to them one at a time.

They were scattered around the region, each pointing to a solar system.

<<Don't tell me you didn't see it!>> Lydia said quite angrily in disbelief after Gruber hadn't said anything in a while.

Gruber didn't understand what she meant and made no effort on covering it.

<<Oh for Five-Three-Five's sake,>> she cried out and took the communicator from Gruber's hand. She tapped it a few times and then gave it back to him. It now showed all the 10 stars highlighted at the same time.

Gruber looked at it in amazement.

"Well I'll be damned," he said, accidentally in English.

"Captain!" Gruber shouted from across the bridge and hurried to Zelnick's side, tailed by Lydia. He then explained what Lydia had found from his encrypted log entries and that they were in fact coordinates. He sent the information to the bridge's star map and did the same Lydia had just done to the communicator's map. He highlighted the finding even more by connecting the stars with lines.

The image of the map was projected on the main screen. It showed that the 10 stars in question were organized in two straight lines that intersected at Groombridge, forming an arrowhead pointing towards the galactic core.

"So why would these coordinates be in your log?" Zelnick asked, sounding a little less impressed than Gruber had expected.

"I don't know," Gruber replied, "but one of these points to a rainbow world and one to the mysterious Groombridge. We'd be fools if we ignored them. I strongly recommend we'd check these out as soon as we have the chance."

"If we were on an exploration mission and had plenty of fuel," Zelnick speculated, "I would order us to check the nearest one of those – that's Epsilon Lipi – right away. But…"

"Of course, captain," Gruber agreed. "When we get the chance."

Zelnick nodded and they clearly understood each other.

"Speaking of chance," Zelnick began, "we picked up a few spoors on the radar a while ago. They are still far away and won't intersect our route to Alpha Eridani, but their speed matches that of an Ur-Quan Dreadnought pretty closely."

Gruber checked the radar.

"They are far towards the positive Y," he observed. "According to the Melnorme, their war with the Kohr-Ah was centered around the Crateris constellation. If we believe that, and assume that those ships are not on some random mission, their sphere of influence must be huge."

"At least 400 units in diameter," Zelnick continued the thought. He either picked it up really fast or had thought of it already. "Let's just wait and see. We still have almost two days to our destination."

The Vindicator had already passed the Fornacis constellation when Zelnick and Gruber were watching the radar very closely – and they were worried. Several new spoors had been detected, most of them matching the Dreadnought's maximum velocity. The spoors still wouldn't stop them from reaching Alpha Eridani, but it started to look like if they were to spend any significant amount of time there, two of the spoors would get between them and Sol. Circling around the spoors wouldn't be possible either if the other contacts kept their course.

"We still have a few hours to turn back and avoid this blockade," Gruber pointed out.

Indeed, if they were to turn around and fly at full speed towards the positive X, none of the spoors could catch them.

“Where would we go?” Zelnick asked, obviously not happy with this option.

The problem was that there were no super-giant stars in that direction. In fact, the only one reachable with their fuel reserves was Alpha Eridani. Gruber didn’t have an answer for the captain.

“We could only circle around and hope that we find an opening to Alpha Eridani,” Gruber figured. “In the worst-case scenario, we will run out of fuel hundreds of units away from the previously known frontier, surrounded by the Ur-Quan and the Kohr-Ah.”

“And we both know what that means,” Zelnick said, meaning that it wasn’t an option. “So what happens if we proceed?”

“In the worst-case scenario,” Gruber explained again, “We will encounter a superior enemy fleet and will be forced to escape in true space. Since they are not the Vux*, we could probably avoid them for a long time, but I doubt that our enemies would just give up and let us go.”

“So we would once again end up surrounded by the Ur-Quan and the Kohr-Ah,” Zelnick concluded.

“If only the Tobermoon and all those Zoq-Fot-Pik ships were with us…” Gruber thought out loud.

“At least in this latter scenario we would have fuel,” Zelnick pointed out. “And there is a chance the spoors won’t surround us completely.”

“True,” Gruber agreed. “If our fuel tanks are full, we can take as long a detour as we want.”

“That’s it then,” Zelnick decided. “We shall continue on course and afterwards take what’s coming to us. Let’s just hope that we can really find the Melnorme there.”

---

* Because of their superior mathematics, the Vux are able to jump into true space with the accuracy of a few meters. They have designed their ships accordingly and can deal heavy damage in the first few seconds of combat.

There were no sudden changes in the movements of the spoors so, upon entering the vortex to Alpha Eridani, the situation was as they had predicted. There was no way to leave without encountering at least one of the spoors.

"Any sign of the Melnorme?" Zelnick asked Dujardin immediately after they had entered true space.

There were only two planets in the system so at least they wouldn't have to spend days searching for something that might or might not be there. The faster they got back to hyperspace, the more options they might have on choosing their encounter.

"Yes," Dujardin replied, "we are receiving their open invitation."

Gruber was as relieved as Zelnick's sigh sounded.

"Where are they?" Zelnick inquired as there were no contacts on the radar.

"According to the broadcast they are in orbit around the second planet," Dujardin explained.

"It will take us about three hours to reach it," Samusenko estimated.

After three exceptionally long hours they saw a Melnorme ship similar to the one they had encountered at Alpha Illuminati over two months ago. There was an incoming transmission to which Katja responded as always.

"LOOK OUT!" a Melnorme identical to the earlier one frantically shouted immediately after the link had been established. It looked to its side and fell silent for a few seconds. Then it continued with a normal voice: *"Hoy! What a close call!"*

Zelnick was just as puzzled as everyone else.

"Captain Zelnick," the trader accusingly said, *"why did you try to run down that Keel-Verezy vessel? You almost smashed it into flinders!"*

Gruber didn't understand what the Melnorme meant, and apparently neither did Zelnick.

"What vessel?" Zelnick asked innocently.

"What? You didn't see it?" the Melnorme continued, still with a slightly accusing tone. It seemed to be waiting for Zelnick to defend himself somehow, but then suddenly looked like it remembered something.

"Oh..." it said and calmed down. *"Never mind."*

"What was that about?" Zelnick asked, and this time he was the one sounding accusing.

"I apologize for this misunderstanding," the trader apologetically said. *"Now then, I am very pleased to meet you and am looking forward to the excellent deals we'll be making today. I am Trade Master Magenta in command of the starship 'Realm of the Best Deals You Will Ever Make'."*

Regrettably there was no time for chit-chat.

"Nice to meet you and I accept your apology," Zelnick replied. "Listen, we're in kind of a hurry today, so could we get down to business right away? We found one of those rainbow worlds you were so interested in."

The bridge of the Melnorme turned from red to purple.

"When I had itchy pods this morning, I knew this was going to be a great day!" it triumphantly said. *"If you don't mind, I could scan the log of your ship and thus verify the coordinates."*

"Alright," Zelnick agreed. "How are you going to do that?"

"It is done," the trader answered.

Zelnick opened his mouth to say something, but the trader continued.

"According to your ship's log, you have found ***two*** *rainbow worlds."*

"Huh?"

"Your credit balance is now 1000."

"What do you mean?" Zelnick asked. "What was the second one? I only know of the one at Beta Leporis."

"Don't worry, Captain," the trader assured him. *"We already checked this information and found it to be credible. The coordinates we gave you the credits for are 853.4 : 879.7 and 996.0 : 904.2. The credits are now yours no matter what happens after the transaction."*

Gruber checked the coordinates even though he remembered them all too well.

"They are Beta Leporis and Groombridge," he whispered to Zelnick.

"What are we going to do with 500 extra credits?" Zelnick whispered back.

"We could ask for some assistance on getting us home safely," Gruber suggested.

"What kind of assistance?" Zelnick asked skeptically. "Are you talking about mercenary work?"

"I don't know," Gruber admitted. "Whatever they could offer us."

Their whispering had caught the attention of everyone on the bridge.

"Is there a problem?" the trader asked.

"No, nothing like that," Zelnick said. "Bear with us for a moment." He then turned back to Gruber.

"But if Groombridge also had a rainbow world, shouldn't we assume that all of your mysterious coordinates point to some of those"

"I think we should," Gruber agreed. "The question is: Will those coordinates be enough for the trader?"

Zelnick turned back to face the screen.

"We… might have information on some more rainbow worlds," he began.

"Either you do, or you don't, Captain," the trader said sounding awfully neutral. *"Please keep in mind that we don't deal in uncertainties. We don't buy or sell rumors."*

"Well, we have this set of ten coordinates," Zelnick tried. "We have only visited two of those systems and they both contained a rainbow world. Are you interested in that set of coordinates?"

"No," the trader bluntly answered.

"Why so?"

"It is more profitable for us to use our time on other business. If you verify the existence of rainbow worlds at those coordinates in the future, we will gladly buy the coordinates from you at our list price."

The Melnorme clearly knew what they were doing and there was no point in pushing the matter. Obviously realizing this, Zelnick moved on.

"In that case we would like to make a purchase," he stated.

"Ah, excellent," the trader joyously said. *"What can we do for you today?"*

Zelnick and Gruber had agreed that they would first fill their fuel tanks and then use the remaining credits primarily for improving the weapons of the Vindicator. Of course now that they had many more credits than they had planned on, they might have to rethink their strategy.

After the first purchase, the trade vessel latched its fuel lines into the Vindicator. A few minutes afterwards the tanks were full. It happened a lot faster than at the starbase.

"131 units of fuel have been transferred to your vessel," the trader reported. *"Your credit balance is now 869. What else can we do for you?"*

Where the hell do they keep all that fuel? Gruber thought. The ship itself wasn't much bigger than three of the Vindicator's fuel tanks put together.

"As for our next purchase," Zelnick began. "We seem to be surrounded by hostile ships in hyperspace… Is there any way you could provide us a safe passage out of the region?"

"Absolutely," the trader immediately said. *"However the cost for such action is 16 000 credits."*

"Darn," Zelnick replied and thought for a moment before continuing. "Is there anything you can do to help us with 869 credits?"

"Captain Zelnick," the trader began as if explaining something to an idiot, but not at all impolitely, *"we do not know what is currently happening in hyperspace outside this solar system. We hope that you live long and continue this mutually beneficial relationship with us, but with our knowledge on your current situation being so limited, there is little we can do to help you... at an affordable price."*

Once again they made it very clear that there was no point in pushing the matter further. Zelnick turned to Gruber for help.

"Should we just get on with the original plan?" Zelnick whispered and Gruber nodded.

"Let's see what they have for sale."

Zelnick faced the trader again.

"Could you please show us what kind of improvements you have for sale for this ship of ours?"

"Of course!" the trader enthusiastically said. *"As I'm sure we have told you earlier, we have the blueprints for several new modules designed for your ship type. We will gladly sell you these plans for 150 credits each. These modules are:"*

The trader then used part of the communications screen to display detailed pictures of the modules.

- *a point-defense laser system, which will give you highly effective protection against small fighter ships.*
- *new fuel-tank design, which has approximately double the capacity of your current fuel tanks.*
- *a blaster weapon utilizing super-heated fusion balls, which we calculate to be twice as destructive as your current ion-bolt guns.*
- *and this one... If you are looking to do some serious damage, I suggest taking a closer look at the 'Hellbore Cannon'. The destructive force of their*

projectiles is beyond compare. We estimate that a single hit is enough to completely pulverize most ships you'll ever encounter.

There was a slight pause in the sales pitch to give the prey some time to think things over.

"So what's the catch?" Zelnick asked. "Why would we take the less powerful weapon if we could get the… Hellbore Cannon at the same price?"

"Ah, what a good question!" the trader commented, skillfully making himself as pleasant as possible. *"The Hellbore Cannon is a heavy piece of equipment and its energy consumption is as impressive as its destructive force. We fear that in its current state your ship would be incapable of firing it. BUT! There is no need to get depressed..."*

Another new type of module was displayed on the screen.

"...We also offer you this! The 'Shiva Furnace' creates a vast amount of energy for your combat batteries. With one of these on board, you are good to go even with the Hellbore Cannon."

The next pause gave the impression that the speech was over.

"So... What module designs would you like to buy?"

Zelnick turned to Gruber.

"What do you think?" he asked, not whispering.

"I think we should buy both weapon designs," Gruber proposed. "That way we wouldn't have to rely on one powerful main gun only. And the point-defense laser would also come in handy. In fact, I think the only thing we don't need right now is the fuel tank upgrade. If we run out of module slots in the future, then we could buy that."

"That's… 550 credits then?" Zelnick calculated. "Counting the energy-creation-thingy."

"600" Gruber corrected him.

"Oops. So we'd have left… How many credits did we have again?"

Gruber had made a note of it and checked.

"Our current balance is 869," he said. "After my suggested purchases, we would have 269 credits for future use."

"Should we use it all now?" Zelnick raised a question.

Gruber thought for a while.

"At least not all of it," he then said. "Synthesizing fuel is a huge drain on our resources at the starbase, so we should buy our fuel primarily from the Melnorme for some time."

"That's a good idea," Zelnick agreed. "But I'd like to ask them for some info on what's going on with the Hierarchy as well."

"Well, they said that they'd give away pieces of information for 75 credits on average," Gruber remembered. "One question would be fine."

Zelnick nodded and turned back to the trader.

"We'd like to purchase all the module designs you described with the exception of the fuel tank."

"A fine choice, Captain!" the Melnorme cheerfully commented.

"There's an incoming data transfer from the trade ship," Katja reported and Zelnick gave the approval to accept it.

"The designs have been transferred to your ship's data banks," the trader reported. *"Your credit balance is now 269. What else can we do for you?"*

"We'd like to buy some information," Zelnick readily said. "Can you give us 75 credits worth of information on the current activities of the Hierarchy?"

"Absolutely. I'm sure you're aware of the Ilwrath gods Dogar and Kazon whose every word all Ilwrath obey? Well, lately those words have been the words of the Umgah, who found a way to impersonate the gods, making the Ilwrath follow ***their*** *every command. As a joke, the Umgah ordered*

the Ilwrath to attack a race called the Pkunk in the Lacaille and Krueger constellations. This fighting goes on as we speak."

Those pieces fitted nicely into the big picture, Gruber thought. The Ilwrath they had defeated in Sol had mentioned that they were preying on the Pkunk. And in addition, there was that mysterious Ilwrath fleet on the move near Procyon.

The Melnorme clearly indicated in a non-describable way that it wasn't going to continue for the price paid.

"Your credit balance is now 194. What else can we do for you?"

Zelnick verified from Katja that the plans of the modules were indeed in their data banks.

"That's all for today, I think," he said. "We are in quite a hurry as you remember."

"Of course. It has been a pleasure dealing with you, Captain. We look forward to your next visit."

"Likewise," Zelnick concluded and cut the transmission.

"Mr. Samusenko," he then immediately ordered, "take us to hyperspace as quickly as possible."

Zelnick was about to say something to Gruber when Steinbach addressed him.

"Sir," he said, "if we're **really** in a hurry, we can use the emergency warp… now that we have lots of fuel again."

It was an unexpected suggestion, but very rational.

"Good thinking, Otto," Zelnick praised him, using his first name probably for the first time. It came as a surprise to Gruber that Zelnick actually knew Steinbach's first name.

Indeed, the only problem with the emergency warp was the five units of fuel it would consume. But now that their tanks contained 160 units, they could afford that, especially since the few hours saved might mean all the difference in the world.

"Please proceed with the emergency warp," Zelnick commanded.

There was an alarm siren and red lights began flickering. The emergency warp hadn't been tested on the Vindicator, but presumably it would result in quite a jolt.

Steinbach counted down from five to zero as the warp engines had charged. At zero, just as they had predicted, there was a feeling of extreme acceleration, which would have knocked over anyone not prepared for it.

CHAPTER 22

THE ESCAPE

June 23rd 2155, just outside Alpha Eridani, 587.5 : 772.9

And they were in hyperspace.

"Fwiffo, are you still there?" Zelnick checked.

Fwiffo pulled himself up from the floor, his eyeball rolling.

"I suppose," he replied and took support from the control sticks, which made the Star Runner lurch forward, tipping Fwiffo over again.

Zelnick and Gruber checked the hyperspace radar. Just as they had feared and anticipated, the spoors had surrounded them completely. There were numerous contacts in almost every direction. If they kept still, the closest ones would reach them in less than ten hours from the direction of Gamma Fornacis. They couldn't push their way through without having to encounter several spoors, and even then they would have to destroy their enemies quickly to avoid the other spoors swarming on them.

"What do you suggest?" Zelnick asked Gruber after a while.

There were slightly fewer spoors in the direction of the Geminorum constellation. If they were going to make a break for it, that's where they should aim, and it wasn't too far off the course to Sol. Gruber asked Dujardin to run a simulation of what would happen if they took off at full speed with the heading of 190 degrees*.

According to the simulation, they would encounter one spoor at 571.9 : 770.2 in approximately 15 hours. A second spoor would reach their position soon after that and a third one in the next few hours. If they could deal with the first three, they would have over ten hours until any more arrived.

"I think that's our best bet," Gruber suggested after the simulation was over.

"I think so too," Zelnick agreed. "Mr. Samusenko, proceed accordingly."

The Vindicator accelerated to full speed with bearing 190°. There weren't any stars on their way and it was highly unlikely that any ships would just emerge from true space up ahead, so it shouldn't get any worse than the simulation.

"It looks like we have 15 hours to come up with a plan," Zelnick stated.

"Right," Gruber replied, "and we definitely need to be well rested."

15 hours later they were as ready as they could be. Some were better rested than others, but at least they had come up with some strategies. Fwiffo had been exceptionally helpful – after all – escaping dangerous situations is what the Spathi do best. But of course everything would depend on what kind of a battle group they would encounter.

The simulation of the spoors' movements had been pretty accurate. The first one was just about to reach them.

"This is it then, ladies and gentlemen," Zelnick addressed the crew on the bridge. "If there ever was a time for you to be at your best, it is now."

---

* The number is the angle relative to the positive X-axis, increasing counter-clockwise.

And right after he had said that, the spoor was so close that it began to interfere with the Vindicator's hyperdrive.

Katja had prepared the ansible for sending a report to the starbase along with everything they purchased from the Melnorme (not including the fuel, obviously) as soon as they were in true space. Dujardin was ready to report the number and locations of all enemy ships. McNeil was ready to fire the main weapons, and Steinbach was ready to activate the emergency warp. Samusenko was an observer since Zelnick had assumed control of the helm.

The few seconds of transition from hyperspace to true space seemed to take forever. Finally, when the space around them was black again, they could see what they were up against.

Dujardin swallowed before reporting.

"There are seven Dreadnoughts, sir. One is very close behind us."

"Dammit!" Zelnick said loudly and hit his fist on the armrest of his chair. "There's no time to charge the emergency warp, is there?"

"Not a chance," Steinbach replied.

If the emergency warp was charging, the ship's engines couldn't do anything else. The Vindicator would be a sitting duck for almost half a minute, which was more than enough time for a nearby Dreadnought to wipe it out of existence.

"Captain, they're hailing us," Katja reported.

"Well, we can't afford not to try diplomacy now," Zelnick remarked. "Let's hear what they have to say in just a few seconds… Fwiffo!"

Fwiffo was doing some kind of a ritual which involved keeping his eye closed and mumbling something to himself.

"mmmm— yes?" he opened his eye and spoke with a relaxed voice.

"If they try to contact you, don't respond," Zelnick ordered.

"Affirmative," Fwiffo responded, closed his eye and continued the mumbling.

"Alright, Katja, put them on," Zelnick said.

An image of every earthling's nightmare was soon displayed on the communications screen. Just as he did at Vela, Gruber felt uneasiness and pressure which could probably be more commonly described as fear. The Ur-Quan, however, looked like it couldn't believe any of its eyes.

"WHAT!" ~~it exclaimed~~ the talking pet exclaimed as indicated by the exclamation mark. *"A human in a Precursor service vehicle?!"*

Gruber had of course assumed that the Ur-Quan knew a great deal about the Precursors. But he hadn't paid any attention to the thought that the Vindicator in the hands of their slaves might be quite a surprise. And this time, unlike the time in Vela, the Ur-Quan couldn't be shot into silence. Even if they managed to escape, the Ur-Quan would now know that there was an uprising. In the worst case they would march straight to Earth and kill everyone.

"How did you escape the slave shield, human?" the creature demanded. *"Or are you a rogue?"*

Gruber had instructed Zelnick that there was no point in lying to the Ur-Quan.

"I guess we can tell you that we come from outside the slave shield," Zelnick explained. "We do not represent the people of Earth."

Zelnick seemed a lot less defiant than at their last encounter with the Ur-Quan. Gruber wanted to think that the captain had matured, but then again, it had only been three months since their visit to Vela.

"Human, over 20 years ago your species made the wise decision to accept our slave laws and remain forever on the surface of your home planet. Your presence here is a direct violation of your oath of fealty. You have intruded upon the

battleground of our Doctrinal conflict with the Kohr-Ah. This is not tolerable. We must maintain our concentration on this war. We must win. Should we lose, the consequences to you and all other sentient life in this part of the galaxy would be very grave."

The speech was very impressive. It made you feel like not arguing. Gruber noticed again the twisted thought that maybe the Ur-Quan were indeed ultimately on their side.

"What do you mean by Doctrinal conflict?" Zelnick asked, rather politely.

It seemed to work since the Ur-Quan continued:

"The Kohr-Ah follow the Eternal Doctrine. They strive to eliminate all sentient life before it becomes a threat to their existence. We believe they are wrong, so we fight them – to protect you."

"Well in that case," Zelnick wistfully began, "why not let us help you? We need to form a strong alliance to stop those madmen!"

The Ur-Quan obviously didn't consider the offer.

"This is an Ur-Quan matter. Your assistance is not required. All we want from your species is that you will refrain from distracting us."

This line was clearly what Zelnick had hoped to hear.

"Very well," he obediently said. "We shall leave now."

"No," the creature said strictly. *"Your independence is too dangerous for us to tolerate. In addition, your insubordination towards the slave laws has guaranteed your death, there can be no alternative. If you surrender now, we promise your crew a safe transport back to Earth."*

Zelnick glimpsed at Gruber with his 'so it's these terms again' look.

"I'm afraid we can't do that," he responded to the offer.

The Ur-Quan immediately seemed a lot more threatening.

"Although we must now punish you," the creature said in a matter-a-fact tone, *"your species has not yet crossed the*

threshold of disobedience that would require us to decimate Earth. You can die in peace. We will only kill everyone on board your ship."

And the transmission was cut.

"Fighters incoming!" Dujardin reported. "There's several from every Dreadnought. They're everywhere!"

"The Dreadnought behind us is in firing position!" Samusenko continued the report. He had assumed the role of secondary radar operator.

This might be it then, Gruber thought. They had gotten a lot further than he had initially expected, but they were still overwhelmed by the Ur-Quan's superior forces. It was a damn shame, really. If only they had gotten the plans from the Melnorme sooner… They might have taken the Ur-Quan by surprise with the so-called 'Hellbore cannon'.

The fighters blocked all the holes in the surrounding blockade and the Dreadnoughts were all positioned to destroy anything trying to get past them, but they didn't make any offensive moves.

It was a siege. Apparently the Ur-Quan wanted to neutralize the Vindicator with the fighters without completely destroying the ship.

Zelnick steered the ship away from the firing line of the Dreadnought behind them. He then set course directly towards the swarm of fighters.

"Captain, we can't ram that many of them," Gruber pointed out. "It wouldn't work like last time."

Zelnick ignored him for now.

"McNeil," he addressed the weapons officer, "get ready to fire."

"Yes sir," McNeil replied. "What am I aiming at?"

"Nothing in particular," Zelnick answered. "You'll clear a path for us."

"Steinbach," Zelnick then addressed the engines officer, "give us everything you got until I command otherwise."

"Aye-aye, sir," Steinbach replied and the Vindicator started to accelerate ferociously.

"Fwiffo, follow us as close as you can," Zelnick commanded and then turned to Gruber.

"It would be unhealthy to hit too many fighters, yes, but our hull will definitely withstand their shots if we can make them scatter a bit first."

"I see," Gruber agreed, impressed. "So we'll fire in the shape of a cone at the center of the fighter swarm?"

"That's the plan. McNeil, don't worry about the batteries, just fire as much as you have to."

"Roger that."

The Vindicator was still accelerating and from the tactical display they could see the fighters up ahead arranging themselves into a pyramid formation.

"All the data has been sent via the ansible," Katja reported.

"Good," Zelnick acknowledged it.

They were already moving so fast that, no matter what happened, they wouldn't stay inside the blockade. The Dreadnought closest to their path was positioning itself to fire right in front of the fighter formation.

"McNeil, now!" Zelnick ordered and McNeil fired as rapidly as the ion-bolt gun allowed. The fighters broke the formation slightly to avoid the incoming shots.

"Fire the last shot here," Zelnick instructed and pointed at one spot in the formation that looked just like any other.

"Yes sir," McNeil said while continuing to fire. Gruber had counted 10 shots already. Their combat batteries would soon be dry, but an opening was really starting to emerge in the formation. It was maybe just big enough for the Vindicator to squeeze through.

"This is the last one," McNeil reported and fired where Zelnick had instructed.

Just then they entered the Dreadnought's firing sector and a blast of fusion plasma was fired at the spot where the Vindicator would be in a few seconds. There was no way to dodge it.

But then something happened. The fighters that had evaded the last shot from the Vindicator had just moved into a position directly in the Dreadnought's line of fire. Now they didn't have enough time to dodge the friendly fire in any organized manner. The fighter in the unluckiest position made a panicky move that resulted in a collision with another fighter. The other fighter had just initiated a powerful thrust, but the sudden impact turned its prow towards the direction where the other one had come from – namely – the line of the Dreadnought's shot.

A single fighter wasn't nearly enough to absorb a Dreadnought's fusion blast completely, but it slowed the blast down just enough for it to miss the Vindicator by an immeasurably small margin.

The Vindicator, followed closely by the Star Runner, was now inside the swarm of fighters. Thanks to McNeil's firing, the fighters had had to scatter and they weren't all ready to fire right away. It bought them a few extra seconds.

"Steinbach, shut down the engines and charge for emergency warp," Zelnick commanded.

The fighters had now regrouped and started pounding the Vindicator with their lasers.

"Hull temperature is rising," Iwasaki reported. "Nothing serious yet."

All of the fighters' fire was concentrated on the Vindicator, which probably suited Fwiffo just fine. The Star Runner fired several B.U.T.T. missiles from inside the cloud, targeted at the nearest Dreadnought, which had two effects: It forced the Dreadnought to take evasive action, not allowing it to fire towards the Vindicator again, and it also caused a hassle within the fighter cloud, as they tried to keep out of the missiles' way.

Soon the Vindicator had cleared the fighters.

"Iwasaki, report," Zelnick requested.

"The hull is intact," he replied.

"Fwiffo, what's your status?" Zelnick then asked.

Fwiffo was still mumbling to himself, but at least he kept his eye open.

"I'm still here," he replied with a distant voice.

"I can see that," Zelnick said. "Have you taken damage?"

"I don't know. There was a little shaking at one point, but it was probably just a decoy projection getting destroyed."

Indeed the Star Runner seemed to be one sphere short.

"Warp engines are nearly charged," Steinbach reported.

The fighters weren't fast enough to catch them and the Dreadnoughts were either too far or facing the wrong direction to fire.

"Five," Steinbach began counting down, "four, three, two, one… warp."

The stars stretched into long thin lines and space turned red. They had managed to escape the first ordeal, but there were more enemies waiting for them in hyperspace. There was no way to avoid the second spoor coming their way. It would pull them into true space in a matter of minutes. During those minutes they needed to get as far away from the previous spoor as possible. Then they might have a chance to escape with the emergency warp if they were able to use it quickly.

Gruber used the few minutes they had in hyperspace to appreciate how well the captain had handled the previous encounter. He couldn't have done it better himself. In fact, he couldn't have done it himself at all. Zelnick is not just a Precursor prodigy, he thought. He also has strategic insight which might grow to become equal to Trent's.

If they survive, that is.

The next spoor soon pulled them back to true space again and they could see what kind of a fleet they were up against this time.

"I'm picking up eight Kohr-Ah Marauders, captain," Dujardin reported as soon as the radar was ready. "We are, again, surrounded."

The data was sent to the tactical display. It looked hopeless. Gruber couldn't think of any scenario where they would survive. In comparison to the Dreadnoughts, the Marauders were a lot more difficult to pass due to their fire defense, which the Zoq-Fot-Pik had given the semi-official nickname 'the Fiery Ring of Inevitable and Eternal Destruction.' A close proximity fly-by was highly inadvisable.

"Hail them," Zelnick told Katja.

The Kohr-Ah answered swiftly. It looked just like the last Kohr-Ah they talked with. And to them all humans probably look exactly the same. Zelnick was ready with a question:

"Will you let us go without a fight?"

"No. You are filth. We will cl—"

Zelnick cut the transmission immediately.

"I like to keep things simple," he said to everyone on the bridge and got a few chuckles.

It's small things like this, Gruber thought, that make the crew perform at their best. The captain had become a person you really wanted to follow.

"Sir, they're firing at us," Dujardin pointed out.

Several spinning blades were coming at them from different directions. The enemy ships were still pretty far so there was no immediate danger, but they had to take evasive action anyway.

"Fwiffo!" Zelnick called out and Fwiffo's 'face' appeared on the communications screen. "We need to split up. Your objective is to stay alive for as long as you can. If you see a chance to warp out, take it and fly back to Spathiwa."

"That's the way of the Spathi!" Fwiffo declared. *"I feel I can now tell you that meeting you has made my life a lot more fun. It's a shame that we die today, rather than at some other time in the distant future."*

There was a small drop of tear-equivalent in the lower part of Fwiffo's eye.

"This is not necessarily the day," Zelnick disagreed. "If we're still alive when the Ur-Quan catch up with us, anything might happen."

"Aw," Fwiffo said in disappointment. *"I had already made my peace. Well, I guess I'll have to give it my all then. Good luck to us all!"*

"We'll show 'em," Zelnick encouraged him and ended the transmission.

Samusenko was already making moves to avoid the first wave of shots. The Star Runner made a series of powerful thrusts and diverged from the Vindicator towards its starboard side. Zelnick took the helm and steered the Vindicator in the opposite direction.

This time they weren't in that much of a hurry to push through the enemy lines since there was no enemy ship right behind them and no incoming swarm of fighters. However the range of the Marauder's main weapon was extremely long, so they could just shoot from their positions far away and wait for the prey to make a mistake.

Half of the enemy ships targeted the Star Runner, so at least the number of the enemies shooting at them was reduced.

Another round of spinning blades was launched towards them. Zelnick steered clear of them with ease, but more and more shots followed soon afterwards.

"It's like playing dodgeball when you're the last one inside!" Zelnick agonized while constantly observing the trajectories of the projectiles and trying to find a safe path between them. One mistake and an unlucky hit could mean the end of everything. There was no chance for the Vindicator to shoot back.

"We can't keep this up forever," Zelnick pointed out after narrowly evading one shot. "Any ideas?" he asked Gruber.

One of the Marauders targeting them was a bit further from the rest. There was another one close to it, but that one was targeting Fwiffo.

"That's our only chance," Gruber stated and pointed at the lone Kohr-Ah ship. "If Fwiffo can keep the others busy, we might be able to take that one head on, one on one, like we did at Alpha Tucanae."

"That wasn't really one on one," Zelnick remarked and made a quick turn to dodge a shot, barely. "But I guess you're right."

Zelnick navigated so as not to make their plans obvious. For several more minutes they just evaded incoming shots.

"That's our path!" Zelnick suddenly declared and it took a while for Gruber to understand what he meant. He could see an opening – a way to fly aggressively towards the 'lone' Marauder without getting pounded by the others.

Just then there was a bright flash from the direction of the Star Runner.

"No!" Zelnick cried out. "Not now… Fwiffo, are you still there? Fwiffo?"

Fwiffo appeared on the communications screen again.

"Still alive," he said. *"But I'm running out of decoy projections."*

Indeed the Star Runner was now two spheres short. The next hit would have a high probability of hitting the main crew areas.

Zelnick let out a sigh of relief and asked Fwiffo to carry on.

"We're going in now," he then stated. "Mr. Steinbach, full throttle if you please."

The Vindicator accelerated furiously. For a short while they would only have to worry about shots from the ship up ahead.

Suddenly Gruber's communicator beeped. It was Lydia again. Every time she had called, she had had something important to say so Gruber answered.

<<The Orz has gone crazy,>> she said. *<<It's hammering on the airlock doors, screaming about happy time.>>*

A distant banging noise could be heard. Gruber wasn't sure whether it came from the communicator or if the hull carried the sound all the way to the bridge. Maybe the Orz wanted to do its thing and board the enemy ship. It was worth a shot. He relayed the information to Zelnick.

"Good idea," Zelnick agreed. "Let it out."

Gruber talked to his communicator again.

<<Is there anyone else in the hangar?>>

<<No.>>

<<Can you operate the airlock?>>

<<Of course.>>

<<Open the inner airlock doors and let the Orz enter if it wants to. Hurry.>>

Judging by the wobbly image, Lydia was running to the airlock controls. Soon Gruber heard her shouting 'Go!'

<<Alright, the fish is in the airlock. Now what?>>

<<Open the outer doors.>>

<<Are we going to just leave it here in space?>>

<<Hopefully not, but if it wants to go out and fight so badly, we're not going to stop it.>>

<<Well, okay... It's banging the outer doors now, still screaming the same thing.>>

The banging kept on for a while and then suddenly stopped.

<<Alright, it's gone.>>

<<Well done. Thank you.>>

Gruber paid attention to the battle again. They soon got into firing distance of the ion-bolt gun. One of the Marauders chasing after Fwiffo was turning to intercept them, but it looked like it wouldn't make it in time. They should be able to just barely make it past the line before the other one would be in firing position.

Fwiffo was still playing dodgeball quite successfully. He also managed to land a few hits with his Backwards Utilizing Tracking Torpedoes.

"McNeil," Zelnick addressed the weapons officer, "prepare to intercept incoming projectiles. I'll try to steer us past as close as possible from the port side, but still far enough to avoid the fiery ring."

The Marauder fired. The blade was coming straight at the Vindicator.

McNeil fired four shots, three of which hit the blade and destroyed it. They were now so close to the enemy ship that dodging was out of the question.

Zelnick had to change their course slightly to steer clear of the possible ring of fire. For a short while the Vindicator's prow was pointing too far away and the enemy ship slid out of their firing sector.

And of course it fired just then.

"I can't intercept that shot!" McNeil frantically shouted.

There were a few seconds of silence during which everyone had time to accept that they were going to get hit. Zelnick sounded an alarm and a very loud beautiful female voice advised everyone to get a hold of something.

Zelnick lowered the prow slightly to avoid a direct hit on the bridge. Gruber grabbed a hold of the captain's chair since it was the only thing nearby. He watched the last second before impact on the tactical display. From the corner of his eye he could see a quick flash on the main window and then…

An irresistible force pulled him to the floor, making him hit his mouth into the structures of the chair he was holding on to. A very loud and unpleasant sound echoed through the hull.

"Iwasaki! Damage report!" Zelnick immediately demanded.

Iwasaki pulled himself up. Apparently he had also fallen to the floor. A structural image of the Vindicator appeared on one of the screens, the fifth module slot blinking in red.

"We've lost the ansible," Iwasaki reported. "There's no signal whatsoever from the module."

"Seal off the module," Zelnick ordered. If the module had been manned, as it should have been, everyone inside was surely dead. And if they weren't, they would soon be after sealing it off.

But they had managed to break through the enemy line. Now they were heading straight towards an enemy ship targeting the Star Runner. They were approaching the Marauder from the side, catching it with its pants down.

Gruber's communicator beeped again. This time the caller was Ivanova from the engine room.

"Roberto is injured," she said in a panicky voice. *"He hit his head in the impact... badly. We're taking him to the infirmary."*

"Copy that," Gruber acknowledged.

He closed the connection and was about to report to Zelnick, when a drop of blood fell on the screen of his communicator. He put a hand on his face to check where it came from and noticed that his lower lip was bleeding.

As there was no time to bleed, he went along with reporting Roberto's situation to the captain.

"You're bleeding," Zelnick pointed out.

"I don't think I'm the only one," Gruber replied, implying that there might be more casualties that they weren't yet aware of.

"Fwiffo, fly over here right now," Zelnick ordered and pointed at the ship in front of them so that Fwiffo would see it on his display. "Together we could do some damage to it."

"Good idea," Fwiffo commented. *"I was just about to run out of space here."*

They had almost reached firing distance. The Marauder switched its target and slowly turned towards the Vindicator, but it wouldn't make it in time. It could defend itself only with the fire ring.

"McNeil," Zelnick said, "when you have the chance, hit it with everything."

"Will do, sir," he replied.

After a few seconds they were close enough for the ion-bolt gun to be effective.

"Eat this, ogres!" McNeil taunted and fired rapidly.

As was expected, the Marauder used its flame defense, which swallowed the first shots. However the consecutive shots made a pathway through the flames, allowing many of the latter shots to land on their target, causing severe damage. At the same time the Star Runner was closing in from the other side.

Zelnick apparently wasn't going to go around the fire ring.

"We're going to use the same opening," he said and followed the path cleared by the bolts.

It was a narrow hole in the ring of flame, but the Vindicator managed to squeeze through. Their combat batteries were now empty so they flew right past the damaged Marauder.

"Fwiffo," Zelnick hailed again. "Do one attack run and then follow us."

"I'm on it," he confidently said.

They could see the Star Runner fly straight toward the enemy ship and fire its rarely seen forward gun. Then Fwiffo broke away in the direction of the Vindicator and fired three missiles.

Now all of the enemy ships were behind them. A few spinning blades were fired their way, but at that distance they had little chance of hitting.

"If we're ever going to do an emergency warp, now's the time," Zelnick stated and commanded Steinbach to initiate the charging.

It looked as if they were going to make it. It was unbelievable, but they were really about to escape from seven Dreadnoughts and eight Marauders. Actually now it was only seven Marauders, since the last missiles Fwiffo fired were enough to break the hull of the enemy ship. Dujardin put the view of the collapsing ship onto one of the screens and there were a few cheers.

"Thirty seconds to warp," Steinbach reported.

They had dealt with this battle so quickly that the third spoor in hyperspace shouldn't be too near yet and they should be able to circle around it.

"Twenty sec—" Steinbach was about to report, but stopped in mid-sentence, because he saw what was just happening in front of them.

An Ur-Quan Dreadnought warped right into their path, and what's more, almost directly facing them. Immediately as it emerged into true space, it fired a shot towards the Vindicator. They had no choice but to dodge it and lose the charge of the emergency warp.

"Damn those caterpillars!" Zelnick fretted. "Couldn't they wait twenty more seconds?"

More Dreadnoughts were warping in all over the area. Without hesitation they engaged in combat with the Marauders. For a few tranquil seconds the crew of the Vindicator observed the beautiful sight on the tactical display as both their enemies were at each other's throats. The only thing ruining the moment was the one Dreadnought focusing fire on them and sending out fighters to block their path.

"This might work out after all," Zelnick said rather lightly as he dodged another bolt of fusion plasma from the nearest Dreadnought. "We'll just try to keep our nose clean and wait for them to wipe each other out. If it's just this one ship after us, we can manage."

Fwiffo made a nice sneak-attack and landed a few B.U.T.T.s on the enemy.

"McNeil, how are our combat batteries?" Zelnick inquired.

"Still at very low charge, I'm afraid," McNeil checked. "At our current state we could fire only one shot."

"And I thought we would never have a use for those 'dynamo' modules," Zelnick laughed at himself while steering the Vindicator away from an incoming squadron of fighters.

After a while their waiting strategy was starting to seem a lot less effective. The Kohr-Ah were clearly winning. In addition to the one the New Alliance of Free Stars destroyed, the Ur-Quan had managed to sink only one Marauder. The fleet of Dreadnoughts on the other hand was down to three ships.

"We could offer our temporary assistance to the Ur-Quan," Gruber suggested.

Zelnick agreed and asked Katja to contact the ship still firing at them.

"You are fighting a losing battle here," Zelnick told the Ur-Quan after communications had been established. "If we make a short truce, we can help you out and you can in exchange let us go afterwards."

The Ur-Quan seemed to be thinking for a while.

"No," it finally replied. *"If we lose this battle then so be it. Your freedom is not permissible under any circumstances."*

Then it cut the transmission.

"Idiots," Zelnick declared.

A few Marauders were now coming their way. They were about to get trapped like in the beginning of the battle and the Kohr-Ah surely wouldn't allow them to escape the same way again.

"We still have energy for only a few shots," McNeil reported.

Two spinning blades were simultaneously fired in the direction of the Vindicator. Zelnick was able to dodge them, but one of them hit the Dreadnought behind them.

"Fwiffo," Zelnick called out and Fwiffo's eyeball appeared on the screen again. "Don't fire on the Dreadnoughts anymore, even if you have a chance to sink them. We'll concentrate all our efforts on the Marauders."

A bright flash in the distance marked the destruction of yet another Dreadnought. Once again the situation was starting to look hopeless.

"Well Mr. Gruber," Zelnick addressed him, "I'm out of ideas. What do you propose?"

Gruber wanted to suggest they start crying like little babies, but that would have been somewhat unprofessional. Instead he said:

"We'll have to continue this game of tag and look for an opening to use the emergency warp."

Even if the Ur-Quan captain refused a truce, the fighters were clearly not really trying to fight them anymore. Even the Dreadnought itself hadn't fired at them for a while now. The two operational Dreadnoughts joined forces and together they prepared to face the oncoming Kohr-Ah armada.

The opposing force fired several shots at the Vindicator. Zelnick dodged in the direction of the Dreadnoughts.

"Do you think they'll fire at us now if we get too close?" Zelnick asked. The question was probably meant for Gruber.

Gruber checked the tactical display and noticed that the Marauders were herding all their prey together.

"It looks like we'll have to trust that they won't," he replied.

"You know," Zelnick began, "I could think of a way for us to escape if both of the Dreadnoughts sacrificed themselves for us… Do you think they'd agree to that?"

Gruber wasn't sure whether he should answer that. He put his money on not answering, which turned out to be the right choice.

The Marauders were now positioned in a circle around the Vindicator and the two Dreadnoughts. Soon it would be dodgeball all over again, only this time it would be like standing inside a five-meter circle with six pro golfers swinging their clubs at the same time, trying to hit you – with the balls.

"What if…" Zelnick tried, "… if the Dreadnoughts get destroyed and we… use their wreckages as a bumper and ram one of the Marauders?"

"That's thin," Gruber realistically estimated. "But I'll admit that I don't have any better ideas."

The firing began. The Dreadnoughts were a lot less agile than the Vindicator so they were soon both hit and sunk. The resulting debris was one more thing to evade.

"How about we fly in the middle of the debris and then try to charge the emergency warp?" Zelnick suggested.

"That would be like taking cover from rifle fire inside a cardboard box," Gruber replied. "But that was good thinking."

The tactical display showed a more and more hopeless situation.

"This is it then," Zelnick stated as a new wave of spinning blades was fired towards them. "We can dodge these and maybe the next wave, but then we'll be driven there."

He pointed at a location in space. It was a position in close proximity to two enemy ships where dodging would be futile. Gruber was amazed that Zelnick could calculate their position that much in advance.

"We have an option," Gruber said as the thought came into his mind.

Zelnick motioned to him to spit it out. Gruber then pointed at one of the Marauders.

"Instead of being torn to pieces by the blades, we could ram that one."

Zelnick pondered the option for a second.

"I guess that's the way to go for the flagship of the New Alliance of Free Stars," he agreed. "Mr. Steinbach, give us ramming speed."

"Ramming speed, aye sir," Steinbach replied.

Then there was a silence. Hopefully everyone used it to make peace with themselves. Their whole mission flashed before Gruber's eyes and then he came to a conclusion.

"It has been the greatest pleasure of my military career to serve under you, captain," he proudly proclaimed.

"I second that," Samusenko joined in.

"Me too," Dujardin agreed and soon every officer on the bridge stood up to salute Zelnick, who was taken aback and couldn't find any words.

Gruber understood him very well. It was an emotional moment and it was a lot better not to say anything than to say something stu—

"What the hell is happening?" Zelnick then asked in disbelief.

There was an awkward moment of "uhh"s and "err"s, but then Zelnick pointed at the tactical display that was now flashing like it had way too much information to show at the same time. According to the display, numerous ships were warping to the area.

"Danielle, what the hell is happening?" Zelnick repeated the question, this time addressing it to the one who should know the answer.

Dujardin and the rest of the officers sat down again.

"Just a second, sir," Dujardin said as she put her headphones back on.

They could now see multiple flashes looking out the window. Apparently the Marauders were getting a pounding.

"It's the Orz!" Dujardin triumphantly yelled. "There's at least 30 of their Nemesis starships!"

Gruber let out a sigh of relief and wondered how long he had been holding his breath.

"Oh shit!" Zelnick then nearly shouted and Gruber immediately realized what he meant by that.

They were still flying straight towards the Marauder they had planned on ramming. They would be able to avoid the collision, but they were now right in the middle of its firing sector and so close that there was no chance of dodging any shots. In addition, any shots fired would probably hit right in the middle of the bridge.

"Shit! Shit! Shit!" Zelnick continued and grasped the controls.

There were a few seconds during which Gruber just wanted to close his eyes and wait for the grim reaper. Actually, he would never admit it to anyone, but that's exactly what he did.

"But why isn't it firing?" Dujardin justifiably asked.

…

After a few seconds they picked up an incoming transmission from inside the enemy ship in question.

*"*Happy time* is best!"* a familiar voice declared. *"*Extra silly cows* are *dissolved* for better alliance *enjoyment*. GO is always *favorite dance*."*

Everyone at the Vindicator's bridge joined in on a triumphant cheer while Zelnick steered the ship clear of the apparently neutralized Marauder ahead.

"Well done," Zelnick then praised the Orz.

The tactical display soon showed that all enemy ships were either destroyed or immobilized.

"Do you want us to pick you up?" Zelnick asked the Orz. "Or do you want to join your own kind?"

*"You are *party people*,"* the Orz joyfully responded. *"Being your *close relative* is best. More *happy time* in *not yet happened* I am sure!"*

"I'm going to take that as a yes," Zelnick joyously said to Gruber. "Mr. Samusenko, take the helm and get us near that Marauder. We're bringing our guest back on board.

"Yes sir!" Samusenko cheerfully responded.

"Katja, contact the Orz fleet," Zelnick then commanded and soon they got a visual link to one of the ships.

*"It is the *happy campers*!"* the creature rejoiced.

"Yeah, we're pretty happy right now," Zelnick agreed. "How did you know to come here?"

The Orz made a funny face and a gush of bubbles came out of its gills.

*"You are asking if Orz are *knowing before*. It is not *magic* if you know. Your *close relative* Orz *sister* *tell* of fun to the extreme *playground* at your *silly* numbers 996.0 : 904.2. Orz go for better enjoyment!"*

Gruber noted that this time he thought he actually understood what the creature was saying.

"Captain," he reminded, "we're still on a tight schedule here. We should get going as quickly as possible to reach Sol safely."

"Ah crap," Zelnick said, but clearly agreed. "I was so hoping we could salvage all this and maybe tow that intact Marauder back with us."

"We can't risk that now," Gruber pointed out. "And we could use some extra escorts."

Zelnick agreed and addressed the Orz.

"Would some of you like to join us on our trip to Sol?"

It was difficult to interpret the expressions of the Orz, but this one was definitely positive.

"I am told you are fun," the Orz said. *"Some *heavy ships* will choose to *play* with you!"*

"Great," Zelnick said, cut the transmission and then changed the topic entirely

"I wonder how Fwiffo is doing," he pondered and contacted the Star Runner.

There was nobody at the communications screen. Zelnick called for Fwiffo a few times, but got no response. He then turned to Gruber.

"Get someone to check the ball pool again."

"Aye," Gruber responded.

"Mr. Samusenko," Zelnick then addressed the navigation officer. "When everything's ready, prepare for jump and get us safely to Sol."

"With pleasure," Samusenko replied.

CHAPTER 23

REUNION

July 24th 2155, Sol, 175.2 : 145.0

Gruber was reading some of his log entries to pass time before they could contact the starbase with conventional means.

June 24th 2155: There are several casualties. I stopped by the infirmary as soon as I got the word that Lydia was there. She and a few crew members had taken a bad fall when we were hit by that Kohr-Ah Marauder. Roberto is dead. Novak was in the ansible module and is now missing, so we can assume that he is also dead. Belov got a severe concussion, but according to Mehul he will recover fully. Jenkins twisted her ankle and Vargas and Lydia both got a broken arm. Others, myself included, got away with cuts and bruises.

Lydia doesn't seem to mind being stuck in the infirmary for a short while. She almost didn't notice me when I came to check up on her. She was too busy discussing something psychological with Vargas, who later summed it up for me as "some very deep shit about alien encounters".

Anyway, now that we're accompanied by four Nemesis starships, we should be somewhat safe on our trip home.

June 25th 2155: Everyone seems to be in high spirits despite the casualties. I guess the fact that we're still breathing after a nearly hopeless situation overcomes the death of two crewmen. It's just a shame we can't contact the starbase now. Once again they must assume that we've kicked the bucket.

July 6th 2155: Stopping by the Zoq-Fot-Pik homeworld was a good idea. After all, it was less than a day off our course. Understandably they were a little worried after hearing what had happened to their finest ships and crew, but at the same time they were happy that we paid them a visit. We assured them that a rescue operation would be our top priority.

July 11th 2155: Vargas raised a good point. Why have we not considered the possibility that Lydia is an Androsynth? All we have is her word that she isn't one of the so called 'smart ones'. But she is a wizard with numbers and seems to have a special connection with the Orz.

And speaking of the Orz, the individual who boarded and neutralized an entire Marauder on its own has been standing around in the hangar just as it did before, as if nothing had happened. Creepy.

July 12th 2155: Alright, so maybe Lydia is an Androsynth, but so what? We might all be better off not knowing the truth and not even thinking about it. She deserves a normal life.

Gruber didn't open any other log entries and started writing a new one:

July 24th 2155: There are a few things at the starbase I am anxiously waiting for:

The first thing I'm going to do is give my encrypted log entries to Matthewson. There are so many questions there that I can't even begin to write them down.

Secondly I will—

Gruber stopped there and gave it serious thought. He had been so engulfed in the mystery of his log that he truthfully had forgotten to think about much else. What **would** he do after leaving Matthewson's office?

After drawing a blank for a few minutes he gave up and went to the bridge. The communications officer was in the process of trying to contact the starbase. Zelnick was, as a captain should… no, wait, no he wasn't… He was doing pushups at the front, near the main window. And judging by the lack of looks, and the pace he was doing them at, it wasn't his first time.

"We're getting through," Katja soon said, giving the captain a heads up.

Zelnick very quickly put on his uniform and prepared to converse formally. Then the link was established and they saw the familiar face of Commander Hayes.

"Welcome back," he greeted, happy and disciplined at the same time. *"Some of us thought that we'd never see you again."*

"Likewise," Zelnick put it shortly.

Hayes seemed to take a look at another screen and then put on a funny face.

"Is that the Star Runner with you?"

"What's left of it," Zelnick replied, agreeing that it looked very little like an Eluder starship.

Fwiffo then joined in on the conversation.

"Hello, boss-hunam," he said. *"My ship might need some minor repairs."*

"Sure looks like it," Hayes agreed, *"and the Vindicator too. By the way, there's someone else here who'd like to say hello."*

Gruber tried to think of everyone Hayes could have meant, but when the person in question appeared on the screen, he had to admit that it wouldn't have been among his top ten candidates.

It was Trent – and a trio of the Zoq-Fot-Pik was hovering around him. The Zoq waved its green limbs, the Pik was audibly jumping in place and the Fot stared at them silently as always.[*]

"It's damn good to see you're alive," Trent said and even smiled a little, which was rare for him.

"That's my line, you bastard!" Zelnick laughed. "But… How? Are those with you Dip, Por and Pak?"

"Hello captain!"

"It's us alright!"

Hayes took the stage again.

"Look over there and you'll probably understand," he said and sent a series of proximity coordinates to the Vindicator.

The locations were highlighted on the radar screen. Dujardin zoomed in on them with the optical telescope and put the view on one of the screens for everybody to see:

There were three Arilou Skiff vessels docked with the starbase, along with one Earthling Cruiser, two Spathi Eluders, one Zoq-Fot-Pik Stinger and one Orz Nemesis.

"A lot has happened since your last ansible message," Hayes continued in a more serious tone. *"And I dare say you also have lots of stories to tell. We'll immediately start repairs on the Vindicator and the Star Runner – and any of the Nemeses if they so require – after you have docked. Then we'll have plenty of time to talk."*

"Will do," Zelnick agreed.

When the shuttle had touched down and the exit ramp was lowered, Gruber wanted to ~~walk~~ run straight to Matthewson. It turned out to be difficult since the hangar was packed with people again and Hayes and Trent were

---

[*] Since the Zoq-Fot-Pik themselves didn't know who was who, it was decided for convenience that the green one was Zoq, the silent brown one was Fot and the blue one was Pik.

waiting for them at the end of the ramp. As Gruber and Zelnick emerged from inside the shuttle they received cheers and applause, which felt surprisingly good.

"It's damn good to see you," Hayes said while saluting and they all shook hands. "Let's go to the conference room right away. There are lots of things to go through."

Gruber greeted almost everyone in the crowd on the way and got several handshakes and pats on the back. There was also quite a nice diversity among the crowd. The New Alliance of Free Stars now consisted of the Humans, the Spathi, the Zoq-Fot-Pik and the Orz. In addition, there were the Arilou, whose status in the alliance was currently unknown to Gruber.

He then tried to spot Matthewson from the crowd. It was of course futile, since the man was always in his lab. Instead, he spotted Veronica, who gave him a warm smile and a wave. He responded with similar actions.

The four of them finally made it through the crowd and entered the main elevator.

"Did you notice that the Cruiser we have here is not the Amateras?" Hayes asked.

Gruber hadn't noticed and apparently neither had Zelnick, judging by his expression.

"Captain Halleck and his crew did a fine job scavenging the wreckages at Rigel," Hayes explained.

The elevator reached its destination and the four of them started walking towards the conference room.

"Soon after they had returned," Hayes continued, "they took off to find that lone Shofixti individual you had mentioned. If everything has gone according to plans, they should return from Delta Gorno in about a month."

They reached the conference room and Hayes opened the door. There were lots of people again – Fredrikson, Chu, Hawkins, Snurfel, a Zoq-Fot-Pik trio that looked just like any other, one Arilou and – for some reason – Wu.

Hayes walked beside Wu, who was sitting near the door and got up as the four entered.

"Meet Lei Wu," he said, "the captain of our new Cruiser, Seraph."

Zelnick didn't seem to know Wu so he just shook his hand without any questions. Gruber, on the other hand, had a question.

"Captain? I didn't know you were qualified for that."

Wu gave him an understanding smile.

"I always considered myself a better engineer than a starship officer," he explained. "But right now we seem to have more use for officers, so when I heard the position was open, I applied."

Hayes notified everyone that the meeting could now start.

A lot had indeed happened. After the Vindicator had been sucked into the quasispace vortex, the Tobermoon and all four of the Stinger starships had investigated the site, but found nothing. After about a day they had decided to pool their fuel reserves, pack everyone into the Tobermoon, and fly to the Spathi homeworld. The Zoq-Fot-Pik homeworld was a little closer, but to get there they would have had to cross Umgah territory again, and that was too risky with a slow ship such as the Earthling Cruiser.

Just as they were about to leave, a group of Arilou Skiff vessels had appeared and offered to transport them all safely to Sol. The Tobermoon, the Voyager, the Seeker, the Traveler and the Tracker were stashed on the surface of the fifth planet of Gamma Circini, where they hopefully still were. Getting them back would be a priority.

The Spathi had delivered the special hyperwave transmitter to the starbase and it indeed had turned out to be powerful. With it, according to Dr. Chu, you could easily send a signal through a mile of steel, not to mention through a slave shield. They had sent a few messages to Earth already, although there was no way of knowing if anyone was listening. That should not be the case with the Chenjesu.

Thanks to all the materials scavenged from Rigel, the production facilities were operating at full capacity. They were currently constructing ansibles for the Spathi, the Orz and the Zoq-Fot-Pik. The Arilou hadn't officially joined the alliance, but the three Skiff vessels and their crew would give their full co-operation.

The Spathi had weird news regarding the Umgah. Normally the Umgah would make fun of them at every possible chance, but lately it had almost seemed that they were avoiding the Spathi. One Spathi patrol had encountered a group of Umgah Drone vessels near their border, but the Umgah didn't even hail them. The only response the Spathi got was a weird zombie-like phrase *"We. Funny. Umgah. So. Funny."* In fact, it was so scary that the Spathi were, according to their report, forced to make a tactical retreat.

Fredrikson's team had studied the new module designs very carefully and they were ready to start production whenever needed. Based on the designs, the energy output of the Hellbore cannon was so high that there was no way of estimating its destructive force. They would have to do field tests, but only after they had constructed a Shiva furnace module as well. Both of those modules required a great deal of valuable materials so they couldn't produce everything right away.

Then there was all the news from the Vindicator. The materials they scavenged from the wreck of the Marauder back at Alpha Tucanae would be a great help to the production facilities.

Now they knew that the source of the red probes, which had been making increasingly frequent visits to Sol as well, was in a gas giant in a solar system directly in line with Alpha Tucanae and Epsilon Muscae. There weren't that many possibilities in the region so they decided to try and check those out as well.

Then there was the mystery of Groombridge. Dr. Chu in particular was highly interested in the time-lapse of the event. He agreed that the encrypted log should be delivered to Matthewson as soon as possible.

Zelnick called Skeates to attend the meeting and help him explain what they had learned of the Ultron, which wasn't much. Zelnick was sure that it was of Precursor origin, but that was pretty much it. Skeates could say that it was missing some parts and that with the device in its current condition he couldn't even guess what, if anything, it was meant to do. Fredrikson's team could try to figure out more.

What the Melnorme had said about the current affairs of the Ilwrath was also a curious piece of information. If they were really fighting a race called the Pkunk just a bit over 100 units away, the Alliance had a very good chance of recruiting a new member. In any case they should check it out as soon as possible.

And the casualties... They had reported Bukowski's death via the ansible, but the people at the starbase hadn't known that Roberto and Novak were lost as well. It was a sad thing to hear, but, as Zelnick pointed out, their casualties had been minimal, considering what they'd been through.

Everyone had lots of work to do, so they concluded the meeting swiftly. Gruber was finally free to go to Matthewson. On his way to the lab he realized that Lydia might also have some valuable information for Matthewson, so he called her.

She didn't answer.

Gruber soon exited the elevator on level 9. The place looked exactly the same as the last time he was there, asking about the Cruiser's computer systems. In the office room to his left, between piles of junk, the only source of light was that of one computer display and the only things moving were the hands of the man sitting in front of it. Matthewson didn’t seem to pay any attention to Gruber wading through all the debris towards him.

Gruber had almost reached Matthewson’s desk when something suddenly grabbed his leg. It was so strange and unexpected that he accidentally let out a non-cool little scream.

A second afterwards he saw what had grabbed him. It was still surprising, though. He was staring at the gleeful face of Lydia.

<<Why are **you** here?>> they both asked in unison.

Gruber then politely let the lady talk first.

<<I wanted to see the central computer,>> she explained.

Gruber was surprised that she was by herself.[*]

<<I tried to call you just now,>> he said. <<Why didn’t you answer?>>

Lydia showed her empty hands.

<<I don’t have it anymore… the communicator, I mean. It wasn’t mine to begin with, so I left it at the ship.>>

Indeed the communicator she had used was Bukowski’s. They could get her one of her own here at the starbase.

<<Well I’m glad you’re here,>> Gruber truthfully stated. <<I would have asked you to come here with me. Do you know who this guy is?>>

<<Yes,>> Lydia replied proudly. <<He is the **only one** who understands the central computer.>>

It looked like Matthewson had at least introduced himself to Lydia. So far he hadn’t seemed to pay any attention to the conversation. Gruber decided to get to the point.

“Richard, I have something very interesting for you…”

It took a while to explain everything to Matthewson, but at least he started getting interested half-way through. Lydia

[*] Matthewson doesn’t count.

was also helpful in the explanation. Matthewson took the communicator from Gruber's hand and started tinkering with it before Gruber had even finished talking. Gruber decided it would be best to leave him at it.

"Let me know if you come up with something," Gruber said as he was about to leave.

"Your communicator's here," Matthewson pointed out, not moving his eyes away from his work. "How will I contact you?"

"I'll go get a substitute," Gruber replied, deciding it just then. "I'll send you the contact info soon."

He then switched to German.

<<Lydia, come with me and we'll get you settled in here.>>

Lydia requested that Gruber gave her a tour of the starbase first, which wasn't a bad idea. They began by getting their hands on new communicators. Lydia seemed to be excited and interested about everything around them. Hayes agreed with Zelnick that Lydia was now Gruber's responsibility, at least until the Vindicator took off again.

After going through all the most important areas of the starbase, Gruber noticed that it was getting late in their sleep cycle. He had to find a bunk for Lydia. Now that the Vindicator had returned, there wasn't too much space in the living quarters. There were plenty of sleeping mattresses, but it would have to be set up in an appropriate location.

<<Can't I just stay with you for this night?>> Lydia asked after a while of searching.

Gruber was too tired to argue and they were somewhat close to his quarters anyway.

<<Alright then,>> he agreed, <<but only for tonight.>>

<<Yay!>>

There was plenty of space for Lydia on the floor. She joyously made her bed and started undressing without warning. Gruber considered himself too old and too decent to watch a 15-year old girl changing clothes, so he just lay down and turned off the light.

Once again, Gruber woke up to a knock on his door. According to his communicator he had slept for five hours. He pulled himself up to a sitting position and lowered his feet to the floor. It wasn't the usual cold, metallic floor. No, there was a mattress there. *Oh, right, Lydia is sleeping here.*

And then the lights were turned on and the door opened. Gruber was too slow to do anything about it. Lydia had opened the door wearing nothing but a shirt that covered her bottom only half-way down and now he was standing behind her, wearing nothing but boxer shorts.

The one who had knocked was of course Veronica. For two frozen seconds she didn't say anything, only looked at the sight. Then she turned around and walked away. Gruber didn't show any signs of doing anything, so Lydia shut the door again.

<<Was that your woman?>> she said in an overly cheerful way, apparently hoping for a positive answer.

Gruber burst into laughter and sat back down.

<<You could say that, yes.>>

Lydia was smiling in her own funny way.

<<I shouldn't have opened the door,>> she said and joined the laughter for a while. <<Maybe you should explain this to her?>>

Gruber thought about running after her, but discarded the idea.

<<Nah, I'll tell her when our sleep cycle is over,>> he decided. <<Turn the lights off, please.>>

The next few days consisted mainly of construction, repairs and research. It would still take at least a week before the Vindicator's ansible module was repaired, or more accurately, replaced with a new one. They had agreed on scrapping the Ion-bolt Gun and replacing it in the first module slot with a Hellbore cannon. The required Shiva Furnace was assembled into the eighth slot next to the storage bay. Zelnick and McNeil had suggested adding two Fusion Blasters to accompany the Hellbore Cannon so they wouldn't have to "shoot flies with a bazooka". It was a good idea, but they didn't have enough materials for that. However, they managed to get just enough for the point-defense laser system, which was constructed in the seventh slot. The crew pod would remain in the fourth slot and the ansible would be reconstructed into the fifth. The three fuel tanks would remain in slots 13, 14 and 15.

Gruber watched the construction from the hangar. The Vindicator was starting to look drastically different. There were now more module slots in use than there were free. They were saving a huge amount of resources by not synthesizing any fuel for the Vindicator. The plan was to use the Melnorme as gas stations for now.

The Spathi delegation was also in the hangar again. They were looking more cheerful every day. Gruber still suspected that they were up to something, but there was little he could do about it.

The Orz were making themselves useful by working with the loaders and Lydia was making many new friends among them. From Gruber's point of view they all looked, talked and acted exactly alike. But since the Orz had saved the lives of everyone aboard the Vindicator and the Star Runner, they were quite well-liked and Gruber didn't have a problem with that.

When the Spathi weren't too busy being suspicious, they were playing some kind of a sport with the Zoq-Fot-Pik, who called it “Frungy”. The Spathi called it “The Fun Ball-Throwing Game” even though it was questionable whether throwing a ball was really the essence of the game.

The Arilou mostly kept out of the way, but tried to act like humans when interacted with. Gruber once sat down at the cafeteria with one of them and offered him a beer. The Arilou got all nostalgic and talked about some memories of cows, wheat fields, farmers and the North American mid-west as it had been 200 years ago.

Then Gruber got the report from the team of scientists trying to figure out the Ultron. Apparently they had put it through every test they had and always gotten the same result as if they had used a fork. At least they were certain that whatever its function was, the device didn’t work now. Without Zelnick’s insight they probably would have used the remains of it as raw materials for something else already. It might be worth a shot to ask the Melnorme if they knew anything about it.

Then there was the Groombridge Log, as Matthewson called it. He hadn’t made a breakthrough yet, but kept on saying that he was close. At least he had confirmed that the set of ten coordinates were all supposed to point at rainbow world locations.

Still no information on what happened at Groombridge. We’re leaving on our next mission soon and I was hoping to—

Gruber stopped mid-sentence typing a log entry on his new communicator as there was an incoming call – from Matthewson.

“Can you write in Precursor language?” he asked.

“Huh? Of course not,” Gruber replied. “Why?”

“You’d better get over here.”

Matthewson was courteous enough to turn on the lights as Gruber arrived. Lydia was there too. She had helped Matthewson a lot along the way.

"Check this out," Matthewson said and showed the screen to Gruber.

The symbols, picture, text, or whatever it was supposed to be, didn't mean anything to Gruber.

"What am I looking at here?" he asked.

"This is something – let's call it writing for simplicity – the Precursors used for… something," Matthewson tried to explain. "Similar 'writing' appears on some Precursor artifacts and sites."

"Okay," Gruber said. "Why show it to me now?"

Matthewson took Gruber's old communicator into his hand and pointed at it.

"The log entries weren't really 'encrypted' in the sense we use the word," he explained.

He showed the communicator's screen to Gruber. There was similar gibberish as on Matthewson's work-screen.

"This is from your personal log," he continued. "These are not just some random pictures you could have downloaded from anywhere. These are 'written' with this device."

Gruber had thought of all kinds of wild theories about his log, but none this wild.

"By whom?" he asked.

Matthewson looked at him.

"I'd like to say by you, but then again…"

"If you have a theory," Gruber began, "out with it!"

"But then again…" Matthewson continued by repeating. "This is pretty advanced stuff. This isn't just a set of log entries. I could make a living out of this. I doubt any human mind could do this."

Gruber looked at Matthewson, who looked back at him. Lydia gave Gruber more pressure by staring with Matthewson. Gruber was starting to get annoyed.

"Are you saying that the **Precursors** went out of their way to rise from the dead to write some puzzles on **my diary**?"

Lydia seemed highly amused, but Matthewson didn't.

"Well, no," Matthewson replied, "we don't know if they're dead."

Gruber tried to sit down, but there was nothing to sit on, so he took a deep breath instead.

"We should get Captain Zelnick to take a look at this," he then decided.

August 5th 2155: The Vindicator is ready for its next mission and we are leaving in ten hours. There are lots of places to be again: the Pkunk, the Chenjesu, retrieving the Tobermoon and the Stinger ships, refueling, checking for more rainbow worlds, salvaging the Ur-Quan warp-pod, finding the source of the red probes, making contact with the Yehat...

It's a shame the mystery of the log entries regarding Groombridge must remain a mystery for now. Even Captain Zelnick couldn't make any sense of them, so I'm pretty sure that no human can.

In any case, the strength of the Alliance is growing. We are a diverse bunch, but I'm feeling it is just one of our many strong points.

Lydia has found her place on the starbase quite nicely. The science staff has started to educate her, but I dare say they'll also learn something in the process. I'm glad we rescued her from the Androsynth ruins. If this war ends someday, she might get to see what a normal life could be.

When I first saw Zelnick, I thought he was just a brat who somewhat accidentally became the captain of a starship. (Actually, that **is** *what he is.) But now I can say that there is nobody I'd rather have as my captain. And since the Vindicator is now more powerful than ever, I can also say that I feel quite safe. I can't wait till we reach the asteroid belt and get to try out the Hellbore Cannon.*

I should get some sleep now. It will be a long time before I can sleep in this bed again.

- Adam Gruber, First Officer of the Flagship Vindicator

Lightning Source UK Ltd.
Milton Keynes UK
UKHW010949251021
392802UK00002B/296

9 789515 684189